TENDER SEDUCTION . . .

"Hold still, Sunflower," Cole whispered. "I'm not going to hurt you." Enveloped by a cloud of silky black hair, consumed by its sweet, earthy fragrance, he kept a firm grip on her wrists. His head dropped lower, and his mouth brushed the velvet skin at the base of her throat. Her pulse hammered against his lips. She was so soft, so sweet and clean, yet wild as the country surrounding them.

He lifted his head and stared into her eyes. "Have you changed your mind?" he whispered. "Is this all you wanted from me?" Not waiting for an answer, he teased her upper lip with a gentle sweep of his mustache, then suddenly eager for her taste, claimed her mouth with his . . .

Diamond Books by Sharon MacIver

DAKOTA DREAM
RIVER SONG

River Song

SHARON MacIVER

DIAMOND BOOKS, NEW YORK

RIVER SONG

A Diamond Book / published by arrangement with
the author

PRINTING HISTORY
Diamond edition / October 1991

ISBN: 1-55773-592-1

Diamond Books are published by The Berkley Publishing Group,
200 Madison Avenue, New York, New York 10016.
The name "DIAMOND" and its logo are trademarks
belonging to Charter Communications, Inc.

PRINTED IN THE UNITED STATES OF AMERICA

10 9 8 7 6 5 4 3 2 1

To:

Marge Campbell and the Thursday group:
Audrey Austin, Helen Barkdoll, Maureen Brown,
Marilyn Forstot, Kate Higuera, Juanita Kline,
Diana Saenger, Jan Toom, and Billie Wade—
for the encouragement, the honesty,
and most of all,
the friendship

AND

Ruby Brucker,
with love and many thanks.

PROLOGUE

Arizona City—1866

She kept her silence.

In the way of her ancestors, the Indians of the Quechan nation, Moonstar suffered the agonies of childbirth with a stoic heart. But unlike other Quechan women, she suffered alone.

Droplets of sweat began to pour down her bronzed cheeks and blazed a path across her heaving breasts. She arched her back as the final stages of labor tore through her exhausted body and struggled to bring forth her third child.

During a precious moment of calm, that coveted segment of time she likened to the stillness just before a sudden storm, Moonstar glanced out through the door of the hut. She cast lusterless black eyes on her two young sons as they drew stick people in the sun-baked earth of their desert home and noted how waves of heat distorted their images. Early April, and already the sun was high and relentless. It would be a very long and dry summer.

Another, stronger contraction pulled her up on the straw mattress into a sitting position. *Soon it will be over,* Moonstar thought. *Soon there will be another child brought into this strange world of many cultures, a child who will belong to none of them*. The most powerful contraction yet obliterated all thought, and she focused her energy on the emergence of her newest child.

When it was finally over, after Moonstar had severed the cord and disposed of the afterbirth in a crockery bowl—all things an Indian midwife would have done for her had she remained a true Quechan—she wiped the baby clean and placed it at her breast. Then, exhausted, she beckoned her husband with a high, thin wail. "Patrick!"

The restless father burst into the hut, too concerned about his wife to inquire about the child first. "Are ye having a wee bit of trouble, Star? Shall I try to find ye some help?"

The dusky-skinned woman shook her head and pushed a length of damp hair off her broad cheekbone. "We're healthy, my husband. See what I have brought you this time." Moonstar opened the blanket to reveal a plump, raven-haired daughter.

"For the love of sweet Jesus," the ruddy Irishman proclaimed, "I finally got me a flower to bloom amongst the cactus!"

This brought a warm smile and a sudden vision to the new mother. She looked back out the doorway, past the saucer-eyed stares of her sons as they peered into the hut, and let her gaze linger on her favorite crop. This daughter would bloom under the desert sun, open her petals, and sprinkle the earth with the seeds of her multifaceted heritage.

Her smile more serene now, she said, "You have your Mike and Sean, my husband. I wish to name this child Sunflower."

"Sunflower Callahan?" Patrick Callahan's booming laughter threatened to crack the mud cementing his pole and brush home. "Now there be a name to keep the little dickens on her toes!"

ONE

Sunny dipped her small, tapered fingers into the cool spring water and painted her copper-colored arms with its moisture. This was her spot, a secret place in this arid land where vegetation grew without soil, where soil lay barren.

And she waited. Hoped, in the way of her mother's ancestors, for a vision—that elusive dream showing her the path she would follow in the next phase of her young life. But it didn't come, *wouldn't* come. Had that part of her heritage been left in her mother's womb, the void filled by a healthy dose of her father's blarney?

Sunny giggled at the thought, then craned her neck until the heavy mass of her waist-length hair fell into the pond. After squeezing the excess water from her tresses, she flipped the long coal-black strands across her shoulders and sighed as the coolness penetrated her checkered shirt.

Patrick Callahan wouldn't approve of his daughter's attire. She could hear him bark in his faint Irish brogue that his little Sunflower didn't belong in her brother's shirt, breeches, and wide-brimmed hat. Guessed he would take a mesquite shillelagh to her backside if he knew of this place, this strange oasis of cool spring water shaped by one lone

3

palm tree in an area surrounded by nothing but sand and cactus. But then, he wouldn't have permitted her to ride off in search of a vision, either.

Moonstar understood her need. She had encouraged Sunny's journey to the secret spot shortly after Patrick and his eldest son Sean left on yet another search for an undiscovered vein of gold in La Paz. Her mother knew she hoped for a vision, some sign at least, to tell her in which world she belonged or what the future might hold. Of course, one had to be in a trance or asleep in order to have a vision. Sunny had never been able to accomplish the former, and the latter only served to confuse her further. Her dreams, when they came at all, were always cloudy and obscure, filled with a hunger she didn't understand.

She regarded the copper hue of her skin, a creamy blend of her mother's berry-brown and her father's ruddy pink. She was neither red nor white, Indian or Irish. A half-breed, she thought with a shudder, remembering the ugly snarls of those who would call her by that name. What would become of her if she didn't have that vision soon? Moonstar said the marriage time was upon her, that she must choose a husband. How could she when she couldn't even embrace a culture to fit her needs?

"A husband," she muttered through a bitter laugh. "Now there be a kettle full of malarkey."

Sunny checked the position of the sun, noting the late hour, and picked up her moccasins. She would have to search for this vision another day. She peered inside each leather shoe then shook them, making sure an enterprising scorpion hadn't used one as a refuge from the sun. What would she do with a husband even if she found one, Sunny wondered as she covered her bare feet. She could fish, hunt, and shoot as well as her brothers. Her father, hell-bent on education, had taught all his children to read and write from an early age. What could a husband do for her that she couldn't do herself?

That mating thing, Sunny remembered as she dusted off her breeches and launched her agile body onto the back of her pony, Paddy. She'd observed breeding practices among the desert creatures near her home and at neighboring cattle ranches on several occasions, and had no intentions of allowing some man to spend ten seconds slamming against her soft body. Her vision, when it came, would show her something far better—something that wouldn't include marriage or men.

After tucking the bulk of her raven hair up inside the hat, Sunny leaned forward, pressing her thighs and heels into the pony's rounded sides, and urged him into a slow gallop. Her course back toward Yuma zig-zagged throughout the rocky, sandy terrain as she sought the less-populated trails and kept one eye out for outcast warriors or lone drovers. An unescorted woman in these parts, especially a lowly half-breed, would make a tasty morsel for many a lonely man, regardless of his lineage.

An hour later she reached the Callahan farm situated near the green ribbon-like banks of the Colorado River. She slowed Paddy to an easy trot, then abruptly reined him in as her senses warned her all was not right. It was too quiet. There was no beckoning aroma of corn flour cakes roasting in her mother's new cook stove, and no movement of any kind—not even the whisper of an early evening breeze.

Then a sudden movement from overhead caught her attention. Sunny jerked her chin up and scanned the heavens. A sense of foreboding twisted in her gut when she spotted several turkey buzzards circling the farm in their eerie, ghostlike spiral down towards her home.

Suppressing the strong urge to call out her mother's name, she slipped off Paddy's comfortable back and quietly inched her way towards the adobe brick dwelling. Skirting the creaky wood porch, Sunny crept silently to the side window and stole a quick glimpse inside. The scene turned her veins to ice.

Sunny dropped to the ground and slapped her hand across her mouth. Her throat convulsed, but she managed to keep her silence.

Trembling with shock, her eyes focusing through tears, Sunny forced her shaking hands and knees to move in a soundless crawl around to the back of the house. Then she gave up the remnants of her midday snack to the sandy earth.

Where was her brother Mike? And what of the animals who'd ravaged and bloodied her beautiful mother's body? Did they hide in her home, awaiting her arrival, still hungry for Quechan blood? Or had they done their murderous deed, then ridden off in directions unknown?

Taking great gulps of hot dry air, Sunny stood up, straightened her strong shoulders, and crept around to the front of the house. She kicked in the door, then stood back listening for sounds of reaction. When there were none, she cautiously entered her desecrated home and quickly checked the two bedrooms and curtained closets and pantry.

Satisfied she was alone, Sunny hurried to where her mother lay and sank to her knees beside her. *So much blood!* she thought, reaching a tentative hand toward her. *Too much blood.*

"Mother?" she choked out in a feeble voice. "Oh, please, please be alive."

But Sunny knew she couldn't be. Not with all that blood. Grief swelled in her breast, crowding her heart, and fingers of pain seized her windpipe as she gathered her mother into her arms. "Oh, *kw'ailee*, my mother, *quoann kn'aait*," she cried, pressing Moonstar's brown face to her breast. "Oh, God and please allow the Seven Saints of Ireland to accompany her on her journey into heaven."

Later—it might have been hours or minutes, but in her aggrieved state Sunny couldn't be sure—she finally stopped rocking her mother's bruised body and ceased wailing bits of Quechan chants mingled with Irish prayers. Her features, painted with tears, were wooden and filled with hatred.

Rising from the plank floor, Sunny surveyed the scene with cold calculation. The Irish twinkle in her midnight-blue eyes dimmed, fading like the last sparks of a campfire as she put the pieces together. Although she was unfamiliar with the mating act, the raised skirt, grotesque angle of her mother's legs, and pool of blood beneath her exposed buttocks, told Sunny the intruder had violated her mother in the worst possible way.

Another crimson stain spread beneath Moonstar's shoulders from the bullet that had pierced her loving heart. Sunny prayed it had entered her mother before the man, then spotted another trail of blood. But this life's fluid did not connect in any way with her mother's.

Then, Sunny saw the reason why. Near Moonstar's body lay her favorite carving knife. The shiny blade was mottled with drying reddish-brown flakes. For the first time since she'd ridden away from her secret spot, a tiny smile flickered at the corners of Sunflower's rosy mouth. Her mother had managed to gain some measure of revenge against her attackers before she'd been given up to the heavens.

Sunny followed the trail toward the doorway, and by the time she reached the porch, the stains had become clear enough to identify. Her mother's killer wore a bloody boot on his right foot, which left a perfect outline of the heel with each step he took. He was bleeding badly, she surmised—probably from a large gash in his calf muscle, or even across his thigh. She crossed the steps and examined the dusty ground, confirming her first suspicions. Her mother's visitors were white men. And there were two of them.

The murderer's mounts wore horseshoes, something of a rarity among the inhabitants along the Colorado River.

Indians didn't shoe their horses, and neither did most farmers in this region. The intruders were probably miners, ranchers, or maybe outlaws. She shaded her blue eyes from the afternoon sun and followed the impressions as far as she could. The men had ridden south toward Yuma, and hard.

How could this have happened? Sunny's heart cried out. Where had her oldest brother been during the vicious attack on their mother? In town selling Moonstar's carefully woven blankets? On the reservation visiting the comely daughter of the tribe's shaman? The sudden rustle of the turkey buzzards' great flapping wings and screeching provided Sunny with a clue.

"Mike?" she called with a sliver of hope. But when she turned her gaze on the young crop of corn and spotted the depression amongst the budding green stalks and a glimpse of blue plaid, Sunny gasped. Heartsick, she hurried through the flooded field and collapsed in the mud at her brother's side. Robbed of life's shining luster, Michael Callahan's ebony eyes stared towards the heavens as hard lumps of charcoal.

"No!" Sunflower cried, throwing her arms and head across Mike's rigid chest. "It can not be! This can not be true!"

But it was.

She slumped in despair. After the final bitter tear burned its way across her dusky cheek, when hatred's acid began to eat away at the hurt, Sunny lifted her head and turned eyes as cold as death on the landscape.

Her father and remaining brother, Sean, were busy navigating the upstream waters of the Colorado to the northwest. The animals who'd murdered half her family had ridden southeast.

In which direction should she travel? North, fighting the current, fending off the lonely miners she was bound to encounter as she searched for what was left of her family? Or south, tracking and identifying the killers? Sunny glanced down at Mike, then towards the farmhouse. Her first priority had to be the building of a funeral pyre.

Maybe then, as she stared into the flames and smoke that would carry her fallen family's souls to their reward, she would finally have that elusive dream. A vision would tell her in which direction to travel.

Several miles to the northeast, near the Gila River, Cole Fremont leaned back against his saddle and positioned his bedroll in the hollow of the back of his neck. With a grimace that spread his mustache beyond the width of his jaws, he raised his injured leg and propped his boot heel on the stump of a dead mesquite tree.

After carefully rolling a cigarette, Cole lit it in the campfire and regarded the rabbit roasting on the makeshift spit. He glanced at the dimming sky, drawing a deep breath of tobacco.

"Dammit all, anyway," he complained. His injured leg would have him eating in the dark and had rendered him nearly incapable of hunting for his own supper this evening. Maybe by tomorrow the pain would ease enough for him to get around in his usual fashion.

He sat listening to the cry of a lone coyote and pondered his future, Arizona's future, and the many reasons for his long trek to Yuma. He had finally sold his last herd of cattle on behalf of the family ranch. From now on, Cole would center his thoughts and actions on *his* ideas for the future, not on his father's. Grinning broadly through his thick mustache, he reflected on the new direction he'd taken— and the order he'd placed for his unusual livestock. He laughed thinking about the bizarre creatures, and as he did, several other coyotes joined the first, creating a musical celebration of the night's kill. Then he heard something else.

Cole sat straight up and pulled his rifle from the nearby gun boot, listening. Somewhere, off to the left behind a stand of mesquite and palo verde trees, something or someone crept in the darkness. Ignoring a fresh stab of pain in his right calf, Cole quietly got to his feet and circled down further into the arroyo. Then he began the return journey.

Halfway back to his camp, Cole's hunting instincts were rewarded with a glimpse of a shadowy figure just ahead. As he watched, the figure moved toward his fire with great stealth, stole through the night like an Indian—one of Geronimo's small band of dissidents?

Adept as any savage in moving through thorny bushes and cactus without a sound, Cole advanced on the intruder and caught up with him as he squatted at the edge of the empty campsite.

Pointing the barrel of his Winchester at the back of the wide-brimmed hat, Cole cocked the lever.

"Hands up, mister, and be quick about it!"

With a gasp, Sunny instinctively leapt forward and slithered across the sand like a sidewinder.

"Stop, you little bastard!"

But startled and frightened Sunny continued to snake her way across the sand.

"Dammit all anyway," Cole muttered as he tossed his rifle aside and launched his six-foot frame across the back of the smaller man. Although the intruder struggled valiantly, he was no match for Cole's superior strength. The angry rancher buried the man's face in the sand with one hand as the other hand, well-trained by his years of bulldogging, quickly bound the tiring renegade's wrists behind his back with the short length of rope he wore tied to his belt.

When the struggling ceased, Cole released his grip on the man's neck and slid down across his rounded buttocks to his feet where he secured the slender ankles with his belt.

Panting, Cole got to his feet and waited as his captive spit and coughed the sand from his mouth. When the intruder's breathing eased, Cole slowly circled his prisoner, rolling another cigarette as he regarded the man. Even in the dim light of the fire, he could see the man's skin was a shade darker than his own. Pulling a match from his pocket, Cole struck it with his blunt thumbnail and lit the cigarette.

Trying to keep his tone casual, even though his hatred of Indians ran deep, he said, "Are you Apache? Did Geronimo or Mangus send you on some kind of mission?"

Knowing silence was her only real option, Sunny pressed her sand-painted lips together, and squeezed her eyes shut.

"Talk or I'll kick the answers out of you!"

Still, she remained mute.

"Come on now, speak up." Impatient, his leg throbbing, Cole dug the toe of his boot into the Indian's ribs. "What evil are you up to, disguised as a white man? I want some answers, Apache."

She gave him one. Sunny turned her head to the side and spit on his boots.

"So that's how it's going to be, is it?"

Cole lashed out with his injured leg and kicked the Indian in the shinbone, drawing a groan from both himself and his prisoner. Hobbling, he backed away.

Sunny peered out from under the brim of her hat, her eyes following the movement of her captor's boots as he crossed back and forth, circling her body. There was no mistaking the awkward gait. He limped badly on his right foot. Had she found her quarry so soon?

In no mood to keep up the one-sided conversation, much less stand on his leg any longer, he threatened, "Fine. Have it your way. I'm tired and hungry. If you get thirsty, all you have to do is talk."

He stalked over to his saddle and removed a coil of rope. Then he returned to his prisoner, fastened one end of the rope to the ankle bindings, looped it through the coils joining the Indian's wrists, and wrapped a length around the man's neck before tying it off on the sturdy trunk of a mesquite tree. This renegade might try to slither off during the night, but if he did, he would find it difficult—if not damn near impossible—to breathe.

Her eyes dark, the color of a thunderstorm at midnight, Sunny watched the killer return to his fire and pull the rabbit from the dying flames. Hatred for the man nearly drove all thoughts of her hunger and thirst from her mind as she plotted her revenge.

Nearly two days ago she'd lost the tracks of the horses she followed, and allowed instinct to lead her on a more northerly route toward Phoenix. She'd been preparing camp for the night a few yards down the side of this rocky slope, when the aroma of roasting meat guided her to the clearing.

Directed by the customs of her ancestors, she'd survived during the past few days by eating only a few sweet beans plucked from the branches of mesquite trees along the way and an occasional bite of her mother's corn flour cakes. No meat, fish, or salt were allowed in the first few days following the death of a family member. And only a few cupfuls of warm water, just enough to sustain life, were permitted.

Sunny stifled an ironic laugh as she thought about how the ravenous appetite brought on by her mother's death had led her to the very man who'd caused it. Lifting her chin, then settling it in a pillow of soft sand, she cocked her head for a better look at her captor. She would commit his features to memory in case he slipped away from her, and hunt him down again if it took the rest of her life.

Trying to ignore the hunks of tender white meat he consumed, Sunny examined the profile he offered. A straight aristocratic nose rested above a drooping mustache the color of pale mustard, but his thick wavy hair beckoned her gaze to return again and again. Illuminated by the glow of the dying fire, its blond strands glistened like the shafts of new wheat on her father's farm, and reminded her of her mission.

There could be only one solution to correct the wrong that had been done. The man would have to die. And for that to happen, Sunny would have to find a way to gain an advantage over him. What were his strengths, his weaknesses?

He was a remarkably handsome man, almost too well-dressed for the trail in a pair of blue denim pants, grey shirt with a plain blue scarf tied around his throat, and a black leather vest. A gentleman, some would say.

He would be the kind of man who attracted white women of all ages, Sunny supposed, the kind who'd broken numerous hearts along the way, tickled thousands of mouths with the thick brush he wore on his upper lip. A dandy. A bully. A murderer.

She had to find a way to blindside him, catch him off guard when he would least expect it, but her mind wouldn't cooperate. Exhaustion, hunger, and thirst overwhelmed her concentration.

Sunny squeezed her eyes shut, determined to get the rest she needed to carry out her plans. She squirmed in the sand, trying to ignore the strips of cloth she'd bound around her breasts to flatten them, but the material bit painfully into her tender flesh. Sharp pebbles and rocks poked at her hips and ribs, and her grandfather's war club dug into her waist. Somehow she would sleep. Tomorrow, she had to be clearheaded enough to think of a way to escape from this madman, and then kill him.

After he finished the last of the rabbit, Cole tossed the bones in the campfire and cleaned the remnants from his fingers with a handful of sand. He glanced over to his sleeping prisoner and shook his head. What could Geronimo be thinking of? This was no angry warrior—he knew that much from the softness of the boy's body during their struggle. In the morning sun, Cole was sure he'd be looking into the large frightened eyes of a child barely old enough to leave his mother's breast. That would be proof to him that these murderous Indians had as little regard for their own young as they did for the children of white settlers. Cole gritted his teeth against memories of long ago and added this evening's experience to the growing list of reasons to get the Indian mess taken care of and the hostiles under control.

With a heavy sigh, Cole spread his bedroll across an area he'd cleared earlier and stretched his lanky body across it. Tomorrow he would have to make a decision about the Indian. If released, the kid would probably continue to follow him and ambush him at the first opportunity. If he kept the young brave prisoner, what would he do with him? Take him all the way to the San Carlos Reservation? Tomorrow would be soon enough to worry about it, and by then he would be able to make the correct decision.

At dawn the following morning, the first thing Sunny noticed was the size and texture of her tongue. It seemed to fill her mouth with the bark of a cottonwood tree and begged her to soak it with a cup of water. Pins and needles stabbing at her flesh alerted her to the bruised and stiffened condition of her body.

Then, a miracle. Drops of cool, fresh water sprinkled her cheeks and rolled into the corner of her mouth. Sunny turned her head skyward and opened her eyes.

"Could you use a swallow or two?"

The killer loomed above her, his cool green eyes guarded. Her first impulse was to tell him to go to hell, but Sunny knew that if she continued to refuse food and water, she would be unable to carry out her purpose. She dropped her head to the sand and nodded.

"That's more like it." Cole set the cup of water aside, then released the length of rope binding the Indian to the tree. He slipped his hands beneath the boy's armpits and helped him to his knees, then to a standing position.

After reaching for the cup, he pressed it to the boy's mouth. The Indian drank greedily from the cup, choking and spitting as the fluid tried to find passage through a swollen throat.

"Take it easy," Cole ordered. "There's more where this came from. A sip at a time will ease your thirst faster than those horse-swallows you're taking."

When the cup was empty, Cole tossed it towards the campsite, then grabbed the young brave by the shoulders. "Now you're going to tell me who you are and why you were following me."

As he waited for a reply, Cole noticed the strange shape of the young man's torso. With a sharp rap against the Indian's chest, he demanded, "What do you have in there? Weapons?"

She shook her head, even though the man apparently realized he'd neglected to search her the night before. Then in one quick movement he pulled the tattered brown shirt from her breeches and jerked it open.

An eyebrow shot up in surprise as Cole studied the cloth wrapped around the boy. A hiding place for extra weapons—or bindings for a terrible wound? Tiring of asking unanswered questions, Cole shrugged and pulled his Bowie knife from the sheath near his back pocket. After grabbing the bottom of the material, he slit it up the middle.

"No!" Sunny cried at the same moment the knife touched her skin.

But he was too fast. She was exposed.

Cole gasped and staggered a few steps back. The knife dropped to the sand. His mouth fell open as he stared at the full up-turned breasts peeking out at him from the opening in her shirt. She was like a mirage shimmering up from the Sonoran Desert. He closed his eyes, shook his head, then opened them again. But the ripe buds were still there, more beautiful and beckoning than any he'd ever seen.

"I—I," he choked out, momentarily at a loss for words.

He averted his gaze, collecting himself, and took several gulps of air before remembering that, woman or not, she was a savage and would probably kill him if given a chance.

Cole turned back to her, angry to have been fooled, embarrassed for her. He hastily crossed the torn edges of her shirt to cover her breasts and said, "Why didn't you tell me you were a woman last night? Do you think I'd have left you tied up like a calf at branding time if I'd known?"

Looking for a way to gain his confidence, Sunny lowered her head and spoke in hushed tones. "I was afraid."

"Damn," he muttered, touched by the frightened tone of her voice. Tired of talking to the brim of her hat, Cole reached over and gently removed it. Thick sheets of ebony hair tumbled down her shoulders and across her breasts. Slowly, she lifted her chin and turned mournful cobalt-blue eyes on him.

Cole's throat suddenly constricted, and he had to work at clearing it before he softly said, "Don't be afraid of me. I don't want to hurt you. Why were you following me?"

In the same tiny voice, she murmured, "I was hungry. I smelled your meat cooking."

A sense of guilt played skip rope with his gut and he said the first thing that came to mind. "Damn."

Now what? He could hardly leave her tied and hobbled, and yet she looked to be at least part Indian. What might she do if he freed her? He still hadn't searched her for weapons. It hardly seemed likely she could survive in this land without them.

Absently stroking the silky corners of his mustache, Cole studied the young woman. She was sturdy and broad shouldered, yet remarkably lithe and fragile to the touch. He'd noticed that much after he'd bulldogged her last night. Shrugging off the warmth growing in his abdomen, Cole gazed at her features and tried to guess her tribe. She was lovely, quite beautiful in fact, with high strong cheekbones and a nose much too small and pert to be Apache. What was she doing out here alone? Or was she so alone?

His suspicions growing, Cole glanced around the campsite, then said, "Why are you traveling alone in these parts?"

Working to keep a pitiful, helpless expression, Sunny said, "M-my father and I, we . . . we were heading to the Superstition Mountains to look for gold when Apaches surprised us in the night. I escaped on my pony, but my father, he . . . he was killed."

"Damn. Dammit all, anyway."

Sunny twisted away from him and slumped her shoulders, giving the appearance of a weeping attack.

"Oh, come on—please don't cry."

Her lip curled in amusement to know the man was so easily fooled, and she nearly laughed out loud as she imagined his expression when she drove her father's knife into his belly.

A gentle hand on her shoulder sobered her expression. She stiffened but did not turn around.

"I'm sorry I added to your grief," Cole whispered in a low, soothing tone, "but I thought—well, you know what I thought." Filled with compassion for her plight, he reached for his knife and cut the bonds from her hands, then removed his belt from her ankles.

Relief and pain flooded her aching joints and shoulders. Sunny stretched her arms, then made an adjustment on Cole's attempt to cover her. She tied the tails of her buttonless shirt in a knot just below her breasts, then faced him.

"I am very hungry," she murmured quietly. "And I have not yet quenched my thirst."

"Oh, sure. I have some—" Cole cut off his own words when he noticed the strange bulge beneath her breeches, an oblong outline clearly revealed now that her shirt no longer hung down to her thighs. He pointed a long, tanned finger toward her waist. "What have you got in there?"

A blush raced up the sides of her neck and spread to her cheeks when she realized her grandfather's war club was practically in full view. She hedged, kicking a small pebble as she searched for a reasonable explanation. "I—it is only a small piece of wood—" she stammered before hastily adding, "it is my only protection."

Cole frowned and extended his palm. "May I have a look at it?"

Sunny's fists coiled at her sides when she realized she had no choice. She must be patient. When the time was right, she would know it. Besides, giving up the club would convince him she had no other weapons. He wouldn't dare search her right thigh, the private place she had chosen to tie her father's hunting knife. But then, she reminded herself, he'd dared much more with her mother.

Sunny managed to keep her innocent expression as she surrendered the weapon, but couldn't keep the defiance out of her flashing eyes when the killer began to unwrap her grandfather's *kelyaxwai*.

After removing the canvas covering, Cole stared down at the object in disbelief. Not more than a foot long, the piece of wood was shaped much like a potato masher with a thick, jagged block at the end of a grip-sized shaft. What caught his attention and raised his brows, however, was the two-inch spike protruding from the handle.

"That's some piece of wood you got here, young lady." Cole squinted a green eye in her direction and swung the club back and forth between them.

"What do you suppose a fellow might do with it? I expect the business end," he patted the block, "might soften even the toughest piece of meat. And this?" Cole fingered the needle-sharp tip of the spike, never taking his eyes off her. "This probably makes one hell of a toothpick, huh?"

Pressing her lips together, Sunny stared down at her boots and said nothing.

"Then again," Cole continued thoughtfully, "your little piece of wood could be a handy thing to have in a fight. Just bash a fella over the head, twirl the handle, and stick him in the heart before he hits the ground. Do I have it right yet?"

Sunny raised her head and met his gaze. Her blue eyes sparkled with hatred. "I said," she hissed, forgetting her little girl voice, "it is my only protection."

Cole stepped back and raised his eyebrows. He rolled a cigarette and regarded her over his cupped hands as he lit the tobacco.

Blowing a puff of smoke in her direction, he grinned.

"I'll be happy to provide protection for you for the time being. I think it's best if we retire your club to my saddlebags. Wearing a thing like this inside your trousers could—well, you could hurt yourself real bad."

Cole strolled over to his saddle, motioning for her to follow, and buried the war club in the depths of the bag. Then he pulled out a small package and offered it to her. "Sit down. There's some biscuits and jerky in there. The biscuits are a little stale, but the jerky is good forever. I'll get you some more water."

Easing down in the patch of soft sand, Sunny sat cross-legged and studied the man as she stuffed chunks of dry biscuit in her mouth. His limp was barely noticeable this morning. The injury was healing. Soon, she mused with a coldness that surprised her, he would have a wound that would never heal.

Cole returned with a canteen and cup, then propped his long body against a tree stump across from her. "I expect it's time we were introduced," he laughed. "My name's Cole Fremont from the Triple F ranch just east of Phoenix."

Sunny took a long drink of water, wondering how much she should tell him. She wiped her mouth and said, "I am called Sunflower."

"Sunflower? Hmm. A pretty name for a pretty girl. What's your last name?"

She tore off a piece of jerky, muttering, "Just Sunflower."

Although Cole didn't want to make her feel as if he were interrogating her, he was intrigued and interested in knowing more about her, sensed she was a lot more complex—and intelligent—than she let on. "Do you have family near here? I'd be happy to escort you back home."

Refusing to meet his gaze, Sunny shook her head and continued to fill her belly.

"Oh, I—I'm sorry."

When she didn't respond, Cole reached for his black Stetson hat and dropped it in his lap. Dragging a hand through his hair, he pondered his next move. Should he question her about her heritage? She looked Indian, and yet she didn't. Her high slashing cheekbones could have come from anywhere, he supposed, but the light copper complexion, the thick, straight, jet-black hair, not to mention the brutal club, all cried out Indian to his way of thinking.

Then he thought of her striking indigo-blue eyes, eyes she carefully hid from him most of the time. Cole chuckled to himself as he recalled their response when he'd discussed the uses of her club. Those expressive, captivating eyes had flashed round and wide, showing him a spirit and sense of independence he'd never seen in a woman before.

He'd never seen a woman quite as tall. Around five foot six or seven, she was especially tall for an Indian. And her body was soft and rounded, not like the square, bony shapes of the tribes he'd been exposed to. This thought prompted an image of her bare, dusky peaked breasts.

Taking a deep breath, he addressed her again. "Are you Indian, Sunflower? Maybe I can escort you back to your people."

This caught her in mid-chew. She looked over at the stranger, her mind a blank. She'd thought of everything but that. If she told him she was Quechan, he would know she belonged in the Yuma area. He might guess her true purpose.

Sunny blurted out the name of the first nearby tribe she could think of. "My father was Pima."

Cole raised his brows. He'd crossed paths with some of the Pima on the Fort McDowell Reservation, and while they were easier on the eyes than the Apache or Navajo, none possessed the strikingly beautiful features of this enchanting creature.

"And your mother?" he ventured softly

"White." She bit off the word, daring him to make something of it.

Cole knew better than to challenge her. Interbreeding was a touchy subject, especially if the white involved was female. Even though he wasn't sure where he stood on the issue, he wasn't surprised at the slight wave of disgust rippling through his innards when she explained her ancestry.

Her appetite and thirst sated, Sunny wrapped the remaining supplies and worked on giving him a smile. "Thank you very much for sharing your food with me."

"Anytime, Sunflower." Cole replaced his hat and hopped off his makeshift stool. "It really isn't safe for you to travel alone. Why don't you ride back to my ranch with me? It's about three days from here and very near Fort McDowell, where some of your people might live. You can rest and clean up at the ranch before you decide what you want to do."

Perfect. She would have her chance tonight as he slept. This time, her grin was genuine as she said, "I appreciate your offer very much. Let me help you load up."

Together, they gathered Cole's saddle and supplies, then Sunny stood quietly and waited for him to saddle the buckskin stallion, Sage. She glanced down at the ground, trying to appear disinterested, and studied the animal's tracks. Her blood ran cold when she found a set of clear prints; they matched the ones at the farm. If she'd needed any further proof this man had been in her home, this was it.

As Cole tightened the cinch around Sage's belly, he noticed her intense gaze and the strange, glazed look in her eyes. "Is something wrong?"

"What?" Sunny snapped her head up, caught again.

Stumbling over her tongue, she explained, "It's your horse's tracks. They are very unusual."

"Oh? In what way?"

She pointed at one print in the soft sand. "The front shoe makes a small dent in the earth at the toe, but here," she directed her finger to the print directly in front of her, "on the back shoe, there is no dent. The hoofprint is smooth and longer than the one in front."

"Oh, that," he laughed as he secured the saddlebags and rifle. "Those back shoes are our blacksmith's idea. The ranch horses are used primarily for herding and roping cattle and they have to do a lot of sliding. The smooth surface makes it easier on the horse and the rider." He picked up the stallion's hind leg and pointed to the extension. "The extra length protects the back of his hoof and helps prevent injuries."

"Oh." She shrugged, uninterested in his explanation, burning inside with the discovery of the extra proof of his guilt.

Cole swung onto his saddle and looked down at her. "Are you on foot, or do you still have your pony?"

"He's down at the foot of the arroyo."

"I'll take you there." Extending his hand, Cole directed her to slip her boot into the stirrup, then he swooped her onto the stallion's wide rump behind him. "Hang onto me. The trail here is a little steep." Then he lifted the reins and coaxed the animal in an affectionate tone, "Head on out, Sage."

Sunny had no intention of touching the man until she could do it with the tapered end of Patrick's hunting knife. She clung to the edge of the leather saddle, her chin set defiantly, and rode that way until the horse slipped in the loose rocks and nearly lost his footing.

This immediately sent her arms flying around Cole's trim waist, and her head slamming against his broad shoulders. She remained pressed against him until they were back on level ground, her nostrils forced to breathe his unique man-odor—a mixture of mesquite smoke from the campfire, a hint of rich tobacco, and a curious musky aroma that made her feel strangely warm inside.

Sunny lifted her head and accidentally brushed her lips against the long blond curls at the back of his neck. Some primitive Quechan instinct urged her to take her revenge now, to drive her teeth into his neck and claw at his eyes. Surprise would be on her side. But his strength still gave him an advantage she couldn't afford to ignore. And, she suspected, there would be only one chance with this man.

Frustrated by these sudden feelings, impatient to have her revenge over and done with, Sunny leapt from Sage's strong back while he was still moving at an easy trot. She ran on ahead, deftly sidestepping mounds of barrel cactus and leaping over numerous underground dwellings.

Startled, the curious rancher spurred his mount on and caught up with her at the same time she reached Paddy. "Are you trying to break your neck or something? All you had to do was say stop."

Her breathing rapid, as much with anger as from the short dash, Sunny avoided his gaze. "I—I was worried about my pony. He's been alone a long time."

While she bent to release the animal's hobbles, Cole grinned at her discomfort. Even with her doeskin coloring, the deep flush staining her cheeks was as easily seen as the shallow rise and fall of her full breasts in the shirt he'd rendered buttonless. She'd covered herself as well as possible, but couldn't quite hide the inviting swells or the soft moist valley between them, begging to be explored.

Cole looked back at her flushed cheeks and wondered if she felt the same way he did. Had his touch affected her as much as her small delicate hands had affected him? Those hands, and her moist warm breath against the thin material of his shirt, had almost been enough to turn him weak and helpless. And when she pressed her lips to the back of his neck, he'd damn near fallen out of the saddle. There was no denying the attraction he felt—and no denying that it touched and angered him as well.

Frowning now, he watched Sunny mount astride her pony, then he laughed. Cole imagined the faces of his sister and her women friends if asked to perform such a task. White women only rode sidesaddle—no *real* lady would ever spread her legs over the back of a horse. Cole found himself wondering what harm these ladies thought would befall them if they rode a horse the way God had intended. Regarding his new charge as she rode up beside him, he noted that she seemed comfortable enough, maybe even more so than he.

With Cole in the lead, they rode off together through endless dry gullies, through parched dry creek beds and surprising areas of green and water. Although he was a tough and wiry Mustang, Paddy's short legs and relatively soft life in Yuma made it impossible for him to keep up with Cole's superior purebred. The pace slowed, giving the couple a chance to admire the yearly spring bloom of the devil's coachwhip, a long, spiny-limbed plant with fiery torchlike blossoms—and the time to think about the evening's activities.

Sunflower's thoughts were consumed with murder—a terrifying act she'd never witnessed, much less performed. But it had to be done. There was no one else to make this man pay for her mother's life, her honor. As nightfall began, she knew they would make camp soon and the time would be upon her. Could she do it? He seemed such a nice man, had treated her respectfully and with a gentleness she'd seen in few whites. How could one so kind have performed such a savage act on her mother?

Looking for a perfect spot to bed down for the night, Cole kept a sharp lookout for just the right combination of sloping hills and creosote bushes to guard them from the sudden sand storms prevalent during the spring. As he studied the terrain, his thoughts centered on the dreadful way he'd treated Sunflower during her first night in his camp and the resulting guilt he felt. No matter that she was dressed as a boy. He could have investigated a little further, especially after he'd felt the soft flesh beneath him as he bound her wrists. Cole grimaced when he remembered how he'd driven her delicate features into the sand, the way he'd crushed her glorious breasts against the rocky earth. He swore under his breath. Tonight, he would make it up to her somehow.

When Cole found a suitable campsite, he went off to hunt for a couple of cottontails for dinner, leaving Sunny to prepare the fire and water their horses at a nearby spring. After they'd eaten and the sky had turned as black as Sunny's hair, Cole tossed more mesquite branches on the fire and invited her to join him.

"Thank you," she managed through clenched teeth, "but I did not rest well last night. I am very tired."

Cole got to his feet and tossed his cigarette into the fire. "Sure you are. I should have known that."

He walked over near the base of the small mountain and spread his bedroll in the softest patch of ground he could find. "Sleep here. I'll set up near the fire."

"B-But I can't take your bed. I will sleep on the ground."

Cole gripped her shoulders and pulled her close. "Not for all the silver in Tombstone. After the night I put you through, you ought to demand I build you a rope bed!"

His kindness confused her, but she knew if she stood here and argued with him any longer, she would weaken and later find herself too weak to use her father's knife. Sunny looked into his eyes for one last time, ready to accept his offer and be on her way, but his gaze left the words scrambled in her mouth. He was staring at her, through her, in a way no one ever had. It made her feel warm and liquid, like a barrel of her mother's homemade mescal—and just as fiery and potent.

Cole's golden head inched towards hers. With sudden certainty, Sunflower knew he meant to kiss her. Dear God, why wouldn't her feet move? And why was she so intrigued by the thought of his inviting mouth brushing against hers?

He was a whisker away from her trembling lips when, mercifully, an image of her mother's battered body gave her the courage to jerk away.

Sunny managed to snap off a quick, "Good night. Thanks for the bed," then spun around and lowered herself to the blanket. Rolling on her side, Sunny offered her back to the rancher, and waited for the sounds of his boots fading as he crossed the camp to his own bed.

But it didn't happen. She could feel his hot green eyes boring into her back. Did he mean to attack her? Had his kindness been a trap, a way to catch her off guard? It would be impossible for her to reach her knife with him standing behind her. She was nearly defenseless. Sunny lay still, coiled like a cougar, ready to spring. This rancher may try to kill her, but he would not have an easy time of it.

Just when she thought her muscles would burst from tension, she heard his low sigh, retreating footsteps, and a heavy groan as he stretched out on Sage's blanket for the night. Then she waited. Every sense on alert, Sunny breathed deep. The fresh desert air mingled with the comforting aroma of mesquite wood smoldering in the dying fire and the biting odor of a nearby creosote bush. She listened to the plaintive call of the quail, to the mournful song of a lone coyote, and finally . . . to the light snoring of her prey.

Normally a light sleeper, Cole had dropped into a deep slumber almost as soon as his head touched the blanket. His dreams swirled around him like strands of long ebony hair, the shadows punctured only by an occasional flash of twinkling blue eyes. For a long time, he was unaware that the woman crept around him, preparing for her attack.

When his excellent instincts finally warned him something was amiss, Cole automatically reached for the Colt .44 lying near his head.

The holster was empty.

Fully awake now, some sixth sense telling him to move, and move fast, he rolled over on his side.

But it was too late. He felt the fire of the knife as its tip burned into his flesh.

TWO

A vivid nightmare woke him with a start.

Sean Callahan jerked to a sitting position and wiped the sweat from his brow. He shook his head as if to clear the terrible dream from his mind, but the images returned, clearer and more prophetic than before.

He gasped for a breath of fresh air, but the atmosphere in the steamboat's hold was suffocating. Sean turned to the bulky figure lying beside him on the wooden planks and tapped the man's burly shoulder.

"Pop," he whispered. "Come on, wake up."

Patrick Callahan grumbled and groaned, his mind hazy from too much mescal the night before.

"Wake up, Pop. I have to talk to you," Sean pleaded.

With great effort, Patrick rolled over on his back and lifted one eyelid just enough to make out his son's form in the darkness. "Ohhh," he groaned, " 'tis the breath of a Gila monster I find in me mouth this morning."

"I'll not be arguing that." Grimacing, Sean got to his feet. "Come up on deck with me for some air."

He helped his swaying father off the floor and gave him a few minutes to get his bearings. Then the pair crept by the other passengers who couldn't afford private staterooms, and past the assortment of chickens, wagons, cordwood, and various animals entombed in the hold. After climbing out the hatch, Sean led his father to the rear of the stern-wheeler and leaned against the rail.

" 'Tis still nightfall, son!" Patrick barked. "Why are ye waking me at this ungodly hour?"

"It's closer to dawn than you think, Pop. I brought you out here to tell you . . . to explain . . ." But he couldn't finish the sentence—knew if he didn't choose his words correctly, his father would dismiss the dream as so much blarney and then amble off to the hold.

"I'm a listenin', son. Get on with it."

Sean stared down at the churning wheel, comparing the big paddle's struggle against the upstream current to Patrick Callahan's stubborn mind, and let out a long breath.

Finally, he looked over to his father and said, "I had a vision."

Patrick cocked a bushy brow and squinted an ice-blue eye in his son's direction. "This is why you shortened me rest and robbed me brain o' the time needed to ease the throbbing?"

"Sorry, Pop, but it was so clear, so real, I had to tell you now." He lowered his head and voice before adding, "We have to go back home."

"Turn back? Blarney!" Patrick bellowed. "And *dooble* blarney!" he tossed in as he rapped his fist against the wood railing.

Sean had expected that reaction, and in spite of the terrifying vision, he had to grin. Placing a gentle hand on his father's shoulder, the young man explained the mayhem and horrors the dream had shown him. By the time he finished his story, the sun had crept over the foothills along the Colorado River and splintered the dark night with fingers of gold.

Staring down into the turbulent waters, Patrick shook his

head in disbelief. It couldn't be true! Or could it? Had Sean inherited this prized gift from Moonstar's forbearers? Although Patrick understood many of his wife's beliefs and customs, accepted them as he accepted her, he'd always been uncomfortable with her search for spiritual power—and the fact that she looked for it in their children. The acquisition of this power had always been far more important to Moonstar than new dresses, fancy buggies, or her husband's endless search for gold.

Patrick shuddered as he continued to ponder Sean's words. The only thing he knew for certain about attaining these visions was that they only occurred during sleep. The Quechan could not induce a vision through drugs, fasting, torture, or ritual as some tribes prescribed. This power always took form through a dream. The nightmare could very well be true.

Regarding his son, the troubled Irishman spoke in hushed tones. "Ye haven't been nipping on yer mum's poteen, have ye?"

Shaking his dark head, Sean said, "No, Pop. I wish I could blame it on mescal, but I can't. It just happened."

With a short nod, Patrick studied the young man's expression. Whether this vision was real or just a bad nightmare, one thing was clear. Sean *believed* it was real. Could Patrick afford *not* to?

With Sean, anything was possible. Of the three Callahan children, this one had always been the one most at odds with his mixed heritage. Even his physical characteristics couldn't seem to decide if he was Irish or Indian. Sean's hair, cut short at the neck, appeared as black as Sunny's on first glance. But in the sunlight or upon closer inspection, amber strands glistened with Irish pride.

And those eyes, Patrick thought with a sigh, Sean's eyes told the real story. Clear and shining one moment, they battled from within, turning a murky hazel color when he was angered, to a surprising deep river-blue when pleased.

Even his body showed a distinct division. At six feet, the young man was four inches taller than Patrick, yet of average height for a Quechan male. But in place of the lean, slender silhouette of a Yuman Indian, he'd inherited his father's muscular arms, powerful shoulders, and thick chest.

Patrick returned his gaze to the river, to the frothy wake kicked up by the rotating wheel. He had no choice. If there was any chance at all that the lad's dream had indeed been a vision, he would have to put off his own dream of finding gold. Again.

"So ye really b'lieve yer mum and Sunny and Mike are in danger?" Patrick said quietly.

"Yes, I do," Sean replied, but he didn't mention the vision had also told him one or two of them were already beyond danger.

Patrick moved his gaze to the southeast and settled his sky-blue eyes on the strange configuration known as Castle Dome. This giant rock formation, hundreds of feet square and shaped like a great castle, could be seen for many miles in several directions. To Patrick, its base represented a one-day journey to his home.

"How long a ride do ye think it to be from Ehrenberg to Castle Dome, lad?"

With a shrug, Sean guessed, "Around two days or so."

"Then we won't be waitin' around for another steamboat. We're due to dock in Ehrenberg this morning. The minute they lower the stageplank, we'll get on the mules and head home."

With an anxious glance to the south of Castle Dome, Patrick quietly added, "Faith, and I hope we'll not be too late."

But they were. Seven days late.

"Oh, me darlin', me second son," Patrick cried as he buried his greying head in his palms. Resting his trembling elbows on the dining table as an anguished sob nearly tore him in half, he glanced around his once-happy home.

Patrick could almost hear Moonstar's shy giggles, Mike's deep voice as he teased her and Sunny with her unmerciful good humor. *Sunny,* he suddenly thought, worry tempering his grief. Where was his mischievous little Leprechaun? How had she managed this terrible ordeal alone?

When he and Sean had ridden into the farmyard an hour ago, the first thing Patrick spotted was the remnants of the funeral pyre. Obviously, Sunny had dug a small pit, dragged Mike's rope and wood bed out to the yard, and positioned it above the hole. Then she'd surrounded the bed with the family's entire store of firewood, and arranged the bodies of her loved ones and their belongings above their final resting place. After the fire burned out and the ashes had fallen into the pit, Sunny had covered the grave with earth and ridden off.

Moonstar would have burned the house as well. He supposed he should be grateful Sunny was either unaware of that custom or hadn't been able to destroy her desecrated home. All Patrick had left of the woman he'd loved so long and so well was a few beads and shells from her marriage necklace. Had it been torn from her throat during the attack? In shock, he fingered a single blue seashell, the center and most precious part of the necklace.

"Oh, Pop," Sean moaned after he read Sunny's note again. "What are we going to do?"

But the older man continued to stare at the floor, his heart and spirit broken.

Resting a comforting hand on his father's trembling shoulder, Sean considered the information in Sunny's letter. Devoid of detail, the note informed them only that Moonstar and Mike had been murdered by two white men riding shod horses towards the direction of Yuma. Sunny was in pursuit and would send a wire once the killers were identified. And then what? Had she seen the men commit their deed, could she bear witness against them in a court of law?

He thought of his younger sister—innocent, beautiful, and alone in this untamed land. He thought of the outlaws—ducking, hiding, ambushing many an unwary traveler in their attempts to survive unpunished. Then he thought of the few bands of renegade Indians, especially of Geronimo's last escape to freedom and the havoc he was causing settlers and army alike. Sean's heart grew cold.

"Pop," he said, fighting the tremors in his voice. "Our grieving must come later. Sunny's in danger."

With a heavy sob, Patrick took a great lungful of air and pointed to the corner of the cabin. "A cup of yer mum's poteen, son."

"We'll be needing clear heads, Pop. We have to—"

"A cup of poteen!" Patrick shouted in a hoarse voice.

Pressing his full Quechan lips into a thin line, Sean gave his father a short nod and did as he was ordered.

After the last trickle of mescal burned its way down Patrick's throat, he shuddered and got to his feet. "Now 'tis a clear head I'm havin'. Now I'll be thinkin' what to do."

With great deliberation, Patrick walked through his home, his keen eyes searching for clues, for anything disturbed or out of place. His gaze came to rest on the blank spot above the hearth of the fireplace he'd built with his own hands.

"Yer grandfather's war club is missing. Do ye think yer sister's planning to take revenge herself?"

Although that was exactly what Sean thought, he shook his head. "Probably took it for protection, Pop. That and a couple of knives, if I know Sunny."

"If she had our rifles and pistols as well, she wouldn't have protection enough!" Patrick boomed. " 'Tis a fool's errand the lass has taken on. Saddle up the mules. We'll be looking for her trail before sundown."

"Pop, I've another idea."

"Time's a wastin', son o' mine!"

"Please, Pop," Sean pleaded. "Listen to what I have to say. There's no need for both of us to go after Sunny."

Patrick swallowed his protest and regarded the young man with a skeptical eye. "What's yer plan, then?"

"I think you should go into town and tell Lieutenant Wallace at Fort Yuma what's happened. Maybe the army will help us find Sunny and the murderers."

Raising a bushy brow, Patrick grumbled, "And what if the men were some of his own troops, boy?"

Shrugging, Patrick guessed, "If they were army, it'd be all the reason more for Lieutenant Wallace to help out. I'll go after Sunny myself."

"No, no, lad. She's my girl, I'll be findin' her—"

"Pop!" Sean exploded. "Think about it. I can make better time than you. I move faster, quicker, and make a lot less noise. If Sunny's in trouble, my chances of helping her are much better."

Muttering to himself, the troubled Irishman paced the dusty wood floor of his home. "I kin help ye on the trail, son. I know I kin."

"You'll be more help here. What if Sunny sends a wire? Who'll be here to read it?"

With a sigh of frustration, of resignation, Patrick slowly nodded. "Aye, yer right, lad. Let's get ye packed up."

Silently, their thoughts and prayers centered on their terrible loss, father and son gathered food supplies, a rifle and two pistols for Sean's journey. After loading everything on the back of the strongest mule, the younger man, his eyes a hard, murky hazel, swung into the saddle.

"Don't worry about me or Sunny, Pop. We're Callahans— we're tough." Giving his father a tight grin, he added, "I'll send a wire as soon as I have any leads."

"Aye, and may the seven saints of Ireland protect ye both," Patrick whispered as his only living son, and perhaps his only child, rode off. Then he saddled up the older mule, Flossie, and headed south for Fort Yuma.

Just after bypassing Yuma and changing his course to a more easterly direction, Sean lost the faint trail left by Sunny's pony, his tiny hooves swallowed up by the many riders using the same path running parallel to the Gila River. He thought briefly of turning back, of riding southwest to the Gila/Colorado River junction where the Quechan leader, Pasquel lived. The great *kwoxot* might help him decide in which direction to travel, may even have given the same advice to Sunny. Had she sought help from him before her journey took her east?

Sean pressed his fingers into his temples, praying for a sign leading him to his sister's route. The scant trail he'd followed from the farm was at least a week old. Time was not on his side.

Without a look back, Sean dug his boot heels into the mule's belly and headed east, allowing instinct and his Quechan blood to guide him. He rode hard through the night, stopping only when the mule, Whiskey, refused to move any farther. During those times he walked, encouraging the animal to follow by an occasional jerk on the reins, and he thought back to his childhood. Of his mother and younger brother. Of Sunny.

In the entire Callahan family, he and his younger sister were the most alike, felt their Indian heritage the strongest. And because of this, he would have the best chance of finding her, by thinking the way she did: the way of Moonstar.

With a heavy heart, his mind turned to Mike, two years his junior, his opposite in every way. With the exception of his coal-black hair and eyes, the younger Callahan brother was as Irish as their father, as boisterous and full of pranks. Had his death been merciful and quick, a surprise, or had he been killed defending their mother?

Sean suppressed a shudder, felt a growing lump of anger in his throat as the first rays of dawn led him and Whiskey to the banks of the Gila River. He splashed cool water over his dark head, allowing the mule to drink to his content, then began to fill the canteens. He was tying the water pouches to his saddle when a flash of yellow off to the side caught his eye.

Sean crept over to the tall cottonwood tree, his gaze darting in every direction before he plucked the piece of material from the branches.

"Sunny!" he gasped when he recognized the cloth as a length of her favorite calico. Surely she hadn't ridden off alone in her best dress and bonnet!

"No," he muttered under his breath, "she wouldn't." More likely, he surmised, she'd be wearing Mike's clothes the way she did when their father wasn't around. Dressed, as Patrick might say, like a refugee from a potato famine. Calico strips would be her way of marking her trail, of leading him to her mother's killers.

For the first time since he'd had the vision Sean chuckled, confident in his sister and their mission. Then he mounted Whiskey and veered to the northeast, allowing the Gila River to guide his path towards Maricopa Wells and Phoenix.

Driven by his purpose, Sean rode for the next two days aided only by his instincts and two more strips of calico. At dusk on the third day, he came upon a suitable wash in which to make camp and rest the tiring mule. He led Whiskey to a small spring for water, then spotted a familiar piece of yellow calico at the base of a mesquite bush.

Grinning, he bent over to pick it up, but froze instead— his hand in midair. For the first time since he'd left Yuma County, he saw the welcome sight of Paddy's tiny hoof-prints in the sand. Walking up the arroyo, Sean followed the trail until another set of prints materialized. These were much bigger, the impressions clearly made by horseshoes.

His gaze moving up the wash, Sean noted how both sets of prints mingled and overlapped. His sister was no longer alone. Balling his hands into tight fists, squeezing until his brown knuckles blanched, Sean wondered about the indignities Sunny might be suffering at the hands of her captor and how long she would be able to endure the agony.

She was close, he sensed. Close enough to risk the life of his tired mule? He glanced back at Whiskey then back up the arroyo. His sister, though wily in the Quechan manner, was pure, ignorant of men and their ways.

His mind made up, Sean stalked back to his mule and mounted him. Soon, his gaze would rest on Sunflower—his rifle sight on the bastard who held her hostage.

THREE

She'd had several chances to finish what she had set out to do. Yet when Sunny hovered over the killer, poised and ready to strike, she found she wasn't ready to become a killer herself. Not until she was absolutely certain this man had been involved in the attack on her mother.

At first she'd been convinced his injured leg and the hoofprints were enough to convict him. But what if he'd only sprained his ankle? What if many other horses were shod in the same manner as his? Why did she suddenly want him to live so badly?

It was the way he looked at her, the strange fluttering she felt in her lower abdomen when she thought he meant to kiss her. Why hadn't she felt that way before, back when the son of her tribal shaman had helped himself to a taste of her lips? How could just the mere *thought* of kissing this evil stranger magnify those sensations tenfold? What did those feelings mean?

Sunflower had no problem staying awake as she struggled to ignore her wandering mind and confused body. By the time she heard his light snores, her resolve dangled by a thin thread, and she knew she wasn't quite ready. She would have to search for more proof of his guilt before she could carry out any kind of revenge.

Sunny's ability to move through the night like a cat served her well until Cole wakened and ruined everything. Just when she was about ready to prod him from sleep to ask a few straightforward questions—with the tip of her knife resting against the skin of his throat, of course—he surprised her.

Sunny tried to draw back, but Patrick Callahan's hunting knife moved on its own, slashing her victim as he rolled away.

"Are you loco?" he spat as he tried to stem the flow of blood from his upper arm.

"I—I am Sunflower!"

"Well, Sunflower, would you mind telling me what the *hell* is the matter with you?" Cole demanded as he tightened the tourniquet he'd fashioned from the tail of his shirt.

"*I* will ask the questions now, dog," she said with an authority she didn't feel.

"The hell you will!" Cole snapped. He leaned forward, struggling to get to his feet, but the click of the Colt's hammer froze him to the spot. Swallowing hard, he spoke in an even tone. "Put my gun down, Sunflower. It's loaded."

"I hoped it was. Now sit down you miserable dog before I part your hair!"

What the hell had he done to deserve this treatment? Angered, assuming she was playing some kind of game, he began to move forward again.

"I said put that gun down and stop fooling around before you accidentally shoot someone!"

"And I said, sit down!"

A bullet shot past his head and ricocheted off a rock in the distance.

"All right!" Cole raised his hands, wondering if the girl had gone loony, and muttered, "Just take it easy, Sunflower." Cole sat back on his haunches and peered at her through the hazy firelight. "Would you mind telling me just what *is* going on here?"

"I am asking the questions—remember?" She took a backward step and squatted near the fire. "First, I want you to remove your trousers."

"What?"

"Take off your breeches, you idiot! Can you understand the King's English?"

Uncertain which unnerved him the most, the immodest order or the change in her dialect, Cole slowly began to unbutton his jeans. The crazy girl leaned toward the fire, stirring it with a curved hunting knife, while his gun dangled from her left hand.

Cole studied her as he eased his jeans down over his slim hips, then realized she'd eaten with her right hand. Dear God, he thought with horror, she'd shot at him with her *left* hand? It's a wonder she hadn't blown his head off! What in heaven's name did she want from him?

His pants circling the tops of his boots, Cole twisted his mouth into a smirk. "All right, they're down. Now what, young lady? Do you intend to have your way with me?"

Incensed, Sunny advanced a few steps but stopped short of his reach. "Enough of your questions, dog. Take off your boots and slide your pants all the way down." She pointed the .44 at his head.

"All right, all right." Grumbling, Cole followed her orders. His eyes narrow and thoughtful, he looked up at her, gave her a wicked grin, and said, "Anything else you'd like me to take off?"

"No!" Waving the pistol toward the fire, Sunny took a few steps back. "Slide over to there and stick out your right leg."

"You plan to roast me like a jack rabbit?" he blurted out, surprised.

"Maybe later," she threatened. "For now, I just want to have a look at you."

Cole inched closer to the flames until his leg was illuminated. His mind galloping at full speed as he thought of ways to disarm her, he was careful to keep one eye on Sunflower as she crept closer for a better view.

His heel propped on a stone from the fire ring, Cole's long muscular leg glistened with coils of blond down. But where was the mark of her mother's revenge?

Leaning closer, she peered at a peculiar mark near the thick part of his calf. Unlike the slash of a knife, the healing wound was nearly round, and had the shape of two quarter moons fitted together. The wound resembled a small bite. Had she followed the wrong man?

Cole sensed her confusion, guessed she was faltering in whatever plans she had for him. With lightening quickness, he leapt to his feet and lunged for his gun. Her responses sluggish, he was able to duck his head as the slow-moving knife arched towards it, then he reached up and gripped her right wrist.

The two circled for several seconds as if dancing to some primitive ritual, their arms high over head, Cole's hands clamped firmly around her wrists. Then Sunny's boot caught the back of a large stone and the two dropped to the ground.

Like a large tumbleweed, they rolled over and over in the sand and rocks, startling a pair of roadrunners. The birds skimmed across the sand, half-running, half-flying at the disturbance, and caught Sunny's attention for a split second.

Cole took that moment to shout, "Dammit, hold still!"

Sunny answered him by raising her head up hard under his chin.

"God *dammit*," he screamed just as they bumped the base of the cliff where Cole's bedroll was spread.

"Let go of me," Sunny demanded, fighting like a wounded lion. Knowing he would kill *her* if he got the chance, she pounded his back with one small fist and strained to bring the barrel of the pistol to his head with her other hand, but she was no match for the hardened rancher.

"What in *hell* is wrong with you?"

This time, she answered him by poking at his eye with her free hand.

Ducking her, Cole's strong fingers circled the delicate wrist holding his gun. Then he hooked his boot around her leg, flipped her over onto her back and straddled her.

"Hold still!" he gasped, out of breath.

But Sunny renewed her attempts to break free, still convinced he was trying to kill her. She squirmed beneath the prison of muscular legs and heaving chest, and sputtered a long string of Irish curses between breaths. Patrick's knife had been knocked from her hand during their tumble, leaving the Colt as her only defense. She struggled, trying to find a way to free the gun and use it to gain her freedom—or end his.

Sunflower's vain attempts to escape inflamed Cole as her soft full breasts pressed against his chest and her hips writhed between his legs. A fire grew in his loins, even though he understood the pleasurable distraction might cost him his life. His mind rapidly losing sight of the warnings, Cole lowered his head and repeated the request, but this time the words were soft and low.

"Hold still, Sunflower. I'm not going to hurt you."

Wary, but confused by his sudden gentleness, Sunny tested her rapidly tiring body for a quick burst of energy with which to fight him off. Then it occurred to her that she might not need her strength. The rancher had a new look in his eye, a gentler hold on her than before. Was he thinking of using her, of sating his lusts in her copper body, then discarding her?

If so, she would allow his disgusting advances.

She would *encourage* them. Then, when some sixth

sense told her he was beyond control, she would point the
gun at his head and demand her freedom.

Sunny stopped her struggles and willed her body to relax.

Enveloped by a cloud of silky black hair, consumed by its
sweet, earthy fragrance, Cole kept a firm grip on her wrists,
not realizing the girl had given up the fight. His head
dropped lower, and his mouth brushed the velvet skin at the
base of her throat. Her pulse hammered against his lips. She
was so soft, so sweet and clean, yet wild as the country
surrounding them.

Cole lifted his head and stared into her eyes. Then he
noticed the compliant limbs, the inviting expression looking
up at him in the moon-bathed night.

"Have you changed your mind?" he whispered. "Is this
all you wanted from me?"

Not waiting for her answer, Cole teased her upper lip
with a gentle sweep of his mustache, hoping to draw some
kind of response from her. The gesture only served to
inflame him further. Suddenly eager for her taste, he took
her up on her invitation and claimed her mouth with his.

Keeping her purpose in mind, Sunny squeezed her eyes
and mind shut to what was happening, and accepted his
kiss. Her first sensation was one of surprise. Instead of the
stabbing broom-like prickles she expected from the growth
of hair on his upper lip, the feeling was akin to a caress from
a length of the finest fox pelt. Her mouth wrapped in this
wonderful silky fur, Sunny allowed instinct to guide her,
and matched his kiss with the same heat and intensity. But
when his tongue slipped between her lips, when the tip
sought passage between her clenched teeth, she stiffened.
What did he mean to do to her?

"Open your mouth, little flower," Cole breathed against
her fiery flesh. "Let me taste your sweetness." Then he
crushed her mouth, determined to invade the honeyed
sanctuary.

If she relented, allowed him to perform this unnatural act

with his tongue, would he finally be rendered helpless? Could this concession give her the opportunity she sought? It was a chance she decided to take.

Steeling herself against the wave of nausea she was sure to have, Sunny slowly parted her teeth. But Cole didn't plunge in as she'd assumed, didn't ravage her tender flesh or bite her. Instead, he slowly circled the tip of her tongue with his in a lazy swirling motion. In place of the expected revulsion, she was hit with a stunning series of new and terrifying sensations. She was on fire everywhere at once. Her skin burned where he touched her, yet begged for him to return and add to the flames. As if it had a life of its own, her body arched against his, demanded that he fill the aching voids she never knew existed within her.

And then she became more aware of Cole, of the hard length of his body pressing against hers. Of his immediate need. Clad only in a shirt and his loose summer drawers, Sunny could feel every angle in his body, every muscular ridge as he pushed against her thin cotton breeches. For the first time in her life, she knew what it was to have a man want her, to feel his arousal thundering against her core. Suddenly confused, wondering why her most sensitive area was so alive with a deliciously painful ache—and worse, why she wanted the feelings to continue—she struggled to clear her mind and ignore the sweet torment.

Cole moved from her mouth and spread a trail of hot kisses across her cheeks to her earlobe. One big hand slid along her ribs until it found, then cupped, a full breast. And when his lips began the return trip to her open mouth, this time sweeping across her forehead and down to the tip of her nose, he began to murmur hoarse words of encouragement against her flushed skin.

Instinct told her he was ready to mate.

Her brain told her he had only that purpose in mind and it was time for her to make a move.

Her body told her an entirely different story.

Her body won. Just a couple more of those wonderful exciting kisses, she convinced herself. Then she would be ready to do what had to be done.

Not thinking of her own slipping control, Sunny reached up with her free hand and sank her fingers into Cole's flaxen hair. She guided his mouth back to hers as if it were an act she'd performed a thousand times, and buried her lips in his.

Suddenly bold, wanting to know everything at once, Sunny didn't wait for his exploring tongue, and instead drove hers into his mouth and mimicked his swirling motion with the expertise of a far more experienced woman. She was drowning in him, savoring the exquisite sensations and marvelous texture of his mouth as the kiss deepened. His aroma, that same blend of fresh tobacco, of the earth and his horse, nearly drove her mad as her senses heightened. Unaware she'd become as helpless as her victim, or that the gun had fallen from her suddenly boneless hand, Sunny wrapped both of her arms around Cole's broad back and dug eager fingers into the hard muscles of his shoulders.

She was even wilder than he'd first imagined, as schooled as any courtesan in the art of driving a man into a frenzy. Where had she learned her skills, how many men had shown her the way? Cole flinched at the thought, then dismissed it—along with the fact that she was Indian—as a wave of urgency shook him. Impatient to possess her, to know what other delights she had in mind for him, he slipped his hand between their damp bodies and began to fumble with the knot in her shirt.

Singular in his purpose, aware only of the beautiful, sensual woman he held in his arms, Cole failed to pick up the ominous signals of impending danger. By the time he heard the distinct click of a rifle hammer, it was too late.

"Now ain't this an interestin' sight for these tired ole eyes," a deep whiskey voice commented.

Cole jerked as if ready to leap to his feet, but the barrel of the rifle dug into the center of his back.

"That wouldn't be too smart, stranger. Just slide to the side of that little gal and keep your face hugged to that there blanket."

Silently cursing the lapse in his usually excellent instincts, Cole inched his body off Sunflower's and pushed his head into the bed roll.

A shrill, appreciative whistle cut into the calm night before the man said, "Can't say as I blame ya, mister. She your squaw?"

"I am no man's *squaw*," Sunny snapped. "I am not a squaw."

Heedless of his own danger, Cole whipped his head towards Sunflower. "Shut your mouth and lay still," he hissed under his breath.

Through cackling laughter, the man said, "Better listen to him, squaw. You and me can have us a real good time if you don't give me any trouble. But if you insist on misbe-havin'," he ran his fingers over the rifle as if it were a woman's body, "I'd just as soon splatter your pretty face all over the sand."

Confident and suddenly hungry for the squaw, the outlaw spread his legs wide and added, "Be a real waste, tho."

His mind exploding with rapid-fire ideas for their escape, Cole glanced at Sunflower, hoping she'd remain quiet and go along with him. "No need to threaten the squaw, buddy. She'll do anything you want."

Sunny gasped, but something in Cole's cool green eyes and low, even tone prompted her to lie back and press her lips together.

"That's good. That's real good," the outlaw remarked lustily. Then he took a few steps back and picked up the coils of rope he'd left at the edge of the campsite. When he returned to the pair, he tossed two short lengths to Sunny. "Be a good little injun and tie your friend up for me," he ordered harshly. "Hands behind his back, legs at the ankles."

Realizing that for the first time since she'd left her mother's home she was in real danger, Sunny shook off a cold shiver and got to her knees. She began to bind Cole's hands, careful to leave the coils loose enough for him to maneuver out of them, when the barrel of the rifle suddenly cracked against the side of her head.

"Nice and tight, honey. We don't want your friend interruptin' us, now do we?"

Wincing in pain, Sunny refused to give the outlaw satisfaction by bringing her hand to the lump forming on her scalp. With a burst of anger, she yanked the loops tighter and twisted the ends into a knot, then moved down to Cole's ankles and performed the same task.

When she finished, the outlaw reached down, grabbing the back of her shirt, and jerked her to her feet. "That's real good, honey."

Terrified, but with her Irish eyes flashing defiance, Sunny got her first good look at the man. Not much taller than she, he was thick and barrel-chested with the flat cold eyes of a rattlesnake. Stubbles of a week-old beard poked out of his puffy cheeks, and strands of silver popped through the muddy brown hairs. Sunny grimaced when his sour breath reached her nose. He smelled of whiskey and rotted vegetables, sweat and damp rawhide.

"You're gonna have to wait a bit for your reward, squaw," he said with a throaty chuckle. "I got to collect my horse and gear."

Moving quicker than she imagined he was capable of, the man grabbed her hands and bound her wrists together. Leading her by a long length of rope, they walked past Cole's head to a nearby mesquite tree. Pulling her hands over her head, the man looped the rope over the tallest branch and tied a knot at the base of the tree.

"Now you just stand there and think of all the fun we're

gonna have, honey." He turned to walk away, then suddenly pivoted. "Say, where's the gun, squaw?"

"Gun?" she squeaked out.

"Yeah, gun. You know—bang, bang, you're dead? I heard the shot from your camp, brought me to you like one of your smoke signals." Bellowing an ugly laugh, he turned his rattlesnake eyes on Cole. "I see he ain't wearin' no gun. He ain't hardly wearin' nuttin'."

Cole had spent the minutes since Sunny tied him searching the sand for that very item, and had discovered the butt of his Colt poking out from under the bedroll not three inches from his head. Thinking quickly, he explained, "I lost my gun several miles down the trail. You heard my rifle when I shot at a coyote. It's over by my saddle."

"Rifle, huh? Didn't sound like no rifle to me."

The skeptical outlaw scoured the campground for the weapon, and dug through Cole's saddlebags, but found only the rifle. Taking the Winchester with him, he disappeared into the bushes at the edge of the campsite.

Cocking his head until he could look up into Sunflower's eyes, Cole whispered, "Can you get loose?"

"I'm trying," she answered quietly, "but my hands are swollen."

"Damn," he muttered under his breath. "Keep trying. I'll think of something in the meantime."

He glanced at her silhouette, illuminated by the moonlight as she struggled against her bonds, and cursed his negligence. How could he have been blindsided, and because of an Indian squaw of all people?

Disgusted with himself, Cole snapped at her, "You did a hell of a job tying me up. You have a better chance of getting free than I do. Do it!"

Sunny nodded, renewed her efforts, then glanced toward the bushes where the outlaw had disappeared. "And if I do, what then? I think this man means to kill us."

"Not as long as I can draw a breath, he won't. If you

manage to get free before I do, the gun is under the blanket by my chin. Do you know how to use it—*really* use it?"

Hearing the stranger's approach, Sunny kept her silence and gave him a short nod.

Satisfied she could handle the pistol, Cole eased his head back down on the blanket and watched the outlaw tie his scraggly mount next to Sage.

"Nice horse you got here, mister. Damn fine animal." He swaggered past the fire and headed for the mesquite tree, taunting Cole as he walked by him, "What do you say to a little swap? Sound fair? It does to me," he rambled on to his silent prisoner. "Yep, I think that's exactly what I'll do."

When he reached Sunny, he stood before her, eyeing her from head to toe. "Let's see what kind of swap you and me can cook up, honey," he threatened before he planted a wet sloppy kiss on her mouth.

When his fat, slimy lips touched hers, Sunny jerked her knee up and drove it into the man's groin.

"Shit, oh . . . *shit*," he groaned, grabbing his crotch as he staggered backwards. "Y-you r-rotten . . . *bitch*," he managed to add, the words strangling in his throat as he fell to his knees and rested, panting between groans.

After he recovered enough to move again, the outlaw lurched to his feet and began to stalk her. His features twisted in a murderous rage, he raised his thick arm high above his head. "You stupid, stupid bitch."

Then he whipped his open palm across the side of her face with enough force to knock Sunny off her feet.

"Think you're a real wildcat, huh?" he bellowed. "You miserable excuse for a half-breed whore! I'm just the man to take all the fight out of your kind. When I'm done with you, you won't have the strength to feed yourself!"

Stunned by the blow, Sunny hung by her wrists until the man untied the rope. Then she dropped to the ground. Grabbing her shoulders, the man pulled her to her feet and gave her a vicious shove towards the fire. "Go rustle me up some grub, squaw. Then I'll be happy to show you how a real man tames a no-good savage."

Disoriented, Sunny stumbled and nearly fell several times as she crossed the opening. When she reached Cole's saddlebags, she thought of digging deep and retrieving her grandfather's war club, but the click of the hammer on the stranger's gun pushed the thought from her mind. She would have her chance. She would *make* her chance.

Thick cords stood out along the sides of Cole's neck as he fought to keep his temper and struggled to remain silent. Watching the outlaw strike Sunflower sent a burst of white-hot anger coursing through him, tensed his entire body, and paled the skin on his knuckles the way the desert sun blanched the skull of a dead steer. Disregarding the pain of skin rubbed raw by his bindings, Cole worked at loosening the ropes. He couldn't take much more, couldn't bear to witness the next chapter in the man's plans for Sunflower. Somehow, he would break free. Then, if he had to, he would kill the bastard with his bare hands.

Sunny hung her head low, her eyes cast to the ground as she served the outlaw a supper of leftover rabbit, some jerky, and a couple of biscuits.

"That's better," the stranger growled. He waved her away with his pistol. "Go sit across from me where I can keep an eye on you."

Obediently, Sunny sidestepped the campfire and sank cross-legged into the soft sand. She watched the man stuff the food in his mouth and wash it down with a swig of whiskey, and wondered how she might gain an advantage over this cunning animal. Would he drink enough poteen to slow his responses? Or would she have to pretend to submit to this disgusting creature and wait for him to lose control, as she'd tried to do with Cole?

She glanced over at the blond rancher, warming inside in spite of her predicament, and picked out the gleam of his watchful eyes. She gave him a shy smile, then dropped her gaze to the sand. It wouldn't be the same with this ugly beast. She didn't need experience to know that this man could never make her feel the way Cole had, to know that instead of setting her on fire with longings and pleasures she didn't understand, this stranger's touch would make her wither inside—make her wish she were dead.

"Toss me that there pouch of tobacco, woman!" the whiskey voice bellowed.

Startled, Sunny scrambled over near Cole's saddle, then threw the bundle across the fire.

The outlaw held the pouch near the flames and read the inscription on the canvas bag. "Bull Durham, huh?" He turned his gaze on Cole. "Mighty fancy smokes ya got here, fellah. Mind if I have one?" But he turned his back to the prisoner, not interested in his response. "I didn't think you would," he said with a hoarse laugh.

Guessing the time in which to save herself was running short, Sunny desperately searched her mind for a way to disarm or disable the man. If she moved without his permission, she had no doubt he'd shoot her on the spot. What ploy could she use to get up and walk around the campsite?

Unwittingly, the outlaw provided one for her. "Let's have a better look at you, squaw. Stand up and walk around to the front of the fire."

Taking a deep drag on his cigarette as she followed his directions, the outlaw peered at her through rings of blue-white smoke. "Damn half-breed, all right. Do you even know the name of the bull that sired ya?"

Her heart pounding in her throat, Sunny bit her bottom lip and slowly shook her head.

"Didn't think so," he grunted with a disgusted sneer. "The only thing your kind is good for is a little relief at the end of the trail. Then—" He pointed the pistol at her head and made a popping sound with his mouth. Laughing, he looked back at Cole. "You don't mind if I pick up where you left off with the little gal, do you?" Again swiveling back to the fire, he grunted, "I didn't think you would."

Measuring the distance between herself and the man, Sunny took a tentative step in his direction. "I am good for much more than that," she promised. "If you will take me with you, I can make your journey very pleasurable."

"Yeah? What can a half-breed whore do for me except slow me down?"

"I—" Sunny swallowed the lump in her throat before she went on. "Besides warming your bed at night, I can cook for you."

"Cook for me?" he snorted. "If them biscuits are your idea of cookin', I'm better off chokin' down cactus needles!"

"M-maybe I could—"

"Shut up, woman! I don't want to listen to your yammering. I want a look at you. Take off your clothes."

Sunny bit her bottom lip again, this time hard enough to bring the salty taste of her own blood to her mouth. With a terrified glance in Cole's direction, she brought trembling fingers to the knot in her shirt and slowly began to untie it.

The look on Sunflower's face was too much for Cole.

Swearing hotly under his breath, he jerked and twisted his hands, caring little if he tore off his fingers in his efforts to save her from the ultimate indignity. Sunflower's expression showed him much more than her terror. She had a look of innocence, of an almost virginal fear of what was about to happen. With a great effort, he jackknifed to his knees, still twisting his raw and bleeding hands against the bindings.

Then everything seemed to happen at once.

Her shirt removed, it dangled in Sunny's hand as she took a couple of bold steps towards the man. Her head held high, her eyes cold and hard, she arched her back and presented her upturned breasts for his inspection.

"Nice," he grunted thickly. "Real nice. Now the drawers."

His lust-glazed eyes and complete attention focused on her dusky nipples as she'd hoped, Sunny made her move. She tossed the shirt over the man's head, then scrambled over to the bedroll—and Cole's .44.

Her back to the outlaw, Sunny could hear him screaming curses as he struggled with the shirt. Frantically searching for the gun, she finally found it and pulled it from its hiding spot.

Still fighting his bonds, Cole saw the outlaw get up and charge through the sand and rocks like an enraged bull. Unable to do anything else, he called out a warning.

"Behind you! Quick, turn and shoot him!"

Wheeling around as she stood up, Sunny raised the pistol and aimed it at the man's chest.

"You no-good bastard daughter of a diseased whore!" he bellowed, a murderous gleam eclipsing the lust in his eye. "I'll teach you a thing or two! You don't know who you're messin' with, squaw!"

Then he saw the gun and froze.

Advancing a few feet, Sunny cocked the hammer. "Sit down or I will blow a hole in your black heart!"

"Stupid injun squaw. Gimme that gun!" he growled as he lunged towards her.

Sunny's moment of indecision gave the outlaw enough time to grab the barrel of the Colt. The pair grappled, the outlaw's curses jumbled with Cole's frantic words of encouragement.

Then the thunderous crack of gunfire splintered the night air.

Patrick Callahan's daughter dropped to the ground with a sickening thud.

FOUR

She was swimming.

She swirled down, spiralling into the deep dark waters.

Sunny was cutting through the strong current of her beloved Colorado River as if she swam in melted butter. She felt the cool water washing over her, through her hair, soothing her. Then she felt a sharp sting on her cheek.

"Sunflower. Wake up, it's all right."

The waters called her name over and over. It had never sounded more beautiful. Then she realized the voice did not belong to the river but to a man. And she wasn't swimming, she was lying amongst rocks and sand.

Alarmed, Sunny bolted upright, her eyes wide and fearful.

"Easy, Sunflower," Cole reassured. "It's over. He's dead."

Wild-eyed, she looked around the campsite and spotted the evil stranger sprawled in the sand a few feet beyond the fire. "W-what happened?"

"You caught the recoil of my Colt right between your eyes. You knocked yourself out, Sunflower." Cole brushed the back of his fingers across her cheek, then continued in a soft comforting tone. "The minute the gun went off, you both dropped to the ground like a couple of sacks of feed. I wasn't sure who shot who at first."

She *had* shot the stranger. Sunny buried her face in her hands and tried to stifle a heavy sob. Salty tears streaked across her palms as she realized the enormity of her deed.

"I killed him," she cried. "I have murdered another human being."

"No, no. Not exactly." Cole gathered her in his arms and pressed her head against his shoulder. Stroking her satiny hair, he began to rock her. "He tried to pull the gun out of your hand. It was an accident. If anything, he killed himself."

"B-but—"

"No buts about it. You're not to blame. I just wish I could have gotten free sooner."

He continued to stroke her ebony hair, allowed her the silence and chance to weep away the terrors of the night until he could no longer ignore the heat of her bare breasts pressed against his chest. She'd endured the humiliation of one madman's lust this night. She wouldn't have to deal with yet another. Cole released her and got to his feet.

"Wait here for a minute, Sunflower. I'll be right back."

"Sunny," she said in a small voice. "My family and friends call me Sunny."

"Sunny?" He repeated the name several times thinking how well it fit her, how like a ray of sunshine she seemed to illuminate a corner of his life. *In what capacity?* he suddenly wondered. She was lovely, exciting, and spirited. But she was also Indian. How could he be so attracted to her?

A toddler when the Fremont family made the dusty, danger-filled trek from Texas to Arizona, Cole's only memories of Indian attacks during the journey were supplied by his father, Nathan. But Cole needed no reminders of his eleventh year, of the vicious Chiricahua ambush on the Triple F ranch and the painful losses that nearly tore the Fremont family apart.

As if it were yesterday, Cole could see his mother, Olive, writhing on the floor of her burning home, delivering Nathan's third son too early, stillborn. No stories from the past were necessary to prompt the image of his fifteen-year-old brother after the Chiricahua were finished with him, either. The day after the attack, when they were certain Olive was out of danger, Nathan and Cole had set out to search for the youth.

The Chiricahua had released the boy, using his body as a warning, a message to all ranchers in the area. The youth's flesh was a pincushion of arrows, each carefully placed so they wouldn't pierce a vital organ. The eldest Fremont brother's death had been agonizingly slow and painful, its message forever stamped on Cole's heart.

Shaking off his ugly thoughts, Cole spun on his heel, catching his bare foot on the corner of a jagged rock, and hobbled off to his saddle. After slipping into his jeans and boots, he fastened his holster around his waist and sheathed the Colt. Then he picked up Sunflower's shirt and took it to her.

"Cover yourself," he said more harshly than he'd intended.

Startled by the change in his attitude, Sunny grabbed the shirt and quickly dressed. Why had he changed so? He'd been so warm, so tender, before the man had come and again after he had died. What had she done to displease him?

Sunny's puzzled expression, the hurt in her eyes, told Cole more than anything she could have said at that moment. Although his memories and Nathan's bitterness towards all Indians were a part of his life he couldn't ignore, Cole was not without sympathy for these native Americans, especially for the gentler tribes like the Pima. He could hardly blame Sunflower for the tragedies in the Fremont family.

His voice cracking, he said, "I'm sorry for barking at you like that. I—I'm tired. Let's use what's left of the night for some rest."

Cole reached for Sunny's hands, pulling her to her feet, then impulsively scooped her into his arms. "You've had a rough night. I'll stay by your side." Inclining his head towards the fire, he added, "I'll take care of our *friend* in the morning. Then we'll talk."

Suddenly exhausted, Sunny nodded weakly and allowed her head to drop to his shoulder. When they reached the bed roll, Cole positioned himself with his back to the cliff, then fit Sunny's body against the curve of his.

"Goodnight, Sunfl—Sunny. Rest well, little flower."

"I will try. Goodnight."

Cole's arm rested on her hip, but it was more protection than embrace. She needed more. Gripped by an overwhelming sense of loss, of isolation, Sunny longed for Cole to gather her in his arms. Never had she felt so alone, so vulnerable, or in such need of another's strength and touch. What would he do should she turn to embrace him?

Did he, like the disgusting outlaw, look on her as a half-breed whore? A nuisance? What of the kisses they'd shared? *Mother would know*. Sunny mouthed the words silently, missing her so much she thought her breastbone would split from the ache inside. Rage slowly replaced self-pity, and even in her exhausted state, she resumed her plans for revenge. If Cole's offer to escort her to his ranch was still good, she would take him up on it. Continuing east, there was a chance she might encounter her mother's killers on the way—west toward home would mean defeat and allow the murdering scum their freedom.

It was a very long time before sleep came to Sunny that night, and the following morning she slept well past the dawn. When she finally did awaken, it was with a start. She was alone. Propping herself on one elbow, she glanced around the campsite and found Cole at the edge near a stand of Palo Verde trees. He was piling stones on the outlaw's grave.

After dragging her fingers through sleep-tangled hair, she approached him. "Why didn't you wake me? I should have helped you bury the viper."

Wiping the perspiration from his brow with his sleeve, Cole turned to face her. She was even more beautiful this morning than she'd been in the moonlight, her sleep-drugged eyes languid and seductively stunning. Wheeling around, Cole resumed piling rocks on the fresh mound of earth before he trusted himself to answer her.

"I thought you'd seen enough of his ugly face. You needed the rest."

Again she sensed a coolness in his attitude. Puzzled, Sunny circled the grave and began piling rocks across from him.

"You said we would talk this morning." She heaved a large stone onto the center of the grave, then brought her hands to her hips. "If you will spare me the blarney, I would like to know what I did to raise your ire so."

With a heavy sigh, Cole reached into his shirt pocket for his tobacco pouch. As he loosened the drawstring, he wondered how he could explain his feelings without hurting hers, skip over the "blarney" as she'd put it and . . . *blarney*? Cole's upper lip curled in amusement as he thought of the Irish phrases scattered throughout her speech, not to mention the string of curses she'd spat at him during their struggle the night before.

Striking a match to his cigarette, he cocked a suspicious blond brow. "I'll be happy to dispense with the blarney if you will."

Sunny lifted her chin. "I will not be handing you any."

"Good." He took a deep drag and blew a long stream of smoke down to the outlaw's grave. "How does a young woman of Pima extraction happen to be so full of Irish expressions?"

"Oh," she laughed lightly, "that."

Stalling, Sunny began to carve a series of circular figures in the sand with the toe of her boot. Should she tell him everything? Could he *really* be trusted with the truth? Before the outlaw had come upon them, her suspicions about Cole had nearly vanished, and now that their moments of terror were behind them, the last little nagging doubts seemed to be dissolving as well. Maybe if she told him everything, he might even be able to help her. Maybe if she— But an impatient Cole sliced into her thoughts.

"All right. If you don't want to explain that, perhaps you'd like to shed some light on your midnight attack on me." He rubbed his aching shoulder where the knife had pierced his skin. "You know, when I woke up and saw you at the business end of my gun, I actually thought you were trying to kill me."

"I was," she admitted, remembering the struggle and how close she'd come to slitting his throat.

"You were?" Stunned, Cole lifted his brows. "Why? All I did was try to help you. Why would you want to kill me for that?"

Suddenly remorseful, Sunny lowered her lashes. "I thought— I was following a trail from Yuma."

"You followed me all the way from Yuma? Why?"

Sunny's heart constricted at this. Had she been wrong about his innocence, made another mistake? Until now, she'd only guessed he'd been in her homeland. Still able to hope that he could not have been involved in her mother's murder, she became the interrogator.

"I followed two riders from Yuma. Men whose horses bore the same prints as yours."

Cole shrugged. "I rode out alone. As for the prints, I suppose other ranches have horseshoes made in about the same way." He took a deep drag on his cigarette and tried to make sense out of all she'd told him. "Why were you on my trail?"

"I told you. I am looking for two men. One of them has a nasty wound on his right leg. When I came into your camp, I saw you were limping."

With a short laugh, Cole said, "You'd limp too if you were stupid enough to sit on a Gila monster. Damn thing chewed through my jeans and started working on my leg before I could get his teeth pried apart with my gun barrel."

"You have been bitten by a Gila monster!" she gasped. "Why aren't you dead?"

"I didn't give him enough time to chew his poison into me. He just got enough in to give me a belly ache and a damn painful swollen leg."

"Oh?" she breathed in awe. "My mother's people believe the breath of a Gila monster is enough to kill a man. How could you survive the bite?"

Familiar with the old Indian tale, Cole chuckled softly. "Don't tell me you believe that. Only Indians—" He cut off his words when he remembered the girl's description of her family. "You're *mother's* people? You told me she was white."

Certain now that Cole was not one of the men she hunted, Sunny resumed drawing figures in the sand. "I was afraid to tell you my mother was Quechan, afraid if you were the man I sought, you might guess my true purpose." Her large dark eyes glistened with tears as she explained. "My mother and older brother were murdered by the men whose trail I followed. I thought you might have been one of them."

"Oh, Sunflower." He groaned, thinking of her pain, remembering she'd also lost her father. "I'm sorry for your terrible losses, but please believe me. I had nothing to do with their deaths."

"I realize that." She nodded. "And I am sorry for the wound I gave you. Is it deep? Does it give you much pain?"

"Don't worry about me," he assured, wondering how he

could feel such compassion for an Indian—one who'd tried to kill him at that. "It's just a scratch."

Still feeling a deep empathy, Cole approached her and slid a comforting hand along her shoulder. "You're not alone, Sunny. You may have lost your entire family, but my offer is still open. Come to Triple F ranch with me. You might even find some relatives at Fort McDowell."

Taken aback at first, Sunny recalled her earlier story about mining the Superstitions. "There is one more thing you should know. My father is not a Pima Indian. He's Patrick Callahan, straight from Killarney, Ireland."

Surprise trapping a puff of smoke in his throat, Cole coughed and tossed his cigarette on the grave. He'd expected the Gaelic bits of her conversation had come from an educator, mentor, or perhaps even a husband, but her father?

Cole stepped away from her and stood with hands on hips. "You said, *is*. Am I to assume your father wasn't murdered on the—"

"No, I forgot to set you straight. My father and older brother, Sean, are seeking gold somewhere north of Yuma. They should be in La Paz or maybe Fort Mohave by now."

"I see," he muttered thoughtfully, but he really didn't. She'd told him so many stories, he didn't know what to believe. Had she lied about anything else? Did she have other surprises planned for him if he went ahead and escorted her back to the ranch? He'd let his guard down around her once and it had nearly cost him his life. It wouldn't happen again. "I think it's time we had a very long and *truthful* discussion. Join me at the fire."

Sensing an underlying storm in his words, Sunny followed him to the campfire and accepted the cup of coffee he offered. Settling cross-legged into the sand, she took a cautious sip of the hot brew and waited for Cole to take the lead.

"All right," he said after rolling and lighting another cigarette. "I want the truth from you. Every bit of it."

"But I have told the truth," she objected, suddenly indignant. "There is nothing more."

"And the truth is—your mother was Quechan, murdered by unknown assailants, and instead of going to your Irish father for help, you took off, *alone*, with the idea of taking care of the varmints by yourself?" His tone incredulous, Cole raised it another notch and added, "You really expect me to believe that?"

" 'Tis the truth!" she snapped, banging the tin cup against her knee. Wincing as droplets of hot coffee burned through her cotton breeches and shirt, Sunny tossed the cup across the fire towards Cole's boot. "Believe what you wish you—you yellow-haired leavings of a bull-headed coyote— but I swear by Saint Patrick, those are the facts."

As he regarded the dark coffee stain spreading across the toe of his boot, Cole's mustache began to twitch, but even he couldn't be sure if it jerked with anger or mirth.

Chancing a glance into her midnight-blue eyes, he said, "You expect me to accept the fact that a smart girl like you didn't think of the danger she'd be in crossing Arizona alone?"

"I knew of the danger," she sniffed. "But if I had gone alone after my father, the danger would have been no less." Indignation gave way to anger and Sunny jumped to her feet. "I suppose you think I should have stayed at the farm, *alone*, wailing and weeping for the next two or three months until my father returned."

His ire rising to meet hers, Cole got up and stood facing her across the dying fire. "You might have at *least* gone to the sheriff and let him handle things!"

Sunny's laugh was bitter as she said, "You actually think the sheriff would go out of his way to find the murderers of another damned Indian?"

With an inward groan, Cole shrugged. "Some might."

·"Not this one." Holding her head high, Sunny tossed her long raven hair over her shoulders, clearly signaling Cole to make the next move.

Uncomfortable, he took a couple of steps around the outside of the smoldering fire, kicking pebbles and rocks out of his way as he went. "What about your mother's tribe? Don't you have some kind of leader who would have helped you?"

"I thought of that," she bit off. "Our leader is Pasqual, a man of great vision. But if I had gone to him, if I tried to—" Sunny let out a long sigh and looked into Cole's green eyes. What she saw, either skepticism or disapproval, made up her mind for her. "You have the head of a pig-eyed goat. You would not understand."

Sunny whirled on her boot heel and stalked off towards Paddy, mumbling over her shoulder as she kicked up the sand, "If I may have a minute, I will be happy to give you your rid of me and all the doubts plaguing your blitherin' fool for a brain!"

Cole rolled his eyes and blew out a long exaggerated breath before he approached her. She'd managed to put *him* on the defense, and while he didn't understand that, or her solitary journey into the badlands, he knew one thing for certain. He couldn't just let her ride off alone again.

"Don't be in such a hurry to run off, Sunflower," he began softly. "I'd like to understand, and could if you'd just give me a chance."

Her back to him as she arranged her traveling sacks across Paddy's neck, Sunny gave him a sideways glance. This time, his springlike eyes reflected only sincerity, honesty. Keeping her back to Cole, she stroked the pony's mane.

She would try one more time because she really did want his protection on the trail. "If I had gone to Pasqual, it would have been a waste of my time."

"I still don't understand, Sunny. Surely he would have

sent some braves—men adept at tracking—after your mother's killers, and saved you the trouble."

Sunny turned and faced him at this. Fighting to keep the hostility from her eyes, she said, "He would have wanted to track the men, of that I have no doubt. But," she lowered her head and stared down at the earth, "the cost would have been too great. If Pasqual sent a few braves after these men, they surely would have found then killed them as honor demanded."

"As you set out to do. I don't see the difference, except you were alone and put yourself in grave danger."

"And if Pasqual chose the same path as I, which he would not have, the entire Quechan nation would have been in grave danger. We are a peaceful tribe, and love our land and the relative freedom we enjoy." She turned a frosty indigo eye on him as she added, "Surely a man as *smart* as you can guess the price our nation would pay should a band of savage Quechans attack a couple of innocent white men."

"Damn," he muttered under his breath. Cole shook his head then pulled his fingers through his wavy hair. "I suppose General Crook would pull some of his troops off Geronimo and send them after your people."

"See how smart you can be, bucko?" Sunny turned back to Paddy and grabbed a wad of his mane.

Just as she prepared to launch her body onto the pony's back, Cole reached out and slipped his arm around her waist.

"Not so fast," he said as he dragged her into his arms. "If you can keep that flaming Irish temper of yours in check for a minute, I'd like to apologize. I didn't understand how limited your choices were before, but I do now. Please forgive my ignorance and allow me to escort you to the Fort for some well-deserved rest. Who knows, our path might cross the men you're looking for."

It was what she wanted. After spending these past few

nights on the trail alone, her few moments of sleep constantly interrupted by the cacophony of desert life celebrating the darkness, the thought of resting in a quiet room safe from all predators, human or animal, was too tempting to ignore. Exhaustion made the decision for her.

Sunny tilted her chin and looked into his hypnotic green eyes. "Thank you. My father will find some way to repay you."

Far too aware of her softness, wondering why he'd found it necessary to gather her in his arms, Cole released Sunny and stepped back. How would her father repay him for the thoughts he was entertaining at this moment?

He cleared his throat and nodded. "Then it's done. We'll spend one more night on the trail, and by tomorrow night we should be at the ranch." If they rode hard. If he could manage to keep his eyes and hands off of her until she was safely locked in her own room at the house.

Cole quickly cleaned up the campsite, tied a rope around the thick neck of the outlaw's Appaloosa, then he and Sunny rode off to the east. They progressed much slower than Cole had planned, Paddy still unable to keep up with Sage, the Appaloosa, windbroken and ill-used. More than once Cole thought of shooting the unfortunate animal, but sensed Sunflower would find a way to stop him and insist on bringing the poor horse back to health. By the time they stopped and made camp for the evening, he knew they would never reach the gate of the Triple F ranch by the following night.

Glancing over at Sunny as she stacked rocks to form a campfire, Cole considered his options. Maybe the extra time would work in his favor. Even if Paddy slowed his pace further, they would still make Phoenix by sundown tomorrow. He studied the young woman, following every movement of her fluid body as she worked to bring life to the mesquite twigs, and flinched with a new thought. How would his father, a fierce hater of all Indians, react to their houseguest?

Although ill-fitting, Sunny's breeches afforded Cole a rare opportunity to admire her long legs and tiny waist, making him uncomfortable when she turned, giving him an unobstructed view of her neatly rounded derriere. And that tattered shirt. The thin material barely covered the swell of her magnificent breasts and couldn't begin to hide the protruding nipples he knew to be a breathtaking dusky-rose color.

Cole took several deep breaths and turned his attention back to the horses. Nathan Fremont would never allow this disheveled Indian squaw into his home no matter how hard Cole tried to convince him otherwise. Taking a room in Phoenix would make that task much simpler. After a good night's rest in the Goldwater Hotel, he would purchase a suitable traveling ensemble for Sunny and the two would arrive at the ranch in a fresh and respectable fashion. Maybe Nathan Fremont wouldn't even notice Sunny was half Indian.

And maybe he wouldn't notice his only son had finally returned home.

The pair finished their supplies that evening, dining on leftover jerky, biscuits, a corn flour cake, and the few pumpkin seeds remaining in Sunny's pouch. When it came time to bed down, Cole made it a point to arrange Sunny's bedding on the opposite side of the fire from his own.

"Try to enjoy your last night on the trail, little flower," he laughed as he stretched the length of his body across the blanket. "Tomorrow I promise you'll be sleeping in luxury."

But tomorrow didn't interest Sunny. Tonight did. Why had he separated their sleeping quarters? She needed his comfort, the sense of security his arms brought her during the night. With a pout and a determined toss of her head, Sunny jerked the bedroll from the spot Cole had chosen and marched over to his side of the fire. She dropped the bedding next to his and began to spread it out.

"What do you think you're doing?" Cole demanded.

"Sleeping. As I did last night."

"I don't think it's such a good idea for you to bed down here. Go back to your side of the fire."

But Sunny continued to make the area beneath her blankets soft and rock-free. When she was satisfied with the arrangement, she curled up beside Cole.

"Didn't you hear me? This isn't a good idea."

"Oh?" Sunny leaned up on one elbow and propped her head with her hand. "Is it a good idea to leave me alone, unprotected on the other side of the fire? I would be at the mercy of the cougar and other men like the outlaw."

Mercy. She didn't know the meaning of the word or she would show him some. "Oh, all right," he complained, also knowing she was right, "but stay on your own bedroll and try to hold still. I'm beat."

Remaining propped on her elbow, Sunny stared down at his closed eyes, his tousled blond hair, the inviting silky mustache, and softly whispered, "Goodnight, Cole."

In spite of the little warning at the back of his mind, Cole opened his eyes and found his gaze immediately locked in hers. "Goodnight, little flower. Sleep well," he managed through a suddenly thick tongue.

"I would sleep even better if you kissed me the way you did last night."

He stared at her for a long moment, surprised by her boldness, then shook his head. "Don't test me, Sunflower, I'm only a man, and a pretty weak one at that right now. Roll over and go to sleep. I won't be held accountable if you don't."

Although she didn't understand what he meant by a test, Sunny was determined to feel his mouth on hers again, to know if she'd imagined the wonderfully delicious feelings or if they were indeed real.

She leaned over and slid her hand across his chest. "If you will not kiss me goodnight, then I shall kiss you."

When Cole opened his mouth to launch a feeble protest, Sunny lowered her head and took her fill. The moment their lips met, his reluctance vanished and she felt his hungry tongue searching her sweet mouth for some unknown fulfillment. The sensations she sought thundered throughout her, and her heart soared with the pleasure of his touch.

Again flames of passion licked at her, teased her with promises and left her eager and desperate to know how this inferno might be quenched. She wriggled across the bedroll until half her body lay draped over Cole's, then reluctantly pulled her mouth away from his.

Leaning back just enough for a clear view of his handsome features, Sunny struggled for air and moaned breathlessly, "Umm, that was wonderful. Kissing you is very pleasant. Can we do it some more?" And then she puckered her lips, tilted her chin, and closed her eyes.

Caught off balance, Cole was temporarily at a loss for words. He'd usually been the seducer. Even on those few occasions when some bold female had chosen that role for herself, never had he been approached so brazenly and yet so innocently at the same time. The effect nearly drove him mad.

"You don't leave a fellow much choice," he said with a throaty growl. "I've tried to play the gentleman, but I guess you don't appreciate the effort."

Cole laced his fingers across the back of her neck and pulled her within inches of his mouth. "I always try to oblige a lady. You'll get everything you want and more." With that, he quickly flipped her over on her back and straddled her, promising as he covered her body with his, "But we'll do it my way."

Startled, but still waiting for another kiss, Sunny did nothing to stop him when Cole began nibbling moist kisses behind her ear. All she could think of was how her skin responded to his hot breath, how his touch made her tingle all over—and how badly she wanted him to kiss her again. She drove her fingers into his thick hair and tried to pull his head to her waiting mouth, but he jerked her arms to her sides and continued the assault with his fiery mouth, this time journeying into the valley between her breasts.

Then he slid his hand between their writhing bodies and deftly untied the knot in her shirt. When his fingertips followed the contours of her body from her flat tummy, across the soft dunes of her ribs, and finally to her throbbing nipples, an alarmed Sunny fought her way through the fog of pleasure and gasped, "What are you doing?"

"Nothing you didn't ask me to do," he moaned just before he took her exposed breast in his mouth.

Sunny tried to squirm away. "Stop this. I only asked you to kiss me."

Disoriented, feeling as if he were slightly drunk, Cole muttered thickly, "What do you mean, *stop*? You started all this. What the hell are you talking about?"

Embarrassment flooded her cheeks when Sunny realized what he must have thought she wanted. She pushed him away and sat up.

"I am sorry if you misunderstood. I—if you think I intended to mate with you, you are mistaken. No, thank you very much."

In spite of his frustration, Cole had to laugh before he said, "That's precisely what I thought, although I wouldn't have used those terms."

He sat up behind her and draped a length of her hair across one magnificent breast. Stroking her nude shoulder, he whispered against her dusky skin, "If it's not what you had in mind, why did you lead me to believe you wanted to make love?"

Had she done that? Did merely kissing a man lead to this "making love"? Sunny shrugged off his kisses and pulled her shirt back over her shoulders.

"If making love is the same thing as mating," she said with a confident air, "I know all about it and it does not interest me one bit. All I wanted was a kiss goodnight."

Cole's brow furrowed as he tried to understand, and when it occurred to him that her only experiences may have been with white men who used her only for their own pleasure, Cole moved to her side and reached for her hand.

"Has no one ever really made love to you?" When she didn't answer, but drew her brows together instead, he came to his own conclusions and softly murmured, "If all your experiences with men have been little more than what you call mating, I think it's time—"

"I do not need experiences with men to know I won't be joined to one," she sniffed, cutting him off. "I learned of mating by myself."

"By—by yourself?" Cole shook his head and strangled on a burst of laughter.

"Why do you laugh?" Sunny demanded. "I am not stupid. I can see dogs and bulls slamming against their helpless females. I need no man to show me that which I can observe for myself."

Shocked into silence for several minutes, Cole just shook his head again and again. How could he have been so wrong about her, misread her boldness for promiscuity and overlooked her obvious inexperience? Whatever made him think she was anything *but* innocent?

But he already knew the answers, could almost hear his father's voice sneering, mocking the immoral behavior of all Indians. And Nathan's only surviving son had listened well. Cole shrugged off a wave of self-loathing before he brushed Sunny's cheek with gentle fingertips and eased her back down on the bedroll.

"We've both made some mistakes tonight, my sweet little flower. Some day you will find out how wrong you are about what passes between a man and a woman," he breathed. "I only hope you are lucky enough to find a man who knows how to please a passionate woman like you."

"Th-Then there is a . . . a difference between this making love and mating?"

At his abrupt nod, she said, "Then I would ask you to please tell me about this difference."

Cole laughed before he said, "It's not really something I can tell you about. Making love is something that is best explained by showing."

Sunny considered this for only a moment before she said, "Then I ask you to please show me what these differences are."

Unprepared for her answer, Cole stared down into dark eyes wide with curiosity and trust, and knew he could take her now—that she was ready and eager for her first lesson. But how could he? She needed, *deserved*, something more than he could offer. She was entitled to a man who wouldn't see the arrow-riddled body of his brother every time he looked on her dusky skin. A man who could offer her a happy future, a husband whose family would welcome her as one of their own. Cole Fremont could offer none of those things.

"I wish I had the right to show you the difference, little flower, but I don't. Just let me say goodnight. It will be easier for both of us that way." And before she had a chance to protest, he quickly kissed her forehead then rolled over onto his own bed.

More confused than she'd ever been in her life, but knowing from the rigid outline of Cole's back she would get no more answers from him this night, Sunflower breathed a heavy sigh. If only she'd accepted the advice and information her mother had tried to give her, maybe she would be able to understand what had happened just now. But, stubborn and independent as she was, Sunny had convinced Moonstar she knew all she would ever need to know about what goes on between a man and a woman. Insisted she knew more than she ever wanted to know. She'd been so wrong! How she longed to have one more conversation with the gentle woman who had raised her.

Sunny rolled over on her side and wiped a sudden tear from her cheek. She missed her mother, the comfort and understanding Moonstar would have given her at this junction in her young life. And she missed her father, his boisterous Irish brogue, his strong, protective arms. Where was he? Still fighting the strong current of the mighty Colorado, or breaking his back in a pointless search for gold? If only she could see him and talk to him, the confusion she was feeling would evaporate and she would be in control of herself once again. If only her thoughts could reach him.

That night Sunflower Callahan dreamt of her beloved Colorado River, but she swam in the murky depths, unable to see or find her way to the surface.

Back in Yuma, Lieutenant Andrew Wallace pointed a manicured fingernail at a man in the chair across from his desk. "Your heart will explode if you don't calm yourself, Patrick, my friend." He pulled the bottom drawer of his desk open. "Maybe a sip from what's left of my private stock will cool your temper."

"Thank ye and I'll be acceptin' yer kind offer, but nothin' except justice will cool me temper." Patrick Callahan dropped into the chair and slammed both palms against the desk. "Now will ye be helpin' me or nay?"

"And how am I to do that, Patrick?" Andrew poured two glasses full of amber liquid and slid one across the polished walnut desk top. "My troops pulled out of here four months ago and all I got left is a half-dozen infantry who are more boys than men. Even if I wanted to, I couldn't spare them."

"Then borrow some troops!" Patrick took a swig of whiskey and swished it around in his mouth before he swallowed. "Fort Mohave's still running at full strength, is it not?"

"Yes," Andrew said with a heavy sigh, "and no."

Patrick squinted an ice-blue eye at the lieutenant and leaned across the desk. "We've a sayin' in the old country. 'Tis a dark day indeed when a cloud obscures an Irishman's smile." Patrick's expression was grim as he added a warning, "If ye and that miserable excuse for a sheriff do not stop the malarkey ye've been ahandin' me, I'll be makin' bad cess for the pair of ye 'til I'm lyin' beside me faithful wife."

"Take it easy, friend," Andrew comforted. "Star was a fine woman, and Mike was a son any man would be proud of. I'd do anything to help you, but my hands are tied."

"Then untie 'em. Wire the commander at Fort Mohave."

"You're not listening to me, Patrick." Andrew refilled the Irishman's glass but bypassed his own. "There are no available troops. Forty-six companies of infantry and forty companies of cavalry—the entire army—have been called to Fort Bowie, orders of President Cleveland himself."

"What fer?"

"To rid Arizona of Geronimo and the Apache problem once and for all." The lieutenant's laugh was caustic as he added, "That figures out to be around one hundred and twenty-five troops per Indian. What do you think of those odds?"

Patrick took a large gulp of whiskey as he did a little arithmetic in his head. "Five thousand troops chasin' forty Apaches? And Geronimo with 'em? I heard tell General Crook brought him in this past month."

"He tried," Andrew grunted. "Geronimo and his followers surrendered to General Crook at Canon de los Embudos in Mexico, but on the way to Fort Bowie, some idiot bootlegger sold them whiskey and convinced them that as soon as they crossed the border into Arizona, the army planned to shoot them all. Can't say I blame Geronimo for waiting until nightfall, then heading back to his hideout in the Sonoran Mountains."

"Nor kin I," Patrick agreed, "but I do not understand why Crook needs so many men fer so few Apaches. Ye'd think he could spare a few for me troubles."

The lieutenant laughed at this, but more due to the irony of the situation than the humor. "Just between you and I, the orders from Washington are from men working out of West Point textbooks. They don't seem to understand we're facing a small but clever band of Indians who do not stand and fight on a broad front, who do not think it honorable to fight to the death rather than retreat. This war could go on forever."

"Aye," Patrick agreed with another swig of his drink. "But Crook is a good man; he understands the way the Apache think and they seem to trust him. I still do not see the need for so many troops."

"There lies the problem, friend. It no longer matters what the general wants to do. President Cleveland has relieved him of his command at the Department of Arizona. He wants those Indians rounded up and turned over to civil authorities to stand trial. The new commander, General Nelson Miles, will be conducting the latest attempts at surrender."

"Then I'll not be wishin' him luck." Patrick tossed the remainder of his whiskey down in one swallow, then pushed his chair back and rose. "I thank ye for yer time, if not yer aid."

After getting to his feet, Andrew circled the desk and took Patrick's hand. "I know it's not much, but I can promise to keep my ears open and make a few inquiries around town. If those animals are still in Yuma, they'll be bragging about their adventures, and sooner or later I'll hear about it."

"And when ye do," Patrick said as he shook the lieutenant's hand, "be sure to save 'em fer me."

Then the broken man turned a little unsteadily and ambled slowly out the door. He walked aimlessly through the dusty street for an hour, stopping only once at the depot to check on incoming wires, then found himself standing in front of Yuma's most notorious saloon, The Bucket. Not realizing or caring that the seedy establishment had become his home since the devastation of his family, Patrick Callahan crashed through the swinging doors and slumped onto the first empty bar stool he came to.

"Whiskey," he barked to the bartender, "and leave the bottle."

Then he turned his thoughts to the only bright spots left in his life. Did his children still glow with life's precious light, or had their flames also been extinguished by the harsh land in which they'd been sired?

Patrick closed his eyes, and swimming in an alcoholic haze, saw the image of his beautiful daughter, Sunflower. But the thought that she, alone and unprotected, might have met with the same fate as her mother was too much to bear. Groaning heavily, he rubbed at his eyelids as if he hoped he could wipe the terrible nightmare from his life, but when he opened his eyes, nothing had changed.

He was alone with a bottle of whiskey. His wife and youngest son were dead. Sunflower was somewhere in the vast desert. And Sean was hot on her trail.

If the lad had somehow managed to find it.

If he hadn't already been murdered by the very men he sought.

FIVE

Just as Sean started up the wash, he spotted another set of hoofprints mingled with the others he'd been following. There were three riders, not two as he'd first assumed.

With a yank of the reins, Sean jerked Whiskey to a stop, then whirled the animal around and backtracked to the area where he'd picked up Paddy's trail. As the mule plodded slowly along, Sean kept a sharp eye out for the point where the pony's tracks originated, and where they were joined by the others. In the wash, all the prints seemed to blend into one, but just past a large clump of creosote bushes and barrel cactus, three clear sets of hoofprints gouged a winding path down the side of the mountain. Should he go up?

Realizing any clues about who or what he might be up against were better than what he had, Sean elected to scour the mountainside. And even though it appeared as if the riders had already left the area, he knew surprise would be his best weapon against two adversaries if they hadn't yet broken camp. He tied Whiskey to the bush where he'd discovered the bit of yellow cloth, then silently climbed up the side of the hill on foot. At the crest, he peered between the branches of a palo verde tree and discovered an abandoned campsite. A quick glance around showed him a hastily covered campfire, a couple of small clearings smoothed out as sleeping circles, and at the far edge of the plateau, a large pile of rocks.

Curious about the stones and what they might be concealing, but still cautious, Sean cut a wide circle around the campsite and quietly made his way to the spot. Once he recognized the mound as a crude grave, he quickly forgot about his own safety and crashed through the trees.

"Sunny?" Sean called as he reached the pile of rocks. But the only response was a hot breeze whistling through the trees. Swallowing his fears, he took another look around the campsite and walked over to the fire.

Squatting down beside it, Sean sifted through the ashes. They were at least two, maybe three days old. He rose and crossed over to the area where Paddy and the two horses had been tied to the trees. Three mounts added up to three riders, and yet there were only clearings for two bed rolls. Had the third horse carried not a man, but a corpse?

Sean took off his hat and ran his fingers through his sable hair as he walked back to the grave. Then another thought occurred to him. It was just possible the riders only required sleeping quarters for two because they passed Sunny from blanket to blanket during their nights on the trail.

Sean's nostrils flared and his fists curled into tight balls as he realized he'd come up with the most reasonable explanation. The only thing keeping him from screaming his rage while he contemplated her predicament was the knowledge Sunny wouldn't be making life easy for her captors. He knew she would fight their indignities with every ounce of her strength, would leave her mark on any man who tried to— A horrifying thought cut off his reassurances.

His eyes wide, his stomach rolling like a pair of loaded dice, Sean looked down at the pile of rocks. Who *had* died on this spot—and why?

"Sunny!" he gasped as he dropped to his knees and began frantically tossing aside the large rocks as if they were pebbles. When the stones were all removed, Sean's hands became shovels, and sprays of loose dirt and sand fanned out behind him like a cloud, until his fingertips finally connected with something other than soil.

The sensation sickened him. Sean recoiled and sat staring at the object for a long moment before he could be certain his eyes hadn't deceived him. He gazed on two thick, gnarled fingers. When at last he was able to accept the body as that of a man, not the young beautiful woman fueled by the same blood as he, Sean breathed a long, hoarse sigh.

Sunny lived.

At least she'd lived through whatever happened here. Certain until now he'd been following only Paddy and one horse, Sean surmised the campsite had probably been a pre-arranged meeting site for the two outlaws who'd murdered half of his family. He could only guess that once the men joined up again something, possibly Sunny, had put them at each other's throats.

Now his sister rode towards Phoenix with the stronger of the two. Would she be able to hang on until he reached her? Or had her spirit already been irreparably broken?

Sean fingered the pistol he carried in the waistband of his trousers and made a deadly vow.

This man, this *murderer* who'd forced Sunflower to accompany him, would pay dearly for that atrocity.

More than a hundred miles to the east, Sunny and Cole crested the last red-rimmed ridge before the short ride into the town of Phoenix. Although the farther they traveled, the more the landscape changed from sandy browns and cloudy greens to terracotta and rich emeralds, she was unprepared for this oasis in the Sonoran desert. Gasping as the town and its lush valley came into view, Sunny said, "Your Phoenix is very beautiful. You must be so proud of it."

"Proud?" Cole shrugged and slowed Sage to a trot. "I don't know, it's not something I think about much. My father is the one who's so proud of this little city. Nearly twenty years ago, he was part of the citizen group which founded the town. He's been active in Arizona politics ever since."

"Then," she laughed, "you must be very proud of your father."

Again he shrugged. "I suppose so." He was proud in many ways, but in many others, more and more Cole found himself questioning Nathan's ethics and prejudices, his rules and his methods. How would the old man react when he learned Cole no longer shared his goals, that his return to the Triple F ranch was only temporary?

Fascinated by the scenery, busy comparing the tree-lined town to the only home she'd ever known, Sunny didn't realize her escort was deep in thought or that she spoke only to herself.

"I cannot believe how much greener Phoenix is than Yuma. And the streets are so clean! Is that because you do not have a railroad yet? What about a fort? Does Phoenix have a fort? You know, the Army pulled out of Fort Yuma a few months ago. There is talk they might even turn the abandoned buildings over to the Yuma Indians. I think that is the least the Army can do for my people. Cole?"

"Huh?" He swiveled around in his saddle and looked at Sunny as if seeing her for the first time. "I'm sorry, I wasn't paying much attention." He reined in Sage and caught Paddy's bridle. "Look, ah, I think it'd be a good idea to fix you up a little before we go any farther."

"Fix me up?" she said with a raised brow. "I spent nearly an hour in the Gila River this morning. I do not know what else you expect me to do."

"I didn't mean that, I meant . . . here." Cole reached over and pulled Mike's hat off her head. "I plan to take you right to the general store for some decent clothing. I thought you might want to look a little more like a lady."

Sunflower cast her gaze to the ground and buried her hands in Paddy's mane. Cole was ashamed of her. Embarrassed to be seen with her in the town where his father was so highly regarded. She examined her torn shirt and dusty trousers and had to agree they were shabby, but that was all she'd admit to.

"I seem to have left my best dress behind during my hasty departure from home. Perhaps you will be more comfortable riding into town alone."

"Damn," he muttered under his breath. The last thing he wanted to do was hurt her feelings. How could he make her see he was only thinking of her? Cole nudged Sage until he pressed up against the pony's shoulder.

"I just thought you might want to fix your hair before we go into the store. You look fine to me." Beautiful, in fact. And so damn desirable with that fire burning in her dark eyes, he felt paralyzed by a sudden tension in his loins.

But Sunny could sense none of his thoughts, and remembered only the utter disdain in his voice when he first set eyes on her and thought her to be an Apache brave. There was no question about it; her benefactor, the first man who'd ever made her curious about what it meant to be a woman, was repelled by her heritage.

Sunny raised her chin and faced him. "And how would you have me fix my hair, Cole Fremont? Wound in a ball at the back of my neck like a white woman, or shall I braid it and be an Indian squaw?"

He stared at her a long moment, as irritated with himself as he was with her. His voice harsh, he finally said, "Do whatever pleases you." Then he kicked Sage in the side and continued into town.

Sunny picked up Paddy's reins as quickly as she picked up the rancor in Cole's tone, and she prepared to spin him around and ride as fast as she could back to Yuma, but her heart wouldn't let her move. She suddenly couldn't stand the thought of never seeing Cole again, of never understanding what it was that drew her to him, or not having another chance to feel his hot kisses.

Sunny nudged Paddy forward as she reached into one of her pouches. There she found the last strip of yellow cloth. Her original idea of marking a trail that wouldn't be searched for weeks had been a feeble one. She had a much better use for the colorful material now.

Glancing up at Cole's broad shoulders, Sunny grinned and urged her pony to catch up with him. Then she pulled a length from each side of her hair and fastened the strands with a cloth bow at the back of her head. She was in Cole's territory now. She would act and dress in the manner he expected. She would learn to curb her temper and keep her tongue in check. She would behave like a lady—at least she could try.

When Sunny rode up beside Cole, he gave her a sideways glance and a short nod of appreciation, then the trail-weary pair came to the end of their journey in strained silence.

They'd traveled only a few feet down the main street of Phoenix when Cole pulled up his mount and gestured for Sunny to do the same. After helping her down off Paddy, he quickly led her into Goldwater's Mercantile Store.

"Wait here a minute," Cole instructed as he hurried off to greet the distinguished looking gentleman approaching them.

"Cole! Good to see you. It's been a long time," the proprietor said as he extended his hand.

"Hello, Baron." Cole accepted the warm greeting and sighed, "It's good to be back."

"I would imagine so. Your father was in yesterday and told me you decided not to take the train to Maricopa, but that you chose to ride all the way back from Yuma."

"I had a few decisions to make and decided I could use some time alone." Cole glanced over his shoulder, wonder-

ing briefly how he would explain Sunny to Goldwater.
"Right now," he continued quietly, "I need a few . . .
things. Is Mrs. Brown working today?"

"Why, yes, she is." Baron Goldwater looked beyond
Cole to where Sunny stood, and frowned. "You, ah, need
some clothing for . . . *her*?"

"I—er, yes, she—it's a long story. Have Mrs. Brown get
her anything she wants and put it on my bill."

"Of course." Baron gave him a tight smile, then turned
and disappeared into the storeroom.

"Everything's taken care of," Cole explained as he
returned to Sunny. "The clerk, Mrs. Brown, will help you
with whatever you need."

"B-But I have no money, I cannot—"

"I have credit here," he assured. "You can worry about
paying me later. For now, just make sure you get outfitted
from . . . er, from head to toe." At the sound of footsteps
approaching, Cole added, "I'll take care of the horses and
get us registered at the hotel. It's next door. When you're
done shopping, meet me there in the lobby."

A quick nod was all she could manage before he spun
around and hurried out the door.

"Excuse me?"

Sunny wheeled to meet the owner of the bird-like voice.

"Mr. Goldwater said—" The woman cut off her own
words as she studied her customer. "Oh, my."

One look in Mrs. Brown's eyes told Sunny exactly what
she was thinking. She'd seen that expression of disapproval
all too often from the fine white ladies of Yuma—women
who thought it disgusting to find the proof of this vile
practice of cross-breeding walking around town for all to
see.

Lifting her chin, Sunny also raised her brows and squared
her shoulders. She ignored her vow to keep her tongue in
line, and whispered conspiratorially, "Mr. Goldwater said,
'Oh, my'? Whatever do you think he meant?"

"N-No, no," the clerk sputtered, "he didn't say that, he, what I meant to say . . . I thought, I—"

"You thought what, Mrs. Brown?" Sunny demanded.

"I—I—" She seemed to regain her composure. She flashed a confident smile and said, "When Mr. Goldwater asked me to help a lady friend of Cole Fremont's, I just naturally thought he was talking about Elizabeth Scott. Please forgive the mistake."

Sunny felt like a snake-bit rabbit. She couldn't breathe, talk, or move any of her limbs. Why hadn't she even *considered* the possibility of Cole and another woman? Men as handsome, and apparently well to do as he, probably never wanted for female companionship. *Of course* he had a sweetheart or fiancée waiting for him in his hometown— any blitherin' fool should know that.

With a feeling akin to despair, an awareness she really didn't understand, Sunny turned away from the clerk and strolled over near the dresses. "That is all right, Mrs. Brown. Everybody makes mistakes."

She fingered a grey serge travelling dress, knowing it would be the proper garment to purchase, but a frothy calico frock emblazoned with tiny yellow roses seemed to cry out to her.

"Oh," Sunny breathed, " 'tis perfectly lovely!"

"We just got it in," Mrs. Brown proclaimed as she held the dress in front of Sunny. "And it looks like it's just your size, too. Wait until you see the matching bonnet."

But Sunny wasn't interested in bonnets, she was interested in fastenings. She turned the dress in a circle, relieved to see that it buttoned up the front, then said, "I would like just the dress and a length of yellow ribbon—oh, that and some new drawers . . ." Sunny paused and took a quick inventory of herself, then amended, "and a camisole, a petticoat, some stockings, and I guess I should have a pair of shoes."

Mrs. Brown lifted her nose. "No corset or bustles, dear?"

Sunny thought of making excuses, but looked her straight in the eye and said, "No corset—I have no one to lace it." The bustles were another matter, however, and an item she knew next to nothing about. Raising her chin level with Mrs. Brown's, Sunny sniffed and said, "I do not like bustles—dear."

"I see." Withholding further comment, the size of her commission reflected in the clerk's eyes as she suggested, "What about a reticule? I may have one in yellow."

Sunny hesitated a moment, more attracted to the color than the item, then shook her head. "I have no use for one. Please wrap those items. I must be on my way."

While she waited for her purchases, Sunny helped herself to a licorice drop and strolled around the store examining bolts of expensive imported yardage. When the clerk gave her the packages, Sunny added a pound of the delicious black candy to her bill then stepped out into the late afternoon sunshine. More aware of her appearance than ever, she kept her head down as she made her way across the wooden planks to the next building and quietly slipped into the hotel lobby.

Only then did she lift her gaze to search the room for Cole. He was engaged in conversation with an older gentleman and a well-dressed woman. As she pondered whether to call out to announce her presence or simply approach the trio, Sunny noticed the desk clerk move out from behind his station and take several determined steps in her direction.

"The letters on the front of this building spell hotel," he began impatiently. "We don't allow injuns in this establishment. Skeedaddle on out of here," he finished with a wave of his hands.

His tone low and dangerous enough to strike fear in a wounded grizzly, Cole's voice sounded over the clerk's shoulder, "The *lady* has a room in this two-bit establishment." Cole circled the man and stepped between him and

Sunny. "I just paid for it. Do you have a problem with that, mister?"

"Oh, Mr. Fremont, I—no, of course not. I thought she was, you know, that—"

Cole cut him off with a cold green gaze before he muttered, "I'm not interested in what you thought. Are those baths ready yet?"

"I'm sure they are, sir."

"Then if you have no further objections, we'll take our rooms now." Not waiting for or interested in a reply, Cole spun around and relieved Sunny of her burden. Then he extended the crook of his elbow. "Shall we?"

This time remembering her vow to curb her temper and tongue, Sunny settled for spearing the clerk with a scathing glance before she tossed her head and accepted Cole's arm.

When the pair reached the top of the stairs, Cole turned to her, his voice low and sincere. "I'm really sorry for the way that idiot behaved. It can't have been a very pleasant experience for you."

"It is an experience I have had many times in the past. I am very aware of the way white men look on me. You have no need to apologize."

"Well, just the same I—"

"Please," she said curtly. "I would like to forget it. Where is my room?"

Cole's lips were pressed together so tightly his mustache obliterated his mouth. Inclining his head down the hall, he walked a few more feet then slipped a key in the lock of room seven. He pushed the door aside, leaving it open intentionally, then gestured for her to enter.

"I hope it suits you. This is the best hotel Phoenix has to offer."

Trying to conceal the wonder she felt from her lack of exposure to the world outside her home, Sunny stepped into the room and indulged her gaze with the sheer luxury of her accommodations. A large inviting bed dominated the room, its spread made of the same colorful chintz as the curtains hanging over a double window. Trellises of amber roses seemed to leap out of the beige paper covering all four walls, and a milk-white wash basin and pitcher awaited her on the dressing table.

"I—I, this is very nice, Cole," she managed to say as her gaze brushed over the crystal chandelier and came to rest on the steam rising from the claw-foot bathtub in the center of the room.

"Good. I'm glad you like it." He began backing out of the door, adding, "I'll let you take advantage of your bath while it's still hot. Bang on the wall if you need anything. My room is right next door." Cole pointed to the left, then pulled the door closed behind him.

Once inside his own room, Cole breathed a long sigh and stripped off his clothes. He sank into the warmth of the burnished copper bathtub and lay there, mindless, for several minutes. And then his thoughts returned, centered as they seemed to be of late, on Sunflower.

Had he been mad for bringing her to his town, his home? The reception she got from the desk clerk was a simple prelude to what might await once Nathan laid eyes on her. Maybe, he groused to himself, he'd made a mistake. Perhaps even though his plans had been to help her, he'd only added to her problems.

Just how honorable *were* his intentions, he suddenly wondered? If he'd had to spend another night on the trail with her cuddled up next to him, odds are he would have snapped, taken her like one of the wild animals their campfire sought to drive away. He might have behaved no better than the disgusting outlaw who'd tried to rape her.

Scrubbing his scalp with a vengeance, Cole submerged his head in the tub and hoped somehow the act might cleanse away his lustful thoughts. But when he came up for air, he had a vision of Sunflower in her own bath. She would be soaped, her slippery body reclining, and her glorious hair would be floating beneath her like a cushion of ebony satin.

Cole leapt from the tub, frustrated, confused, and aroused. He needed a drink. He needed to put more distance between himself and the beautiful Indian maiden who called herself Sunflower Callahan. And, damn his wayward body, he needed her.

Back in room seven, Sunny had already washed from head to toe in fragrant lilac-scented soap, but she couldn't seem to pry herself from the luxury of the hot bath. Never had she felt so pampered, so spoiled. And it was all because of Cole. She rolled his name off her tongue, savoring the sound of it, then remembered Mrs. Brown's defensive remarks. How long before Cole would go to this Elizabeth? Was he on his way now, while she lay in the water like a stunned squawfish? The thought startled and troubled her. A special seed was growing between her and the rancher, something so wonderfully delicate that Sunny sensed the bud might easily wither before it had the chance to bloom. If only there were a way to detain him for a few more hours, a few more days, or weeks . . .

Several sharp raps against the door jolted her to a sitting position. She tried to calm the suddenly turbulent water, working unsuccessfully to dam a large wave as it spilled over the side of the tub and doused the floor. "Y-yes?" she called out, distracted.

"It's me, Cole." His voice filtering through the thin wood, he announced, "I'm going on downstairs to arrange a good hot meal for us. Take your time joining me and don't worry about a repeat of what happened the first time you were in the lobby. I'll be looking for you."

"All right," she sputtered, giggling at her vain attempts to keep the water inside, rather than outside, the tub. "I will be down in a few minutes."

After Cole's footsteps faded down the hallway, Sunny reluctantly emerged from the comforting bath, and quickly dried her hair and tingling skin. Dressing carefully but quickly, Sunny slipped on her new undergarments, buttoned the sleeves of her new dress at the wrists, then fastened the bodice up to the lacy opening at her throat.

Thrilled with her image in the dresser mirror, she twirled and contemplated a new way to fix her loose hair. How did fine ladies convince their tresses to curl so uniformly? Surely they couldn't all have been born that way. With only a single yellow ribbon to aid her, Sunny didn't have many options. She chose to catch the length of her hair with the ribbon, then swooped the strands back into a thick cascade and tied a bow at the top of her head.

Satisfied she'd done her best to look presentable in Phoenix society, Sunny glided out of the room and made her way towards the steep staircase.

Downstairs, a frustrated rancher complained, "I'm a tellin' ya, Fremont, Swain's herd is growin' mighty quick. I swear his cows have a calf every washday."

Cole laughed as he polished off the rest of his drink. He took another glance at the empty stairway, then answered his neighbor. "Like I told you, Tom. It's way past time for you to invest in fencing like the rest of us. That, and a damn good brand are the best ways to guard against these settlers and their 'borrowing' ways."

"Ah, hell, Fremont. 'Twixt the drought and all those damn squatters and their stinkin' sheep grazin' up the good grass, we didn't get diddly-squat for our herd. Where's the money s'pposed to come from for all that wire?"

There wasn't much Cole could say to assure the rancher. The past two years had been tough on everyone. Even the big ranches like the Triple F felt the blade of a depressed economy cut into their profits. "Have you checked with Harvey over at the bank? Maybe he could—"

"Come on, Fremont," Tom interrupted impatiently. "Even you couldn't get a penny out a that ole skinflint. He sits on his assets like a brood hen hatchin' her chicks."

"Well then, how about this," Cole offered without much conviction. "My brother-in-law, Buck Wheeler, is in Maricopa right now trying to secure a loan from Darvey Tymes. If he's successful, maybe he could put in a word for you."

"That'd be an idea. Why don't you have him—" Tom left the sentence unfinished when he realized his words fell on deaf ears. His friend's mouth had dropped open and his gaze rested on something other than the frustrated rancher.

"Excuse me, Tom," Cole said with effort as he pushed his chair back from the table and rose. "I'll let you know what I find out."

Tom's reply was lost on Cole. All his attention and senses honed in on the vision descending the stairs. When Sunny gracefully swiveled as she reached the bottom step, then began to float across the room towards him, his breath caught in his throat and he froze.

Sunny noticed his peculiar expression, the strange waxy appearance of his flared nostrils. Was he angry again? What had she done wrong? She slammed her hands to her hips and came to a halt. "Faith and begorra, Cole Fremont! What does a girl have to do to be 'fixed-up' in your eyes?"

Still, he was speechless. During the past few days together on the trail, her brother's clothing had given him ample opportunity to study the outline of her long legs and curve of her well-rounded bottom. The tattered shirt encouraged glimpses of her full breasts, and the rope belt repeatedly brought his gaze to her tiny waist.

He had had no trouble imagining that beautiful body stripped of civilization's garments, but somehow the thought of her in a fine dress had escaped him. Had his father's prejudice colored his own viewpoint to the extent he could only think of her as an Indian squaw, not as a lady? If that were the case, he thought with sudden awareness, his attitude was no better than that of the desk clerk.

More crestfallen by his silence than indignant at his reaction to her, Sunny's voice became a whisper as she suggested, "Maybe it would be better if I returned to my room."

"No!" Cole moved swiftly, catching her arm as she turned to walk away. "Please, listen to me. You look so beautiful, so different, I—" He recalled the way he felt when he saw her on the stairs and softly said, "You took my breath away."

Unaccustomed to such remarks, Sunny lowered her lashes and fumbled with a length of lace and ribbon tied at the front of the dress. Her cheeks grew warm as she tried to think of the proper response to his compliment, but her mind was as empty as a roadrunner's nest in winter.

Cole's strong hands stilled her busy fingers as he brought them to his lips and brushed them with a tender kiss. "Come on, little flower. Let's have supper. I'm so hungry, I could eat a side of beef."

With a short nod and nervous laugh, Sunny slipped her small hand in the crook of his arm and strolled, her head held high again, into the dining room. After they were seated, Cole raised two fingers, signaling the waitress, then settled back in his chair.

"I hope you like steak, Sunny. If you do, you're in for a taste of Triple F's finest Hereford stock."

"Oh? Your ranch supplies this hotel?"

"This and several other establishments in town. If all goes well, the Triple F will also be shipping to parts of California by next year." That is, he thought, if Maricopa County got some much needed rain—and they could find a way to keep the homesteaders from crowding them out of any more precious grazing land.

Famished beyond caring about what she consumed, Sunny was equally hungry for more information on her handsome companion. She smiled across the table and said, "Did ranch business bring you to Yuma?"

"That," he nodded, "and a few other things." But he chose not to elaborate about the other things and instead explained the ranch's plans for the future. "The Phoenix and Salt River Railroad is due to be finished next year. It'll connect in Maricopa where we can pick up the Southern Pacific and run through Yuma all the way to San Diego."

Although she listened to the words, Sunny was more intent on watching Cole as he spoke. She loved how his mustache drooped past the corners of his mouth, treasured the way it hugged the upper curves and gave her a full view of his sensual bottom lip. She could still feel the heat of that mouth pressed against hers, remembered the surprising yet electrifying sensations when he drove his tongue—

"Sunny?"

That sensual mouth was lop-sided now, grinning at her as if it knew exactly what she was thinking. With a start, she looked up into his amused eyes. "What?"

"Aren't you hungry?"

She glanced down at the table, astonished to discover a plate filled with steak, fried potatoes, and biscuits staring up at her. When, *how*, had they arrived?

"Oh, I—yes. I am." And with that strange heat tickling her cheeks again, Sunny spread a napkin across her lap and focused on her supper.

Aware of her embarrassment, guessing he had something to do with it, Cole gave her some privacy and turned his attention to his meal. But he found he was no longer interested in eating. He cut off a few chunks of meat and chewed them absently as his gaze returned again and again to Sunflower. She was radiant, practically glowing. Was it the hot bath? The new dress? Or, was it possible he made her blood run hot just by being in the same room with him? She certainly affected him in that way, he acknowledged as ripples of desire rolled down his belly.

Even the way she ate was an erotic experience. Sunny didn't nibble at her food or cut tiny pieces of steak only to leave most of them on her plate in ladylike fashion. She literally dove into the meal, relishing the taste and texture of each morsel, drenched her biscuits in rich honey, then licked the excess from her fingers with a sensuality that nearly drove him wild.

His senses heightened to the point where he could almost feel her tongue mimicking the gesture around his own fingertips, Cole's fist curled around his fork with enough force to bend it. She would be an absolute wildcat in bed. Instinct, coupled with that independent and curious nature of hers, would have her relishing each touch, every sensation possible, whenever she gave herself to her lover. The lucky man honored with the responsibility of educating this little beauty in the ways of lovemaking would be rewarded beyond his wildest fantasies.

Cole shuddered as an intense jealousy of the faceless man surged through him. He didn't have the right to be that lucky man. Would never have the right. Sunflower Callahan would belong to someone who held her dual heritage in high esteem, a man whose family would welcome her for the beautiful woman she was. A man like Charlie White, Pima Indian and blacksmith for the Phoenix livery stable.

A sudden picture of Sunny nestled in Charlie's arms turned Cole's blood to crystals of ice. Now that the man had a face, the surge of jealousy became a flash flood, cutting a painful gorge through his gut, his heart. With something that felt like anger, Cole slammed his fork to the table, then took a deep breath before he trusted himself to speak in a rational tone.

"If you're finished, I think we ought to go to our rooms now. We're long overdue for a good night's rest."

Her dark eyes wide, Sunny cocked her head. "But you have not yet finished your supper."

"I wasn't as hungry as I thought," he snapped.

Her hunger more than satisfied, a puzzled Sunny slid out of her chair. "I am ready to retire."

Cole tossed a few coins on the table, then escorted her through the lobby and up the staircase. The only overture he made after seeing her to her room was a gentle squeeze on her arm as he softly said, "Sleep well." Then he closed the door and was gone.

Sunny wandered over to the dresser, took a piece of licorice from the bag, and wondered as she popped the candy in her mouth if she had done something to annoy him again. She'd noticed the way he stared at her during their meal, knew instinctively the glazed look in his eyes had more to do with desire than anger. So what had happened? Why was Cole so difficult for her to understand?

She peeled off the new dress and petticoat, carefully draped them across a chair, then slid between the flannel sheets with a heavy sigh. Maybe she'd been right all along. This business between men and women—this love, mating, and marriage thing—was not for her. It was so hard to understand, so complicated. And, she thought with a heavy heart, it was beginning to hurt.

But she wanted him. Exactly what she wanted from him was still nebulous, but with each passing day it became a little clearer. For now, all she wanted was his touch, his silken mouth on hers, the sound of his rich voice murmuring in her ear. With a mind of its own, her tongue caressed the piece of candy, suckling it as her thoughts spread a warm ache throughout her abdomen and below.

Sunny finally drifted off to sleep with the licorice drop stuck to the roof of her mouth.

A short time later, she was brutally torn from a deep slumber by the sound of gunfire outside her window. She bolted upright in the bed and inclined her head towards the source. Angry voices punctuated the dark night. More shots were fired. At the same time, she became aware of boisterous laughter in the hallway. This was quickly followed by several loud bumps against her door. Then silence.

Unused to city noises, uncertain whether this was the norm or if she were in danger, Sunny jumped out of her bed.

She wrapped a thin blanket around her shoulders and scurried over to the door. She pressed her ear against the wood and listened. More silence. Either the men who'd stumbled down the hallway were gone, or they waited like patient buzzards for their prey.

Too nervous to stay alone any longer, Sunny opened the door a crack and peered down the hall. It was empty. Moving with featherlike steps, she hurried to the room next door and knocked several times.

"Cole," she whispered loudly. "Cole, wake up! It is Sunflower—let me in!"

When the door finally opened a cautious inch, she railroaded her way through the tiny opening.

"What the hell—"

Cole's sleepy protest was cut off as Sunny threw herself in his arms and buried her head in his shoulder. "I am frightened," she cried. "I cannot sleep in this town! This place is dangerous."

When he felt her body tremble against his, Cole closed the door and swaddled her in his strong arms. He, too, had heard the gunshots, but undaunted by them, he'd drifted off to sleep as quickly as he had awakened. Sunny on the other hand, was obviously shaken, unfamiliar with the sounds of ranch hands cutting loose on payday. He would give her time to collect her wits, then escort her back to her room.

Calmer now that Cole was so close, Sunny leaned back and looked into his eyes. "I have changed my mind. I do not think I like your town of Phoenix after all."

Chuckling, he countered, "Have you ever spent the night in a hotel in Yuma?"

"No, but I—"

"Trust me, little flower. You wouldn't like it any better." Far too aware of her soft breasts rising and falling against his chest, of her heart thundering in time with his, Cole released her and stepped back.

"I doubt you'll be disturbed any more tonight. The sheriff

has probably put the fear of God in those boys by now. I'll take you back to your room."

"You will not!" She tugged the blanket tighter around her body and stepped further into the room.

"Do you want to stay here a little while longer?"

"I will stay here all night, Cole Fremont. I will not be alone in this hotel."

"But you can't do that," he objected, advancing on her.

"Of course I can, and I will."

"You will not!"

"Why not? Have we not slept together these past nights on the trail?"

"Yes," he grumbled, "but this is different. I—it just wouldn't look right."

"Then," she said with a wink and a curve of her mouth, "we simply will not allow anyone to look."

"Oh? Oh, really?" he finally said, unable to come up with a logical retort.

"Yes. Really."

Her smile triumphant, Sunny spun around and marched over to the bed. "Now, which side do you wish to sleep on?"

Cole pressed his lips together and narrowed his eyes as Sunny cast her blanket aside to reveal a low cut camisole and long ruffled drawers. When she actually climbed between his sheets, he rolled his eyes towards the heavens and spit out a muffled curse.

The pristine girl really meant to climb into his bed and actually expected they would *sleep*? Maybe what he ought to do was climb in there with her, show her she was in more danger in his room than she could ever be in her own. If he didn't think of a solution soon, he was certain to forget his good intentions and lose what little control he still possessed.

Cole opted to give reason one more try. He approached the bed, his arms spread wide. "This really is a bad idea,

Sunflower. I just can't do it. If you insist on staying here, I'll have to go to your room."

Alarmed, wanting him near for more reasons than security, Sunny sat up and blurted out, "Would you send this Elizabeth person from your bed?"

"What?" he croaked, his throat strangled. "Where did you hear that name? Who told you about Elizabeth?"

Distressed by his sudden burst of temper, Sunny pulled the sheet up around her neck. "M–Mrs. Brown said—"

"Mrs. Brown? That woman has the tongue of a rooster at dawn. She ought to keep the damn thing inside her mouth instead of wriggling it at anyone who'll listen."

Cole blew out a frustrated sigh, then glanced over at Sunny. He saw fear and amusement in her eyes. What if he accented that fear, made her see what an impossible request she'd made of him? It might be his last chance to convince her to return to the relative safety of her own room. It was a chance he knew he had to take.

"I hope you understand if you stay here with me, I can't guarantee you'll leave this room with your virtue in tact."

When she didn't answer and sat there instead with an intriguing combination of anxiety and curiosity flickering in her Irish eyes, Cole slid his fingers around to the front of the pants he'd thrown on when she knocked at his door. "All right, Sunflower. You win."

Then he stripped off the jeans and slid in beside her. "Just don't try to say I didn't warn you."

SIX

Panic and disbelief widened Sunny's enormous eyes. "You would not—you *could* not."

"I can, and I will."

"You—you will not!"

Cole fit his hands around her tiny waist and dragged her beneath him. "We've got better things to do than talk. Besides, I think we've already had this conversation."

"B-but, I only meant to, I—"

"What you mean and what you want no longer matters, woman. You've pushed me too far." Done with words, he pressed down on her opened mouth in a brutal kiss. He would teach her a lesson, show her the folly of her insane proposal, drive her from his room, his heart, with sheer masculine lust. But the mouth he sought to turn away, to harden against his, was soft and yielding, encouraging rather than fighting his savage invasion.

Cole could taste no fear as he plunged deeper into her sweetness, and found instead a delicious curiosity, an eager response he hadn't considered in his plans to dissuade her. Sunny's essence swirled around him, clouded his thoughts, his purpose. She smelled like lilacs and sunshine, tasted of licorice and honey, moved with an innocent abandon he'd never felt before. He couldn't seem to get enough of her.

He was losing control, his objectivity, and for a crazy moment, Cole had to wonder who was teaching the lesson here. With the last of his strength, and as savagely as he'd come to her, he tore his mouth away.

His voice strangled and husky, Cole turned his head from her and muttered, "Go to your room, Sunflower. This really is your last chance."

Dazed, her head spinning, Sunny's lashes fluttered as she tried to catch her breath. This *was* her last chance, she suddenly understood, maybe her only chance to be part of the one man who'd ever mattered to her. Once they arrived at the ranch tomorrow, he would be different. He would return to a life which didn't include her but this Elizabeth person instead—and this Elizabeth probably knew how to warm his bed properly, had most likely done so often. A shiver of anticipation skittered through Sunny as she thought of his kisses, his touch. So far, this lovemaking was not at all objectionable. She would not, could not let this chance slip away.

"No," Sunny breathed in a smothered whisper.

Cole groaned and mouthed a silent curse. "You really expect me to lie next to you on this small bed all night and *not* touch you? Do you have any idea what you're asking of me, for God's sake?"

Sunny turned languid, expectant eyes on him. "No."

"No," he echoed with a sigh. "Of course you don't."

Cole released her and rolled onto his back. This had been a very stupid plan. He'd wanted to scare her off, send her back to her room, not rouse her curiosity, inflame *himself* beyond rational thought. Now what? he wondered as he fought to get his desire, his emotions, under control. How would he be able to convince her to leave when he wasn't sure he could still convince himself?

"Cole?"

Her voice fragrant with the hint of anise, he answered the call and unwisely chanced a glance into her moist, dark eyes. "Damn," he muttered.

"Damn?" Sunny moved closer to him and slid her hand across his bare chest. With soft, inquisitive fingertips, she traced the tawny map of hair shaped like dove wings, then cocked her head and raised her brows. "What do you mean by damn, Cole Fremont?"

"I mean—" Captured now by those midnight blue eyes, his flesh tortured by the simple gestures she made with her inexperienced fingers, he gripped her shoulders. "I mean, damn I want you, Sunflower." And until he'd said the words, he didn't realize how much. Every fiber of his being cried out for her, his skin came alive with jolts of lightning everywhere she touched, and her scent smothered him in a dark cocoon of passion.

His need, his desire, grew huge as he tried to make her understand. "I *want* you, do you have any idea what that means?"

She lowered her lashes, stared at the springs of blond curls circling her fingertips, and nodded. "I think I want you in the same way."

"Oh, Sunny," he moaned, "you don't know what you're saying, what you're doing to me!"

"Show me what I don't know, Cole Fremont."

"I can't." He tried to push her away, but she resisted, slid under his grip, and began to finger the ridges of the wound she'd sliced into his arm.

"Does this still hurt?" she purred, lightly kissing the healing injury.

"I—no. Leave it alone. Leave me alone." Again he tried to push her away, but this time the attempt was feeble.

"Why should I leave, Cole Fremont?"

"Because . . . because I don't have a right to anything you offer. Don't you understand—?"

Sunflower cut off his protest by sliding her fingers up his

chest, past his throat, to his lips where she buried the tips in his thick mustache. "It is my right to give myself to whomever I choose, is it not?"

"Well," he said against her soft fingertip, kissing that dusky finger in spite of himself. "I suppose in a way it is, but—"

"Then I give that right to you."

Cole's breath caught as he studied her trusting, orphaned-calf expression, and he wondered briefly if he might be teetering on the brink of madness. Somehow, using the last sliver of his control, he made a final effort to explain. "You have a right to much more than me, little flower. I can only give you tonight—you deserve a lifetime with the first man who comes to you."

Although she wanted that and much more, Sunny replaced her fingers with her lips, and whispered against his mouth, "Tonight will be enough, Cole Fremont. Tonight is all I ask from you."

As if to bind her promise, convince him of its legality, Sunny pressed her lips to his, opened her mouth in invitation, and awkwardly tried to straddle his legs. Her uneducated body moved across him in a timeless, instinctive rhythm, yet the direction of her passion was blinded by the newness of its birth.

She was everywhere at once, unbridled, unguided. Cole gripped her shoulders and flipped her over on her back. "Are you sure this is what you want, Sunflower?" But even as he said the words, Cole suspected if she said no, he would be unable to honor the request.

Her breathing suddenly ragged, Sunny chewed her bottom lip in anticipation, and nodded.

"Then relax," he whispered as he ran a gentle fingertip across her throat and down to the outline of her breasts. "You asked me to show you—lie back and let me."

Cole lifted a length of satin from the center of her camisole, then pulled it, releasing the bow. He stared down at the loosened garment, at the dewy sheen of her dusky breasts, and considered tearing her underclothing off now and granting his eyes their fill of her. But instead, he reached for the lamp on the bed table.

"What are you doing?" Sunny gasped, her breath coming in erratic gulps.

"I thought you'd be more comfortable if I blew out the light."

"Oh, will you please leave it on? How can I learn everything if I cannot see what is happening, if I cannot look into your eyes and know that I have pleased you?"

With a sigh that was more of a groan, Cole slid the lamp across the tabletop. She was unlike any women he'd ever known, would ever know. She was real and utterly guileless, beautiful, but refreshingly unaware of her charms. At that moment, he was stunned with the realization he could never touch another woman without thinking of Sunflower, understood she'd stirred him deeper and roused inaccessible corners even he wasn't aware existed in himself. He would find her secrets, he promised silently, find them and make the night something she would remember and cherish forever. The way he would.

Cole finished unlacing the white satin ribbon, then drew the camisole away from Sunny's body. His breath whistled through his teeth as he gazed on her soft breasts, their rigid peaks beckoning him through the flickering light. Fighting the urge to take her now as his body demanded, Cole gently took one breast in his mouth, teasing the crown with his tongue and caressed its twin with feather-like fingertips.

Sunny's response was instant, and so filled with pleasure she bit her lip to keep from crying out. His mouth and hands roamed over her body, sparked fires every place they touched, and ignited an inferno when they brushed across the dry tinder of her abdomen. Impatient to know everything at once, she loosened the drawstrings of her drawers when Cole tried to slide them lower on her hips. With only a moment's hesitation, she wriggled out of them and awaited the next lesson.

"Easy, little flower," he said with a lusty chuckle. "If you rush me, I might hurt you more than is necessary."

"More than is necessary?" Her mind swimming through all the new sensations, she tried to understand what he meant. "I thought you cared for me. Why do you plan to hurt me?"

"It's not my plan, little one. It's nature's, but I'll try to make everything as painless as possible."

Cole brushed his fingers along the inside of her knees as he spoke, and she rewarded him by opening her long swimmer's legs without shame or coyness. Spasms of desire, and something else, ricocheted throughout him as he gazed on the lush raven mat of curls. When he realized his hands, his body, would be the first to touch hers so intimately, it was all he could do to keep his movements slow and gentle.

Strong hands capable of twisting a thousand-pound steer to the ground, became velvet gloves of tenderness as he stroked her trembling body from head to toe. Wet kisses punctuated by occasional flicks of his exploring tongue made her want to giggle with delight yet scream with sweet agony at the same time. She was a mass of contradictions, wanting but holding back, needing yet keeping something in reserve.

Cole massaged and teased the flesh of her upper legs and inner thighs until Sunny thought she'd go mad for wanting something . . . anything to ease the terrible ache between her legs. And when he finally stroked her in that private place, Sunny's breath sucked in painfully, then ceased altogether. She arched and bucked, uncertain if she wanted him to stop or to go on forever, ravage her or leave her in this virginal state for the rest of her life. As new sensations washed over her, each one higher and more intense as his caresses increased, Sunny thought she would die from the pleasure, fill to overflowing with this incredible joy, and explode.

And then she did.

Confused, embarrassed by her reaction and wondering why her body was suddenly out of control, Sunny thought of fighting against the delicious shudders and rhythmic spasms. But she was already lost, her mind no match for the thunder and lightning bursting through her veins. A helpless passenger, she rode passion's wild pony until the last pulsing hoofbeat faded in the distance. Only then did she open her eyes and risk a glimpse of Cole's reaction to her strange behavior.

But she could read no disapproval in his expression. Averting her gaze, she murmured, "I am sorry. I do not know what happened to me, I have never—"

"Oh, little flower." Cole kissed her trembling mouth, then lifted her chin with his finger. "What happened just now is only one difference between what you call mating and making love."

"It is?" Her eyes wide with wonder and relief, Sunflower's sigh was one of contentment. "Then I like this making love. And it was not at all painful."

"I said," he growled, the corner of his mouth turned up in amusement, "that was *one* difference. We haven't made love yet, Sunshine. I've only made it easier for you to accept me."

She thought of what she'd witnessed among the animals, of his earlier warning, and knew he meant to mount her. Sunny's heated blood cooled and she stiffened in fear, even as her curiosity, her desire to become his, remained potent.

The movement wasn't lost on Cole. "Don't be frightened, sweetheart. There is nothing to fear, only new sensations to experience." He smiled as he took her hand in his. "Do you trust me?"

Her eyes wide, she nodded and admitted, "With my life, Cole. With my very life."

Touched beyond words, past comprehension, Cole groaned and slipped their hands beneath the sheets. When he directed her small fingers between the waist band of his underdrawers and the taut skin of his stomach, Sunny tensed and tried to withdraw. "Don't you want to know me the way I know you, little one?"

"Y-Yes, I do if it will give you as much pleasure."

"Then relax. I have a feeling you're going to give me more pleasure than I can stand."

Suddenly nervous and uncharacteristically shy, Sunny's swollen mouth instinctively puckered, and she felt her cheeks grow hot as she allowed him to move her hand down past a coarse crop of hair to the thick base of his desire. Startled by his size, wondering how they could possibly fit together, Sunny tried to jerk away, but Cole kept a firm grip on her wrist, and urged her to explore the entire length of him up to the soft velvet tip.

Only then did he release Sunny's wrist and allow her to make discoveries on her own. He watched her eyes widen then darken with desire as she explored him, struggled with his sanity as her small hands brought him to unbearable heights of pleasure, and knew after this night, neither of them would ever be the same again. When he was certain he could no longer stand the luscious torment of her touch, he caught her wrists and drew her arms around his shoulders. Incapable of speech, Cole took her mouth with his, tasted its sweet flavor, and found a tenderness within he didn't know he possessed.

He was magnificent! she marveled as his kiss deepened. Magnificent, wonderful, and if only for tonight, hers. As if guided by some mystic force, Sunny's hands fell from his shoulders, slid across his suddenly damp back to the hollow of his spine, then settled at his rigid buttocks. Cole's body, so different from hers, was hard where she was soft, rippled with muscles where she curved gracefully, and she reveled in their contrasts.

Her mouth watering in anticipation, Sunny helped Cole remove the final barrier of his clothing, then sucked in her breath when he pressed his hot pulsing need against the tender flesh of her thigh. She squirmed against him when he reclaimed her breast with his mouth, and heard the sounds of her own voice calling his name, begging him to ease the terrible throbbing again.

"Soon," she heard him promise through the haze. Then, while his tongue continued to tease and circle her captive nipple, Cole slid his fiery hands down her slick body to the place that cried out for satisfaction. This time, her core already hot and damp with passion, she was ready for him, and she cried out in a strangled sob as she begged him to end the sweet torment.

His own need, white-hot in its intensity, urged him to kneel above her where he loomed for a long moment. Recording her expression, the beautiful glow of desire, Cole committed the moment to memory and knew he would carry it to his grave. Then slowly, his gaze locked in hers, he filled her—with his passion, his soul.

Ribbons of sunlight filtered in through the window and bathed Sunny with morning's first glow. A warm breeze pushed the curtains aside and found its way to her sated body, where it caressed her as Cole had the night before. Feeling kittenish and feminine, she lifted her heavy lids and stared into the face of her lover.

Cole still slept, his mustache curled at the corners of his mouth in contentment. The lines fanning out from his eyes were somehow softer this morning, the deep furrows between his brows almost nonexistent. Was she the cause of this newfound peace, or did he awaken smooth and fresh each day and she simply hadn't noticed it before? She smiled at the sight of his tousled blond hair, the way some of the longer curls at his neck, still damp from the night's exertions, clung to his skin. Taking a deep breath, Sunny inhaled his scent, noticed how beautifully it mingled with the clean sweat of their lovemaking and the heady musk of passion.

She tried to change her position for a view of his entire body, but found she was trapped. Reaching up, Sunny discovered Cole clenched a fistful of her hair in each hand, and when she tried to move the lower half of her body, she also realized one of his muscular legs lay possessively across her.

Tickled, hoping he felt as contented and happy as she, Sunflower painted the silk of his mustache with a tentative fingertip. When one sleepy green eye inched open and tried to focus on her laughing face, she grinned and murmured, "Top of the mornin' to ye, *ave ahala*."

This pried the other eye open. His lip curving up at one corner, Cole released her hair and pulled her to his mouth for a long, leisurely kiss. So it hadn't been a dream or mirage, he thought as she opened herself to him. Sunflower was his in every sense of the word. But for how long and to what end? They would arrive at his home before sundown, be smothered by his family and friends. Would she be accepted by them—by *him* on his own turf? When their lips parted, he shook off his concerns and centered his thoughts on her radiant beauty looking up at him. Her cheeks were alive with color, her dark eyes flashing with sparks of Irish mischief. With a hoarse laugh, Cole gathered her in his arms and snuggled her against his chest.

"So," he chuckled. "What's an *ave ahala*—or do I want to know?"

Her laughter high-pitched and delicate like fine crystal, Sunny sprinkled good-morning kisses in the valley of his throat before she answered. "I am not sure, but it is Quechan and I think it has something to do with this private time." She considered telling him the first word meant rattlesnake, then chuckled and decided against it. "I only meant to say, good morning, Cole Fremont. I am very happy this morning."

"So am I, Sunny." Cole slid his hand around to the side of her neck and found his gaze cornered by the unsettling contrast between their skin tones. Hers, a creamy berry-brown highlighted with a hint of copper; his, tanned but more palomino than buckskin. In spite of himself, of the warm feelings growing inside him, a sudden image of his father flashed through his mind.

Cole jackknifed to a sitting position and slid out of the bed. He began to dress, careful to keep his gaze and troubling thoughts to himself, and stated as casually as possible, "If we're going to make the ranch before sundown, we'd better be on our way."

Unsure of his thoughts, Sunny pulled on her drawers and slipped into her camisole. But when she climbed off the bed and looked around, she remembered she was in his, not her own room.

"M-My dress," she sputtered, afraid she would cause him embarrassment. "It is next door with my things."

"Don't worry. I'll sneak you back in there." Cole grabbed the blanket off his bed then draped it around her as carefully as he would wrap a fine porcelain vase. Fighting to think only of Sunny, of the night and gifts they'd shared, he pulled her against the length of his body and lifted her chin with his thumb and forefinger. "I forgot to ask—how are you this morning, Sunshine? Do you hurt? Are you all right?"

"Umm," she hummed, her eyes serene and heavy lidded. "I feel nothing but this happy tingling everywhere. I feel so . . . so alive." She could have added "in love," but sensed somehow that this information would burden rather than please him.

Something in her expression, something other than physical contentment, stirred him even as it set off a series of alarms. He'd promised her nothing and she'd accepted the night spent in his arms as just that. It sounded simple at the time—why didn't it *feel* simple now? Cole indulged himself, gazed on her perfect features and cherry-stained mouth, and suddenly understood that if he didn't release her soon, the promises would fade away.

With considerable effort, he stepped away. "We'd better hit the trail. I feel a change in the weather—one that will have us arriving at the ranch soaking wet if we don't leave soon."

Sensing he'd reached some kind of uneasy truce with himself, Sunny chewed on her bottom lip and gave him a short nod. "My dress?"

"Oh, yeah. Sure." Cole opened the door a crack and when he was sure the hall was empty, he slid over to the adjoining room and fit the key in the lock. Then he motioned, and she scurried past him into her room.

Backing away, he said, "I'll arrange for a quick bite to eat and get the horses ready while you're dressing." At the sound of approaching footsteps, he hastily added, "Stay in here. I'll come back for you after I've made all the arrangements."

After he was gone, Sunny twirled and sashayed over to the dressing table. She pulled the gold and pearl brush through her long hair, still feeling deliciously feminine, and helped herself to several pats of lilac-scented powder before slipping into her new clothes. Was Cole feeling the same things she did this morning? she wondered. What had been going through his mind as he held her near the doorway, or when he held her all through the night? Suddenly missing Moonstar again, wishing she could ask the questions she thought she'd never want the answers to, Sunny drew in a long breath as thoughts of her mother opened the valves of her heart, flooding her with pain and a sense of loss.

Then she waited.

The minutes ticked by to thirty, and then to an hour. Restless and worried, Sunny began pacing back and forth in front of her window. Where was Cole? Had he run into some trouble, found himself short of money, or . . . decided not to take her with him? Her imagination running wild, it was impossible for her to wait any longer. Tucking her brother's clothing in her empty pouches, she draped them over her arm and slid out of her room into the empty hallway.

She listened for several minutes, hoping to hear Cole's welcome footsteps, but all was silent. Cautiously, Sunflower made her way to the top of the stairs, then started a quick descent. Determined to avoid any kind of trouble, she made straight for the front doors, her head low and eyes cast down, and pushed her way into the morning sunshine. Then she collided heavily with the base of a willow tree.

"Hey!" the tree bellowed as it jerked her off her feet and squeezed her against its trunk. "Cain't ya look where yer walkin', squaw lady?"

Sunny's eyes flew open and she pressed her forearms against the chest of the biggest man she'd ever seen. "Let me go!" she demanded, her struggles impotent against such superior strength.

"I ain't gonna hurt you none."

But trapped in the arms of this grizzly of a man, Sunny panicked and began to fight in earnest. She kicked out, catching the man in the knees and shins, and drove her fingers towards his eyes as she cried out, "Let go—let me go!"

"Put her down, Jesse."

Cole's voice, calm and without malice or warning, reached the big man's ears. He lowered the woman to the wooden planks and stepped back, ducking her flailing arms and driving feet.

"Howdy, Mr. Fremont," he said, backing away. "I just ketched her, I didn't hurt no one."

"I know, Jesse. It's all right." Cole waited for the slow-moving giant to make his way inside the hotel before he turned on Sunny. "Dammit all, didn't I tell you to stay in your room and wait for me there?"

Still shaken, Sunny kept an eye on the door where the monster had disappeared and stammered, "Yes, but I—I, you took so long, I—"

"Wasn't your run-in with the desk clerk enough?" he went on as unreasonable anger tore through him. "Do you have to go looking for trouble?"

"I was worried about you!" she snapped, a fever building in her eyes. "All I did was walk out the door and accidentally bump into that . . . that *man*. Then he grabbed me!"

"He didn't mean you any harm. Jesse is a friendly sort." Cole jerked off his hat and dragged frustrated fingers through his hair. "I told you to wait for me. This wouldn't have happened if you'd have stayed in your room where you belong."

"I am thinking perhaps I don't even belong in this town."

"Oh, hell," he grumbled, unwilling to consider her words, afraid she may have voiced his own thoughts. "That's not it at all." Cole brought the Stetson back to his head and worked it into the correct position, then he blew out a heavy sigh. "Let's just forget it and get on out of here before anything else happens."

Sunny measured him for a long moment, that sickening thought swirling in her mind again. He was embarrassed by her, ashamed of her heritage. Would the fact she was a half-breed disturb him as much at his family's ranch?

"Sunny? You coming?" Cole offered his elbow, his green eyes filled with apology.

Shrugging, Sunny accepted his arm and allowed him to usher her back inside the hotel for a meal of fried ham, potatoes, and biscuits. Vacillating between righteous anger and acquittal, she kept her silence as they ate. He *had* told her to stay in her room, *had* come back as he said he would, so why shouldn't he have been angry when he found her outside the hotel captured by what had to be the son of Goliath? She didn't know. And yet she did. She couldn't understand. Or maybe she understood only too well.

Sunny ate without interest, and her meal lay in her stomach like a sack of corn flour while she and Cole walked back through the hotel and crossed the street to the livery stable.

"Charlie?" he called after they entered the barn.

A chestnut-skinned man with long black braids appeared from around the corner of a stall. "Ah, Mr. Fremont. Your mounts are ready."

"So are we. Please fetch them."

His gaze lingering on the half-breed woman, the blacksmith gave a short nod and went after the horses.

Well aware of Charlie's interest in Sunny, remembering his own thoughts about pairing the two of them, Cole grimaced and his mustache twitched as he informed her of the new traveling arrangements.

"The reason it took me so long to get back to the hotel this morning was the search Charlie and I went through to find a lady's saddle for your pony. I'm afraid even the smallest one was too big for Paddy," Cole explained. "I'll tie him alongside Sage and you can ride the outlaw's horse."

Her eyes wide, Sunny gasped as the blacksmith appeared with the horses. "But I cannot!"

"It's all right," Cole assured. "Charlie trimmed his hooves and rubbed him down. He's a little worse for the wear, but he won't have any problem carrying you to the ranch. He can wait to rest up until then."

"You do not understand." Sunny shook her head as she moved to the shaggy horse's side. "It is not the animal. 'Tis the saddle."

His brows knotted, Cole examined the leather seat and shrugged. "It looks fine to me. It's a standard sidesaddle. What's the problem?"

"The problem," Sunny glanced around then lowered her voice. "The problem is that I don't know how to ride on one of those. I would prefer to ride Paddy out of here the way I rode him in."

"Is that all?" Cole laughed. "The way you can handle a horse, this is going to seem like a buggy ride. Come on, I'll help you up."

But Sunny wasn't convinced. She eyed, then fingered the long horn protruding off the side of the saddle. "Cole, I really don't—"

"You just hook your right leg over the horn and sit back and let the horse do all the work. That's all there is to it."

Still skeptical, Sunflower lifted her arms and allowed him to hoist her into the strange saddle. After sitting there a few minutes, her leg dangling off the side of the horse, she nodded, hoping her sense of balance would return before they started moving. "I suppose I am ready."

"Good." After a quick wink and a squeeze of her ankle, Cole turned, thanked Charlie, and mounted Sage.

The pair traveled down the dusty street slowly as Sunny familiarized herself with the odd rhythms atop the sidesaddle. They stopped at the edge of town long enough for her to send wires to her father in La Paz and Fort Mohave, and considered sending a message to Yuma as well, but thought it a waste of money. A wire to her hometown wouldn't be read for at least three months. She would have her hands full repaying Cole for the clothing before she returned to Yuma and didn't need any more extra expenses. Proud of her good sense, Sunny allowed herself to be hoisted onto the sidesaddle for the journey to the cattle ranch.

Back on the trail again, Cole urged her to join him in a slow trot, then onto an easy lope as she became more comfortable. But even with his concern and several rest stops along the way, by the time they reached the arched gates of the Triple F ranch, she was stiff and chafed, her waist crimped on one side and sorely stretched on the other by her unnatural posture.

When they slowed to a stop and Sunny took her first good look at Cole's home in the lower Verde Valley, she forgot about her discomfort. Tall, gnarled junipers lined the endless white fences leading to the house, their twisted branches waving as if to greet her. In between these, bright green palo verde trees bent gracefully in the light breeze, their thick leaves a welcome respite from the setting sun.

"Ohhh," she breathed. "This is even more beautiful than I ever imagined."

Coaxing her down the path beneath the arched branches, Cole glanced around the property. "I suppose it is beautiful," he acknowledged, noting how the much-needed rain had filled the pastures and meadows with lush, tall grass. "Sometimes you have to go away from your home before you can appreciate it."

"Oh, I would never find this place to be anything other than beautiful. Is it always so green?"

Impatient to be off the trail, Cole nudged Sage and the outlaw's mount into an easy lope as he answered. "If there's green to be found in these parts, it'll be here in Verde Valley, but the last few years we've been damn near as dry as Yuma."

Tired and giddy, Sunny laughed and nearly lost what little balance she had. Gripping the saddle horn more tightly, she glanced up the road and spotted a small dust storm heading their way. Inclining her head, she said, "What is that?"

Squinting his eyes against the fireball of a rapidly setting sun, recognition spread a grin across his tired features as the rider approached. "Looks like we've got a welcoming committee," he said as the oncoming horse skidded to a halt and a petite young woman flung herself off the saddle.

"Cole!" she cried, racing towards Sage.

Swinging his long leg over the saddlebags, Cole dismounted and spread his arms wide. The woman flew into his arms, and the two twirled like a top, laughing and muttering words of welcome to one another.

Elizabeth? Sunny wondered, wishing for a reckless moment she had her grandfather's war club in her hand. Or was that another admirer of the handsome rancher? She watched them, a cold knife twisting in her gut, until they finally broke apart.

His arm still wrapped around her shoulder, Cole and the woman approached the outlaw's mount. "Sunny, I'd like you to meet my sister, Nellie." He looked down at the beaming woman and continued, "Nell, this is Sunflower Callahan. She's going to be staying with us for a while."

"Sunflower?" Nellie glanced at Cole, then up at Sunny. "What a pretty name. Nice to meet you."

"I am pleased to meet you, also." Sunny's smile, one of relief at first, quickly became genuine as she regarded Cole's sister. Instantly, she felt at ease, as if she'd just met an old friend. Nellie's expression sparkled with eyes more hazel than green, reflecting sincerity and kindness—along with a disturbing hint of sadness.

Nellie turned back to her brother and patted his shoulder with a delicate hand. "Dad's at the ranch. I told him it was you coming up the road, but he didn't believe me. Let's go show him he's not always right!"

"That'd be a first! Let's get going." Cole laughed as Nellie skipped back to her horse and remounted, but when the trio started down the path again, his amusement quickly faded to apprehension. He'd meant to warn Sunny about his father, at least give her a general idea of the way the old man looked on Indians—*any* Indian.

Somehow, he'd never found the right moment—or the right words. Now, he thought with a heavy sigh, it was too late.

SEVEN

Nathan Fremont filled the doorway of his sprawling home, his hawklike eyes darting from Sunny to Cole and back to Sunny again. Speaking fluent Texan, his voice big and bold, the words hot and spicy, he drawled, "Been a hell of a long time, son. Mighty nice to see you again. Whatcha'll brought home here?"

"A houseguest, Dad." Hoping his father read the clear warning in his eyes, Cole reached for Sunny's hand and pulled her inside the doorway. "Miss Callahan, my father, Nathan Fremont."

"Callahan?" The elder man shook his head, grumbling, "Humph—"

"Excuse us, Dad," Cole sliced in as he coaxed Sunny past his father and into the foyer. "Miss *Callahan* has had quite an ordeal. Nellie's going to take her upstairs for some rest now. You two can make your acquaintances later."

Sunny planted her feet at this. "But Cole, I am not—"

"It's quite all right." He speared her with a meaningful gaze, then inclined his head towards the stairs. "Please go with Nellie and let her help you get settled."

Cole exchanged glances with his sister, then removed his

hat and sailed it toward a set of steer horns mounted on the wall. Turning back to his father, he raked his fingers through his hair. "We've got some catching up to do. Why don't we down a couple in your office?"

Nathan stroked his busy beard and narrowed his scarred left eye until it was a slit. "I reckon we should, Cole. And I reckon we'll be doin' a lot more talkin' than drinkin', too."

Sunny couldn't keep her eyes off the two men, could actually feel the frigid blast of air surrounding them, and realized with a shiver that her presence had everything to do with it. She tore her gaze away and followed the young woman up the gracefully curving stairway to the second floor of the huge home.

"You can have the room next to mine," Nellie said as she opened the door to a luxuriously feminine suite and gestured for Sunflower to enter. "This used to be my room until I got married."

Temporarily ignoring the scene she'd just left, Sunny's brows raised as she studied Cole's sister. "You look so young to have a husband."

"I'm already eighteen," she laughed. "Certainly past marrying age, but thanks anyway."

Nellie's words echoed in Sunny's head, but the voice was that of Moonstar. She thought of her mother, of her insistence that the marrying time was upon her. Sunny lowered her head and closed her eyes, wondering if her own nineteen years were *beyond* the marrying age.

"Sunflower?"

Nellie's voice, soft with concern, snapped her back to the present. "Oh, I am sorry. I suppose I am more tired than I thought."

"That's understandable from what little I heard about your adventures on the trail. Why don't you just forget all that and come look around your room." Nellie spread her arms wide. "What do you think?"

Accepting the invitation, Sunny made a visual sweep of her accommodations and sucked in her breath. Everything seemed made of clouds and gold, flowers, and sunshine. The brass bed was covered with a puffy quilt of ivory and decorated with several lavender pillows. Yards of purple velvet fringed with ivory satin tassels draped the twin windows on either side of the bed and set off the ornate brass headboard. An ivory and gold dressing table with a high curving mirror, and a large wingback chair covered with sprigs of violets on a creamy background, completed the elegant bedroom.

Sunny turned to her hostess, hands clasped at her waist, and said, "This is very beautiful. You are lucky to live in such a home."

"Thank you. This room has always been like a refuge to me. I'd still be in it, but Bucky says it's too frilly and girly for a man, so . . ." Her guard down, Nellie's eyes dulled as she stood silent for several seconds. Then she shook off the trance and went on. "It's become the guest room."

Bright-eyed again, Nell swept over to a large closet featuring twin doors and swung them open. "I still keep a few dresses in here and there's a nightgown on a hook at the back wall." She turned, mentally measuring Sunny, and flashed a broad grin. "I'm sure the clothes will fit you except for the length. All we have to do is add a couple inches of lace or a flounce, and we can build you a whole new wardrobe!"

"Oh, no," she objected. "I cannot—"

"Excuse me for interrupting," Nellie said as she lightly touched Sunny's arm, "but Cole asked me to make sure you have everything you need. I can see you don't have a thing to wear but the dress on your back, and . . . and I can also see my brother cares for you very much."

Sunny's thick lashes brushed her cheeks as she lowered her lids. She began to fidget with the yellow satin ribbons at her waist. "I—I . . . Cole has been very kind to me."

"Yes, well," Nellie laughed, "I'm not saying Cole isn't a kind man—he is—but that's not what I'm talking about. He seems very attentive, almost protective of you."

Sunny fingered an emerald green dress of pure silk, thinking back to the way Cole kept his father from addressing her when they first arrived at the ranch, and wondered what kind of exchange Nathan Fremont might be having with his only son at this moment.

A twinge of guilt spun her around to face Nellie. "You and Cole have both been very kind and generous with me, but what of your father? Perhaps he is not so pleased to offer me a bedroom in his home."

"Oh, just try to ignore him." Nell brushed the remark off with a wave of her hand. "He's set in his ways, but his bark is a lot bigger than his bite. I'm sure Cole can smooth him over."

"And your mother?" Sunny ventured. "Is she not here?"

Nellie's hazel eyes darkened as she drew a honey-colored wisp of hair back from her cheek. "You probably won't meet Mom for a few days. She's in bed with the miseries again."

"I am sorry for her." And, she realized with a start, sorry for Cole. His return home was without joy, and had him facing his father in some kind of showdown she couldn't quite grasp, even though she understood that she was somehow the cause.

Downstairs, the elder Fremont poured another two fingers of expensive brandy and gulped down the burning liquid in one swallow. His fat cheeks ruddy with irritation, he slammed the glass to the desk.

"Why *here*, son? You could have taken the girl anywhere but here! Have you thought of your mother, what it'll do to her when she finds out she's sheltering a goddamn Indian?"

"Sunny's half Irish," Cole fired back, but the moment the words were out, a wave of self-loathing rolled through him. He was thinking of Sunflower on his father's terms, not his own—making excuses for her heritage, not defending her for the fine young woman she was.

His flush deepening, Nathan cut into Cole's introspection. "Irish, smirish! She's a damnable Indian squaw, pure and simple."

Ready to set the old man straight, Cole opened his mouth, but quickly closed it when he noticed Nathan's high color. The time would come for this discussion, a time when Nathan wasn't overwrought by the surprise visitor, or by his concerns for his wife's failing health.

"Sit down, Dad," Cole encouraged softly. "You've got your blood pressure up and racing through your veins like a locomotive. You know what the doctor said about getting excited."

Grumbling, Nathan eased down in his chair. "I wouldn't be so damned excited if you hadn't drug home that stinkin' damn orphaned—"

"I'm going to pretend I didn't hear any of that for now." Cole's angry words arrested his father's dissertation. He backed away from Nathan's desk, and excused himself. "I'm tired and trail weary. All I want right now is supper and my own bed. We'll finish this discussion tomorrow, but I'm warning you now, I'm not going to sit here and listen to you call Sunny anything but what she is—a fine young lady."

Nathan tugged at his beard and glared. "We'll talk," he grumbled with a smirk. "But it isn't going to change any of the facts, or the way this whole thing looks to me."

Cole spun on his heel and headed for the door, but his father's words followed him into the hallway. "I'd like to know what you're thinking about, coming back here, turning this family upside down just 'cause of that trashy little injun squaw. Shoulda satisfied your itch for her somewhere else, boy!"

Sean sat at the edge of a butte overlooking the sprawling town of Phoenix. Unlike the boom towns, places like La

Paz where shops and stores seemed to spring up overnight and without much thought, Phoenix had a look of permanence, of a city with a long and carefully planned future ahead of it. He shivered as the wind increased its strength and chill, then studied the rapidly building clouds. A storm was brewing, one that might even pack the makings of a flash flood. Time was running out.

Sensing he was very near the end of his journey, Sean climbed back on Whiskey and began the descent into town. Knowing the trail he followed would be swallowed up once he reached the outskirts of town, he headed straight for the building any weary traveler would likely make his first stop. The livery stable.

After tying Whiskey to the hitching post outside, Sean ambled into the barn. "Hello?"

"Over here," Charlie White answered from the far side of a wood partition.

"Howdy," Sean greeted as he rounded the corner. "I wonder if you might supply me with a little information."

Charlie frowned as he pounded the last nail in a horseshoe, then he returned the horse's hoof to the floor. Standing upright, he rubbed the ache in the small of his back and regarded the berry-skinned stranger.

"I supply horseshoes and feed. You'll have to git yer information somewhere else."

"Listen, friend." Sean measured the man, hoped he'd feel a kinship in the fact they were both half-breeds. "What I seek is only a member of my family. I have become separated from her and thought you may have watered her pony."

"A pony, you say?"

Almost certain by his expression the blacksmith had seen Paddy, Sean smiled warmly and tried to calm the excitement building in him. "Yes, a pony. My sister rides a small Mustang with a large black ring around his right eye." He studied the man's reaction to this and decided to press him for more. "She is traveling with a man and an extra pack horse. Have they been through here yet?"

Charlie rubbed the tip of his chin with a forefinger, then shrugged. "I don't see no harm in tellin' you. Cole Fremont come through here two days ago with a half-breed woman ridin' a pony what fits that description. Guess it might be yer sis."

Nearly bursting with the discovery, Sean swallowed hard and tried to keep his voice calm and even. "That's the name. Cole Fremont." Trying his best to look nonchalant, he smiled and inquired, "Do you now where I might find them?"

Again, Charlie shrugged. "The Triple F ranch is 'bout a day's ride from town. Head out east 'til you come to the fork, then head north. You'll run right into it."

"Much obliged." His grin wide, his eyes sparkling, Sean shook the blacksmith's hand and went after Whiskey. He would have to wait to savor the end of this trail, make himself stay the evening in Phoenix. The mule wouldn't be much good to him if he didn't give him this full night's rest, and without Whiskey, his journey would be at a premature end. It wouldn't do to let impatience spoil his chances for saving Sunny now that he was so close to her. With the few coins he carried, Sean paid for feed and lodging of his mount, then gratefully accepted the offer of an empty stall for himself.

Tonight he would sleep well.

Tomorrow, he and Whiskey would be refreshed and ready to confront their quarry. Sean drifted off smiling with the knowledge that now his quarry had a name—and soon that name would be carved on a tombstone.

The morning roused Sean from his sleep with a start. He ducked and rolled, forgetting at first that he was no longer on the trail. Disoriented, he looked around the stall and wondered if he'd really heard the sounds of gunfire or if the noise had come from a dream. Then it sounded again. Thunder, steel-edged and razor sharp, fragmented the dawn. The storm was nearly ready to break, making his objective even more difficult.

Sean quickly saddled Whiskey and rode towards the east. With the thunder nipping at his heels from the west, he managed to stay one step ahead of the storm until mid-afternoon. When the rain finally caught up with him, the first droplets, soft and dew-like, were suddenly followed by a tremendous clap of thunder. Then all hell broke loose.

Gnarled fingers of lightning reached out, dug at the earth in a grotesque death grasp as thunder continued to boom across the gloomy skies. The soft droplets of rain became a massive waterfall from above, blinding his vision and soaking his skin. The driving storm assaulted his ears, made him feel like it was playing tricks on him as the howling winds mimicked the screams of children and terrified animals.

Then Whiskey stumbled on a mud-splattered mare.

Sean jumped off the startled mule and shielded his eyes with his hat. The buckskin horse struggled hopelessly in an effort to stand, but her front leg was badly broken. Suddenly aware of a loud rushing noise behind him, of the deadly danger, Sean realized he was standing in the middle of a wash. A torrent of water was building from somewhere behind and soon it would envelop him and the animals in a swirling shroud.

The mare couldn't be saved even if there were more time, but where was its rider? Sean climbed back on Whiskey, keeping one ear tuned to the gaining river and both eyes on the ground as he started for higher ground. Still using his hat like an awning, he squinted through the sheets of rain until he found a bit of color in the muddied landscape.

With the roar of water growing louder, Sean quickly dismounted and hurried to the object on the ground. He took only a moment to identify the lump as the body of a young woman before he scooped the figure in his arms and carried her back to Whiskey. Draping her unconscious form across his shoulder, he struggled to remount the mule, then urged Whiskey up the side of the gorge.

With only instinct to guide him, Whiskey picked his way through the gravel and loose rocks until they reached a plateau well above the rising waters. Sure of their position and safety, Sean dismounted and carried the woman to a shallow depression in the side of the hill.

Still holding the girl, he sank to the ground and positioned her across his lap with her head against his shoulder. Only then did he take the time to examine her. Sean quickly discovered the bit of peach color he'd seen was the dismantled bow at the collar of her blouse, but nowhere could he find the source of her injury. She was pale, her creamy skin cold and nearly transparent against the brown of her skirt and jacket, and her breathing was shallow and raspy.

Quickly releasing the knot of ribbons holding the bonnet together at her throat, he pulled off the hat and started to fan her with it. Then his arm froze in mid-act. Hair the color of the setting sun tumbled down across his arm and her shoulders, captured his breath and gaze with its burnished gloss, made him feel weak and helpless. Never had Sean looked upon anything so beautiful, even with the rain and mud working to dull it.

Sudden concern for her condition brought air back into his lungs. Sean loosened her jacket and gently pressed his ear to her chest. Her heart beat strong through a small breast so soft he had to fight the urge to turn his head and press his lips to it. He straightened and took another deep breath. Then he noticed the angry strawberry-colored mound rising just above her temple.

Sean slid a gentle, inquiring fingertip up to the bruise, then jerked it away when startled ice-blue eyes flashed open. The young woman screamed and fainted.

Eileen's heart fluttered, skipping several beats, as she worked her way up from the depths of unconsciousness again. Deep blue eyes pierced the black corners of her mind, swam in a handsome face framed by shining ebony hair. Was it a dream? Had it *all* been a dream? She remembered trying to outrun the storm, the sickening crack of bones as her father's brood mare stepped in a prairie dog hole, a few drops of rain . . . those eyes . . . a warm breath caressing her breast . . . fingers stroking her cheek.

Eileen's eyes flew open again, and this time she sat up. "Oh, my God, I—"

"Shush," Sean encouraged with a fingertip against her lips. "Careful, do not move. We don't have much room for error on this ledge. Please hold still and I will try to explain who I am and how you got here."

Her spine stiff, Eileen peeked over the edge and down to the raging waters below. With a barely perceptible nod, she avoided his gaze and whispered, "A flash flood. I tried to outrun it."

"I figured as much. My mule came across your horse just before the waters rose. I'm afraid I could not save her, she—"

"I know," Eileen said with quiet pain, "the mare fell in a hole. I knew she was gone before I hit the ground."

Seeing the sadness, the resignation in her timid blue eyes, Sean felt a tug, the tip of a dull knife prodding his heart to life. "She must have meant a great deal to you. I am sorry there was nothing I could do for her."

His remarks brought her chin up, and for the first time she purposefully looked into his eyes. "That's all right. I mean," she stumbled around looking for the right words, "it's not all right that she had to die, but she was my father's horse. He's the one who will . . . he might be kind of . . ." Eileen found that she didn't have the words to explain herself, and immediately lowered her lashes.

Fragile. Frightened. Lonely. Why, Sean wondered, did all these words come to mind as he looked at her? His heart went out to her even as it was drawn to her beauty, ached for wanting to ease her pain, and yet withdrew at the thought of getting any closer to her.

Increasingly aware of her damp body trembling against his, Sean shifted his position, but the movement only nestled her soft bottom deeper between his legs. Ignoring the sudden sensations, the quickening of his loins, he leaned his head against the earthen wall and introduced himself. "My name is Sean Callahan. I'm from Yuma."

Forgetting her shyness, Eileen jerked her chin up and stared into his features, her expression unable to hide her surprise at his name. "Oh? Umm, I'm Eileen Hobbs. M-My father's ranch is a couple miles up the wash."

"What are you staring at, Miss Hobbs? Were you expecting my name to be Geronimo, or Nachez, or maybe something more colorful like 'Red-skinned son of the Irish Mick'?"

"Oh!" Eileen covered her head with her arms and ducked, expecting the angry young man to strike her.

Sean's hands froze in the air a scant inch above her heaving shoulders. What should he do? What had he *done*? A few harsh words, yes, but her reaction surprised and confused him. Maybe he should hold her, take back those spontaneous words he usually spouted when confronted with his Indian heritage, and calm this frightened young fawn of a woman. And yet, if he dared touch her now in this overwrought state, what kind of chance might he be taking? Her response to his words might be nothing compared to his hands on her trembling body, and it could even push her to panic and send them both into the turbulent waters below.

"Miss Hobbs, I'm sorry. I didn't mean . . . Miss Hobbs?" he pleaded, his hands still clutching only air. "What's wrong? Please don't be afraid. I won't hurt you."

Eileen took great gulps of air in an effort to calm herself.

Her neck and cheeks burned with shame at her reaction to his ancestry, and stung with embarrassment over her response to his display of temper. Turning her head aside, she was finally able to say, "You are the one who should forgive me. I don't know what came over me or why I stared at you like that. It was unforgivable."

But her apology didn't interest him. What did concern him was the fear, the near terror in her eyes and instinctive reflexes she exhibited when he barked at her. Was she frightened because he was part Indian—or was there some other cause? Whatever the reason, she was badly shaken and in need of comfort. His hands no longer questioned where they belonged as Sean slid one across her shoulders and the other beneath her chin.

Gently coaxing her head towards his, he waited until she lifted her lids and looked into his eyes before he whispered, "You're wrong. I am the one who should apologize. A half-breed with an Irish name should be used to incredulous stares and occasional remarks by now. I'm afraid my Irish temper has a little more growing up to do. You really did not offend me."

Sean smiled as the fear in her ice-blue eyes began to melt, revealing a heartwarming innocence that touched him deeply. Her bottom lip trembled as he stared into those eyes, and instinctively his gaze gravitated down past her upturned nose to the movement. Her mouth was shaped in a perpetual pout, the full lips curving at the corners, yet dipping on one side making it appear as if it were crooked when she smiled. He wanted that mouth. Wanted to feel those tempting lips part beneath his and welcome him inside for a taste of honey. What would it be like—and what would she do if he were to act on the impulse?

Eileen's eyes grew huge as Sean slowly pulled her face close to his. Cloistered by her father and six brothers, she had never seen any man look at her like this, and wasn't certain if she ought to be frightened or pleased by the attention. He was a bare inch away from her now, his hot breath caressing her lips and offering his own special scent of sweet hay and rain-freshened juniper. She could feel herself growing not just warm, but hot, in some of the strangest places. Her cheeks. She knew her cheeks must be positively glowing. And if the handsome man could see beneath her blouse and chemise, he would find the flesh of her breasts to be feverish and glossy as sun-ripened tomatoes. This thought, and the sudden pleasurable sensations warming the lower half of her body as thoroughly as a hot bath, were too much for her. Eileen's eyelids fluttered uncontrollably and she swooned, nearly fainting again.

"Miss Hobbs? Are you all right?" Frantic, Sean picked up her bonnet and began to fan her.

Again fighting for consciousness, but this time for an entirely different reason, Eileen gasped for breath then forced herself to a sitting position. "Excuse me," she sputtered, trying to think of a logical reason for her behavior. "Maybe I haven't recovered from the blow to my head when Rosie fell."

Thinking of kicking his own behind, Sean muttered an inward oath. That he'd tried to encourage a kiss with a poor white girl who'd never seen him before was bad enough, but he hadn't even bothered to look for, or check her injuries. What could he have been thinking of? Sean pushed a heavy flame red curl off her forehead and lightly touched the strawberry-colored mound.

"This bruise looks very painful. Do you think you might be concussed?" He stared at her pupils looking for signs of dilation or contraction, and waited for some kind of response from her.

Eileen brushed his fingers aside. "It's nothing."

"I'm not so sure about that. It's awfully close to your temple."

"It's all right, Mr. Callahan. This isn't—I didn't fall, well, not here," she stumbled, looking for a way to explain.

"This happened at home. When I fell off Rosie, I landed on the back of my head." Slipping her fingers through her thick waves, she halted when they connected with a huge bump. "Ouch! Right here."

Following the lead of those alabaster fingers, Sean found the egg-sized knot, then reluctantly withdrew his hand from hair soft as the blazing clouds at sundown, and fragrant as a wild rose. Swallowing hard, he worked at a stern expression. "You may still have a fracture or concussion. I should get you home as quickly as possible."

Sean checked the skies, then the water still tumbling through the valley below. "It looks like the storm is ready to break, but I don't think we should chance being trapped down there again. Is the wash the only way back to your place?"

Eileen shook her head, and suddenly realized her hair was falling free. "My bonnet! Where's my bonnet?" she cried.

"Take it easy. I have it." Puzzled at first by what he considered an overreaction to the missing item, Sean waved the hat in front of her then observed as she snatched it away and tucked her glorious hair up inside the brown material.

Guessing the weather had a lot to do with her attitude, he grinned and commented, "Too bad it's raining. You have the most beautiful hair I've ever seen. It's a shame to keep it covered up."

"You like the *color*?" she blurted out, stunned.

"Why, yes, of course I do." She looked so surprised, or perhaps annoyed, he wasn't sure what to say. He shook his head and shrugged. "I can't understand why anyone *wouldn't* like it. It's the most incredible shade of fire and copper, and . . . I don't know. Your hair reminds me of the prettiest sunset I've ever seen on the Colorado River."

"Then you really do like it?" she breathed, not sure she should believe him.

"You act as if no one has ever told you what beautiful hair you have."

With a short laugh, she shot him a sideways glance. "That's because no one ever has."

"Oh, come on, Eileen—ah, Miss Hobbs."

"You may call me Eileen if you wish, and yes, it's true. Papa says my hair looks painted like a fallen woman's, that it's an ugly flag to attract men of immoral character. I've always had to make sure it's covered in public to keep Papa from shame."

Sean had no reply for her, couldn't understand the kind of thinking that would have a beautiful young daughter consider herself as anything less than that, knew he didn't have the right to tell her how wrong she was—or how terribly wrong her father was. He thought of Sunny, of Patrick's protective measures with her, and shrugged. Grown men were funny around their little girls, and fought to keep them that way even after they'd grown. Perhaps this was Mr. Hobbs's way of keeping Eileen as his little girl as long as possible. And even if it wasn't, who was he to judge another man's methods of raising his children?

"I think we'd better get going while we still can," he finally said, with no further references to her hair.

Nodding, Eileen crawled along the ledge until Sean was free to climb to the lip of the hill and help her up beside him. After trying several combinations of positions on the small saddle, they finally settled on Eileen sitting sideways across the leather seat with Sean straddling the mule behind her.

Keeping one arm around her waist to help balance her weight, Sean guided Whiskey along the rim of the shallow canyon leading towards Pleasant Valley. As they picked their way through mud and debris from the storm, Eileen told him of the arduous trek the Hobbs family made just over a year ago from St. Louis. Their objective was to claim a homestead in the untamed territory of Arizona, she explained. Once that was accomplished, she and her six younger brothers worked alongside their mother and father building a meager shelter, raising a few crops, and managing the small herd of cattle they owned. Her tale was one of hope, hard work, and humble beginnings.

By the time they arrived at the patch of ground Dan Hobbs had claimed as his own, Sean felt like he had come to know the small sod house and poorly constructed barn. He slid down off Whiskey's rump and held his arms out to Eileen. She was on the ground, but still in his arms, when he heard a feminine voice cry out.

"Eileen? Oh, thank God. I been so worried." Martha Hobbs stood in the doorway of her home wringing her hands, but made no attempt to approach her daughter.

"Sorry, Ma," Eileen answered over her shoulder. "Please come in, Mr. Callahan. I'd like to thank you proper for saving my life."

"That isn't necessary, Eileen. I should be on my way."

"Where do you have to be in such a rush?"

Sean hesitated a moment, but couldn't find grounds not to divulge his destination. "I've some business at the Triple F ranch."

"Then that's all the more reason to stay. You still have about a two-hour ride from here, and I'll bet the morning's pail of milk that storm hasn't worn itself out yet. It'll be dark soon. Come on." She took his hand and gave it a tug, "You must be ready for a hot meal after the afternoon we spent. Join me and warm yourself by the fire."

The thought of a few more hours with the freckle-faced beauty was more responsible for his decision than consuming the first hot meal he'd had in weeks. Sean allowed her to lead him to the house.

"Ma, this is Sean Callahan. He saved me from being swept away in a flash flood a couple miles up the wash."

Eileen's mother gasped, then grasped Sean's extended hand. "I'm mighty beholden to you. I figgered somethin' awful musta happened to her. Come in. You'll ketch your death in them wet clothes."

Once he was in front of the fire, Sean began to shiver as his chilled skin warmed. Eileen stood beside him, rubbing her hands together as her mother pressed for the details of her journey.

Her once attractive features lined and sagging beyond her years, Martha Hobbs sighed and gasped as she listened to the tale then raised greying brows and relaxed the corners of her sun-cracked mouth as she asked, "Did you git the dress to Mrs. Parson 'fore the rain hit?"

Eileen nodded and turned her back to the fire. "I'd have been home two hours ago if that storm hadn't come on me so fast. Oh, Mrs. Parson did pay me." She reached into her deep pocket, pulled out a few damp coins, and handed them to her mother. Then Eileen took a worried glance around the room and asked in a hushed tone, "Is Pa around?"

Martha shook her head. "All that thunder like to scared the hides off them cattle. Pa and the boys are out roundin' 'em up. Should be back anytime now."

"I've got a problem, Ma. Rosie's dead."

"Oh, Lord, girl!" Martha took her daughter's hand, then turned to Sean. "'Scuse us, please. I gotta help Eileen change into some dry things. Be right back."

"Take your time. I'm going to be awhile thawing out."

After the women disappeared, Sean's brow furrowed. Although her features were completely different than Eileen's, Mrs. Hobbs had some of her daughter's expressions, especially the look of fear in her tired eyes. What frightened them so? This untamed land with its ever-changing weather, bands of hostile Indians and outlaws marauding through the dark nights? Or was it something deeper, more personal. Mrs. Hobbs looked to be at least sixty, but his experience, and just a hint of a springtime in her eyes, told Sean she was probably no older than thirty-five, yet closer to old age than youth.

Hushed, excited voices finally stilled, and when the two women returned to the room their expressions were no less anxious, their voices still muted and cautious. Eileen moved up beside Sean and said, "Ma says you can spend the night in the barn. We have an extra blanket, but I'm afraid I can't offer you a change of clothes."

"I'm drying out just fine. Thanks."

Sean's gaze followed her to the stove where she joined her mother in the food preparation for the evening. She had changed into a simple grey plaid dress, but left her mesmerizing hair uncovered and tied it at the back of her neck with a pink ribbon.

How long, Sean suddenly wondered, before that glossy mane of fire turned dull and lifeless, and her fragile beauty withered like rose petals in the desert sun? Already her delicate hands—beautiful hands that deserved to be kissed and pampered instead of plunged into boiling water and harsh soaps—showed signs of overwork and neglect.

The sounds of approaching riders turned his attention to the door. Sean slowly turned, warming and drying his backside, as he waited to meet the rest of her family.

After several minutes, the door banged open and Daniel Hobbs charged through it. "Ain't that gal back *yet*?" he demanded at the same moment he saw her standing at the stove. "Well, if yer here, where the hell's Rosie? And where'd that old mule come from?"

"Hello, Pa. I had some trouble coming home from the Parsons'." Her voice quiet and more timid than ever, she sidestepped towards the fire. "Mr. Callahan here saved me from a terrible flash flood." Turning to Sean, then back to her father again, she said, "This is my pa, Dan Hobbs."

"Nice to meet you, sir." Sean started to cross the room to greet the man, but Dan advanced on Eileen, ignoring the fact he had a stranger in his house.

"You still haven't told me where Rosie is, girl."

Eileen withered under his gaze and backed into the wall.

"Pa, I—I'm sorry, but she fell in a hole, she's—her leg broke, I couldn't—"

"Rosie's daid?" he bellowed.

"There was nothing I could do, Pa. I swear, she just—"

"You kilt my best brood mare!" Dan stomped towards the frightened girl, his small eyes gleaming with rage. "I'll make sure you never—"

Martha Hobbs stepped between her husband and daughter, pleading, "Dan, we got company. Cain't this wait 'til later?"

Halting, the thick-chested farmer turned in Sean's direction, then spat a wad of tobacco juice across the room. "I don't see no company. I see an injun."

"Dan, please." Martha's hands twisted back and forth, and she took a tentative step towards her husband. "Mr. Callahan saved Eileen's life. I asked him to stay for supper and said he could sleep the night in the barn."

"Did ya now?" Dan Hobbs put his fists on his hips and ambled over by the fire. He scrutinized Sean as if he were checking a side of beef for spoilage, then removed a hunting knife from the leather sheath at his hip. Picking his teeth with the tip, he continued to look Sean up and down. Finally stopping directly in front of his guest, Dan laid the blade of the knife against Sean's chest.

Squinting his eyes until they were no bigger than peas, Dan said, "I'd be a damn sight more hospitable if you'd saved Rosie instead, stranger. But since you chose to save the girl, why don't you just tell me all about it."

Dan inched the knife towards Sean's throat, cutting off any thoughts of reply.

"You and her been out on that trail alone fer some time. What kind of no good you and that little gal been up to?"

EIGHT

His eyes dangerously dark and murky, Sean moved quickly and encircled the old man's wrist with fingers of steel. Holding some of his strength in reserve, he slowly bent Dan's hand backwards until the knife clattered to the floor.

Keeping his grip on the farmer, his lip curled and his tone deepened as he said, "*Sorry* about the horse. It couldn't be saved."

Still painfully squeezing Dan's wrist, Sean propelled him backwards until his knees caught the edge of the chair. With a none-too-gentle push, he encouraged Eileen's father to take a seat, then gripped the armrests and hovered over the suddenly nervous man.

"If I hadn't stumbled across Eileen when I did," Sean explained through tense jaws, "she would have been swept away in a flash flood. Maybe you'd have preferred she had and maybe you wouldn't—that's none of my business. What *is* my business is you suggesting I did anything more than put her on my horse and bring her back home to you."

Sean released his grip on the chair and straightened. "If you have any doubts about what happened after I found her,

I suggest you and I step outside and we'll continue this conversation in private."

Sean could see the man measuring his chances against him, weighing his anger against indifference, but before the decision was reached, the door banged open and a strapping youth rushed inside the cabin.

"Damn they's a chill in the air," he complained as he hurried over to the fire.

His arrival seemed to make up Dan's mind for him. He glared at Sean, then spat, "I got no problem wid you." He rose and addressed his son. "Git the injun's mule rubbed down and bring him round."

"But Pa, I—"

"Do's yer told, Pete!" Dan glanced at Sean, a firm message gleaming in his eyes. "The injun's jest itchin' to be on his way."

Grumbling and groaning, the boy left the warmth of the fire and headed for the barn as Martha Hobbs stepped between her husband and Sean.

"We cain't let him go without some thanks, Dan'l." She pressed a hand streaked with callouses and cracks against his chest. "Let me and Eileen pack him some grub."

Whatever he saw in his wife's eyes, Sean noticed it was enough to soften the harsh farmer's expression. With a short nod, the angry man stomped off to the bedroom and slammed the door.

Martha turned mournful brown eyes on Sean and quietly said, "Please forgive my husband's rudeness. He's had a hard time of it lately. Seems like no matter what he does, things just gits worse."

"No need to apologize, ma'am. I'll be on my way."

"No, please." Martha touched the sleeve of his shirt. "I know Eileen wants to pack some grub for ya, let her. I'll go calm Dan." She slowly turned and headed for the door, then stopped and whispered over her shoulder, "And thanks again for savin' my little girl."

After her mother was gone, Eileen motioned for Sean to join her at the stove. "Sorry about Pa," she said under her breath. "I guess losing his horse was too much for him. Sometimes he gets kind of . . . crazy."

But crazy or not, all Sean could think of was the deep love and respect his father had for Sunflower, and the certainty that he would never have had excuse enough to talk to her the way Eileen's father just did. "It's all right. I'd better go."

"No." She impulsively laid her hand on his arm. "Let me pack some food for your trip. Please?"

Eileen stared up at him through eyes so blue, so clear, he could see all the years of hurt and humiliation looking back at him. Fighting the urge to take her in his arms and kiss away all her pain, he gruffly said, "Sure. Go ahead if you like. I'll check on Whiskey."

When Sean reached the yard, he stopped and took several breaths. The air tasted crisp and fresh, damp and invigorating, with the hint of pine and juniper flavoring the cool edges—a vivid contrast to the atmosphere in the cabin where the warm air was stale with fear. Sean's fists were tight, his knuckles blanched, when Eileen's brother emerged from the barn leading Whiskey.

"Purty sturdy mule ya got here," Pete remarked as he gave the reins to Sean.

"He's served me well."

Pete cocked his head and circled the stranger. He finally stopped and gave him a long look. "Say, you Pima?"

"Quechan."

"Key what?"

"Que—" But Sean changed his mind in mid-word, knowing he would still have to explain to the boy. Using the term white men had coined for all the Indian tribes along the Colorado River—including Maricopa, Quechan, Mohave, Papago, and even some Pima—he said the name more commonly recognized. "Yuman."

"Yeah?" The boy's eyes lit up. "You ride all the way up from Yuma, did ya?"

Sean nodded and turned to Whiskey, hoping the boy realized he was done with this conversation, but Pete persisted.

"Yuman injuns are peaceful, ain't they? They don't git all painted up and go on the warpath, do they?"

Laughing to himself, he thought, *Not since my mother's tribe tried to murder my father and his companions in their sleep*. But before Sean had a chance to decide exactly what to tell him, he heard light footsteps, then Eileen's soft voice.

"That's enough questions, Pete. You'd better get back to the barn and finish your chores before Pa comes out here and tans your hide." As soon as her brother turned and made his exit, Eileen looked up at Sean. "Sorry if he bothered you with—"

"Stop that."

Startled by the abrupt order, Eileen shrank and squeaked out a barely audible, "W-What?"

Softening his tone at her reaction, Sean gave her arm a little squeeze. "Stop apologizing for everyone and everything. It isn't necessary, and from what I've seen around here, none of it is your fault."

Eileen lowered her head and stared at his boots as she tried to think of a response to his words, but nothing came to her mind. She stayed like that until the most gentle touch she'd ever known lifted her chin.

"I really wish I didn't have to leave you here, but I've no other choice," he breathed. "Maybe some other time, some other place . . ."

Sean glanced over at the cabin, making sure no eyes were upon them, then claimed her soft mouth with a quick kiss. "I'll think of you often," he promised as he took the small bundle of food from her hand. With a long look in her crystal-blue eyes, he mounted Whiskey, kicked the animal harder than necessary, and galloped out of sight.

"Some other time," Eileen echoed in a whisper as she watched him fade into the distance.

Touching her lips, knowing they would never feel the same again, she mouthed the words, "some other place," and vowed that somehow, someday, she would find that time and place.

"Then I shall walk."

Sunny flipped her hair over her shoulder and lifted her chin as she began to strut out of the barn, but she'd only managed a couple of steps before Cole's firm grip was on her arm.

"Dammit, Sunflower, hang on a minute." When she halted her stride, he blew out a sigh. "You are the most exasperating woman I've ever known!"

Turning to him, she flashed a haughty grin. "Then I am pleased. It is important to me to be the best at everything I do."

Laughing, he released her arm and shook his head. "I'm not going to win this one, am I?"

"Not for all the water in the mighty Colorado, Cole Fremont," She patted the back of her skirt, then circled him with an exaggerated limp. "My leg and other important parts will never be the same after a day spent in that hideous sidesaddle. If you wish to show me your land, I will ride the way *I* want to, or I shall walk."

"Oh, Sunny." Cole sighed and pulled her into his arms. He stared down at her features, noted the determined set of her strong chin, the stubborn Irish gleam in her deep sapphire-blue eyes. What kind of madness drew him to this half-breed, this woman whose passion had only begun to surface? She had a way of bringing him to his knees, of stripping away all his pretenses, leaving him incapable of any kind of facade. No courting games were allowed with her. This woman demanded the truth—a man's soul.

Chuckling, he rolled his eyes. "All right, stubborn lady. Ride any way you like, but remember—it's your reputation at stake."

"It is also my bottom. I will not have it bruised any further."

Still laughing, Cole kissed her forehead and ran his fingertips down the side of her cheek to her throat. Since they'd arrived at the ranch, he'd been working overtime to catch up with spring calving and going over the books with his father. Glimpses of Sunny had been infrequent, happening most often during mealtimes when they were surrounded by family and ranch hands, all very carefully engineered by Cole.

Now as he looked into Sunflower's eyes he had to wonder if any good had come from the idea to distance himself from her, if he'd helped or hindered his own understanding of what they were all about. Had he really learned anything about their puzzling, forbidden relationship, or about *himself* during the past few days without her? He had hoped to find he'd been caught up in a purely physical flirtation, something that would burn itself out if he were to absent himself from her considerable charms and innocent, trusting nature. But he'd been wrong. The days and nights were consumed with thoughts of her, memories of her spontaneous laughter, her prankish nature, her touch, her scent, the way she looked at him when she wanted something from him. God, how he needed a few hours alone with her!

"I've missed you the last couple of days," he said thickly. "I've missed holding you through the long nights on the trail, feeling your hair against my shoulder as you sleep."

The tone of his voice, the sudden smoke in his eyes, made her heart lurch and her knees weak. Suddenly in need of air, Sunny took a deep breath. "And I you," she murmured softly.

Charged with instant desire, wanting desperately to bury himself in her softness, no longer wondering why, Cole vetoed the urge to keep her in his arms as his father's harsh words of prejudice echoed in his mind.

Abruptly releasing her, he stepped back and removed the offensive sidesaddle from the dark bay mare. "Let's not waste any more time around here."

After stripping the horse, Cole dug out the smallest roping saddle he could find and invited Sunny to mount, wondering what she intended to do with her skirts. But as usual, she was way ahead of him. With a playful giggle, Sunny raised her hem to reveal her brother's trousers, then gathered the bundle of grey serge in one arm and pulled herself onto the horse with the other. Sitting primly, she draped the material over the mare as if she were covering a dining table, then smiled and waited for Cole's next instructions.

Shaking his head, Cole laughed as he mounted and wheeled Sage towards the barn door. With the mare, Dust Bucket, close behind, the chestnut stallion raced down the path leading away from the Triple F ranch.

As they galloped, Sunny fell into an easy cadence with the borrowed horse and marveled at the strength beneath her, the differences between this purebred animal and Paddy, who was still resting in a corral. She could almost feel the ripple of Dust Bucket's muscles beneath the saddle as they bunched and expanded in perfect rhythm with her thighs, and dreamed of one day owning an animal of such magnificence—then suddenly wondered how much longer she'd be in a position to borrow this one. How long *did* she have before Cole, or his father, tried to send her away to a reservation or put her on a train to Yuma? And what about her mother's murderers—how would she ever find them now?

Lost in thought, Sunny was surprised when Cole pulled
Sage to a halt and turned to her. "Well? What do you
think?"

She looked over the red-rimmed crest of the small butte
and sucked in her breath. "Is all this your land?"

Pointing as he explained, Cole's entire manner brightened as he described his property. "It goes all the way to the
Verde River, then as far as you can see to the south and up
to that big stand of pine trees to the north."

Awestruck, Sunny could only sigh.

"Does that mean you like it?"

"That means I think it is truly beautiful."

Grateful for her kind words, he blew her a kiss and
thought back to last year when the land was in its usual
spring condition. "This is nothing, Sunny. The dry winter
has taken its toll, and I don't know if a few more days of
rain like we had yesterday will help or not. The meadow is
far too brown for this time of year."

"You forget I come from Yuma," she laughed. "I see no
brown here!" And again, she sighed as the profusion of rich
colors seemed to blend together, comprising a palette for
even the most discriminating artist. She saw not brown, but
golden burnt sienna mingled with the rich forest green of the
grass and junipers, envisioned Irish shamrocks instead of
dying palo verde trees, and delighted in the rich brick-red
earth in place of the dusty sand of her homeland. But the
Verde River, though not as wide or formidable as her
beloved Colorado, held her captive, filled her with longing
as its inviting red waters splashed up against the willow-
covered banks.

Sunny began to laugh. "Your river is called verde, green,
yet the waters flow red from the surrounding hills. Colorado
means red, but my own river cannot come close to fulfilling
the name the way the Verde does. I think that is very funny
indeed."

Sunny's eyes sparkled as she examined his property,

mirroring his own feelings for the land. Cole felt his heart reaching out for her, a moth drawn to her flame, blindly jumping into the fire of this beautiful and fascinating young woman. Tearing his gaze from her, he stared out to the river and realized he cared little if he should receive third degree burns or perish altogether, as long as she was in his arms. He shook off the implications of those feelings and forbade his mind to condense them to the one word he guessed would describe them best.

Suddenly impatient to hold her, to touch her, not to think, Cole urged Sage forward. "Come on, Sunflower. There's a perfect spot for our picnic down by the red green river."

Dust Bucket began her forward motion the minute Sage started down the hill, and before long they reached a lush, cool picnic area. Cole stripped the horses of their saddles and hobbled them, leaving them free to graze and drink their fill of fresh mountain water. While he tended the animals, Sunny spread a blue checkered cloth over a blanket on a level patch of thick grass, then began to unpack the meal she'd prepared.

Eyeing the fare as he eased down on the cloth beside her, Cole smacked his lips. "Is that the chicken you fried for supper last night?"

"Y-yes," she said cautiously. "Did you not like it?"

"I loved it, and so did everyone else." Impulse prodded him to lean over and kiss her tawny cheek, then Cole settled back on his elbow and hip. "I want to thank you for helping Nellie in the kitchen while Mom's down. It's a mighty big job feeding the Fremonts and the ranch hands."

"Why do you thank me, silly one?" Sunny unwrapped a bundle of sweet cakes spread with currant jelly and offered one. " 'Tis the least I can do for my room and board, and do not forget—I still owe you for my clothing from town."

"You owe me nothing, Sunflower. If anything, it's I who owe you."

"Oh? For what, Cole Fremont?"

"For . . . for just because I say so." Uncomfortable with the conversation, he reached for a chicken leg and sank his teeth in the crispy morsel. He closed his eyes as he chewed and murmured, "Damn this is good. Does Nellie know how to cook this?"

"She does now," Sunny laughed. "We combined the way your mother cooks chicken with the way my mother does . . ." *Did*, she corrected mentally, before she continued. "Anyway, this is what we came up with. I think it is pretty good, too."

But Cole was no longer interested in the chicken. He'd seen the shadow extinguish the sparkle in her eyes, the corners of her mouth droop in sadness. "You miss your mother a lot, don't you Sunshine?"

Warmed by his insight, the sensitivity in his tone, Sunny nodded silently and lowered her gaze.

"I wish I'd have met up with you closer to Yuma, so I could have been some help in finding the men who attacked her." Cole tossed the chicken bone towards the river and wiped his hands on a napkin. "I'm afraid it will take a real miracle to locate them now."

"I know," she agreed with a wistful sigh. "I was foolish to go after them myself or to think I might actually be following the right trail. I should have stayed home and waited for my father."

Inching across the blanket, Cole took her hand in his. "And rob me of the chance to know you? Not on your life." Opening her fingers, he kissed the center of her palm then looked into her eyes. "If it's not too painful, I'd like for you to tell me about your mother."

Tears sprang into the corners of Sunny's eyes at this. Cole really did care about her, her family, and her life before they'd met. Could it possibly be that he cared for her in the same way she cared for him? "You really wish to learn of Moonstar?"

"And your father, if you feel like talking about them

both, but I'm particularly interested in your mother. I have a feeling you were very close to her."

"Oh yes," she sighed. "My father went in search of gold as often possible, and depending on the crop season, took at least one of my brothers along with him. This left Mother and I alone much of the time as I was growing. She was very proud of the English skills Pop and the priests taught her, and by the time I was of age, she decided to be my teacher instead of sending me to the mission school my brothers attended."

"She sounds like a wonderful woman. I wish I could have met her."

Buoyed by his response and her own memories, Sunny rose up on her knees as if in a trance. With a broad, self-conscious grin, she reached behind her neck, untied the yellow ribbon holding the bulk of her hair, and shook her head. A thick ebony sheet of velvet tumbled down her back, swinging before it settled into a soft mass at the base of her spine.

"This," she breathed with reverence, "was Moonstar, only her hair would sweep down to the blanket."

Sunny had taken on an incredible glow, presenting the very essence of pride in who and what she was. Cole suddenly felt humble and small in her company. She had the face of an angel, the body of a temptress, a look of cool innocence, but the radiance of passion's wisdom. At once he wanted to place her beyond the reach of mere mortals, but ravish her himself, lock her in a crystal cage and bury the only key in his heart forever. What was happening to him? Could he be falling into that illusive abyss called love? His discomfort increasing rapidly, Cole shrugged off his inner voices and regarded the vision before him. He cocked his head and swallowed to relieve the tightness in his throat. But he couldn't think of anything intelligent to say. "Your mother looked like you?" he finally managed.

Sunny broke into an impish grin, unaware of the reasons

behind Cole's odd expression. "No. I look like her." And then the spell was broken. Her laughter sprinkled the air like a cool spring breeze as she sat back on her heels and pulled her fingers through her hair.

More relaxed now, Cole breathed easily and thought of the woman he'd never met. "I would imagine your mother must have been very beautiful."

"She was the most beautiful woman ever made, but not just to me. My father has said so many times." She pulled a length of raven-black hair over her shoulder and began to stroke it, as if somehow it might bring her closer to her mother's spirit. "I told you of my mother's hair and how she wore it because I thought you might like to know more of our people. Quechan women do not braid their hair as white men suppose all Indians do. She left it free and wild—like her soul."

Like yours, he thought to himself, more drawn to her than ever. Cole took a long drink of water from the canteen, then shook his head as if to clear it. When he looked back over at Sunflower, she still rested on her heels, her smile almost ethereal.

"Your father," he said with difficulty and a determination to change the subject. "What about him? How did he meet your mother?"

Sunny froze as if struck, then squealed with laughter and collapsed on her side.

"Did I miss something?" he asked, chuckling along with her.

"I—I had n-not—" She laughed, working to collect herself. "I never thought of it before, but th-they met the same as us." And then she doubled over with laughter again.

"Sunny? What do you mean, the same as us?"

"M-My father—he met my mother the night she tried to . . . to *kill* him!" And then her laughter came in spasms so strong, Sunny had to hold onto her stomach for fear it might burst.

Chuckling lightly, for he really didn't understand, Cole waited for her to catch her breath before he tried to get an explanation out of her. "Are you saying she went after your father with a knife in the middle of the night?"

"In a way, she did." Composed again, Sunny thought back to the stories told over the supper table, to the close sense of family, and shook off the pangs of sadness now accompanying those memories.

She pressed the tip of her tongue against her upper lip and gave Cole a shy smile, then she resumed. "As a young man, my father and his family traveled from Killarney, Ireland to St. Louis. When he came of age, he read of the gold strikes in Gila City and took off to seek his fortune."

"As did half the settlers in the state. Is that how he met your mom?"

"No." Sunny picked at a piece of sweet cake as she remembered. "By the time the Butterfield stage coach rolled into town with Patrick Callahan aboard, the gold fields of Gila City were all claimed or played out. So Pop got right back on the stage and headed for the newest boom town. He started out for La Paz. That is where I think he is now."

"Then La Paz," Cole mumbled between mouthfuls of chicken, "is where they met?"

"No. He never got that far." Sunny closed her eyes and hugged her knees to her chest. As she'd done many times before, she imagined the scene, pictured the pair who'd given her life as they first set eyes on one another. Had the sparks been as intense, as immediate, as they were between herself and Cole?

Smiling inwardly, Sunny went on. "Pop got off the stage in Yuma thinking he would rest up and have a look around town before booking passage on a steamship to La Paz, but instead he got caught up in talk about new gold discoveries in California."

Cole gave Sunflower a playful nudge in the ribs and a crooked grin. "But he discovered something better than gold, didn't he?"

Chuckling, Sunny rolled onto her back and began plucking at shafts of new spring grass. "He certainly did. Pop set up camp with a group of argonauts who'd taken advantage of the Quechans' hospitality. The Indians controlled the Colorado River crossing and with it the land route to California, so you might say my father and his friends really had no choice but to throw in with them for the night."

"And your mother," Cole whispered with a conspiratorial gleam in his eye, "crept up on him as he slept and demanded he remove his breeches or else she'd stab him in the heart!"

Sunny slapped Cole's shoulder. "No, silly. My mother's people were generally friendly and not given to attacking white men without good reason." She gave him a sideways grin, then averted her gaze as she added, "They did not, however, see any harm in relieving the travelers of a few 'extra' belongings as they slept off the effects of homemade mescal in the relative safety of the Quechan camp."

"Got him drunk and robbed him, huh?"

"Cole!" Sunny jerked to a sitting position and worked at feigning an injured expression, but it was no use. She shrugged. "It was something like that I suppose. Anyway, Pop came to just as my mother's fingers closed over his pocket watch. They struggled a few moments, then arrived at a stand-off with the barrel of Pop's gun against Moonstar's head—and the tip of her knife pressed against his throat."

"I have to assume they both had a change of heart."

"A change of heart *and* temperature, if I understand what happened after that."

Sunny glanced at Cole, then blushed as her own words

sank in. For the first time in her life, she understood what might have drawn her parents together, how the strength of their attraction must have overridden fear, a sense of survival, and the boundaries separating their cultures. She knew her bonds with the handsome rancher already were or could be as strong, but what about Cole? Would he ever be free to feel the same way? How big a part would their conflicting backgrounds play in the future? And what if he expected her to fit completely into his world, to become a fine lady? Could she do it? Did she even *want* to become one?

She'd already figured out that the reason she'd seen so little of him over the past three days had as much to do with her as the ranch, knew he struggled within where she was concerned, and even understood why. What she couldn't foresee or fathom was what he would do about it, when and how he would find a way to fit her into his life—or send her away. Eventually, he probably would have to do the latter. Her spirits and good humor dimmed as she realized that day would be too soon even if it were a hundred years from now.

"Sunflower?" Cole whispered. "Are you all right?"

Taking a long invigorating breath, she leaned back on an elbow and cocked an eyebrow. "Me? I am fine. Why would I not be fine? You have brought me to your beautiful home, and your sister has been kind and helpful and so very thoughtful, she has made me feel like a friend." Sunny picked up the hem of her skirt and shook it with gusto. "See what she has done? Nellie has put more length on this and some of her dresses just for me. How can I be anything but fine?"

Sensing the undercurrents, the tension in her words, Cole pushed the remnants of the picnic aside and snuggled up next to her. "Something's upset you. Is it Nathan? I know my father has been less than friendly."

Shrugging, she hedged. "He does not disturb me. I

understand how most white men feel. I also understand there is nothing I can do about it, so I do not think about it."

Her candor touched his heart, and his sense of injustice. Why should one as beautiful and sensitive as Sunflower have to accept anger or even indifference from anyone, but *especially* from the father of her lover? Had he encouraged, or even bowed, to Nathan's prejudice by practically ignoring Sunny since they'd arrived at the ranch?

Troubled to think he may have added to her feelings of rejection, Cole drew her down beside him and traced the outline of her strong proud jaw with his fingertip. Trying to provide an explanation for her, and most likely for himself as well, he said, "Dad's problem has nothing to do with you. He's had a pretty rough time with Indians, and because of it he has a hard time understanding they're not all the same."

Knowing she'd be taking a chance, but too curious and proud not to ask, Sunny looked him straight in the eye. "And you, Cole Fremont? How do you see me?"

"I see the most beautiful woman I've ever laid these unworthy eyes on," he said truthfully.

"That is not what I meant. Am I Irish, a half-breed, or do you think I am the same as all Indians, as your father does?"

"Now there's a hell of a question," he said with a lusty chuckle as he buried his lips in the hollow of her throat. But when he looked up and saw the midnight clouds building in her eyes, he realized she wasn't teasing. She was demanding real answers. Leaning back, Cole scrutinized her features and thoughtfully murmured, "Let's see, we have a pair of gracefully arched raven's wings perched over the most incredible shade of blue eyes I've ever seen, a small upturned nose, and the enticing lips of an angel. No," he laughed deep in his throat, "I see nothing about you to remind me of Geronimo, so that leaves 'all Indians' out."

He moved his mouth lower, to the entrance of the valley

between her breasts, and pressed his lips against her softness. "Charlie White at the livery stable has skin about the same color as yours, but his never made me crazy just by looking at it, or touching it, and—" Cole took a deep breath, then groaned as he exhaled, "—the scent never fogged up my entire brain like yours does, so that also leaves out any thoughts of 'all half-breeds.'"

Concluding his mission, Cole reached for the buttons on her white cotton blouse. Slowly releasing them one at a time, he was rewarded by tremors of her heating flesh as he tenderly whispered, "What's my last choice—Irish?" His mustache curled up on one side when he gave her the crooked grin that always melted her heart. "I suppose of all those descriptions, Irish fits you best—especially when you're calling me names or chasing me with a hunting knife."

Aware of the heat rising in her entire body, of the sudden spear-like pain of desire, Sunny fought against the feelings and persisted. "Are you saying when you think of Sunflower Callahan, you think of an Irish woman?"

Uncertain what she wanted to hear, not sure he could give her a completely honest answer, he told her what was in his heart. "When I think of you, I don't see Indian or Irish or anything in between. You remind me of spring and summer, wind and water. You're one of a kind, Sunshine, the most beautiful woman and person I've ever known. There are no mere words to describe you."

Stunned by the depth of his words, by their meaning, Sunny couldn't speak for several seconds. Her mind was satisfied and her body was begging for the same consideration, yet all she could manage was a breathless, "Oh, Cole."

Passion, thick, dark, intense beyond comprehension, swept over them at that moment, drove them into each others arms with near hysteria. Both incapable of speech, they communicated in a timeless fashion with their hands and mouths.

Sunny's long legs slid up along Cole's thighs and she arched her hips against his as shudders of urgency tore through her, and this time she made sure he knew he held no awkward innocent in his arms. The woman she'd become knew what she wanted—and how to get it.

"My God," he gasped as her tiny hands found his belt buckle—and more. "Slow down, Sunshine. I can't last this way."

"No. I cannot," she whispered, struggling for breath, wondering if a demon had taken over her body. This was different, so completely different than two nights ago when he'd showed her how a man comes to a woman. Then, she'd also wanted him, knew something inside cried out for fulfillment, and that somehow Cole could provide the relief she sought. But now she was out of control, focused only on her man and her burning need for him. Tugging at the steel buttons on his jeans, she again cried, "I cannot wait any longer. Please, Cole. Please."

And because her enthusiasm, her demands, had pushed all rational thought from his mind, Cole dove into her, vaguely aware of flying petticoats and tattered trousers, of filtered sunlight and the scent of damp spring grass. He immersed not only his body, but his entire being in Sunny, wondering for a brief moment if he might not die from the experience, and understood that he cared little if he did. To hell with their differences. To hell with his father's prejudices and concerns for his only chance at having pure white grandchildren. To hell with tomorrow. All that mattered now was Sunflower Callahan and, he finally had to admit if only to himself, the love he felt for her.

Sunny's last lucid thought after he filled her was the sensation of being levitated, of being carried to incredible heights by a suddenly volatile sun, of being blinded by the flash from its exquisite glare, then of being warmed as the sunset gently lowered her back to earth. Wondering if she'd lost consciousness, if she were even alive, she lifted one lazy eyelid and found Cole's blond head bobbing up and down on her heaving breasts. Still unable to speak, she moaned and wound a damp wheat-colored curl around her finger.

He heard her voice through the haze, felt her touch through the web that seemed wrapped around him, and finally Cole was able to open his eyes. He looked around, stunned for a moment to discover he was in an open field in broad daylight. Then he whipped his head around and stared into those incredible midnight-blue eyes.

"Sunny?" he whispered, his grin crooked, embarrassed. "I—I don't know what happened. Are you all right?"

But her sensuous smile, the lazy love-saturated expression on her lovely features, told him more than her slow nod and dreamy sigh. Cole glanced down at their attire and shook his head. They almost hadn't bothered to undress. Sunny's blouse, trousers and drawers were tossed on the bank, but she still wore her chemise and skirt. He on the other hand, was fully clothed, except his jeans had been pushed down around his knees.

Giving in to another urge, too weak to fight it, Cole rolled over on his back and began to laugh in a deep throaty tone.

The sound brought Sunny out of her fog. She sat straight up and looked down at him. "What is so funny, Cole Fremont?"

"Nothing," he chuckled. "Everything. I always figured I'd die with my boots on, but never in my wildest dreams did I think I'd do *this* in them!"

While she waited for his laughter to subside, Sunny scanned the length of his body, allowing her gaze to linger on his midsection and the thatch of light brown hair protecting his loins. He looked so different now than he did a few minutes ago, so harmless, she had to wonder at what point during this magical act had he changed and grown? What exact event brought about such a dramatic difference in this nub of man flesh she gazed upon?

His amusement played out, Cole furrowed his brows as he noticed her expression. Afraid he may have hurt her feelings, he explained, "Do you understand what I meant about my boots?"

"I think so," she said absently, still distracted by his manhood. "You are saying that you have never come to another woman's bed wearing your boots." She directed her gaze to his eyes in time to see him nod, then asked, "Is this an honor you pay me?"

Again he burst out laughing, but this time he pulled her down on his chest and wrapped his arms around her. "I suppose," he said between chuckles, "you might call it an honor, if you want to."

"And so I shall, but please tell me this: What does it mean to you, Cole Fremont?"

There was no humor shining in her dark eyes, only a quest for the truth. His expression sober, his heart open, he said, "It means I've never wanted any woman, or anything for that matter, bad enough to forget I was wearing my boots."

Sunny's breath rattled in her throat and whistled out through the tight passage as her pulse hammered against her temples. Did it mean he loved her the way she loved him? Afraid to say the words, to find that he might not share her feelings, Sunny pressed her mouth against his chest instead and murmured seductively, "Would you like to keep your boots on this time, or shall I remove them for you?"

Chuckling softly, he reached down and flicked the end of her nose with his fingertip. "I wish that were possible, you greedy little rabbit, but I'm afraid I'll have to rest awhile before we worry about whether or not I wear my boots."

Running her fingers through the soft down on his chest, Sunny thought about resting, then about the way she was feeling at that moment, and knew he had only to touch her and she'd be on fire again. Dismissing his suggestion, she said, "I am not tired. I would rather make love with you once more."

Trying not to laugh again, Cole pressed his lips together and explained, "You have me at a disadvantage, Sunshine. You can make love all day if you want to, but me—well, men need to rest a while before they can . . . before they're capable again. Understand?"

She raised, lowered, then drew her brows together as she tried to make sense of his words, but still she could not understand. She wanted him now. She wanted him to want her. It seemed a simple enough thing. He could rest some other time. Determination twitching in her jaw, Sunny's eyes twinkled with mischief as she inclined her head and allowed the bulk of her hair to drape across Cole's chest. Then she lowered her head and began nibbling kisses, punctuated by little nips, as she made her way along the hairline leading to his navel.

"Sunny," he warned, "didn't you hear me? I need to—" But the next word was sucked back into his lungs as her delicate hands skimmed like tiny butterflies across his lower abdomen and upper thighs, and came to rest between his legs.

When she felt the flesh of his stomach quiver against her lips, Sunny guessed if the event were to happen, it would happen now. Turning her head slightly, she watched the magical transformation taking place before her eyes, felt her insides dissolve and spill over like warm sarsaparilla as she recognized her feminine power. *Rest indeed*, she thought with a delicious grin. How badly did he want this rest now?

Tremendously proud of herself, Sunny lifted her head and her body, slid caressing fingertips along the length of his desire, lingering for a moment at the tip, then stood up and looked down at him.

Although her heated blood was thundering through her veins, Sunny casually said, "Well, I think I shall leave you to this important rest you must have. I believe I will take a walk in the meadow."

"Sunny," he choked out, "you know I'm in no mood to rest now. Get back down here."

Quickly sidestepping his extended fingers, she strolled away from the blanket. "Oh, no sir," came the breathless reply over her shoulder. "I would not dream of robbing you of this nap men must have."

Awkwardly sitting up, he cautioned, "Sunny, I mean it. Now quit playing around. You can see how much I want you."

She turned around at this, the corners of her mouth turned up in amusement. "The Irish have a saying that is beginning to remind me of you. They say what cannot be had is just what suits."

"Sunny . . ." he warned.

"How much do you want me, Cole Fremont?" she said playfully. "You tell me bad enough to forget you are wearing boots. Do you also want me bad enough to catch me with your trousers down around your ankles?" Then, laughing like a child playing in the river, she turned and skipped off through the tall grass.

Struggling with his jeans, Cole tried to get to his feet, but stumbled and fell several times. He could hear Sunflower's laughter echo through the nearby canyons, whisper through the leaves of the palo verde trees, and the sound only inflamed him further.

When he finally got his pants up far enough to catch one button near the waist, he took off after her, alternately shouting promises of what he would do when he caught her and muttering harmless curses. Twice he caught a bit of material between his fingers when her skirt swirled past as

she dodged him, and twice she shrieked and bolted,
laughing even louder.

The third time his grip held, and the two of them tumbled
into the sweet grass amid the sounds of ripping fabric.

And the crack of rifle fire.

NINE

Sean spent a miserable afternoon on the trail. Although the rain had long since ended its saturation of the powder-dry earth, his damp boots and clothing kept him chilled and shivering as he tried to get his bearings and find a place in which to camp.

Whiskey made slow progress through the cactus-riddled canyons, making the Triple F ranch out of reach for one more day. After passing between a particularly high range of mountain walls dotted with black, unidentifiable shadows, Sean decided to make a final climb for the night. Heading up the side of the hill, he kept watch on the chollas, a pale sage-green species of cactus which had turned a ghastly hue in the twilight. Sprinkled throughout the road and along the steep mountain-sides, several of these chollas were nearly as tall as Sean, and each branch sprouted huge appendages which resembled a human head.

He shuddered as he passed by the ghost-like plants. In the vague light these heads seem to be nodding, beckoning him to come impale himself and Whiskey on their vicious spines. Knowing the long and painful night he'd be in for if he should accept the sinister invitation, Sean found a suitable clearing while he still had enough light to make certain he didn't bed down in the crawling or jumping version of these especially nasty cactus.

After tying the mule near a safe patch of grass, Sean settled down and tore into the supper packet Eileen had prepared for him. He thought of her unhappy life as he ate, wondering what the future held for such a timid and browbeaten young woman, then recalled the kiss he'd stolen. Caught off guard by his advances, Eileen's upturned mouth had been soft, her lips slightly parted when he pressed against them. Sean closed his eyes with a sigh as he remembered the taste, the fresh scrubbed aroma of her skin and hint of citrus laced throughout her hair. Warming as he thought of her, he shifted his position on the damp earth and chewed on a soft biscuit spread with honey.

Still, he thought of her—of her glorious flaming hair, of her full bottom lip and the perpetual pout it gave her expressions, of what it would be like to hold her in his arms in a soft bed of fresh-cut hay. But those thoughts were forbidden to take form, their fulfillment impossible for a half-breed such as he. Although well-regarded in Yuma as the son of an Irish immigrant, as the heir to the Callahan farm—even as a man—that respect vanished when talk of women dominated the conversation. The son of Moonstar would be thrashed soundly for even thinking of fine white ladies, much less trying to court one. And the brief kiss he'd given Eileen was grounds for hanging. Or worse.

Restless and troubled, more at odds with his dual heritage than he'd ever been in his life, Sean fell into a fitful sleep. He slept long past light of dawn. When he awoke, he pushed all thoughts of Eileen out of his mind and began to concentrate on his true purpose—rescuing Sunny and extracting his revenge on her captor. Guessing he was very close to her, he chose to breakfast on leftovers from Eileen's package and wait until the late morning sun finally warmed his chilled bones before resuming his journey. Now was not the time for reckless actions or mindless revenge. He would be one against many at the ranch, a lone warrior whose work would have to be done under cover of darkness. He would proceed slowly from here on out, and take great care to avoid detection.

Sean had traveled less than an hour before he discovered he'd veered too far to the northeast during his detour to the Hobbs ranch and subsequent journey from there. Stopping near the top of a butte, he scanned the countryside and made some calculations. If his senses weren't deceiving him, all he needed to do was turn to the southwest and the Triple F Ranch would stand directly in his path. To make certain of his position, Sean tied Whiskey to a cottonwood tree and hiked to the crest of the butte for a view of the horizon.

Focusing his vision due east, he spotted the red waters of the Verde River dead ahead. His calculations were, in his estimation, nearly perfect. With a somber grin of determination, Sean turned to collect the mule, but stopped when he heard the high-pitched screams of a woman in distress. Was the wind playing tricks on him? Whirling around, he cocked his head and listened intently.

Again, he heard the screams.

Shading his eyes from the noon sun, he looked out over the meadow just as a half-naked woman burst from the trees and shrubs near the water's edge. She ran headlong into the meadow, her long black hair streaming out behind her. Shortly after that, a man emerged from the same spot, his objective all too obvious.

"Sunny!" he choked out, his throat raspy and constricted. Even at this long distance there could be no mistaking his beloved sister. The statuesque appearance, the way she ran dodging the man, and the ribbons of ebony hair trailing down her back all belonged to Sunflower Callahan.

Sean dropped to the ground, the sour taste of hatred and vengeance rising in his throat, and slithered back through the cottonwoods to where Whiskey stood. He quickly

removed his rifle from the scabbard, then crawled back to
his vantage spot at the crest of the hill. Sunny's cries met his
ears just as his vision picked out the man as he bore down
on her. Bringing the gun to his shoulder, Sean struggled to
frame the man in the rifle sights, but by now the pair
struggled together as one, making it impossible to chance a
shot. When they collapsed amongst the tall grass and
weeds, Sean did the only thing he could do from so far
away.

He fired a warning above the spot where they'd fallen.

Then he wheeled and raced for Whiskey. As he mounted
and then whipped the mule into a dead run down the side of
the hill, one thought blazed in his mind. This vile excuse for
a man would pay, and pay dearly, for the pain and horror
he'd put Sunny through. Her ordeal was at an end, as was
the life of the rancher who now tried to defile her.

The crack of rifle fire brought Sunny's playful shrieks
and high-pitched laughter to an abrupt end. She froze as
Cole covered her body with his and admonished her to keep
her silence.

With extreme wariness, he slowly lifted his head until he
could just see past the tips of the grass to the crest of the
nearby mountain. He scanned the rim, straining his eyes,
but couldn't locate the source of the rifle fire.

"Stay flat on your belly," Cole cautioned. "I'm going to
make a break for the river and my gun."

"No, you cannot—"

"Don't move and be quiet! It may be our only chance."

With that, he turned on his knees and began to inch his
way to the clearing, but an inhuman cry froze him to the
spot. Again peering over the grass, he watched as a rider
exploded from the brush at the base of the mountain and
bore down on them at a thunderous gallop.

Quickly measuring his slim chances, the defenseless
rancher coiled his long body for the jack-rabbit start he
would need to reach the trees. But the minute his head

appeared above the grass, the distant rifle fired another deadly warning. He dropped back to the earth, the fingers of unfamiliar panic closing around his throat. After a backward glance at Sunny, he knew her only chance was for him to move, and move now before the rider overtook them. His mind made up, Cole pulled his legs up beneath him and into a crouch just as the rider cut loose with another murderous war cry.

Something in the sound, the tone of voice, gave life to Sunny's dry throat. "Cole! Wait!"

She whirled around and grabbed at his boot just as he started to run through the grass. Her fingers closed over the heel and metal prongs of a spur, bruising her flesh, but still she hung on. Once again, Cole dropped to the ground.

"What the *hell* are you doing?" he raged as he tried unsuccessfully to get his balance. He turned, prepared to hurl a string of curses towards the foolish woman, when instead the words died in his throat. Sunny was standing upright, a full-sized target for the rapidly approaching rifleman.

"What in God's name is *wrong* with you?" Cole spat as he scrambled to his feet. "Get down, dammit!" He took a couple of angry steps in her direction, but she dodged him, never taking her eyes off the rider. "Sunny, are you trying to get yourself killed?"

She could hear Cole's voice, but it sounded as if it were muffled and a long way off in the distance. Her incredulous eyes said her *brother* was riding towards her, and yet . . . how could that be? He was in La Paz or Mohave, anywhere but here! She blinked several times, then stared at the horse—the *mule*—and its rider again, but her brain received the same message. Sean and Whiskey. Certain now that she did not behold a mirage, Sunny found her voice and turned to Cole.

"Do not worry," she whispered breathlessly. " 'Tis my

brother, Sean. He will not harm us." Then she spun around, lifting her skirts, and ran through the grass to greet him.

Again the rifle fired, its message clear that the bullet was not meant for Sunny as it passed over her head and continued on towards its intended victim.

"NO!" she cried as Whiskey skidded to a halt and Sean leapt from his back, the rifle cocked and ready for another try.

Screaming in fright, begging him to stop, Sunny raised her arms in submission and charged toward her brother. But she was too late. The gun sounded again and this time, Cole Fremont spiraled down and disappeared in the thick grass.

Horrified, sick to her stomach, and angry all at once, Sunny cried out in a long wail, "Nooooo," then buried her face in her hands.

Sean dropped the rifle and pulled a pistol from his belt as he approached his anguished sister. "It's all right, Sunny. I'm here now," he assured as he slipped an arm around her shoulder for a brief hug. "Stay here a minute. I'll just be making sure he's dead."

"Take another step towards him," she warned through her tears, "and ye'll rue the day you were born."

Not giving him a chance to move another step, Sunflower grabbed her skirts as she wheeled and rushed to her fallen lover. There she dropped to the ground beside him, her heart breaking, a sob wrenching her throat. As she bent over him, searching for the wound, she wailed, "Oh, Cole! What has he done to you?"

"Not near as much as he had in mind," Cole whispered out of the corner of his mouth. "Where the hell is he?"

"Oh!" she gasped. "You *live*!"

"So far I do." Cole raised his head a few notches and peered over her shoulder. "Good God, here he comes and . . . he's got a pistol aimed at my head!" He quickly flattened out in the grass again, then scowled at Sunny. "If that madman really is your brother, isn't there something you can do with him—like disarm him?"

"Oh!" she cried, so delighted to find Cole in good health, she'd nearly forgotten about the danger. "Of course."

"Get out of the way little sis," Sean warned as Sunny jumped to her feet and turned to face him. Pulling back the hammer on the gun, he stood his ground and announced, "This son of a bitch is long overdue for his last breath."

"This son of a . . . a *bitch*," she bit off, using a word she'd only heard infrequently, but never used before, "saved my life. Do you still wish to shoot him, my lizard-brained brother?"

Momentarily speechless at this information, Sean's anger and determination returned as he recalled the way he'd come across them. "You don't owe him for that, pumpkin. He may have saved your life, but I could see he had no intention of saving your honor. For that alone, he dies." Sean raised the pistol, his lip twitching as he eyed her disheveled appearance. "Get out of the way, Sunny."

"Never." With a dramatic sigh, she flung herself, spread-eagle, across Cole's prone body. "If you wish to shoot him, your bullet will have to pierce Callahan flesh first."

"Sunny," Sean growled between his teeth. "You don't have to do this." And then a thought occurred to him—a delicate, disturbing thought, but one that had to be dealt with. "Look, pumpkin, if he, if you've . . . What's already happened doesn't matter. You can go on as before. No one will ever know if he's already shamed you."

Convinced at first that silence would be his best weapon against Sean's anger until Sunny had a chance to explain, Cole now found he couldn't keep his tongue or let him think what he was thinking. He blurted out, "I wouldn't *shame—*"

But Sunny had other ideas. She slapped her hand across Cole's mouth and narrowed her eyes. "Quiet, Fremont," she said under her breath, "they don't call Sean 'Crazy Callahan' for nothing. Let me handle him."

Thinking quickly, Sunny craned her head until she made eye contact with her enraged brother. She had to find a way to calm him, make him listen to what she had to say— before he lost all control. "All right," she said with a composure she didn't feel. "I understand what you must do, but first let me tell you all that has happened. If you still think he must die, I will not stand in your way." She felt Cole's body stiffen beneath her at this, but he kept his silence. "Fair?"

Sean had never killed a man before. And this dog of a man was unarmed. A sense of relief flooded him as he thought over her suggestion. "All right, but I keep the gun on him while we talk."

"Fair enough." Again Cole flinched, but Sunny went on with her instructions. "Back off, Sean. What I have to say must be said in private. Move to the edge of the meadow and I'll join you."

Against his better instincts, he did as she asked, knowing the only Callahan with a stubborn streak bigger than Patrick's now challenged him with a pair of determined indigo blue eyes.

When Sean was in place, Sunny whispered quickly, "Do not try to move or join us. I will explain the situation to him." Then she scrambled to her feet and hurried to her brother, careful to keep her body between the pistol and Cole.

"He can't hurt you anymore," Sean assured as he gathered her in his arms. "Say the word, and I'll take care of him."

Pushing back from his chest, Sunny vigorously shook her head. "You are not listening to me. He has done nothing to hurt or shame me. I have come to care for him a great deal."

"B-but—" Sean gestured towards her torn skirt, her immodest attire. "You are half-dressed, he has torn the clothing from your body. You wish me to spare a man who has ravaged you so?"

"My brother, I—he—" She stumbled over her words, worried about Sean's reaction. But she was a very poor liar and would telegraph the fib through her eyes if she should try any explanation but the truth. With an anxious sigh, Sunny lifted her chin and stared into the features that so closely resembled her own. "Cole Fremont has never shamed me or forced me to do anything I did not wish to do." A sudden pride burned in her as she added, "I am his woman."

"His *woman*?" Sean said with a harsh laugh. "Have you forgotten you are Quechan, a half-breed, little one? You cannot be the woman of a white man. If you are anything to this snake, it can be nothing more than his *puta*."

An enormous anger tore through her like a runaway train, towing a burden far more weighty than Sean's stinging words or the fact that he'd said them. There was a truth in them that couldn't be ignored, an unjust fact of life separating Indian and white man with a cruel and biased sword. But just as suddenly as the anger came over Sunny, it left when it occurred to her that she didn't really care about facts and words. The only thing she intended to care about now was Cole. And as long as he wanted her, he would have her. No matter what Sean, or anyone else called it. She swallowed her anger.

Sunny tilted her chin and lowered her lids. "Say what you will about me, but know this and know it well. I love Cole Fremont. I will not allow you or anyone else to harm him. If you do not believe me, raise your pistol to him and see that you will be killing your sister first."

Stunned by the admission, Sean regarded her words carefully. Did she speak the truth, or did this miserable cur have some kind of hold over her, something to make her so afraid that she would lie? His voice barely above a whisper, he pressed. "Sunny? Be very sure of what you say to me, of what has happened between you and this man. You are safe now, you need not pretend."

"I love him. I swear it on my mother's grave." She leveled her gaze and made a final statement, one last plea. "Put the gun away, or shoot me with it now."

The last time he'd seen that look, it radiated from the face of his mother as she stared down a sheriff intent on arresting him or his brother Mike for horse theft. Unquestionable proof, the missing animal, stood in the yard of the small Callahan farm, yet Moonstar was adamant in the defense of her sons. When they were eventually cleared, the sheriff's sheepish apology was met with the identical stubborn lift of the chin his sister now displayed—and the same love and blind faith he saw in her eyes.

With a grunt of frustration, Sean pushed the pistol into the waistband of his pants. "All right, little one, but if he so much as—"

Sunny jumped into his arms, smothering his words with grateful kisses and a string of Irish phrases. "Faith, and I knew you would understand if only you took the time to hear what my heart had to say!"

Cole discreetly inched his lean body to stretch its full length as he watched the siblings' reconciliation. Convinced he should take this opportunity and run to the river's edge for his weapons, he quietly started in that direction. If Sunny's brother really was called "Crazy Callahan," it wouldn't hurt to be armed when, or if, they were formally introduced. He'd only taken a few steps towards his objective when Sunny whirled around, her brother's hand clasped in hers.

"Cole?" she called out, her voice wavering with tension. "Umm, my brother would like to talk with you."

The top half of his body seemed to understand he really had no other choice, but the rest of him, his feet in particular, leaned towards gathering the weapons on the bank. Cole stumbled and nearly fell as he approached the Callahans.

"Cole Fremont," he supplied as he wiped a suddenly

damp palm on his jeans, then greeted the grim-faced man
with an outstretched hand. Looking for a way to thaw
Sean's frozen features, he added, "Sunny's told me a lot
about you and her family."

Although he'd accepted her story, conceded she at least
believed she loved the rancher, Sean met Cole's handshake
with something less than enthusiasm. His answer to the
friendly smile beneath the golden mustache was a short nod
and low grumble in his throat. "And she has told me
nothing of you, *ahata*."

Sunny's gasp confirmed Cole's assumption that he had
just been called something other than "friend." Keeping
one eye on Sean, he addressed her. "I get the feeling your
brother isn't too happy to meet me. Maybe we ought to head
back to the ranch and give him some time to cool off."

Knowing Sean would never allow such a plan, Sunny
made light of her brother's attitude, and completely ignored
the fact that he'd called Cole a dog. "Sean is known as one
who keeps his feelings inside. He is very pleased to know
you."

Before he could disagree or add to the already tense
situation, Sunny knotted her brows and faced Sean. "What
in the name of all that's holy brings you here in the first
place? Why are you not up river with Pop, where you
belong?"

His acceptance of the blond rancher far from complete,
Sean kept his eyes trained on the man as he answered. "I
had a vision, little one. Pop and I didn't get any farther than
Ehrenberg after that."

"A *vision*?" she gasped. "A true vision?"

Sean turned his full attention on Sunny after Cole raised
the expected brow. "We'll talk of my vision later—
privately," he said with conviction. Having no intentions of
discussing the spiritual gift bestowed on him by his mother's people in the presence of a white stranger, Sean
concluded his explanation. "After reading your note at the

farm, Pop and I decided it would be best if I went after you while he did what he could in town. I followed the trail you left behind until I caught up with Paddy's hoofprints outside of Phoenix." He leveled a thoughtful gaze on Cole. "The rest was easy."

Taken aback by the inference, not the words, Cole took a forward step. "It should have been easy to track us because I made no effort to hide our destination. I had no reason to do so." Then the rest of Sean's story sunk in. "And what do you mean, you followed a trail? What kind of tracks did we leave besides hoofprints?"

"My sister is clever," Sean replied with a jerk of his head, "smart enough to tear strips of material from her dress and tie them to shrubs and trees along the way without your knowledge."

"Oh?" Cole's eyebrow rose again, but this time it was joined by its twin as he placed his hands on his hips and turned to her. "Is that so, my sweet trusting love?"

Sunny's breath whistled out as she took a couple of backward steps. Shrugging innocently, she said, "I may have accidentally dropped a few scraps of calico along the way, but not after we arrived in Phoenix."

"I see." He nodded, his mustache twitching more with humor than anger. "And why did you stop then? Why not lead your family, and lord knows who else, all the way to the ranch?"

"I—I—" Again she shrugged, thinking now was the time to tell him how much she had come to trust him, but instead she laughed. "I ran out of calico."

"You little devil," he said, his voice thick and gruff. Cole dragged her into his arms, temporarily forgetting her brother stood behind them, and playfully threatened her. "I ought to take you over my knee and whip the tar out of you, truss you up like the little, the little—"

"Leprechaun," Sean supplied, reminding them of his presence.

"Yeah," Cole agreed, vaguely uncomfortable with Sean so near. He released Sunny and turned to her brother. "She's a sneaky little leprechaun all right, whatever the hell that is."

But Sean ignored Cole's attempt at levity and gave him a short nod instead of the expected chuckle. "I thank you, Fremont, for escorting my sister safely through her ordeal." Dismissing the rancher, he beckoned to Sunny. "Now it's time we returned to Yuma where we belong."

She'd known all along that day would come, but never had it occurred to her it would be so soon, so abrupt, or that the reality would hurt so much. "But Sean," she cried, frantically searching for a reason to stay, "I am not ready, I—I cannot—"

"She's only had a couple of days rest," Cole cut in, determined to keep her with him. "Taking her back out on the trail now could be very dangerous." He noted the dark circles under Sean's eyes, his weary expression, and added, "You look as if you haven't had a decent night's rest or a good meal for a couple of weeks yourself. Why don't you come on back to the ranch with us and rest up. We can talk about your departure later."

Shaking his head, Sean muttered, "Our father is already sick with worry over his hotheaded daughter. I'm sure she doesn't want him to suffer any more than he already has." He fixed a pointed gaze on Sunny, then looked back at Cole. "Again, I thank you for—"

"She's *not* leaving." Cole advanced a couple of steps, examining the younger man. Sean stood two inches taller than his own six feet and looked to be carrying twenty or thirty more pounds—all of it muscle. He studied the determined square-shaped jaw and the tenacity in his unusual hazel eyes, and knew this Callahan would be a wily and menacing fighter. *This fella could squash me like a bug,* he thought, also suspecting Sean wouldn't let up until he'd accomplished just that.

But Cole wasn't ready to let Sunny go, wasn't sure he could *ever* let her go. He hitched up his jeans and chose his best weapon. "Let's talk about this, friend," Cole began. Sean started to object, but Cole eased his hand onto the half-breed's thick shoulder and urged him to walk towards the river with him.

Sunny's first impulse was to follow the men and join their conversation, but she thought better of it and instead took a parallel course to the picnic blanket to collect her drawers and blouse. Concealing herself behind a cottonwood tree, she dressed while the man she loved tried to convince her brother to let her stay.

"I understand how much Sunny must mean to you," Cole went on as they reached the river's edge. "She has become very important to me as well. Because of that, I simply can't let you waltz in and take her away so easily. I need some time to think, and I believes she does, too."

"But our father," Sean cut in, "also cares deeply for—"

"I've thought of that too," Cole assured. "Every spring my family holds a huge barbecue at the ranch and invites all our neighbors and the townsfolk. That party is scheduled for this Saturday, and because of it we have to make a run into town for supplies tomorrow."

"And so?" the younger man shrugged.

"So, I thought you might be interested in riding along with the hands and sending a wire to your father. I'm sure if he knows you're both safe and staying at the Triple F, he won't mind if your return is delayed a few weeks." Or, in Sunny's case, months or maybe even years.

As he considered Cole's proposal, Sean dropped into a squat and scooped up a handful of pebbles scattered along the shoreline. After regaining his footing, he skipped the stones, one at a time, across the surface of the reddish water. The rancher's offer was inviting, he had to admit. He was bone-weary from his long search, wanted nothing more than a hot bath and a real bed on which to rest.

There was also the problem of Sunny herself. She would not leave this valley without a fight, would give him a battle he was mentally unable to meet at this time. Cole's plan made good sense. What would be the harm if they should stay on for a week? Their father would be happy simply knowing they were alive. His mind made up, Sean turned to the rancher with an extended hand.

"I thank you for your kind offer. I look forward to visiting your home and accepting your hospitality." As the men shook hands, Sean narrowed one eye and said, "I hope you understand this, however. Sunny and I will be leaving the Triple F one week after your barbecue."

Cole had to force his hand to keep pumping, hoped Sean hadn't noticed the hesitation in his grip. Preventing Sunny and her brother from departing so soon was a problem he would have to deal with later.

For now, he had to figure a way to convince his father to welcome another half-breed into his home.

TEN

Nellie sewed the final length of frothy silver grey lace to the bodice of Sunny's ball gown, then bit off the thread at the knot. "There," she said with a satisfied grin. "That ought to cover enough of you for decency."

Sunny pressed the dress to her bosom and swirled like a ballerina before stopping in front of the full-length mirror to examine the fruits of her labor. She and Nellie had worked on altering the dress almost since her arrival at the Triple F. Now, with only a couple of days before the barbecue, it was almost finished.

Sunny studied her reflection, delighted with the effect the fabric had on her appearance. The gown, made of fine silk in a bright peacock-blue color, matched her eyes in intensity and spirit, brought out the creaminess in her complexion, and complimented the ebony gloss of her hair. Never before had she touched, much less worn, anything so beautiful and elegant. Running her fingers along the smooth fabric, Sunny closed her eyes and sighed.

"You'll take my brother's breath away," Nellie whispered, guessing her new friend was thinking of Cole's reaction when he saw her in the dress.

Sunny laughed as she picked out Nell's image in the mirror. "I suppose he might have cause to suffocate when he sees his little Indian captive dressed up in one of his sister's gowns."

"That's not what I meant." Blushing, Nellie chewed on her fingernail and averted her gaze. "We don't all think like Father. I don't, and I don't believe Cole does either, but sometimes it's hard to go against our stubborn father." Jerking her head up as if slapped by a sudden thought, Nellie blurted out, "Oh! Are you upset about your brother's arrangements? If you are, I could try to talk to——"

"No, no," she assured the worried woman. "Believe me, Sean is too tired to argue or care where he beds down tonight." She thought about it a minute, and realized no matter what Nathan or anyone thought of him, Sean was probably exactly where he wanted to be. "I can assure you my brother will be very comfortable in the barn. Even if your father had insisted he stay in the bunkhouse with the ranch hands, I am certain he would not have accepted his offer."

"Well . . ."

"Please, do not give it another thought." It was impossible to explain Sean's attitude to someone like Nell. She would be unable to put herself in his place, couldn't understand how difficult it would be to live in the same room with a group of strangers—white men who'd been subjected to bloody Indian attacks with unnerving frequency. It would take only one ranch hand, bitter over the death of a friend or loved one, to end Sean's life with no more regret than he'd have if he'd killed a rabid dog. That fact wasn't worth a rope bed, no matter how comfortable.

Determined to end the disturbing conversation and shake off the fears welling up in her, Sunny turned back to the mirror and regarded the ball gown. "Would you mind showing me what is left to be done so I can finish the work myself? You have already spent too much time on me. I think your husband must be eager for your company."

The fire in Nellie's cheeks flared again as she scooped the dress into her arms. "Bucky's still talking to Father and Cole. He won't miss me for a few more minutes. I'll help you find some ribbon to match the piping."

Chuckling to herself at Nell's discomfort, Sunny thought back to the confusion of a few hours earlier. She, Cole, and Sean had arrived at the ranch at almost the same moment as Buck Wheeler and the ranch hand who'd accompanied him on his month-long journey. Caught up in questioning his son-in-law about his adventures, Nathan had taken little notice of the newest half-breed Cole had brought home and seemed, in fact, to believe Sean was a hired hand rather than the brother of his houseguest.

This, Sunny noticed, had set well with Sean. And she knew the reason why. He wouldn't want to be beholden to Cole or any member of the Fremont family; he would rather work for his keep than accept their hospitality in order to make it easier for him to leave when the time came. No matter that Sean was a farmer who'd hired himself out to a cattle ranch. No matter he had no idea how to perform the tasks that would be required of him.

The only thing that seemed to matter to her stubborn brother was the fact that when he was ready to leave, he would try to take her with him. Well, she thought angrily, she would not permit it. She would find a way to stay for a while longer, to convince Sean to return to Yuma alone and leave her to—

". . . should be wide enough. What do you think?"

"What? Oh." Sunny pressed a finger against her lips as she realized that strange buzzing noise she'd vaguely heard in the back of her mind must have been the sound of Nellie's voice. "I am sorry. I was thinking of other things and did not hear what you said."

"That's all right." Nellie draped the gown across the back

of a chair and stuck the needle in a pin cushion. "Maybe we have done enough sewing for this evening. And I suppose you're right," she sighed as she crossed the room, "Bucky is probably in our room waiting for me now. I'd better not keep him waiting. Goodnight, Sunny."

"Goodnight, Nell." Sunny fought the sudden and unreasonable urge to offer her sympathies as Nellie closed the door behind her. Odd, she thought. Why should she be feeling sorry for a woman who was on her way to her husband's bed after a month's absence? She and Cole had only been apart for a few hours now, and just knowing he was only a couple of doors down the hallway was almost enough for her to risk the ultimate breech of good manners and sneak into his room. Why did Nellie seem so reluctant to join her love in their bridal chamber?

Maybe, she speculated as she changed into a borrowed nightgown, this attitude came with the years, and that which had once been new and exciting was now boring and commonplace. But recent memories of her mother and father, of the deep affection they openly displayed towards one another, convinced her this was not inevitable or likely.

Sunny blew out the lamp and buried herself beneath the huge patchwork quilt on her bed. Snuggling into the warmth, she thought back to when Nellie had confided in her and told about the Apache raid on the Triple F ranch several years ago. Nell said the attack had caused the horse she'd been riding to rear and tumble over backwards. The animal then landed on her, crushing her pelvis. Perhaps, Sunny surmised with a sad heart, the injuries from that riding accident had not only left Nellie incapable of bearing children, but had also affected her intimate life as a woman—or made it impossible all together. Troubled to think her new friend couldn't experience the kind of pleasures Cole had brought to her just by brushing her lips with his, Sunny drifted off to sleep.

The next two days left little time for worry over anything.

The ranch was teeming with party preparations and enthusiasm, involved hired hands and guests alike in a flurry of baking, barbecue pit preparations, and decorating.

Caught up in the excitement on the morning of the big day, Sunny fidgeted at the dressing table as Nellie removed the rags she'd carefully wound throughout Sunny's long coarse hair the night before.

"It worked!" Nellie cried, draping a perfect ebony tube down the front of Sunflower's dressing gown. "I wasn't sure your hair would hold a curl, but look at these ringlets!"

Nell's request was unnecessary. Sunny couldn't look at anything else, could hardly believe she'd allowed Cole's sister to turn her head into this tumbleweed of tangled logs!

Nellie happily bounced each coil, her pale blue eyes bright with her victory over the stiff, straight shafts of hair. "Well? What did I tell you—are you surprised?"

"To say the least," Sunny answered honestly. "My, my," she added, craning her neck to assess all the damage. "It is curly. Should I leave it this way, or would it look better if I tie it back with a ribbon?"

"Oh, I'm not done yet." Nellie stood back and examined Sunny's profile from every angle. When she'd decided on the perfect style, she splayed her fingers and announced, "Sit very still. When I'm done with you, you won't know yourself."

For Sunny, those words unfortunately proved to be prophetic. When Nellie finished her masterpiece, a long uncomfortable hour later, she finally allowed her victim a look in the mirror. An Indian disguised as a white woman stared back at Sunny.

Most of her hair was slicked back then piled high on the back of her head and artfully woven together with strips of blue silk and smoke grey velvet. The few long tendrils left free hung down to the middle of her back or could, if she were feeling coquettish, be draped over one shoulder. The look was one of elegance, of prosperity. Some people would even say she was beautiful. But it was not the look of an Indian/Irish half-breed named Sunflower Callahan. What would her mother think of this transformation? Or her father?

Nellie chose that moment to let Sunny know what she thought. "You're absolutely beautiful. The men will be falling all over themselves to get a dance with you tonight!"

Sunny turned to disagree, to tell her she couldn't go through with this charade, but stopped herself as she realized the girl actually believed her own words. What about Cole? Would he have the same reaction as his sister? She whirled back towards the mirror, hoping to find this beautiful woman, but the reflection continued to mock her, to laugh at her attempts to be something she was not. Sunny opened her mouth, tried to form the words she knew she must say, but the words wouldn't take shape.

"I understand," Nellie comforted, patting Sunny's shoulder. "I remember my first big dance and new hairdo. The excitement kinda turns your tongue to a washboard, doesn't it?" Laughing, Nellie squeezed Sunny's shoulders then flounced over to the closet. "You just sit there and admire yourself in the mirror. I'll lay your day dress and petticoats out for you, then I have to be getting dressed myself."

Any thoughts Sunny had of gently convincing Nell to dismantle the creation and wash the coils out of her hair vanished. She had no choice but to carry this burden through the process of meeting the guests then later at the dance. Her only hope was that as the festivities spilled over into tomorrow, no one would notice if she should revert to her old, comfortable self.

Resigned to the idea that she must at least start out acting and dressing in the same manner as the other female guests, Sunny even allowed Nell to stuff her into a rib-pinching corset before the delighted hostess would think of going to her own room to preen for the party. And if that wasn't bad enough, she also had to stand still while Nellie tied the tapes to form the proper rear height of an underpinning called a bustle.

After Nellie was gone, Sunny took a moment to examine the strange undergarments. Unused to anything more restrictive than a belt about her mid-section, she poked at the white duck corset material and fingered the ridges of whalebone sewn inside it. How was she expected to endure this contraption all day and then all night at the dance as well? She would never be able to do it! Sunny inhaled, testing the limits of her freedom, but could only fill her lungs to half their capacity. When she turned sideways to examine the bustle in the mirror, she groaned when she saw the shape of the ridiculous contraption. She already had a bottom—why did she need another?

Guest or not, she thought with a stamp of her foot, these little items would be discarded along with the day dress or she would faint before she ever got to her first dance. Grumbling to herself, Sunny stepped into a red flannel petticoat, careful not to snag it on her new pointed-toe shoes, then slid two more petticoats of white taffeta over her head. Finally ready for the dress, she struggled with the skirt portion, a mass of pink organdy with a large pouf of material gathered and draped over the rear bustle.

After pausing for a breath of air, she forced the tight sleeves of the plum velvet basque over her arms, then pushed an endless row of ornate cloth buttons through the embroidered buttonholes. When Sunny was completely dressed, she fastened a pink broach at the throat of the ruffled collar and turned toward the mirror. She was presentable. She could pass as a fairly cultivated guest. She was also seriously in need of oxygen. Sunny backed over to the edge of her bed and sat panting until someone knocked at the door.

"Yes?" she called out weakly.

"I got a message for you if you're dressed."

Sunny recognized the voice as that of Buck Wheeler,

Nellie's husband. She pushed herself off the bed, taking one last glance at her barely recognizable reflection as she passed by the mirror, then pulled the door open.

"Well now," Buck said with a low whistle. "Ain't you somethin'. That Nellie's dress?"

"Uh, I, yes, it is," Sunny stumbled, unused to such bold flattery.

"Well, it looks a damn sight better on you, darlin'."

Uneasy, wondering how she should respond to Buck's compliments, Sunny took a backward step. "Ah, thank you. Did I hear you say you had a message?"

But he didn't answer immediately. Instead he popped a toothpick in the corner of his mouth and regarded her through his small, muddy brown eyes. When she'd first met him, she thought the color was unusual, a striking blend of brown and gold. Now, as he stared at her, *through* her, they began to look predatory—mean and hungry like the eyes of a coyote. Sunny shivered, tensed as she realized his thick bull-like frame filled and blocked the doorway. Was she trapped like a frightened rabbit in the confines of her room, or was her imagination running wild?

Amused by her wide round eyes and sudden spasm, Buck laughed and said, "Relax, darlin'. The message ain't gonna hurt you none. Cole is waitin' for you downstairs in the library." He backed away, flipping the toothpick to the floor, and added, "Some of the highfalutin guests have already arrived. I reckon he's anxious to show off his little prize." Buck winked at her, then strolled off, chuckling and shaking his head.

For a long, soul-searching minute, Sunny stood rooted to the spot. Buck's attitude, while disrespectful and rude, really wasn't so unexpected, and would most likely be exhibited by others once she joined the party. Was she a fool for thinking she might fit in? Was she asking too much of herself? Of Cole? It would be so simple to strip off Nellie's dress and tear the miserable corset from her body. She could plead sudden illness, take to her bed, and remain there until the last guest had gone home—even if it took three days. Sunny glanced back at the bed, then down the hallway.

Her father's encouraging voice echoed in her mind, assured her she had as much right to enjoy this festive occasion as anyone. But she wasn't able to move until a sudden dose of her mother's pride practically shoved her through the doorway.

Downstairs, Cole passed through the living room on his way from the library to the front door of his home. He paused at the foot of the long curving stairway and lit a cigarette. Where was Sunflower? He'd sent Bucky upstairs with a message for her fifteen minutes ago, and now he couldn't wait any longer. Down the road puffs of dust rose like storm clouds, announcing the impending arrival of more guests. His chances of finding a few moments alone with Sunny would be practically nonexistent from here on out, and now it didn't look as if it would be possible at all.

In frustration, he blew several smoke rings to the ceiling, then took a final hopeless glance at the top of the stairs just as Sunny stepped into view. The cigarette dangled from the corner of his open mouth as she cautiously began her descent. Too involved with keeping her skirts away from her feet to notice his presence, Cole was able to study her, undetected, as she drew closer to him.

She was a vision, a frothy pink model of femininity. She was impeccably groomed from the top of her carefully coiffed head to her white silk stockings and pointed-toe shoes. She was a woman to do any man proud. But she wasn't Cole's woman. She wasn't the Sunflower Callahan who had managed to get a hold on his heart.

Flipping his cigarette into a milk pail filled with sand for just that purpose, Cole made his presence known. "May I escort you outside, you gorgeous stranger?" He'd kept his voice soft and low to avoid startling her, but she lurched at the sound anyway. Cole offered a gentle hand, steadying her as she negotiated the last step.

"Oh, thank you." Sunny gladly accepted the crook of his elbow and worked at appearing nonplussed in spite of her discomfort. How would a fine lady excuse this sudden clumsiness? "I think my feet are not used to these shoes just yet. Perhaps a stroll outside would ease their grip on my toes."

She looked at him expectantly, and suddenly, Cole Fremont had no idea what to do. She was talking like a proper lady from back East, presenting herself to him as if she were indeed a stranger. If she were, he would have had no problem with his next move. He would escort her outside. And leave her there.

His smile grew lazy, crooked, as he thought of pulling the ribbons from her hair and dragging his hands through it until all the tight little curls had relaxed. His cool green eyes warmed, turned potent with the promise of spring as his memory returned to their playful pursuit through the tall meadow only a few days ago. And then his mind forced his thoughts to the present, told him he had to stop daydreaming about what had been, what could be, and get on with the present. But it didn't stop him from sliding his hand around her waist, or pulling her close and whispering the words he knew she wanted to hear.

"You look beautiful, Sunshine." Cole slipped his finger under her chin and tilted her head to receive his kiss, but she resisted, stiffened her entire body to match the rigidity he felt surrounding her waist.

"Please, I—I cannot." Sunny wasn't sure if it was the excitement of the party or just the damnable corset squeezing the breath out of her, but she was certain of one thing. If she stayed in Cole's arms or allowed him to kiss her, she would faint dead away, and most likely ruin her chances of fitting in with the other ladies in the bargain. She tensed her spine and he released her.

"Sorry." Cole's apology was awkward and uncertain. How should he behave around this new version of Sunflower Callahan? Contrite and remorseful? Or playful and honey-tongued? Working at blending all those sentiments, he tipped his hat and bowed at the waist. "Please forgive me, Miss Callahan. I know this isn't the time or place to show you how I feel, but you just look so doggone beautiful, I couldn't help myself."

And at least that much was true, even if his other thoughts had been selfish and impulsive. His needs and his desires would have to wait. Sunny had to be nervous about meeting his neighbors, as well as excited about wearing these fine new clothes and having her hair arranged so fashionably. She'd informed him how limited her knowledge was of these things and expressed her curiosity about the fine ladies of Phoenix several times. How could he spoil her debut by showing anything less than respect and enthusiasm for her efforts and new look?

And she was beautiful, he had to admit. Breathtaking, even if she wasn't as he first knew her or what he wanted her to be. She could be very happy for the next couple of days as she stepped into a world that had always been denied to her, might even find it to her liking. Something deep inside told Cole to encourage her foray into the world of socially prominent white women. He owed her that much, even though it might turn her from him—and the woman he'd come to love might fade as this new lady emerged.

Love? Cole's breath caught with the realization, and he reached out to the bannister to steady himself. When had *that* happened? he wondered with a start? Was that the thing, that nebulous feeling clouding his thinking since his return to the ranch? Was love, not his father's prejudice or his own ranching plans, the thing he'd been struggling with all along? Cole looked into Sunny's puzzled eyes and let his breath out in a long sigh. He could hear the rumble of wagons arriving in the yard. He would have to sort these feelings later. Now it was time to present Sunflower to his guests. And dammit, he would present her in grand style and encourage her entrance into Phoenix society. He would support and accept anything she wanted to do over the next few days, as long as she didn't pick up too many flirtatious habits or start batting her eyelashes at him the way Liz Scott always did.

Proud of his insight, of his decision, Cole turned, clicking his boot heels together, and held out his arm. "My dear Miss Callahan, I believe the guests have arrived. Would you care to join me in the yard?"

Sunny's smile was as enthusiastic as it was prim, and she gave him a proper little curtsy. "Thank you, sir. I would be delighted."

Then she accepted his offer wearing her most saucy expression, and batted her eyelashes as if they were on fire.

Daniel Hobbs pulled on the reins as the wagon rounded a curve and the rooftop of the majestic Fremont ranch house came into view. "Whoa, now!" he shouted as the wheels slowly rolled to a stop. Swiveling on the narrow wooden seat, he barked an order. "Eileen! Git on up here and squeeze yer worthless behind twixt yer ma and me."

"Yes, Pa." Careful not to catch her only decent wrapper on a splinter, Eileen picked her way past three of her five brothers, then scrambled to the side of the wagon and climbed over. Her legs wobbly from sitting on her knees for the past two hours, she limped to the front of the wagon and made an awkward climb up to the seat.

She was bent over, trying to wedge her slender body between her parents, when Daniel cracked the whip and sent the wagon lurching down the path again. The force snapped her backwards onto the hard seat, and sent a searing bolt of pain up her spine. But Eileen didn't cry out, wouldn't shed her reservoir of tears. She bit her lip until the taste of her own blood seeped into her mouth, but remained silent and uncomplaining.

Daniel turned to Eileen, scrutinizing her out of the corner of a hard, cold eye, and grumbled, "You know there be only one reason I brung you along to this here bar-bee-cue, doncha?"

"Yes, sir, I do." She kept her gaze on the road ahead and folded her hands in her lap.

"Don't get cute with me, gal!" Daniel raised his hand, but lowered it when Eileen ducked, covering her head with her arms. "I axed you a question and I 'spect a real answer!"

"Yes, sir." Her bottom lip trembling, she recited his instructions. "I'm to flirt with Cole Fremont and try to get his interest."

"Not try, gal! Make damn sure he takes up with you! It's high time you earned yer keep. Ownin' part a that Fremont ranch might ease the agony of raisin' a brat like you considerable. Yessir," he grinned, running his tongue along his thick cracked lips, "I believe I could git real used to havin' a Fremont in the family."

"But, Pa," Eileen cried in a soft whimper, "Cole already has a girl, and even if he hasn't spoken for her just yet, that Elizabeth Scott is lots prettier than me. I don't have a chance."

"Then make one!" Daniel's whip cracked, leaving a vicious welt across the back of the roan mare. "Gals like you kin always find a way to snare a man," he spat. "This Fremont boy cain't be any smarter than the rest of us."

He turned, curling his lip into an ugly snarl, and regarded his trembling daughter again. "Could be Fremont takes to sportin' women. He might sit up and take notice if that gaudy hair of yourn shows. Could be a good idear this one time to leave off yer bonnet. What'd you think, Ma?"

Martha's tired eyes darted from her husband to Eileen and back to Daniel again. Shrugging her thin shoulders, she said, "I s'pose that'd be all right. We could comb it around our fingers and make a few curls. Would you like that, honey?"

But before Eileen could answer, Daniel snapped, "It don't matter what she likes. It's a done deal." He looked down the trail, gauging the distance. "Git to it. We're almost there."

Without another word, Martha loosened her daughter's bonnet and the two women set about working Eileen's wavy red tresses into a suitable, if not particularly fashionable, style. Lacking extra hairpins or ribbon to match the green checkered gingham of her wrapper, Eileen tucked the sides of her hair behind her ears and left the rest to flow freely down her back. Daniel grunted and gave her a grudging nod of approval as they pulled into the yard of their host.

"Now just remember what I said," he ordered as he slowed the wagon to a halt. "Mind yer manners, but make damn sure that Fremont colt sits up and takes notice."

"Yes, Pa."

Eileen glanced around the grounds searching for Cole, wondering if he even knew her name, what he'd think of her wild red hair hanging loose for all to see. She felt naked, ashamed, certain Cole would grimace when he saw how cheap and wanton she looked. She'd only met him once, and that had been a brief "how'd you do" at Goldwater's in town. Maybe he wouldn't even remember her. And even if he did, handsome and roguish as he was, the thought of sparking his interest, of actually encouraging his advances, was too farfetched to be real.

"Welcome to the Triple F ranch," a well-groomed man in a fine suit of grey wool greeted. "Nathan Fremont at your service." Always cognizant of his political future, Nathan flashed a toothy grin as he approached the side of the wagon, his hand extended in a warm greeting. "And which of our good neighbors might ya'll be?"

"Daniel Hobbs." He pumped his host's manicured hand,

then gestured to his right. "This be my wife Martha and daughter Eileen. Got five of my six boys in the back."

"Six sons? You're a fortunate man, sir, to leave such a legacy. I'm down to the one boy, but a man couldn't ask for a finer son and heir than I got in Cole."

"So I've heard tell." Daniel worked to keep the greed out of his voice as he climbed off the buckboard and helped Martha and Eileen down. "Where might that boy of yourn be?"

"He's in the barn greeting our other guests with lemonade and iced cantaloupe. Why don't you folks join him and refresh yourselves. I'll have one of the hands see to your horse and rig."

"Thank ye kindly." Daniel gestured to his family, and they dutifully followed him into the huge barn. Cleared and carpeted with fresh straw just for this occasion, the newly painted walls were lined with tables filled with food and drink, and the loft played host to a series of ribbons, bows, and several brightly burning lanterns. The smell was fresh, clean, and inviting—a scent of springtime and new beginnings. When his nose caught the enticing aroma of fresh-baked goods as well, Daniel headed for one of the food-laden tables with his wife and children trailing after him like a column of ducks.

"It's Dan Hobbs, isn't it?" Cole asked as the newcomer reached for a slice of toast topped with a crisp quail breast, and stuck it in his mouth.

"Umph," Daniel mumbled with a nod. He turned, his eyes widening as he recognized the very man he sought, and wiped his hand on his trousers before he offered it to Cole. "Good to see you again." Spinning around, he grabbed Eileen's arm and dragged her along side of him. "You recall meetin' my gal, Eileen? She's growed up some since you last saw her, I 'spect."

"Miss Hobbs." Cole tipped his hat, then looked past her to Martha. "Nice to see you again, too, Mrs. Hobbs. Please have some food and drink and refresh yourselves from your long trip."

"Thank ye kindly." Martha beckoned to her boys, then joined them, trying her best to slow their impassioned assault on the cakes and pies. Her husband moved towards a group of neighborhood men, leaving Eileen alone with Cole.

Untutored in the ways of seduction, Eileen braided her fingers together, squeezing them until they turned white as she frantically searched for something clever to say. Chancing a quick glance into Cole's eyes, she tried to speak in a light, carefree voice, but it came out sounding more like a creaky hinge. "Mighty nice place you've got here. Must be something to live in a big house like that."

"Thank you. It's a very comfortable home."

He said the words politely enough, but they were hollow, distracted. Eileen chanced another look into Cole's handsome features and saw the reason why. He was looking past her, gazing intently at someone or something as it came into the barn. She followed his line of vision to a beautiful doe-skinned woman as she made her way towards them. Although Eileen was sure she'd never met or seen the woman before, something about her was familiar. Who was she?

Trying not to mimic the red-haired creature at Cole's side, and stare the way she was being stared at, Sunny glided up to him. "Nellie asked me to tell you your mother will join everyone later this afternoon. She has decided to rest a little longer so she can enjoy the dancing tonight."

"Thanks for the message." Still unaccustomed to her new appearance, Cole's gaze lingered on Sunflower a long moment before he remembered his other guest. "Oh, Eileen. I'd like you to meet a very special friend of mine. This is Sunny Callahan from Yuma. Sunny th—"

"Callahan?"

The meek redhead suddenly became animated, nearly

pushing Cole out of the way as she approached Sunny. "Are you by any chance Sean's sister? Have you seen him? Did he make it here all right?"

Her curiosity outweighing her suspicions, Sunny regarded the girl carefully before she answered. "Sean Callahan is my brother. Do you know him?"

"Oh, yes," Eileen cried, her ice-blue eyes sparkling with excitement. "He saved my life this past Tuesday. Is he here?"

"Saved your *life*?"

The thought was vocalized by both Sunny and Cole. Glancing at each other, they burst out laughing, then Sunny caught her breath. "Excuse us, but you are quite a surprise. Sean has not mentioned saving anyone's life. And yes, he is here."

"Oh," she laughed, clapping her hands together. "May I see him?" But as soon as the words were out, Eileen realized her mistake. She'd spoken too quickly, with too much excitement. She was supposed to be attracting Cole's interest, not hinting at her feelings for another. Her expression rigid with panic, Eileen glanced around, looking for her father. He was engaged in conversation several feet away, apparently oblivious to his daughter's blunder. He hadn't seen or heard.

Determined to see Sean again, in spite of Daniel Hobbs or what it might do to her chances with Cole, she bit her lip and spoke in hushed tones. "I—I'm afraid in the . . . the excitement the other day, I didn't, well, I never really thanked Sean proper. Where might I find him?"

Sensing the undercurrents but not their cause, Sunny smiled at the nervous girl. "He's at the far table serving lemonade. Come, I will take you to him."

"Oh, no!" Eileen stepped back, ducking as if to hide. "Ah, th-that's all right." Her mind raced as she tried to think of a way to see him without her pa's knowledge. "I was just going outside for a breath of air. If you'd be kind enough to tell him, I'd like to talk to Sean out by that yonder stand of cottonwood trees."

Sunny's muscles tensed and her eyes dulled as Eileen spoke. The girl obviously didn't want to be seen with a half-breed, was much too good even to thank him for saving her miserable life in front of the other fine white folks. Lifting her chin, Sunny replied as respectfully as good manners dictated, but her tone was flat and dull, her expression cold and aloof.

"Of course. I will be happy to tell him." Then she lifted her skirts and flounced off to the other end of the barn. By the time she reached her brother, her quick temper had chilled to contempt.

"Sean?" Gesturing for him to follow, she turned and stomped out through the double doors. When Sean rounded the corner after her, he was carrying two cups of iced lemonade.

"You look like you could use a little cooling off," he observed, handing her the drink. "What's wrong, little one?"

Sunny choked down a swallow of the tart liquid, then shivered and puckered her lips before she explained. "A woman with hair the color of fire has come to me with a wild tale. She says you saved her life. Is this so?"

"Eileen? Is she here?"

"Then her story is true?"

"Yes, I guess I did save her life. Where is she?"

Sunny uttered a short, bitter laugh. "Hiding in the cottonwood trees so none of the fine folks gathered here can see that she would speak to one such as you."

"Eileen's not like that! She's one of the kindest, most gentle people I've ever met. You've judged her too quickly."

His sudden anger, the force behind his words, took Sunny by surprise. She backed further away from the door, urging him to join her. "What is this?" she whispered, incredulous.

"Do you actually think of this woman, look on her as . . . or think of, of . . . *courting* her?"

Sean's sigh was long, more of a groan. He pulled off his hat and ran his fingers through his thick black hair. "No, little one, your brother's no fool." He thought of adding, "like you are," but knew that wasn't completely true. While neither he nor his sister could ever hope to be entirely accepted in white society, Sunny at least had a slim chance. Men like his father had paved the way for her. He, on the other hand, could never hope to make Eileen anything but a casual acquaintance. It would be a deadly folly to try.

"I'm sorry if my temper spoke before my brain had a chance to think, but I wanted you to know that Eileen is no cruel woman who thinks I am less than she. She has a tender heart and a pure soul."

"She has more than a kind heart," Sunny said with a knowing smile. This brother she knew well enough to be her twin was hiding something, denying himself to her. Willing to accept his wrath if she were wrong, Sunny ventured, "I think she may have your heart as well."

"That is impossible! This is something I know to be unthinkable for either of us—even if you don't."

"Oh, my brother? Is this so?" Sunny fingered the soft leather of Sean's vest, plucked at the sleeves of his checkered shirt, and pulled the short hairs at the back of his head, cut just for the occasion. "If not for your skin, I believe you have disguised yourself almost well enough to hide your Quechan blood. Perhaps you think you have the right to steal the heart of a white woman. Was it your plan to forget who you are?"

"No, little one—was it yours?" Caught by the injustice, the prejudices they both must endure, Sean waved his hand from the top of her head to her toes. "I see nothing of the Sunflower I knew from Yuma here. Who do you pretend to be?"

"I pretend to be no one but myself!" she snapped. "And

we are speaking of you and this flaming-haired woman, not of me and my need to borrow some clothing from the generous Fremont family."

"I too have borrowed," he countered, referring to his ranch hand look. "But I know who I am and where I belong. Do you still retain that knowledge, little sister?"

Sunny stamped her foot, but held her tongue. She had no answer, for him or for herself, and wasn't even certain she wanted to look for one. Lowering her lashes, she stared at the red earth. Her brother had turned the conversation around, changed its course to point at her. Was she deluding herself to think of a future with Cole? More and more, she'd considered what life would be like as a permanent part of the Fremont family, and wished in her heart it would come true. Was Sean right? Did she belong in Yuma with her own kind, whatever that may be?

Suddenly jerking her gaze up to meet his, Sunny thought of the party escalating inside, the fun she was missing out on. She would not allow any more talk or thoughts of this kind. Not on this day. And not until she'd really taken the time to think things through.

"This discussion has strayed, my bone-headed brother. I have more important things to do than debate which of us lives in a world of dreams." She picked up her skirts and turned her back to him. "Do what you will with the message I have brought to you. I must return to the barn. Cole is waiting for me."

With that, she flounced off towards the door, and immediately caught the heel of her shoe in a gopher hole and turned her ankle. Muttering curses under her breath, she lamented the birth of the idiot who'd designed the tiny shoes her toes were squeezed into, then limped inside the cool barn. As she waited for her eyes to adjust to the dim lighting, she heard the mellow cords of a violin as the fiddler called the guests to the floor for the first polka of the day.

Sunny glanced through the crowd, searching for Cole's black Stetson hat. When she spotted it, she took a few steps towards him, but froze as she noticed he was not alone on the dance floor.

A beautiful young woman dressed in shiny emerald green taffeta smiled up at him, her adoration complete. Standing very still, Sunny studied the laughing couple, feeling a dull ache spread throughout her breast, increasing the pressure of her corset until she was sure it would burst. They knew each other well, this woman and the man Sunny loved. That much was apparent from the way the woman clung to Cole, the intimate way she moved against his body.

An introduction to the gold-haired woman would be unnecessary, Sunny thought with a heavy heart. No third party was needed to tell her that Cole held Elizabeth Scott in his strong arms.

ELEVEN

"Sean—over here."

Eileen's voice was a faint rustle in the breeze. Following the sound, Sean rounded the base of an old cottonwood tree and nearly bumped into her.

She was a stunning sight, a free and wild apparition with that glorious mane of sun drenched hair bouncing across her shoulders.

Suddenly feeling boyish and awkward, Sean sidestepped, then removed his hat. "Nice to see you again. My sister said you wanted to talk to me."

"Oh, well, I . . ." His very presence rendered her incapable of putting a sentence together, and the thought of soliciting his help actually silenced her. What if her request drew his laughter? His ridicule? Or worse, his anger? Mortified, Eileen averted her gaze and brought her hands to her cheeks in an effort to cool them.

Thinking she was about to faint, Sean dropped his hat and slipped his arms around her waist. "Eileen? Are you all right? Maybe if I get some water."

"No." Her voice returned, yet still, her thought processes trailed behind. "I—I'm fine, really." Unsure what her next move should be, but unwilling to draw away, she rested her head against his chest and draped her hand over his shoulder as she tried to clear her mind. Why was it that every time he was near she turned into a bowl of mush? She was no silly swooning female, and yet here she was, behaving as if she were. Sean must think her mad.

She stepped away and turned her back toward him, afraid to expose her vulnerability. "Thank you for coming. I—I wanted to see you to express my gratitude again for saving my life, I . . ." Eileen let the sentence, the excuse, fade. *Now* was her chance, maybe the only chance she'd ever have. How could she waste it with small talk and half-truths?

Eileen whirled around, her loose hair following the movement like a scarlet whip, reminding her of her immodest appearance. She wavered slightly, but managed to form the words she knew she would have to say if she hoped to persuade him. "I think maybe I just wanted to see you again. I hoped you wanted to see me, too." There. She'd said the words, but she still wasn't able to look into his eyes. What if he thought her unattractive and cheap, or even wanton?

Sean's expression darkened as he said, "I'm going to assume you don't know what you've just said." Even if she did know, he didn't want to hear it, couldn't *bear* to hear it. He forced his goodbye through a tense jaw. "If that's all, Miss Hobbs, I'd better be—"

"No!" The thought of his leaving before she'd had a chance to explain her plan spurred her on. "Please, stay and hear me out."

"I'm sure it would be better if I didn't."

"But don't you remember what you said to me just before you left our ranch?" she persisted.

Scanning the trees and shrubs for unexpected visitors, Sean satisfied his sense of caution that they were undetected. Then he thought back to his departure from the

Hobbs ranch, but couldn't figure what she could be referring to. "I'm sorry, but I don't know what you're talking
about."

Eileen swallowed the hurt, the sense of rejection, and
resumed in a smaller, less confident voice. "You said,
'some other time, some other place.' Y-You said th-that,"
she pressed a fingertip against her lips, and finally looked
into his eyes, "r-right after you . . . kissed me."

Her vulnerable, beaten expression sent a jolt through
him. Sean's arms ached to surround her, to crush her to his
chest and murmur words of comfort in her delicate pink
ear. Yet merely to continue this conversation, with no
thoughts of anything more than speaking to her, would
compromise his very life, leave him open for all manner of
punishment—including death. But to end it now would
deprive him of the joy of looking into her crystal-blue eyes,
of hearing her sweet voice call his name, of drifting in her
soft wholesome scent.

A tremendous lump formed in Sean's throat. Forcing a
scowl, he tried to dissuade her with a frosty gaze. "That kiss
was a mistake. It meant nothing. Go back to your family—
now."

Eileen trembled, flinching at the anger in his voice, the
chill in his eyes. But she held her ground. "No. I want to be
with you."

Troubled and frustrated, Sean reached out and gripped
her shoulders as he searched for a way to end this madness.
"Why me, Eileen? Are you another of those curious white
females who seek forbidden pleasure with any savage
who'll have them?" The words were meant to hurt and
anger her, to give her the freedom of choosing to leave him
standing alone. But her reaction puzzled and alarmed him.
She turned pale, nearly translucent as his fingers dug into
her flesh. Rather than the expected anger, her expression
was one of fright, of sheer terror.

His voice gentler, concerned, Sean eased his grip and

said, "This can go no further between us, you must realize that. You will be shunned by your family and their friends, and I, well, I will be dealt with sternly." With instinct guiding him, Sean relaxed his hold and slid his hands around her tiny waist. "Please understand," he pleaded in a low whisper.

Calmer now, Eileen slowly moved her hand along Sean's shoulder, tried to ignore the way the hard ridges and valleys of his muscles felt beneath her fingertips, but still couldn't look in his eyes. Did he mean what he'd said? Was her father right all along when he'd said no man would ever look at her and see a proper lady? What she was about to suggest certainly wouldn't help her cause. But she had no other choice.

Using every ounce of her courage, Eileen forced her chin up and willed herself to examine Sean's handsome features, the truth in his eyes. She saw nothing of her father's prophecy. Clinging to one last hope, she took a deep breath and squared her shoulders.

"You are the one who must understand," she said softly. "Since you saved me from the flood, I've felt we're tied together somehow, that you're destined to save me from *my life* as well. Will you please help me?"

She was talking gibberish. Either that, or her nearness, that soft and desirable body pressed against his, had dulled his mind past the point of comprehension. Against his better judgement, he cupped her trusting face with his big hands and murmured, "What kind of help could you possibly need that I can provide?"

After a moment's hesitation, Eileen gathered all the strength in her bruised body and finally voiced her plan. "I want you to take me away from here when you leave."

Stunned, Sean choked out a feeble, *"What?"*

"I don't care where you are going," Eileen went on, dismissing his distress, "or how you plan to get there, as long as you take me with you. Will you do that for me, please?"

"I can't!" he boomed. Then, remembering their surroundings, he looked around making sure there were no intruders, and finished in a whisper, "You know I can't, and you know why. I can't believe you'd even ask such a thing of me."

"I know what I'm asking, and I've chosen you because I trust you. You're a good man, Sean. You wouldn't hurt me unless I had it coming."

"I wouldn't hurt you for *any* reason." He shook his head, unable to understand. "You're not making any sense. You've got a family, and with your looks you must have suitors lining up to court you. Why would you jeopardize your future to run off with a half-breed?"

"All I'd be jeopardizing," she bit off, "is a life of hell. Surely running off with you couldn't be worse than that."

Sean's hands dropped to his sides as he saw the fire in her eyes flare to match the color of her hair. It was the first real flash of anger, of backbone, he'd seen in her. He wasn't sure what to make of it. "Maybe you'd better start at the beginning. Explain this life of hell, because you won't know what hell is until you go on the run with the likes of me."

"No?" Eileen took his hand and slid his fingers into her hair. "Remember the bruise you found on my forehead the day you saved me? You thought it was from falling off the horse, but I said I got it at home. Well, I got these there, too, and in the same way." She directed his fingertips to a large lump on the side of her head and one on the back. "Pa gets kinda upset if his coffee isn't real hot or I don't get his boots soft enough with—"

"Your *pa* raised those knots on your head?" Sean interrupted, appalled. How could anyone, much less a full grown man, hit a fragile young woman like Eileen? She looked as if she were made of fine porcelain. If what she said was true, why hadn't she shattered?

"Pa did all this and more you can't see," she explained further. "And sometimes, he—he—" Eileen wasn't quite sure how to explain something she didn't understand herself, but she gave it a try. "I don't know what you'd call it, but he looks at me sort of, well . . . funny."

His mind was unable to picture a father even thinking about the kind of look Eileen might be describing, so Sean brushed it off. "I'm sure your father must love you a lot. Maybe you've misinterpreted some of his feelings for you."

Eileen cocked, then shook her head. "I doubt it, but it really doesn't matter right now. All I know is, if I don't get married to some rich rancher real soon, I'm afraid of what he'll do—he might even kill me. Compared to that, I don't think running off with you is such a bad idea."

Sean blew out a heavy sigh, wondering how much of what she'd said might be true. He couldn't believe the girl's own father would actually kill her, but the fact that she thought he would disturbed him a great deal. She'd given him a lot to think about, told him things he had trouble imagining. How could the man beat his daughter so brutally, make her hate him so much she'd run off with a near stranger? Did he have a right to save her from this torment? Or perhaps, an obligation?

"Sean?" Eileen drew his gaze, interrupting his thoughts. "I don't mean to be trouble for you, and I'll understand if you just plain don't want me, but at least think about it. I'll do anything you want. I can clean and cook game as good as anyone, and I know I can learn how to—to make you happy and I'll—"

"Stop it!" he ordered in a whisper. "There's no need for you to grovel to any man, especially to me. I'm just thinking over all you told me, trying to figure a way out. You say your pa just wants you out of the house?"

"Not just out. He wants me to marry someone with

money so he can have a share of it." She looked over her shoulder, making sure they weren't observed, and said with an amused sigh, "I'm supposed to be inside right now making eyes at Cole Fremont. Pa has it in his head I should spin a web around him and convince him to marry me."

Sean barked a short laugh. "Now there's an idea that would get you killed for sure." He answered the puzzled look in Eileen's eyes with another laugh, then added, "Sunny has a bit of a temper. If you so much as lay one of your delicate fingers on Cole, I'm afraid she'd pluck you like a chicken and make a hearth rug out of your beautiful hair."

"Your *sister* and Cole?"

Sean's eyebrows lifted, then fell, and he shrugged. "Yeah. Sometimes, neither of us Callahans are too bright."

"Oh, I wasn't trying to say that. It's just that I didn't know." Did Elizabeth Scott? And what about the rest of the Fremont family? She'd heard they were as anti-Indian as her own father, maybe more. How did the thought of their only son courting a half-breed set with them?

"It could be they don't want anyone to know just yet." Although he didn't like the idea of Cole Fremont keeping his sister on the sidelines as it were, he could see the reasons for secrecy, and understood why Eileen and others were unaware of their relationship. "Maybe you ought to keep that information to yourself."

"Of course."

Her nerves keeping track of the minutes, Eileen glanced towards the barn and saw a group of men milling around in the yard. Her time with Sean had to be cut short before they were discovered. "I'd better get back to the party soon or Pa's going to start wondering where I am." She laid a tentative hand on his forearm. "Will you at least think over my idea and give it a chance to work? I swear, I can't take much more at home."

The best he could give her was a short nod and an answer that skirted the truth. "I'll give your problem some thought."

But Eileen hadn't put her reputation on the line, opened a part of herself no one had ever seen, just to be pacified with an ambiguous statement. "Please understand how serious I am. If I have to, I'll run off by myself."

And then he finally understood. This was no irrational, spur of the moment flight of fancy. Eileen meant to leave her home one way or another. And she'd chosen him as her guide. Suddenly, Sean was as pleased as he was concerned. "Do you realize if I agree to help you, you will be rejected by your kind wherever we go?"

"I'm rejected by my own family here. How can others hurt me worse than that?"

Sean curled up his fist and impulsively wrapped his arm around her. Pulling her close, he voiced his anger. "I simply cannot understand how your father can be so cruel. If you were mine, I would give thanks every day for such an honor, praise God for the beautiful person he has placed on this earth."

"Ohhh." Her breath rushed out and tears sprang into Eileen's eyes.

No man had ever spoken of her in such terms, or with such sincerity. Completely convinced she'd made the correct choice in entrusting Sean with her problems and future, Eileen pondered her next move. She must do something to encourage him to take her along, something to interest him enough to take the risk—but what? She was unschooled in the art of flirtation, and Sean was becoming impatient, nervous. She had to move quickly.

Her fingers trembling, her resolve wavering, she leaned closer to the bronzed half-breed and stroked his cheek. To her surprise, the contact was more pleasurable than repulsive, invoked curiosity rather than aversion. Eileen marveled at the diverse textures, the coarse stubble of a too-fertile crop of whiskers banked by a surprisingly soft patch of burnished skin. Overwhelmed with wonder as she let her fingers drift to his hairline, Eileen shuddered with each increasing sensation.

Sean's tight stomach unfurled at her touch, blossomed and spread hot spurts of desire throughout him as she trembled against him. Sean forgot who he was, where he was, as he gave into a wave of urgency to taste her, to feel her. Not giving his mind a chance to question, to consider the consequences, his mouth quickly claimed hers.

She guessed he was thinking of kissing her, and had a moment of panic wondering if she should turn and run or accept what he so boldly offered. But then he was upon her. Eileen was stunned by the force of his embrace, the depth of his kiss. This wasn't the brief gesture of goodbye he'd bestowed on her a few days ago. This was something new, something exhilarating—and something frightening. Sean's fingers tangled in her hair as he drew her closer, and she could feel the warm moisture of his breath against her skin as he grasped her tighter and tighter. Her first reaction was alarm, a feeling akin to desperation, but Sean coaxed her, urged her to accept him and his explorations.

Eager to please him, Eileen forced herself to relax, to allow his tongue to part her lips, caress the tips of her teeth, then finally slide between them on a shocking journey to the inside of her mouth. She stiffened her body at the first onslaught of sensation, but Sean kept a firm hold on the back of her head, and soon his gentle probing pushed surprise and panic aside and introduced a curious new world of pleasure.

Sean knew he should stop, for his sake as well as Eileen's. But he was drowning in her, lost in her exquisite taste, her supreme softness. Sean muted his inner voices, and opened himself to her in a way reserved for the closest of lovers. When she tensed, pulled back as he deepened the kiss, he thought of releasing her, of apologizing for his lusty behavior and sending her back to the barn. But then she yielded, encouraged his caresses, and followed his guidance until he thought he'd go mad from her naive duplication of his movements.

The sudden cackle of nearby laughter brought them to their senses. As if each had heard the crack of a bullwhip and felt the sting of its leather, Eileen and Sean twisted away from one another and dropped to the ground.

Sean peered through the shrubbery and spotted two male guests walking towards the stand of trees. Keeping his eyes trained on the approaching men, Sean whispered low and urgently, "Back down to the edge of the grove, then slowly come out on the south side. I'll stay here awhile." When he heard the rustle of her petticoats, he quickly added, "I'll have Sunny contact you and let you know my decision about your problem later."

Eileen hesitated as she worked her way out of the tangle of cottonwood trees, but decided against risking a reply. She would thank him later when she hoped she'd have even more to be grateful for.

After she was gone, Sean quickly rolled onto his back and covered his face with his hat. Feigning slumber, he forced his breathing to become slow and methodical, then jerked forward as one of the guests tapped his foot with the toe of a boot.

"Huh?" He jackknifed to a sitting position looking properly disoriented.

"What'cha doin' hidin' out here in the trees, injun? Plannin' an attack on the Triple F ranch?" Both men laughed at the clever remark, then the same one added, "Better wait 'til sundown so's we won't see you sneakin' up on us, tho."

Ignoring their remarks and hoots of laughter, Sean resumed a position flat on his back until they got bored waiting for him to react. They turned away, fumbling with the buttons on their trousers, and left Sean alone. He silently crept to his feet and took a northerly path out of the trees back towards the festivities.

As soon as he reentered the barn, Sean ambled over near the stalls and stood in the shadows. Scanning the crowd, he discovered Eileen dancing a lively polka with Cole Fremont. The blond rancher twirled her, sent her skirts and petticoats flying, and afforded Sean a glimpse of her well-turned ankle just before Cole collected her back in his arms.

Outrage swelled in his throat, but it was directed as much at himself as his host. How could he have lost control so easily in the cottonwood grove and taken advantage of Eileen at such a vulnerable moment? He hadn't been thinking. Now, all he *could* do was think—of Eileen, of their fevered embrace, of finding a way to make sure it never happened again, and of wishing that it could. He'd taken a terrible risk with his life. He couldn't even imagine what might have happened if things went further and he risked his heart as well.

Sean continued to study the dancers, worked at finding a way to deal with his new and conflicting feelings. He knew why she was with the appealing rancher, had noticed Daniel Hobbs observing the pair out of the corner of his eye, but the knowledge couldn't seem to stop a spasm of jealousy from chilling his spine or keep the color of envy from staining his eyes. How could he possibly grant her request and keep his sanity too?

He decided to dwell on his host and assess his sister's chances for future happiness, but all he could think of was his own plight. Cole Fremont could dance with any woman in the room while he, Sean Callahan, descendant of the honorable Callahans from Killarney, Ireland, must stand aside and watch. His mother's equally honorable Quechan blood wasn't good enough to mingle with this crowd, or court their daughters. It wasn't fair. It wasn't right. There wasn't one woman in the room he could invite to— Sean interrupted his own thoughts and nearly laughed out loud as he realized there *was* one woman who might do him the honor of accepting an invitation to dance with him. He continued sifting through the crowd until he finally discovered Sunny standing in the far corner. Alone.

His spirits somewhat lifted, Sean approached her, noticing as he drew closer that her lovely features were pinched in a scowl and her foot tapped incessantly against the dirt floor.

Sean crept up beside her, out of her line of vision, and whispered, "You look as if a coyote has robbed your rabbit trap of its prize, my dear sister. What angers you so?"

After flashing her dark eyes his way, Sunny returned her gaze to the dance floor and grumbled, " 'Tis something very much like that, brother dear. Cole has not yet come to show me how to do this polka dance. First, this Elizabeth creature attached herself to him, and now your little friend with hair the color of an over-ripe pumpkin has lured him into her arms!"

Not ready to tell her about Eileen and what she'd asked him to do, Sean tilted his sister's chin until she had to face him. "My, but you sound off-key, little sister. Has jealousy added a sour tone to your usually melodious voice?"

Sunny's pout lifted at the corners, and she tried to turn away from Sean, but he kept a firm grip on her chin.

"Well, little one? Am I right?"

"Oh," she complained with a chuckle, "I suppose you are, but just a little. I really want to learn how to do this polka dance, and—"

"And you can't stand watching Cole holding another woman," he finished for her.

Sunny opened her mouth to protest, but let out her breath in a long sigh instead. "No, I cannot," she admitted.

"If it makes you feel any better," Sean confessed under his breath, "I'm not too happy about him holding that particular woman either."

Sunny's head jerked towards her brother at this. "I was right?"

First checking to make certain no bystanders could overhear them, Sean pressed his lips together and nodded.

"Oh, my brother," Sunny gasped. "You must be very careful. If anyone finds out—"

"I'm aware of the danger. You don't have to worry about me—yet."

"Yet?"

Again checking for eavesdroppers, Sean leaned very close to Sunny's ear and repeated Eileen's story. When he finished, even though it was against all rational thought, he suddenly had his answer. "I've decided to take her to Yuma with me."

"But Sean! You—"

"Save your energy for the polka. My mind is made up."

Sunny bit her lip when she saw the determination in his eyes. There was nothing she could say or do to dissuade him. "What do you plan to do? Kidnap this girl from her family?"

"I don't have that figured out yet, but when—" Sean cut off his words as he noticed Cole and Eileen approaching. He glanced at Sunny, whispering out of the corner of his mouth, "Get Eileen alone and tell her I'm going to take her away from here. Tell her that when I have a plan I'll send you with another message. Got it?"

Her forehead creased with worry, Sunny gave him a short nod, then turned towards Cole. Masking her concerns, she managed a bright smile and stepped forward. "So nice to see you again, Mr.—ah, Mr.— I am sorry. It has been so long since we met, I am afraid I have forgotten your name."

Laughing as he slipped her hand in his, Cole lifted her fingers to his mouth and kissed each velvety fingertip. "The name is Host. Mr. Host, if you please."

"I am very honored to make your acquaintance," Sunny

grinned. "But I would be more honored if you would please show me how to do this polka dance."

"With pleasure, ma'am." Cole extended his elbow to Sunny, but before she had a chance to take it, Sean stepped between them.

"I hate to interrupt your dance lesson, Sunny, but I'd like a word with Cole. Why don't you show Eileen around while we talk."

Her expression ruffled with irritation, she grimaced. *"Now?"*

"Yes, little sister. Now."

Sunny rolled her eyes and made a face, but she walked stiff-legged over to where Eileen stood. "Join me in a cup of lemonade?" she asked with forced enthusiasm.

Uncertain how much Sean had told his sister, if he'd said anything at all, Eileen lowered her gaze and answered in a tiny voice. "If that's what you'd like to do."

Put off at first by the girl's overly meek nature, Sunny recalled a few of the things Sean told her, and compassion quickly replaced her disappointment. She reached for Eileen's hand, encouraging, "Come on. I think we should go outside for some fresh air."

Afraid to hope that Sean had already entrusted his sister with a message for her, distressed to think maybe he *had* and she was about to receive a stern lecture, Eileen reluctantly allowed Sunny to lead her from the barn to a secluded spot near Olive Fremont's garden.

Her sense of privacy secured, Sunny urged Eileen to look at her. "My brother has told me many things about you. Do not be afraid. I will try to help you."

"Help me?" she said, puzzled and alarmed. "Thank you for the offer, but the kind of help I need is, well, I don't think you'll be—"

"I will help Sean help you."

Eileen's pale blue eyes flew open. "You mean he's gonna take me away with him?"

"Shussshh," Sunny cautioned. "Yes, but I do not think it is a good idea to tell everyone about it."

"Oh!" Eileen's gaze darted around the yard, then back to Sunny. "Sean's planning to take me with him? *Really*?" she cried, her voice barely audible.

"Yes, really." Sunny smiled, her heart warmed by the relief flooding the girl's features. "As soon as he has found a way to slip you away, I will bring another message. In the meantime, I think it would be best to pretend you are not acquainted with him."

"Yes, yes, of course." Her mind racing with possibilities and ideas, Eileen also tried to think of obstacles that might arise in her quest for freedom. "What if I have to get a message to Sean? How will I find him? What if I can't find you either?"

"That is unlikely, but if you think you must go to him, it would be safest at night when others sleep. Sean has made a bed for himself up in the loft in the barn. Please do not," she warned with heavy undercurrents in her voice, "go to him unless you have no other choice. My brother is very important to me. I do not wish to see him harmed."

"Oh, that's the last thing I want, too. I promise, I will be very, very careful."

Not entirely appeased, Sunny thought of seeking further assurances, but then she noticed Nellie standing on the front porch of her home. A small blond woman stood next to her, staring out towards the garden. Olive Fremont?

"Eileen?" Sunny said, never taking her eyes off the porch. "Is that Cole's mother over there?"

Squinting into the setting sun, Eileen nodded. "I think so. Don't see her often, but I think that's her."

Ominous warnings trailed up Sunny's spine as she felt the older woman's gaze boring into her. Should she go to her, introduce herself, and try to become her friend? Or turn and pretend she hadn't noticed her? The decision was taken from Sunny as the blond woman came to life.

Cole's mother stood rigid as a length of bamboo, waving her arm like a bayonet prodding the enemy into a cell. Her target was Sunny.

"I think now it is your turn to help me," Sunny whispered under her breath as she urged Eileen to accompany her to the ranch house. "Cole's mother has been in her sick bed since I arrived. I have not met the woman, but already I have the feeling she does not like me."

Strolling along beside her new friend, Eileen tried to encourage her. "Don't worry. I bet she'll like you just fine."

But as they neared the porch and Sunny glanced at the woman, she could feel a blast of frigid air despite the warm temperatures of early spring. She lifted her skirts, and her chin, then maneuvered the small flight of steps.

"I'm Cole's mother," Olive announced as Sunny neared. "You must be the poor Indian girl he rescued on his way home."

Looking anxious, nervous, Nellie stepped forward. "Mom, her name is Sunny—"

"Yes, sweetheart. Sunflower," Olive sliced in, never taking her eyes off Sunny. "Why don't you see to our guest's needs, Nellie darling." She inclined her head towards Eileen, then raised her skirts and gestured to Sunny. "This little Miss is going with me. We have a few things to straighten out."

"Yes'm." Nellie raised her brow with a sigh, then took Eileen down the steps towards the barn.

Longing to flee with the girls, Sunny's gaze lingered on their retreating figures until Olive's voice cracked like a whip.

"Come, dear! I've guests waiting for me."

"Oh, yes, I—ah, of course." Sunny bolted through the doorway and followed the stiff-backed woman to a small sitting room.

Olive sank onto a comfortable settee, but did not offer a

chair to her guest. "Now then," she began. "Are you enjoying your visit at the ranch?"

"I—ah, yes ma'am," Sunny answered cautiously.

Fanning herself with tedious, well-timed strokes, Olive scrutinized her. "Is that Nellie's dress?"

Sunny hesitated a long moment, uncertain if the woman was merely making small talk or setting her up for some kind of attack. Olive presented herself as feeble and weak, her fine small-boned body covered with pale, crinkled skin, her silver-blond hair thin and several shades lighter than Cole's. She was a starving sparrow of a woman to look upon, but her eyes belied the frailty, the image. Where her son's eyes were a shade of green as cool as spring rain, or warm and lush as a meadow at dawn, Olive's were cold like agate, the bitter green of unripened fruit.

"Well, dear?"

Those tart eyes bore into Sunny, demanding an answer. "Yes, ma'am, the dress is hers. Nellie has been very kind and generous to me."

"So she has." Olive increased the tempo of her fan, then narrowed her gaze. "You may keep the dress when you leave, dear."

Still wary and uncertain, Sunny gave her a short nod. "Thank you."

"And I think it's time we got down to that."

Sunny cocked her head and clasped her hands together. "To what, Mrs. Fremont?"

"Why, your leaving, of course." Now the fan worked in doubletime. "I'm sure you and your brother have had ample time to recover from your long journeys. I also realize that Cole has invited you both to enjoy our barbecue. Most of our guests are staying tonight and joining us for supper tomorrow. You're welcome to do so as well. I see no reason, however, that you and your brother can't be on your way, say, Sunday morning."

Sunny's breath caught in her throat and her mouth

dropped open. Her brows slammed together in hurt and surprise as she tried to make eye contact with Olive, but the fan was moving so rapidly now that glimpses of the woman's face were choppy and distorted. "But Mrs. Fremont," Sunny pleaded, "Cole has—"

"Now, dear." Olive collapsed the fan and dropped it on the settee. She rose unsteadily, then straightened her shoulders. "My son has a great many things on his mind. Don't be bothering him with all this. He has the future of this ranch in his hands, not to mention his own bright future and upcoming marriage."

This couldn't be happening! Cole mentioned nothing of marriage, of his future being tied to the Triple F ranch. There had to be some mistake, some error. "B-But, Mrs. Fremont, you do not—"

"That's enough of this conversation, dear. As I've said, I do have my guests to think of." Olive made her way across the room, leaving Sunny gasping in her wake.

Cole's mother turned back just as she reached the doorway and smiled for the first time. "There is one other thing."

She would apologize now, tell Sunny this was all a mistake, a joke. "Yes, ma'am?"

"Be a dear, will you? On your way out to the barn, please stop in the kitchen and gather up some more supplies. I hear we're running low on chocolate cake."

TWELVE

Cole leaned against the rough wood of the shed and blew a puff of smoke into the twilight. He waved goodbye to the Hobbs family as their wagon rolled past him, then flipped his cigarette to the ground. Turning back towards the barn, Cole caught a glimpse of light coming from his father's study in the main house. He'd last seen him doing a final square dance before the party broke up. Why wasn't he outside bidding farewell to the last of his guests? Had Nathan's bad heart finally caught him in mid-stride?

Delaying his return to the barn and Sunny, who'd been acting aloof and distracted almost since the barbecue had begun yesterday, Cole shifted his direction towards the ranch house. He bounded up the steps two at a time, then hurried down the hallway to the door of the study.

"Dad?" he called out as he tapped against solid oak.

"Come on in, son," came the muffled reply.

Relieved to hear his father's voice, Cole stepped almost lazily into the room. "What kind of vote-gathering do you think you can do in here alone?" He laughed.

"Just taking a little rest and," Nathan held up a bottle of whiskey, "a snort. Join me in a short one?"

"Don't mind if I do." Cole kicked the door shut behind him and tossed his hat on a chair. Maybe a shot of whiskey was just what he needed to bring some order back to his bewildered brain. It suddenly seemed as if everyone he knew and loved had gone crazy as a steer on locoweed. Even his mother, bedridden a good deal of the time due to various female complaints, was acting old and excessively friendly. Elizabeth Scott, an unusually patient woman, seemed desperate for his attention, and left him with the impression she'd known how he felt about Sunny before he'd even hinted at it. And if that weren't enough, Eileen Hobbs, the shyest, most introverted girl he'd ever met, would giggle and fall all over him as if she were madly in love with him one minute, then act as if they'd never been introduced the next. Odd and unusual behavior for all of them.

But most puzzling and disconcerting, was Sunny. Every time he got near her she bolted, her eyes darting back and forth like a wild mare on the end of a rustler's lasso. Was it just the excitement of the party, the new people, and her new look? Or something else? Perhaps some strange little secret was shared among all four women? Hardly likely, he had to admit to himself. Tomorrow, after all the guests had gone home, he would find whatever caused this change in her, would sit her down, talk about it, then make some plans—for his future, her future, and maybe their future together.

"There you go, son." Nathan pushed the glass across the desk. "Here's to another successful spring barbecue."

"I'll drink to that." Cole tapped his drink against Nathan's, then downed the potent liquid in one gulp. He shook his head, and grinned. "Where've you been keeping this stuff?" He pushed his glass across the desk, observing as Nathan refilled it, then settled back in his chair.

"I was saving it for a special occasion—like your wedding, son." Nathan tossed his drink down, then banged the glass on the desk. "But I figured, what the hell—I can always buy another bottle if that day ever comes."

The Fremont men shared a hearty laugh, then Nathan leaned forward, his expression serious, his eyes slightly glazed. "I'm glad you stopped in, son. I been doin' a lot of thinking about you, the ranch, and the way you're dragging your feet about setting a date with Liz."

Cole's moment of relaxation was at an end. He straightened his spine and regarded his father. Nathan had been in the study longer than he'd first assumed, and had obviously finished the contents of another jug of whiskey before opening this "special" bottle. Making a note of his father's crimson cheeks, the flush spreading across his thick neck, Cole also determined his blood pressure was dangerously high for a man with his weakened heart.

"Come on, Dad," Cole suggested, getting to his feet. "Let's hit the hay. I'm bushed."

"Not so fast, son." Nathan bellowed his laughter and directed Cole to return to his seat. "You're not getting away from me till I'm done with you tonight! It's high time you played fair with George Scott's gal. Your ma and I are kinda looking forward to moving to town within the year—be a pure and simple change of residence once you and Liz take over the ranch. I hear she has a hankering to be a June bride."

Nathan wasn't going to be put off this night, that much was certain, but how much of the truth could his heart handle? Especially in his condition? Slowly, carefully, Cole tried to explain his position. "I don't know what Liz wants to do, and frankly, Dad, I don't care. I have no plans to marry her—now or ever."

"Ah, come on, son. You two make a perfect couple, and together," Nathan winked and smirked, "y'all would make perfect babies."

When his father's laughter subsided, Cole made a final effort to convince him otherwise. "I don't love Elizabeth. In fact, I didn't know what love was until I met Sunny. She—"

"That damn *squaw*? Is that what's holding you back?"

Cole watched the color flare in Nathan's cheeks, saw the embers flickering beneath the dry tinder of his beard. "Calm down, Dad. Remember your heart."

"*You* remember my heart!" Nathan boomed, slamming his fist onto the desk for emphasis. "You think real hard about it before you bring up such nonsense as loving a Goddamn injun, for Christ's sake!"

Cole's jaw tensed at his father's words, but he knew better than provoke him any further. The time would come, and soon, but for now he would have to find a way to get Nathan to go to bed. "I'm too tired to talk about this tonight. Let's turn in." Again he started to rise, but his father's voice shoved him back into the chair.

"We're gonna have this out now, boy." Nathan tossed another shot of whiskey down his throat, then pointed a thick finger at his son. "I got no argument about your wanting that little gal. Hell, if I was ten years younger and in better health, I might take a stab at her myself, but as it is—"

"That's enough!" Cole sprang out of his seat, his fists balled tightly in anger.

"Now, don't go getting you dander up, son. I only meant that I can understand your needs, what you're driving at."

"I doubt that you do. Goodnight, Dad."

"Hold on a minute!"

Only the flush of Nathan's skin and the strange gargled noise bubbling in his throat, kept Cole in the room. He would listen, he would have to listen, but he vowed to keep his silence—for now. Slowly turning to face his father, Cole shoved his hands in his jeans pockets and regarded him through cold, flat eyes. "What is it, Dad?"

"You're not thinking things through. son." Nathan wobbled to his feet, straining for balance. "What about your kids, *my* grandkids! You're the only hope your ma and I got to carry on our line. Think of that before you reject the idea of marrying Liz Scott."

Nodding, Cole conceded, "I'll be sure to think about it."

"Don't think you're outsmarting me, boy!" Nathan waved a wild arm harmlessly, then leaned heavily on one elbow.

"Dad, please. You've got—"

"Don't tell me what I gotta do—here's what *you* gotta do! Sleep with that dirty little injun if you have to, empty your loins in her savage body if you think that's what you gotta have, but hear me and hear me good!"

Nathan looked up from the desk, his eyes bloodshot from his exertions, his pupils swimming from the whiskey, and pleaded, "Marry Liz Scott. Keep this little injun gal on the side if you just can't turn her loose, but make your babies with your wife, son. Give me the pretty white grandkids I crave. You deserve that much. So do I."

Sunny leaned against the door jamb of the study and took several deep breaths. Suddenly off balance, sick to her stomach, the words echoed painfully in her mind: *Sleep with that dirty injun . . . keep her on the side . . . marry Liz Scott . . . give me pretty white grandkids.*

She'd been looking through the house for Cole, heard angry voices shouting from somewhere, and found herself standing in front of Nathan's study just a few moments ago. She hadn't planned to eavesdrop. She meant to turn away as soon as she recognized the voices. But then, she'd heard her own name—and the nasty accusations that followed had frozen her to the spot.

Cole? Sunny mouthed his name, waiting, wishing he would answer his father's outrageous demands and profess his undying love for her. But there was only silence. Cole's silence. Cole's concession.

She whirled around, moving on feet made of feathers, and ran blindly from the house. Once outside, Sunny caught her breath and made a dash for the barn, praying as she picked her way across the yard that Sean was inside. After pushing the heavy doors aside, Sunny waited for her eyes to adjust to the semi-darkness, then scrambled up the ladder to the loft.

"Sean?" she cried in a whisper. "Sean, please—are you up there?"

Hay rustled, then Sean stepped out of the shadows. "Sunny? Is that you?"

"Y-Yes," she gasped just as she launched her trembling body across the bedding straw and into his arms. "Oh, my brother, I have been such a fool!"

Her tears fell, splattering the checkered fabric of his shirt, and Sean stood quietly waiting for the storm to pass before he inquired, "What troubles you so, little one?"

"I-I—" But her sobs cut off her breath, made conversation impossible.

Sean dropped the gun he'd grabbed when the barn doors opened, and coaxed his sister to sit down in the straw. "Hush now. Relax and tell me what's happened."

Sunny leaned back, stared up at the ceiling, and took several gulps of air. More in control now, she sat up and murmured, "I do not belong here. Not for the two more weeks I had asked that you allow me, and not for any longer than this night. I wish to go home with you and Eileen."

"And you shall." Her pain cut into him as if it were his own. Sean draped a comforting arm across her shoulders. "Tell me, little one. What has happened to hurt you so?"

But the cruel statements and thoughtless words she'd heard wouldn't form in her own mouth. "I have discovered that you were right, that I have tried to become something I am not. I do not belong here and I know I must go. If I stay, I will only hurt the man I love and tear his family apart." Sunny glanced at her brother, her expression emotionless, shocked, and asked, "Did you make arrangements to meet Eileen?"

He longed to comfort her, to tell her how wrong he'd been, but such a move would only delay the inevitable. The kindest thing he could do was take her away and allow her the time to heal, because he knew she would never forget. "I will leave soon. I have a two-hour ride to the Hobbs ranch, then I told Eileen I'd meet her at a nearby creek. If you're ready to leave now, you can stay up here while I go collect Whiskey and Paddy from the pasture."

"No. I need more time."

"I don't have more time. Once Eileen leaves that house, she will be alone and defenseless. I have to be there for her. I promised I would be."

"I know, and I do not mean to add more danger to your plans, but I must have more time. I must say goodbye to Cole." *In my own way, in my own good time.* She straightened her shoulders and held her head high. "Is there some place I might meet you two?"

Sean thought of arguing, of convincing her to leave with him now, but knew it would do no good. She had to follow her heart—as he did. Shrugging, he plucked at the straw. "Do you know where the road from here forks just outside of Phoenix?" At her enthusiastic nod, he explained, "The road is thick with trees and shrubs, and has plenty of cover for you to hide in the darkness. If you leave two hours before dawn, you will have more than enough time to meet us."

"Yes, I know I can make it. I will be there."

"Sunny, I . . ." Sean hesitated, taking her hand in his before he could continue. "I have to make sure you understand the risk to both Eileen and myself if we wait for you. If you aren't at the fork by dawn, we'll have no choice but to move on without you."

"I do understand, my brother." And, also recognizing that he needed reassurance more than she did, she smiled and promised, "Do not worry about me. When dawn unveils her first ribbons of light, you will see the happy face of your sister and all of her tears will have been shed."

Grateful for her insight, her willingness to put her own hurt aside and free him to go to Eileen, Sean leaned forward and kissed her cheek. "This Cole Fremont is the foolish one, not you, little one."

The corners of her mouth lifted in a half-smile. "I intend to make sure he knows that, too, before I leave this ranch."

With a hoarse chuckle, Sean unfolded his legs and stood up. "It's time I got moving. What will you carry as a weapon?"

"Those I brought with me. Pop's hunting knife is with Mike's clothes in my bedroom, but Grandfather's war club is in Nathan Fremont's study. I will have to sneak in there and get it."

Sean disappeared into the shadows and collected his belongings, then returned and searched through the hay for his discarded pistol. "What about a gun? Maybe I should leave this with you."

Sunny glanced at the pistol he offered, then gasped as the terrible memories flooded her; her near assault on Cole, the vicious stranger and his unholy plans for her, and the subsequent murder of the disgusting man by her own hand. She violently shook her head. "I have no use for a gun. Please take it with you."

"You're sure?"

"I am positive."

Bending down, Sean stroked Sunny's brow. "I'll see you at dawn. Take care."

She blew him a kiss, and whispered to his retreating figure, "You too, my brother. May the seven saints of Ireland protect and guide you."

Sean had to swallow a chuckle at her final words as he backed down the ladder and realized she had offered the same blessing Patrick had bestowed on him as he had left Yuma. That had only been a few weeks ago, and yet it somehow seemed much longer—years longer, at times. How many more days, or weeks, before the Callahan family was finally united again, finally able to grieve together over the loss of their loved ones?

When Sean reached the main part of the barn, he flattened himself against the wall and listened. All was quiet. With the exception of a few inviting aromas lingering from the roast pig and beef, most signs of the party had been removed. Making his way to the doors, he pushed them open a crack and peered out. He must leave the ranch undetected, without suspicion. The longer his disappearance went unnoticed, the longer it would be before anyone thought to connect it to Eileen's departure from her father's home.

From his vantage point, he could see the last of the guests had pulled out of the yard, and could hear the rumble of wagon wheels creaking down the path in the opposite direction he was headed. Looking up toward the house, he noticed most of the lights were blazing as the occupants prepared for their well-deserved rest. Satisfied the grounds were deserted, Sean slipped out of the barn and took full advantage of his Quechan blood to help him move silently out to the pasture where Whiskey stood grazing in the darkness.

After saddling the mule and fastening his belongings with a length of rawhide, Sean quietly led the animals out of the corral and through a wind-break of palo verde trees. Once hidden behind this stand of trees, he mounted Whiskey and rode to the north.

He arrived at the creek near the Hobbs ranch less than two hours later. After tying the mule, then resting by the water for an additional forty-five minutes, Sean grew impatient and worried. He crept panther-like through the cactus and shrubs until he came to the base of a thick, gnarled willow tree. Hidden from the home's occupants,

Sean was able to squat down and observe the house, and hopefully Eileen's expected departure from it.

Only one small light flickered in the window, suggesting that most of the family had retired for the night. Who was still up, and why?

The answer to that question exploded through the front door a few minutes later with a scream that shattered spring's promise of tranquility. The figure was Eileen, and she ran on a reckless path toward the willow tree.

Sean tucked his long body into a crouch and braced himself to spring to her aid. He lunged, one hand sliding across her mouth and the other around her waist as she raced blindly past him.

"Eileen, be quiet—it's Sean!" he urged in a frantic whisper as he gathered her close. When her struggles ceased, he pulled her around behind the tree and pushed her to the ground.

"Easy, honey. It's all right," he comforted as he slowly lifted his hand from her trembling lips. "You're safe now."

"Oh," she cried into his chest, "th-thank God you w-were here. I don't think I could have made it to the creek."

"Hush now. Don't think about what's happened. We have to get out of here before they come after you. Can—" Sean's words snagged in his throat when he realized his hand was wet and sticky with her blood. "You're hurt! Where are you bleeding?"

"It's all right." Eileen brought her fingers to her swollen lip and pressed them against the torn flesh. "Pa didn't think I tried hard enough to get Cole's attention at the party. He said I was worthless and probably already spoilt, too. When he came after me, asking shameful questions and pounding me with his fists, I just couldn't take no more. After he popped me one in the mouth, I busted his head with Ma's frying pan. Oh, Sean," Eileen cried in a soft whimper, "what if I killed him?"

"Hush, hush," he crooned, swallowing his anger—for

now. "I'll never let them find you. Don't worry, honey. Don't worry." Sean began to rock her, but tensed and froze his movements as he caught sight of a shadowy figure creeping through the trees. He was just about to release her and caution her to stay down, when the figure called out Eileen's name in a soft, feminine voice.

"Eileen, baby, where are you?"

"That's Ma," Eileen whispered against his ear. Her mother called again, this time with a note of panic in her voice. "I got to answer her, Sean. She won't tell on me."

But he wasn't so sure. "What if what you said is true and your pa is dead?"

"Who would she tell it to out here?"

Shrugging, Sean reluctantly gestured for her to go ahead.

When her mother had moved close enough for Eileen to be certain she was alone, she whispered, "Ma! Over here."

"Baby? Is that you? Where are ya?"

"Quiet, Ma. I'm over here."

Martha took a few more steps, ducked under a tree limb, and nearly stumbled over her.

"Quick, sit down, Ma!"

Hidden from view by the base of the huge tree, but only inches from Eileen, Sean listened as she questioned her mother.

"How's Pa? Is he hurt bad? I didn't kill him, did I?"

"No, child, he ain't dead, but when he comes to, I bet he's gonna wish he was. You raised some kinda mountain on the side of his thick head."

"I'm sorry, Ma, but I just couldn't take it no more, I—"

"I know, baby, I know. That's why I come out here. I think you'd best leave. No telling what he'll do when he wakes up and's feeling better. You'd best go."

Which is exactly what she planned to do, but why did the idea hurt so much coming from her own mother? "What have I done wrong, Ma?" Eileen cried in a strangled whisper. *"Why do I have to go?"*

"Cause he's gonna be in a heap of misery when that head starts to thumping; cause when he's able, I believe he plans to find out if you been ruint by one a these farm boys." Her shoulders and spirits sagged as she added in a desperate sigh, "Cause I believe one day soon he figures on liftin' your skirts and findin' out for himself, baby."

"Ma?" The word, the thought nearly strangled her. "How could he, how can he be so mean to me, his only girl?"

Martha's head drooped lower.

"Ma? Please, tell me—why does Pa hate me so?"

Her mother's head drooped lower still, but this time she muttered a barely audible answer. " 'Cause a something I should a told you a long time ago, baby. Something your Pa and I thought he could handle, but I was wrong. *He* was wrong."

"What?" Then louder, almost frantically, Eileen cried, *"What?"*

"Honey." Martha finally raised her head and cupped her daughter's distraught face between her hands. "Dan'l Hobbs ain't your pa."

Eileen's eyebrows sprang upward and disappeared beneath her wispy bangs as she blurted out, *"What?"*

"I know it's a shock, but I thought it best you didn't know till now, and your pa—Dan'l," she corrected, "was so good to me, made an honorable woman of me you might say when he knew the trouble I was in, I—I—"

A burst of nearly hysterical laughter obliterated the rest of Martha's sentence, and it took a minute before Eileen realized it came from her. She had the oddest sensations swirling inside her; relief, anger, happiness, surprise, and even joy. But where was the sadness, the sense of loss and humiliation she ought to have upon learning she was illegitimate?

"Eileen? Honey? Please don't be angry with me. I done

the best I could to raise you, to keep you out of Dan'l's way and not let him get too upset with you."

Eileen's laughter subsided, and she looked into her mother's tired eyes. Seeing Martha as a woman for the first time in her life, she kept her voice soft and low, non-judgmental, and said, "It's all right, Ma. It explains a lot, makes me feel better about myself in a strange sort of way. I do have a question, though. Would you please tell me who my pa is?"

Again dropping her gaze to the ground, Martha lifted her bony shoulders and began to fidget with the hem of her dress as if she were a shy school girl. "He was a mighty fancy man," she finally said in a tiny, bashful voice. "Name was Scotty. He come from Tombstone."

"Just Scotty?"

Martha nodded. "I guess so. Never knew if that was his first or last name, or if he were called that because he come over from Scotland. Everyone just called him Scotty." She raised her hand and lifted a length of Eileen's hair. "His hair was even redder than yours, and his eyes were the color of the prettiest blue sky you'd ever want to see."

A lump swelled in Eileen's throat while she watched her mother's features soften and brighten as she drifted in a sea of memories. But time was short, so she cut into her thoughts. "What happened to him, Ma?"

"Huh?" Martha looked startled as reality dissolved her pleasure. "Oh, um, I don't know. He was a gambling man. Moved on to the next town, the next girl, I s'pose."

Although she hated to see pain intrude on her mother's pleasant thoughts, Eileen had to know one more thing before she could leave. "Did you tell him, ah, did he know about . . . me?"

Martha shook her head slowly. "No, girl. By the time I knew about you, he was already gone. But it was just as well," she added in a jovial tone. "Scotty weren't the marryin' kind, that's for sure. Tying him down would a kilt him for sure. I'm just glad I knew him—and that he gave me you."

Eileen threw her arms around her mother's neck and kissed her. "I'm gonna miss you, Ma. I'm gonna miss you a lot."

"Me too," the older woman sobbed. "Me too, but you gotta get out of here. The sooner, the better. It's for your own good, baby."

"I know." Eileen sat back on her heels and dabbed at her nose. "I'm leaving tonight. Right now, in fact."

"But, honey! How can you? Who'll—"

"I got a way and a guide. Don't worry about me. I'll wire you or something to let you know I'm all right. Maybe someday I can come back and see you again."

"Oh, baby," Martha wailed. "None a this is fair to you. You deserve so much more—"

"And I'll find it, Ma. Don't worry."

Martha sniffed as she considered her daughter's words, then shrugged and slowly climbed to her feet. "You best be on your way, then. Who's meetin' you and where?"

"It'll be better for you if you don't know. That way Pa can't beat it out of you if he takes it in his head to chase me down."

"Dan'l ain't never laid a finger on me in anger, you know that, and I ain't about to let him start on me now. Your brothers wouldn't sit still for it, either." Pulling her daughter to her feet, Martha looked into her eyes, pleading, "I got to know, Eileen. Who's helpin' you?"

"I am." Sean stepped out of the shadows, prepared for an adverse reaction.

Martha jumped and gasped in surprise, then strained her eyes in the semi-darkness. "You give me quite a scare! You that half-breed what saved my girl's life in the flood?"

"Yes, Ma," Eileen provided. "It's Sean Callahan from Yuma."

Sean waited for the expected arguments and scolding from the older woman, but she surprised him.

"Then I best thank you for savin' her life again. I believe that's what you'll be doing for her if you take her away from here, and I want you to know how grateful I am. Please be careful tho, and take good care of my baby."

Extending his hands with a warm smile, Sean grasped Martha's wrinkled fingers, and vowed, "Thank you for your encouragement and understanding. Don't worry about Eileen. I intend to guard her with my life."

But when he said the words, he didn't know that was exactly what he would have to do.

THIRTEEN

Cole punched his fist into the pillow, then drove his head into the resulting crater. Sleep eluded him, ducking into hidden tunnels like mice scurrying from the sharp eyes of a bird of prey.

That's exactly the way he felt, as if he possessed the beady, unblinking eyes of a hawk. He'd been staring up at the moonlit ceiling of his bedroom for what seemed like hours on end, his mind cluttered with chaotic thoughts. Staring hard, his brain mired in intense speculation, seeing nothing.

Now the trance was broken, and Cole seethed with frustration. He tried again and again to force sleep the way he could force a young calf to the ground for branding, but this night he was badly outweighed. With a heavy groan, he rolled over to his side and once again gave into his thoughts.

He would have to deal with his father in the morning. He would start slowly, not giving his father a chance to become upset, or to use his bad heart as a way of getting his own way or controlling the conversation. He would explain his plans for the future and make certain Nathan understood those plans did not include running the Triple F ranch. If his father was still with him, hadn't turned purple with rage or short of precious breath, he would continue on and explain about the herd he intended to raise on his own ranch. Nathan might even be impressed by the huge profits forecast for the unusual operation.

Surely the elder Fremont had seen the direction cattle ranching was turning in Arizona. Drought, overgrazing of what little grass grew, and the steady influx of settlers cutting off available land were obstacles enough. But the very lifeline of the Fremont ranch, the Army posts and their steady demands for beef, were dwindling to almost nothing now that most of the hostile Indians had been subdued. If the Fremonts were fortunate enough to feed and water a good-sized herd indefinitely, who would purchase their product? Even the excellent contacts he'd made in Yuma couldn't insure a lucrative future shipping beef to San Diego and the surrounding missions.

Nathan would understand, Cole assured himself. It wasn't as if the Triple F had some great family history behind it, or had been passed down from generation to generation. Only the land they left behind in Texas might have qualified for that honor, but Nathan had picked up, sold the property, and brought his family to the Verde Valley in 1865 to establish his own dynasty. How could he possibly oppose Cole's starting out on his own with the same objective?

Nathan would understand. And when he did, he'd realize he could sell the ranch for a tidy profit or turn it over to Buck and Nellie. In either case, he and Olive would be free to move to town, where she would be closer to the doctor and her women friends, and he could further his political career. Once he accepted the fact the Fremont ranch would no longer operate under the Triple F brand, getting Nathan to see the wisdom in his choice—raising ostriches and selling their byproducts for lucrative profits—would be no problem. No problem at all.

Smothering an incredulous laugh into his pillow, Cole rolled over onto his right side. He slammed his eyelids shut and willed sleep to overtake him, but then his thoughts returned to a far more serious problem. Sunflower Callahan.

How could he make his peace with her? In what capacity and for how long? That he loved her was not an issue. Cole couldn't stifle or hide what he felt for the doe-skinned maiden with the midnight blue eyes, even if he wanted to. He loved her like he had never dreamt was possible, with every aching bone in his body, and as thoroughly as he sensed it was possible for him to love anyone. But where would this love lead him—where *could* it lead him?

If she were a white woman, he wouldn't even have to ask himself the question. He would be spending this night in the same way—sleepless—but his mind would be churning with thoughts of picking out the perfect ring, conjuring up the ideal spot to propose, and making plans for the endless round of engagement parties they would attend in their honor. But Cole Fremont hadn't fallen in love with just any woman, an ordinary white woman like Elizabeth Scott whom his family and friends would welcome with open arms. He'd fallen in love with Sunny, a half-breed, a woman considered much less than his equal by his peers.

What if he said the hell with them all, abandoned his family and friends without so much as a backward look, and made Sunny his wife? He supposed he could live with that decision, but could she? Would it be fair to subject the woman he loved to a life of scorn, of possible ridicule? And what of their future children? How would they be looked on by this perfect society—as Fremonts, or lowly half-breeds? The rejection of his own children was something Cole could not bear to think about.

His fists doubled up as he thought back to Sunny, of the possibilities and the humiliation she might suffer because of his love. Cole could not bear to think of that, either. He prepared to do battle with his pillow again and demand his mind let him sleep, but he tensed instead as he heard the click of his doorknob turning. An inebriated or lost party guest, or someone with an ax to grind? Whoever it was, they moved with stealth and had already entered his room.

His mind raced to the bed table and his Colt .44.

Did he have time to reach for the weapon? Or would the silent intruder attack the minute he heard any movement? Straining his ears, Cole picked out the faint rustle of fabric scraping against skin just as he prepared to launch himself towards his weapon.

"Cole?"

He recognized Sunny's voice in mid-launch. Twisting away from the table, towards the sound, Cole's body reacted awkwardly to the change of direction as his mind sent conflicting messages to his limbs.

He fell out of bed and onto the floor with a tremendous thud.

Her voice louder but still hushed, Sunny cried, "Oh, Cole!" She picked out his form, bathed an eerie silver-white in the moonlight, then rushed to his side. "Are you hurt?"

"No," he grumbled as he worked his way to his feet. "I landed on my head. I'm just fine."

Suppressing a giggle, she apologized. "I am sorry if I startled you, but I was afraid someone besides you would hear if I knocked."

He rubbed at the small bump on the side of his head, then waved her off. "Don't worry about it. What's so important that the proper young lady who insisted she couldn't step one foot in my room while under my father's roof, has made a liar out of herself and done that very thing?"

"I—I wanted to talk to you, I . . ." But the words dissolved, disappeared with her well-planned speech now that she was face-to-face with him. She'd been certain the anger she still carried over Nathan's conversation—and Cole's lack of the same—would make this parting bearable, something she could do without a display of emotion. But now . . .

Maybe if they weren't so close she could think better. Sunny took a couple of backward steps and opened her mouth to say what she had to say. Then she noticed what the moonlight had been trying to tell her at first glance. Cole was completely naked. "Oh!" she gasped.

Following the line of her vision in the dim light, Cole chuckled under his breath. "If I'd known you were stopping by, I'd have dressed for the occasion. As it is . . ." He left the sentence unfinished and spread his arms wide.

"Of course, I should have realized you . . . you know, that . . ." Sunny tripped over her tongue, frustrated and annoyed with herself for not even considering the state in which she might find him. He was in his bedroom, *in bed*, for heaven's sake. How was she going to be able to keep her distance and say goodbye with him standing there, beckoning her, in all his naked glory.

"Come here, Sunny."

That voice, soft and low, deep and seductive, beckoned her with promises she knew he could fulfill. Had she really thought she could make this parting quick and painless, detached but friendly?

Sunny took another backward step. "C-Cole, I should return to my—"

"You just got here, sunshine. What did you want? Why did you come in here?"

His voice remained on the same provocative tone, befuddling her even further. "I—I do not remember."

"Come here, sweetheart."

No perched on the tip of her tongue like a rattlesnake ready to strike. But could she sink her fangs into his heart, allow the poison to spread, hurt him the way she was hurting? Was that what she *really* wanted? She lifted her chin and stared into his sparkling eyes, and found her answer. The answer was no. But it was to her own question, not his. Sunny crossed the room.

"I was cold," she lied, mere inches from his mouth. "I hoped you might be able to warm me."

A little voice in the recesses of his mind told him she hadn't told the truth, that something much more serious than cold feet had sent her to his room. But then he caught her scent, saw the naked longing in her expression and he was lost.

"You've come to the right place, ma'am." Cole took her hand and pressed it against the proof of his desire, and said through a groan, "I've a fire that'll warm you from head to toe all night long."

Sunny's breath caught in her throat as the first wave of desire rippled throughout her, swelled her with longing. Tonight would be like no other. Nothing before, and nothing after, would ever be as special, as wonderful. This she knew in her heart.

She would say goodbye to Cole this evening as planned, but her farewell would be a little different. It would be accomplished with her body, her soul. Words were unnecessary; they would only complicate something she couldn't fully understand anyway. He would know how much she loved him, understand that love had sent her away, and they would forgive one another without a single word passing between them.

Convinced of her course, overwhelmed with sensations, Sunny reached for the ribbon at the throat of her wrapper and gave it a tug. The gown fell open, revealing a lace-trimmed cotton nightgown. "See how the thin fabric chills my skin?" Sunny said, arching her back.

All Cole could see were dusky rose nipples hardened by desire, not the cold, straining against the bodice of the nightgown. A low growl passed, unbidden, through his throat as his hands went to her breasts. "This could be a real problem," he breathed, playing along. "We should get you out of this inferior gown immediately before you catch your death."

With a lusty chuckle, Sunny leaned her head back and squeezed her shoulders together as Cole slipped the straps down her arms, then coaxed the nightgown over her rounded hips. When she was nude, she slid her hands behind her neck and flipped the bulk of her long raven hair over her shoulders and across her breasts.

Although he ached to touch her, to hold her, Cole didn't move at first—found he *couldn't* move. Sunny had been ravishing, a real beauty at the dance last night in her royal blue ball gown and elaborate hair arrangement. But that woman, no matter how stylish or sophisticated she might be, couldn't do justice to the Sunflower who stood before him now. She was every man's dream, the very essence of womanhood. Moonlight caressed her creamy skin, highlighted the tips of her breasts peeking out through strands of raven-black hair, and drew his gaze to her hard, flat tummy and the dark thatch of hair below.

Impatient, he dragged her into his arms and returned the impish grin she'd been giving him during his preoccupation with her charms. "What's so funny, sunshine?"

"Your face." Sunny laughed against his chest, suddenly happier, she knew, than she'd ever be again. "I have seen that look somewhere before, but I cannot remember which of the desert animals wore that same expression."

"Animal?" he said under his breath as he lifted her in his arms. "I'll show you what kind of animal you've got, little flower."

Keeping her firmly in his arms, Cole launched himself into the center of his bed and waited for the mattress spring's rebellion to subside before he went on. "I'm every animal you've ever seen gathered around the last water hole of summer. And you, my lovely maiden, are the last drop of life-giving moisture." He kissed the tip of one breast, swirling his tongue slowly until the nipple was hard and erect, then went on. "I intend to drink my fill of you." He spread wet kisses between her breasts on a journey to the other nipple where he lingered before adding, "And when I think I can't take any more, I'll return and indulge myself until I'm so bloated with your love, I can't move." Cole looked up from her rib cage and grinned, his green eyes sparkling with pleasure.

Her throat tight, aching with her love for him, Sunny could only manage a low, guttural, "Y-Yes, th-that is the animal I saw in your eyes."

She wanted to say more, tell him how she really felt, but the moment she tried to speak again, Cole's mouth resumed its journey. This time, his moist lips and fiery tongue spiraled down on a path to her navel and below. Her breath whooshed out as a sudden rush of intense pleasure assaulted her, and she gripped the bed sheets, both terrified and fascinated by what was happening.

Sunny writhed beneath him, and her long swimmer's legs tensed and locked around his back as he probed at her center. The taste of her passion filled him, swelled him with a love and desire he'd never before known. He was drowning in her, closer to her than he could have imagined possible, and when she shuddered against him, calling out his name in a strangled cry, he thought he'd go mad from the need to be inside her.

Sliding her fingers into Cole's damp curls, she urged him to her breasts, then to her mouth. Out of breath, unable to speak, she communicated with her body—spreading her legs and guiding him into her, to fulfillment. There would never be another moment like this, another love to compare. She would make this a night to remember for them both, for all time.

When their passion finally ebbed, when they lay entwined, their bodies sleek with perspiration, their breathing ragged and slowing, Sunny was overwhelmed with the sudden urge to laugh and cry all at the same time. She tried

to speak, to make light of the insane sensations, but a sob
tore from her throat instead.

"Sunny?" Cole murmured softly. "Are you crying?"

Still unable to speak, she shook her head and sobbed.

Cole's fingertip found the proof of her lie pooled in the
corner of her eye. "Why are you crying, sunshine? Did I
hurt you in some way?"

"No," she gasped, struggling for an explanation. But
still, the words would not come.

"Then what, sweetheart?" Cole lifted his head and stared
down at her features. Instead of the expected look of
rapture, he saw pain and torment. "What is it, Sunny?
You've got to tell me what's bothering you."

Unable to stop them, tears splashed down her cheeks and
onto the sheets. When the onslaught finally spent itself,
she answered him in the only way she could. "I-It is
n-nothing," she said through her sobs, "it is just that I am
so h-happy. Th-That I love you so very much."

"Oh, Sunny," he said with a soft groan, "and I—"

"No, please, don't talk. Don't say anything." To make
sure he didn't utter the words she couldn't bear to hear,
Sunny pressed her lips to his, then drove her tongue into his
mouth with a renewed burst of passion. If he were to
remember this night forever, she would have to make sure
it was unlike any other. She would stay a little longer and
use some more of her precious time. Sunny pulled back
from him and wiped the tears from her cheeks.

"Roll over, my handsome man. I wish to touch you." At
his look of surprise, she sat back on her heels. "I have a
curiosity about the way our bodies fit, something I would
like to try."

Cole laughed and raised up on one elbow. "Just what do
you have in mind?"

Her fingers playful, gentle, Sunny reached forward and
pushed him down on his back. "I learned to ride a pony in
the Quechan way, without bridles or reins, using only my

knees and thighs as guides. I have wondered these past days if this talent might be of benefit to you."

Now it was Cole who had difficulty speaking. With a hoarse laugh and a low groan, he said, "I wouldn't dream of standing between you and your curiosity. Help yourself, you little heathen."

Sunny threw her head back, risking discovery, and cut loose with a lusty chuckle before she set about her task. Showing no signs of inhibition or coyness, she caressed every inch of his body, kissed each damp inch of his skin with near reverence. And when he was ready again, when she knew he ached as much as she did, she finally straddled his fevered body and brought his agony to an end. This time as fulfillment rocked them, it was Cole who cried out, Cole who proclaimed his undying love for her.

Later, when he dropped into a deep sleep as they rested in each other's arms, Sunny quietly slipped from his bed. She dressed, then stood next to the bed, taking a moment for one last look at the only man she would ever love. She could deal with his words of love as long as she thought of them as careless, unimportant mutterings tossed about in the heat of passion. That was the only way she could deal with them.

Unable to resist the urge to touch him, Sunny brushed an errant wave of cornsilk-colored hair off his brow. His handsome face reflected happiness and satisfaction, leaving her with a mental picture she would always cherish. Sunny mouthed a silent, "I love you." Then she closed her eyes—and heart—and stole from his room.

Once back in the bedroom Nellie had provided for her, Sunny moved quickly and silently. She stripped off the bedclothes she wore, and dressed in Mike's trousers and shirt, which she'd hastily repaired only a few hours ago. Dropping to her hands and knees, Sunny reached under the bed and retrieved Mike's hat, boots, and the knapsack filled with leftover party fare for her trip home. Satisfied she hadn't forgotten anything, she crept from her room and tiptoed down the hallway to Nathan's study. The door was ajar, but no light shone through the crack.

What if he were still in the room—asleep in his chair, or worse yet, awake and staring into the darkness? A tremor ran down her spine. Was Grandfather's war club worth the risk? Without it, the only protection she would have was her father's hunting knife—assuming it was still in her saddle-bag in the barn. She really had no other choice but to go inside.

Listening at the door until she thought her eardrum would burst from the strain, Sunny satisfied herself that the room was empty and she pushed the door open. Moonlight bathed the study, showing her instantly that it was unoccupied. Letting her breath out in a long sigh, Sunny quickly discovered the club on a shelf behind Nathan's desk. She grabbed it just as a sudden feeling of panic washed over her.

Desperate to get out of the study, the house, Sunny stuck the *kelyaxwai* in the waistband of her trousers, deciding to wrap it in cloth after she was safely in the barn. Cautious and silent, she made her way through the house and out the front door. Concerned about the wooden porch announcing her departure, she took extra measures crossing it, but once down the steps she silently sprinted across the distance between the house and barn. In her haste, she never noticed a pair of yellowish-brown eyes in the corner of the porch, or that they followed her progress.

Sunny stood for a full minute near the first stall after entering the barn, listening for any kind of sound that might signal another occupant. She heard only silence and the occasional snort of a resting horse. Her eyes quickly adjusted to the semi-darkness as moonlight filtered in through open windows and ventilation slits. Her tension easing, she crossed the center aisle and headed toward the tack room and her saddle.

When Sunny reached the doorway, the rich scent of a

room filled with leather goods caught her attention. At almost the same moment, she heard the creak of the big double doors. Had she left them ajar?

Whirling around, she spotted a wide beam of moonlight where there should have been a sliver. The breeze was gentle, feeble. Was it capable of pushing the door open? She stood silent and observant for a few minutes.

When all seemed normal, she shrugged, muttering to herself, and turned back towards the tack room. "You are letting your nerves rule your actions. If you do not get hold of yourself and use your head, you will never make a safe journey home." With a sudden grin, she imitated her father's voice and added, " 'Tis a fool's errand ye'll run if ye don't, lassie!"

Buoyed by her own words of encouragement, Sunny took a step into the tack room. The double doors groaned again.

Spinning around, she noticed there was now no stream of moonlight at all. Sunny dropped into a crouch. The breeze may have nudged the doors open, but it couldn't have closed them as well. She was no longer alone.

Who had followed her? Cole?

"Is someone there?" she called out in a feeble voice.

The reply was the shuffle of heavy footsteps against the dirt floor. They were coming in her direction.

"Please, is someone there? Who are you?"

Still no answer. The footsteps grew louder, closer.

"Cole," she warned as she inched to her full height, "if that is you, please say so. I do not think this is funny. Cole?"

Silence.

Then, suddenly, a shadowy figure stepped from the shadows.

Sunny's breath exploded in her throat. She clapped her hand against her mouth to keep from crying out. Then, her voice wobbly, she made a final plea. "Who *are* you?"

The form began a slow staggering shuffle up the center of

the barn to where Sunny stood. There was still no response.

The man's shadow loomed above her, reaching almost to the high ceiling of the barn. Sunny shuddered. This wasn't Cole. The physique was too thick, too bulky. This was a very big man. And from what she could tell, a very drunk man, at that.

Finally, the silent figure stumbled into a patch of moonlight. The shroud of darkness fell, revealing his identity.

"Bucky?" she squeaked, incredulous. "Is that you?"

Buck snorted a short laugh. "That's a question I oughta be askin' you." He took a long swallow from the whiskey bottle he cradled, then advanced a couple of steps.

"Strangest thing just happened," he mumbled. "I'm just a sittin' on the porch swing, mindin' my own business, when this boy—*boy*, I tell ya—sneaks outta the house!"

Sunny had no idea how long she'd been holding her breath. She emptied her lungs in a long sigh of relief. "Oh, Bucky. You frightened me half out of my wits. Why didn't you answer me when I called out?"

"Don't be interruptin' me!"

The eyes she'd first thought of as muddy brown sprinkled with golden highlights, turned almost yellow as he scowled drunkenly. Sensing she was not entirely out of danger, Sunny took a backward step. Buck moved up beside her and leaned against the tack room wall.

"As I was saying," he slurred, "I thinks to myself: whar do you suppose that *boy* come from?" He laughed out loud, a deep and bawdy roar from his gut, then went on. "That's about the time I notice the fine li'l ass on that boy, them big juicy tits poking through—"

"Look, Buck—" Sunny cut him off, prepared to add a few indignant thoughts, but kept her silence instead. He would never talk to her like that if he weren't so drunk. Could she risk taking the time, or the chance of discovery, by handing him a lecture?

She'd said goodbye to Cole once this evening. She

couldn't do it again. "I will just forget you said those things, Bucky." Winding her hair in a ball, she began to stuff it inside Mike's hat. "I have to be going now," she said, pointing an authoritative finger at his chest. "And you really ought to get back to the ranch. I imagine Nellie is wondering where you are."

Buck tore the hat from her head and grabbed a fistful of her loose hair. "As I was *sayin'* b'fore I was so rudely interrupted," he growled, pulling the strands tighter. "After I had a good look at the body in them boy's clothes, I seen all this fine long hair swinging down that whelp's back." He gave the wad of hair a jerk, drawing a yelp from her.

Satisfied by her response, he grinned and went on. "So I says to myself, that looks a lot like Cole's injun whore. Yep, I b'lieve that's just who it might be."

Anger and fear commanded an equal measure in Sunny's mind. But anger would cloud her judgment, and might force her into actions that would work to her disadvantage. Something besides liquor ruled Buck's mouth and mind. For her own safety, if nothing else, she had to find out what it was. Sunny pushed her bruised feelings aside.

"Well, my little trick did not work," she said as brightly as she could manage. "I should have known I could not fool a smart man like yourself."

Her answer baffled him at first. He dropped the length of her hair and leaned back, his eyes narrowing, then widening. Finally he grunted, "Humph. Course not. I know'd it was you all the time." He cocked his head to the side, never taking his yellowish eyes off her as he took another swallow of whiskey, then asked, "So why are you dressed in them duds anyway?"

Confident she'd gained an advantage over him, she searched for the right words to end the conversation. Now more than ever, she was anxious to be on her way.

"These are my traveling clothes. I am leaving now,

returning to my home." She turned, dismissing him. "If you will excuse me, I must—"

"You must? *You must?*" he bellowed. "I'll be tellin' you what you must and must not do, squaw! Hear me?"

He'd moved close enough for the odor of stale whiskey to nearly knock her off balance. Struggling for control, assuming that if she were to show Buck any sign of fear she would only agitate him further, Sunny forced herself to stand her ground.

"Sorry, Buck. I meant no disrespect."

"Yeah, of course not. That's better." Pleased with himself, he took another swig of whiskey. "So answer me—why are you dressed up like that?"

"I told you. These are my trail clothes. I have to be leaving."

"For good?"

Sunny nodded, then tried to turn back to the tack room, but Buck caught her by the shoulder and spun her back around.

"I ain't told you you could go yet." He jerked her closer, grabbing another length of her hair. "Cole done with you—that it, squaw?"

Sunny hesitated, not certain which answer would give her the most protection. If she said no, Buck would probably back off, but he might also alert Cole to her plans. If she said yes, what would he do? Let her go or try to sample her himself? She measured her chances against the drunken man. Then she thought of explaining all this to Cole, of trying to say goodbye again.

She had but one choice. "If you must know, Cole has asked me to leave. If that is all," she put her hand on his, hoping to get him to release her hair, "I would really like to be on my way now."

Instead of releasing her, Buck pulled her closer and tossed the bottle of whiskey into the straw. "I figured

Fremont'd throw you out on your ear one day," he leered, "but I didn't think it'd be so soon."

Sunny leaned her head back so far her neck ached. Still he pulled her closer. Buck's smile grew huge and goatish as he stared down at her, licking his thick, filmy lips. His eyes were glazed, glowing as if they were illuminated by the devil himself. She had to think of something, and fast.

"Buck," she began, her voice small and timid. "Please let me go. You are hurting me. I think I shall faint."

Sluggish laughter boomed out of him. When it subsided, he released her hair, but seized her bottom with his huge hands. Banging her slender hips roughly against his body, he growled, "Go ahead and faint if you want to. Don't matter much to me, but think a all the fun you'll be missin'."

Then he fell on her tender, unprepared mouth, bruising her, hurting her with his thick, chapped lips. He used his tongue like a battering ram, but Sunny's teeth didn't budge, wouldn't open for him.

Finally, just as she thought she really might faint from lack of oxygen, from the pungent, unnamed odors fermenting in his hot breath, Buck grew tired of his unsuccessful assault on her mouth. He abruptly released her, then pushed her away with a harsh shove.

"Git on over to that empty stall, injun whore. I got a little farewell present for you." Reaching for his belt buckle, he began to stagger toward her.

Rage swelled up inside her. How could he treat her this way? Drunk or not, this, from a member of the Fremont family, was unthinkable, inexcusable. Sunny straightened her shoulders and glared across the few feet separating them.

"How dare you talk to me this way! You are acting like a disgusting pig, and I will see you pay for your vile behavior. Now," she spat with a toss of her head, "get out of my way."

Buck tottered, rocked on his heels, and stared at her through wide, little boy eyes. Then the wicked gleam returned and he opened his mouth to release an ugly laugh. "You know, for a minute, the way you was talking almost made me feel like I was hearing a white woman. Can you beat that?" He laughed again. "A white woman!"

His expression narrow, he took a step forward. "I guess for a minute we *both* forgot just who and what you are."

Sunny retreated, her outrage replaced by fear. She would have to change her tactics. "Buck, please listen to me." Keeping her voice low, soft, she implored, "You have had too much to drink. Just let me go on my way and we can forget this happened. I know you do not mean to act this way. Think of Nellie, of—"

"Shut up, woman!"

Buck jerked the belt from his trousers. Wrapping the length of leather around his fist, he advanced on her. "Do's your told and everything'll be just fine. Now git in that stall!"

Reasoning with the man and his whiskey was not going to work. Sunny reverted to instinct, employing her survival instincts as a guide. "Get out of my way, Buck. I mean it, or I will scream and wake the whole ranch."

"No one'll hear you out here. But go head, try it," he dared, cracking the belt like a whip, "and you'll be real sorry." His laugh cruel, he added, "Not to mention, real dead."

Alarm raised the hair at her scalp. Would he go that far? Was he that drunk?

"Think, Buck," she pleaded. "I am nothing—a miserable half-breed. What do you want with me when you have a beautiful wife like Nellie to warm your bed."

"Leave Nellie outta this!" he spat, lurching towards her. "This got nothin' to do with Nell anyway. Got to do with you, injun."

"Me? What have I ever done to you?"

"Nothing—yet." He laughed. "I don't know why, but I've always had this hankering for squaw meat. Nothing sweeter than tangling with a red-skinned savage. Nothing at all."

Tired of banter, Buck took a forward step. If he took another, she'd be trapped. She had to try something different—anything. Escape?

Using her rigid arm as a barrier between them, she tried to brush past him. But he was ready for her. Buck grabbed her wrist and twisted, then bent her elbow around behind her.

"Buck," she cried, "you're hurting me—you really are!"

Ignoring her cries, he held her in this position with one hand as he wrapped the other around her neck. "If you insist on being difficult, I got no choice but to quiet you down real good. Understand?"

His fetid breath gagged her, making it impossible for her to speak. Before she could make any kind of movement, he squeezed her throat and threatened, "I could snap your neck like it was a li'l ole twig. *Now* do you understand?"

Sunny squeaked out a breathless, "Yes." She forced herself to go limp, feigning submission. But her mind screamed in fury and plotted her revenge. As soon as she saw an opening, no matter how narrow, she would take it. Then she would run screaming from the barn and announce to the entire ranch what he'd done. Somehow she would find a way to deal with Cole's reaction to her planned departure later. It couldn't be any worse than the mess she was in now.

When Buck realized she'd given him access to her tender body, he grunted, "That's much better." Then he released her and gave her a shove that sent her sprawling in the bedding straw. "Strip off them clothes, injun. I'm done with talking."

Sunny leaned forward, tried to get into a sitting position,

but fell back when her grandfather's war club poked her ribs. She'd forgotten she carried the weapon.

Had she found the way to save herself from this indignity? Did she have the courage or ability to wield such a tool in a death struggle?

She glanced up at the animal bearing down on her and wavered. Could she really smash the weapon against Nellie's drunken husband? Buck wasn't in his right mind, would probably forget all that transpired here by morning. Had she considered every option open to her, short of battle?

Buck's progress stalled as he began fiddling with the buttons on his shirt. Maybe if she kept talking to him, Sunny thought without much conviction, all she'd have to endure would be his filthy words and suggestions. Although talking hadn't worked yet, surely there was a way to convince him to leave her alone without resorting to violence. Maybe if he only *thought* she had the capability to do him harm it would be enough to dissuade him. It surely deserved a try.

Sunny scrambled to her feet and pulled the club from her waistband. Careful to conceal the end with the needle-sharp spike in her fist, she issued an ultimatum. "Stop what you are doing, Buck."

He glanced up from his shirt, working to clear his vision. "Huh?"

"I do not like the things you are saying or doing, and if I have to," she waved the club through the air so he could examine the hammer end, "I will use this on you."

Again he laughed at her. This time, the sound was dark and ugly. "You cain't seem to understand what I'm about, can you? I'm done playing around with you, squaw," he complained as he advanced. "You stupid injuns are all alike—too damn dumb to know when a man means business."

One more step and he'd be too close to use the weapon.

"I mean business too, Buck," she warned, raising the club. "Stop now."

He shook his head and curled his lip. "If I only had my gun, I'd put a hole through you now and be done with it."

He lurched drunkenly forward and reached for the war club.

Sunny's reactions were sober, faster. She swung the weapon in a small arc and caught the back of his hand, smashing the flesh from his knuckles.

"Goddamn bitch!" he screamed, howling in pain. "Stupid injuns think you can attack a white man and live to tell about it?"

He stumbled forward, muttering to himself. Sunny ducked and scrambled to avoid him.

"Guess I'll have to teach you a lesson, too!" Buck's hand shot out, fingers clawing, but Sunny eluded him.

She brought the club around again. This time, she connected solidly and slammed the *kelyaxwai* against his shoulder.

Rage brought his blood to the surface. Pain strangled his voice to a hoarse cry. "Bitch!" he screamed. "You're crazy as your ma, and just as dead!"

Sunny's heart froze. Her lungs collapsed. She couldn't move or speak.

Seeing his chance, Buck lurched forward, ready to claim his prize and extract his revenge. Then he stumbled over the discarded whiskey bottle. His feet slid out from under him and tangled at the ankles. He smashed face-first into the straw.

Buck's groans and struggle to catch his breath jerked Sunny back to action, to lucid thought. She stepped back out of his reach and demanded, "Why are you talking about my mother? What do you know about her or the way she died?"

Gasping for air, Buck only managed to spit out, "Shut up!"

"No, I will not! Tell me!" Sunny punctuated her order by driving the toe of her boot into the calf of his right leg.

"God dammit, squaw!" Buck twisted awkwardly as he tried to reach her foot. "You're askin' for it, just like her!"

"What do you *mean*?" she screamed, even though the answer had already formed in her mind. "Do *you* know something about her murder?"

Buck laughed, an evil gurgle bubbling out of his throat. Then he struggled to his feet, breathing heavily, and leaned against the wall.

"Tell me!"

"I'll not only tell you," he promised with a snarl. "I mean to show you exactly how I done it."

FOURTEEN

"You?" The word slid from her throat like a serpent, and would have spit venom in his eye if it could. "You shot my *mother*?" Her eyes flashing dangerously, teeth grinding, Sunny stalked toward him.

Confused, surprised that he'd made such a careless admission, Buck stood frozen long enough for Sunny to reach him.

Unmindful of her safety, she beat the war club against his chest. *"Why?"* she demanded, her throat swollen with tears. *"Why did you have to kill her?"*

Pain snapped him into action. He drove his fist into her stomach. Sunny flew backwards, groaning with the blow, and collapsed in the straw. Legs spread, Buck loomed above her.

Gloating, he snarled, "She's dead 'cause she wouldn't listen to reason any more than you. 'Cause you filthy injun bitches are just too stupid to lie still and shut your damn mouths when you're told to!"

Ignoring the dull ache in her gut, the taste of bile rising in her throat, Sunny scrambled backwards and staggered to her feet. Her grip on the club tightened.

Buck's yellow eyes shimmered in the semi-darkness, gleaming wickedly. "You might's well give it up, squaw. I cain't let you out of here now, you know that."

He was going to kill her.

Suddenly, it didn't matter to Sunny.

Hatred wound icy tendrils throughout her as she realized those yellow eyes were probably the last thing her mother ever saw. They would not, she vowed, be the last thing she saw as well.

Buck resumed his threats. "I've wasted enough time on the likes of you. Drop that stupid little hammer and do's you're told."

When he was within reach, but before his hands were close enough to encircle her throat, Sunny spat into his face.

This surprised him, stopping him long enough for her to speak. "That was for Moonstar, and all like her who have been degraded by your filthy hands."

Buck slowly wiped the spittle from his eye. Curling his lip in a snarl, he took a step forward and bellowed his rage. "You're dead, injun bitch!"

Sunny whipped the club around through the air with all the force she could muster. It connected with a loud *thwack* against the side of Buck's head.

He didn't react, didn't scream, didn't try to defend himself. Buck remained upright, dazed and bleeding, as if he couldn't quite believe he'd been knocked silly. As he stood there, apparently trying to decide in which direction to fall, Sunny's years of game-playing with her brothers took over. She automatically reversed the club, spinning it expertly as she exposed the spike, and at that same moment, the image of her mother's battered face filled her mind. Then, with a suddenness that surprised her, she drove the *kelyaxwai* into Buck Wheeler's chest.

Someone screamed. But it was Sunny, not her assailant.

Horrified, she jerked the war club out of his body. And

Buck continued to stand there, staring at her as if he didn't understand what she'd done.

Then she looked into those horrid yellow eyes for one awful moment and saw the milky glaze and flat pupils. She noticed the open mouth, heard the strange gurgling sounds coming from his throat, and the enormity of her deed could not be denied.

Sunny was staring into the face of a dead man.

Again she opened her mouth to scream, but this time the best she could manage was a hoarse shriek.

Panicked, she leaned forward and poked her fingertips against his chest. When she gave him a shove, Buck Wheeler tottered for an instant, then fell backward into the straw.

"Oh, my God," she cried, sinking to her knees. "My God! What have I done?" Sunny fought off the dark shadows floating in her head, the terror threatening to shut down her mind and lungs. She took several deep breaths and prayed she wouldn't faint. She *couldn't* faint. Not now. Not in here next to . . . *him*.

Fighting the rolling spasms in her stomach, the urge to be sick and the desire to scream, Sunny clapped her hand against her mouth and buried her face against her knees.

Panic skipped along with her heartbeat as she tried to figure out what to do next. She'd killed a white man— again. Not just any white man, but Nathan Fremont's son-in-law, Nellie's husband, and . . . Cole's brother-in-law.

Who besides the Callahan clan would care that Buck had brutally murdered her mother? Cole would listen, sympathize even, but how could he defend her against his own family? No one else would believe the things she'd discovered tonight. She had no proof of Buck's despicable nature, or of his cruel and murderous acts.

No, the only evidence of any misdeed lay sprawled in this barn. And the finger of guilt pointed straight at her. She had to run now, and get as far away as she could as quickly as possible.

Forcing herself, Sunny got to her feet and stared down at the war club in her hand. Even though her grandfather would have approved of the way she'd used it—her father, too—Sunny wasn't sure how she felt about wielding the family heirloom in such a violent manner. But now wasn't the time to think about it. Now was the time to make a retreat; and a hasty one at that.

Fighting against her rising panic, she rushed to the tack room. There, she gathered her belongings, then dashed to the stalls when she remembered that Paddy was out in one of the pastures. Valuable time would be lost searching for him in the darkness, and time might be the only thing she had left in her favor.

She turned around, scanned the resting horses, and found Dust Bucket, the mare Colt had assigned to her since her arrival at the Triple F ranch. The purebred quarter horse was too much of a temptation to ignore. Not only was she here, two strides away, but she was much faster than Paddy and would serve Sunny for longer stretches, as well. The horse might give her the extra edge she'd need to elude the men who were sure to track her once Buck was discovered.

Her decision made, Sunny hurried back to the tack room, dug out a roping saddle and reins, then returned and prepared the mare for the journey.

As she led Dust Bucket through the double doors, Sunny checked the yard for signs of life, then quietly started down the path to freedom. The horrifying events of the evening swirled in her mind, mimicking the wispy clouds playing tag around the full moon.

In less than an hour, she, Patrick Callahan's fine upstanding daughter, had become a murderer and a horse thief.

Both were grave offenses. In each case, if she were caught, the punishment would be death.

In spite of her predicament, a wan smile lifted the corners

of Sunny's mouth as she mounted the horse. Leaning forward on the mare's neck, she whispered, "Well, Dust Bucket, I suppose they will not have any problem convicting me on both counts; but do not be concerned about my punishment for stealing you—they can only hang me once."

With a bitter laugh, she kicked the horse in the flanks and galloped down the road. She rode hard, making even better time than she'd hoped for, and finally reined Dust Bucket to a sliding halt several yards before she reached the fork in the road.

Sean wouldn't be expecting her this soon; he probably hadn't even gotten this far with Eileen yet. Should she proceed to the fork and veer off the main road, then wait in the shelter of the tree grove until her brother arrived? Or continue on alone?

If she stuck with the original plan, what kind of danger would she visit upon Sean and Eileen? Sooner or later, Nathan would gather up a posse and track her down. What would they do if they found Sean and a white woman on the run with her?

"Shoot first and ask questions later," she muttered to the velvet sky.

Sunny shifted her position in the saddle, finding comfort in the squeaks and groans of new leather as she considered her next move. She really had no choice but to give the pair as much time as possible. She owed it to her brother to lead the posse away, rather than to them.

She was, Sunny decided with a heavy sigh, as alone as she'd been the day she left her desecrated home on a search that had unexpectedly ended this evening. But it had ended. She could now return to her father with that information, that shred of pride, before she had to face the consequences of her actions.

With a breath of renewed determination, Sunny kicked Dust Bucket in the sides and galloped farther away from the

ranch, veering off towards the left—and Yuma—when she
came to the fork in the road.

To the right of the fork, hidden among the trees, Sean
heard the thunder of hooves and knew a rider was approaching from the east. He turned to Eileen, cautioning, "Say
nothing and do not move. I'll be right back."

Then he darted through the opening in the foliage and ran
along the row of trees. As he reached a vantage point near
the apex of the road, he spotted the silhouette of a lone rider
sharply backlit by the first hint of dawn. The mount was a
full-sized horse, not a pony. And the rider never slowed his
stride when he reached the fork, but instead angled away
from the row of trees as if spooked by them.

Muttering to himself, Sean kicked a clump of dirt high in
the air as he made his way back to Eileen. "I wish to hell I'd
have made Sunny come with me when I left the ranch," he
complained. "This waiting around is getting on my nerves."

Fingers trembling, Eileen reached for his hand and
coaxed him down in the soft earth beside her. "There's still
another hour before dawn. We've got plenty of time for our
getaway."

"I don't know," he grumbled, scratching his head. "What
if your mother's wrong and your pa comes after us? I hate
to think we'll just be sitting here waiting for him to come
and shoot us like a couple of crippled prairie dogs."

"Sean," she whispered, "don't fret so. Everything's
gonna be all right now. I feel it. I just know it." To conceal
the fresh batch of misty tears veiling her eyes, Eileen
lowered her lids and smiled.

As a child, her pa had never allowed her to cry, expecting
that even when beaten she should control herself. By the
time she was a young woman, mastery of those undesirable
emotions was complete. Even in pain, Eileen had learned to
rob her pa of the satisfaction of seeing her tears, finding a

way to swallow and choke on them before Daniel Hobbs would have the chance to know he'd made her cry.

Funny, she thought, fresh tears ready to spill from her eyes. Now that she was free and knew he couldn't touch her anymore, she could scarcely keep from drowning in them. She tried to sniff them back, but a sob hiccuped out of her throat.

Sean forgot his agitation and the sense of urgency when he realized Eileen was crying. "Hey, take it easy. Don't pay any attention to me. We're in no danger." He slid a cautious arm around her shoulders and squeezed lightly. "I'm just in a hurry to be on my way and out of this town. I didn't mean to make you worry."

"You didn't," she sniffed as she pressed her head against his shoulder, drawing comfort from his strength. "I'm sorry, but I c-can't seem to stop c-crying." She paused and took a deep breath, hoping to calm her sobs. "I feel so relieved, so *safe* with you, I guess I'm a little over-whelmed."

Her reply touched him in places usually guarded from anyone but his family. With an inward groan, Sean eased back on the soft mat of grass and earth, careful to keep her head cradled against his chest. Using his hips as tools, Sean burrowed out a smooth resting area. Then he stretched out the full length of his body and encouraged Eileen to do the same.

She snuggled against him, curled into a comfortable position, and sighed peacefully. "Rest," she murmured against the cotton of his shirt. "If I could just get a little sleep, I'd be fine."

Eileen's strawberry-colored eyelashes sagged against her freckled cheeks, prompting Sean to blow a kiss and drag a gentle fingertip along the curve of her chin.

"Go ahead, fragile one," he murmured gruffly. "I will watch over you." Noting her bruised and swollen lip, the final monument to Daniel Hobbs's abuse, Sean added, "You are safe now. I will keep you that way."

While he wasn't fool enough to think he could protect her from society's barbs, or their insults, Sean was satisfied he'd just made a vow he could keep. Somehow, he would find a way to keep this promise, even if it turned out to be the last thing he ever did.

A sudden yawn acknowledged his own exhaustion, and Sean rubbed at his burning eyes, then closed them. Maybe it was for the best that they had another hour before Sunny was due to join them. They wouldn't be able to put much distance between the tree grove and Pleasant Valley if they didn't take the time to refresh themselves for the long journey ahead.

Sean's eyes suddenly opened—searching, scanning. He sniffed the air for unusual odors, the smell of death, or fear. And he listened—for noises that didn't belong in the desert, for the telltale sounds of silence.

Satisfied they were alone, that Sunny would be their only visitor during the next hour, Sean relaxed and drifted off to sleep.

Cole approached the bedroom where Sunny slept. He ran his fingers over the scrollwork on the oak door, caressing the ridges and valleys as he'd caressed her body the night before.

"Sunny?" he called softly.

When no sweet voice answered, Cole thought of knocking, of waking her from her slumber, but he shook his head and ambled on down the hallway instead. After the night she'd given him, she could sleep all day if that's what she wanted, he thought with a chuckle.

Halfway down the stairs, Cole heard Nathan's voice drifting up from the landing.

"And make sure that coffee's black as a vulture's heart!"

Cole negotiated the remaining steps and met his father at the bottom of the stairs. "Morning, Dad."

"Oh—ah, morning, son." Nathan fiddled with his shirt tail and made a great show of smoothing the creases into his waistband. "Look, about last night. I was kinda—"

"No need to go over all that." Cole took the Bull Durham tobacco pouch from his pocket and began to roll a cigarette. "Got a minute before breakfast?"

"Sure, son. Sure."

Cole regarded his father through a thin stream of smoke as he lit the cigarette. He took a deep drag of the rich tobacco and motioned Nathan to follow him outside. Once in the yard, the men strolled in silence until Cole finally came to a halt by his mother's vegetable garden.

"I have a few things to tell you, Dad. Tell you, not discuss with you. I hope I can count on you just to listen and maybe try to understand a little."

"I—well, sure, whatever you want."

A puff of blue smoke proceeded his first announcement. "I'm leaving the ranch, Dad. Your ranch. I'm going to start building on my property sometime next week."

"But Cole, you know the Triple F—"

"I asked you to listen, that's all. If you want to get yourself all worked up and blow your heart in a million pieces, that's up to you. You won't do it in front of me, however."

Clearly uncomfortable with anything but the lead in a conversation, Nathan's features puckered up like the pleating on a store-bought dress. But he shrugged and relented. "Sorry. Go ahead."

"I don't have to tell you the trouble the cattle industry is in, and frankly, I'm getting kinda sick of the smell of them." He inhaled another drag of smoke. "I've already put in my order for shipment of the herd I plan to raise over by the Verde River."

"Not sheep!" Nathan bellowed, unable to stop himself.

"No, Dad, you can relax. I wouldn't do that to you or our neighbors."

Nathan scratched his head. "If not sheep or cattle, then what—pigs?"

Cole's grin dropped his mustache on one side. He brushed his finger between his upper lip and nose several times, then shrugged and said, "Ostriches. I intend to build the biggest ostrich ranch this side of the Pacific Ocean."

Nathan's mouth dropped open and he cocked his head to one side. "*Ostriches,* son? You mean them big, ugly birds from Africa?"

Cole nodded and took another drag from his cigarette as his father absorbed the information.

Nathan sputtered and shook his head before he could speak clearly. "Why, that's the craziest thing I ever heard of! It's absolutely ridiculous. What'd you want with ostriches, for Christ's sake?"

Cole leveled his gaze and pointed a finger at his father. "You said you'd listen. Calm down now, or this conversation is over."

Nathan held up his hands in surrender. "All right, you win. Go on."

"I'll give you a brief rundown, but before I do, I want you to remember this is more than a crazy idea. It's done, and there will be no discussion as to whether I carry these plans out or not. Deal?"

Nathan's lips turned white as he pressed them together, but he nodded and gestured for Cole to go on.

"I ordered sixteen pairs of breeders while I was in Yuma. They're due in from San Diego sometime over the next two weeks."

"Excuse me?" When Cole sighed and turned his palm up, Nathan continued. "Just how do these birds plan to get here from Africa and San Diego? Fly?"

"Now, Dad," Cole said with a clear warning in his voice. "In case you're not aware of it, an ostrich can't fly. They'll come from Africa by boat and arrive from San Diego by train. I thought I'd meet them in Yuma and escort them back here myself."

Nathan's lip quivered, but he held his laughter. "That's very thoughtful of you, son. May I ask how you plan to make them feel at home once they're here and feel the blistering heat of Arizona in the summer—and why you even want to?"

Ignoring his father's sarcasm, Cole explained. "First, these birds come from the plains of Africa, remember? A summer in Arizona will be like a vacation in the White Mountains for them. Second?" Cole's grin returned, then doubled. "Profit, pure and simple."

"From what? Feathers? What kinda profit can you hope to gain from a few ostrich feathers?"

"A tremendous profit, Dad. One of these birds eats no more than four pounds of feed a day compared to the forty or so consumed by a single steer."

He watched Nathan calculating the figures and crushed the cigarette beneath his boot heel, before adding, "And water. I can't even guess how much less water I'll need, but the difference is appreciable."

"All right," Nathan broke in, "so it doesn't cost so much to raise these critters. I still don't see how you can make it with them alone."

"Supply and demand. That's all there is to it."

"So the feathers are kinda popular." Nathan shrugged. "How many can you sell, how many birds you got to go through just to put a couple of decorations on a lady's hat?"

"A hell of a lot more than you think, and I don't plan to go through many birds at all. I just have to strip them, and new feathers grow back. I'll have an endless supply and a very tidy profit in the bargain."

Nathan grumbled and shook his head. "I don't know, son. It still sounds crazy as hell and more than a little risky. Don't you think—"

"It's my risk, and I've already taken it. I told you this

conversation was not open for discussion, and I meant it. If you can keep your promise to listen and withhold your opinions a little longer, not to mention, a little better, there's something else I'd like to tell you about."

Nathan took a breath and opened his mouth, but something in his son's eyes changed the course of his tongue. "Sure. I'd be glad to hear what else you got to say."

"It's about Sunny."

"Aw, Cole!" Nathan complained. "Please don't do this to me, I can't take—"

"Then I won't."

Without another word, Cole spun on his heel and started back to the ranch.

"Son!" Nathan called, trailing after him. "Wait up. Can't we talk about this? I'd be glad to hear you out."

The words halted his progress, but when Nathan reached his side, Cole was no longer certain he could keep his temper long enough to tell him what Sunflower meant to him. "Why don't we just forget I mentioned her name."

Nathan's brow smoothed, and his breathing eased. "That's what I wanted to hear! I think it's best we both just plain forget about her altogether."

"No, Dad. You misunderstood." Cole turned and faced him, determined to end the conversation. "I'll never forget her, because I don't plan to let her out of my sight again. I do think it's best if you do, however. In fact, let's pretend this dis—"

"Mr. Fremont! Oh, Mr. Fremont!"

Two heads, one thick with blond hair, one barely covered with silver strands, turned towards the voice.

"Oh, Gawd, Mr. Fremont!" The ranch hand jogged up to them, his hand clutching his chest.

Cole stepped between his father and the hand. "What is it, Stormy?"

"Oh Lord, Mr. Fremont, it's Buck Wheeler!" Although nearly thirty, Stormy's features and expressions were those

of a young boy, and would always give him a look of
youthful innocence no matter how wrinkled and grey he
became. Now in his excitement, his eyes flashed round and
wide, making him look younger still.

"What about, Buck, Stormy?"

"He's hurt, Mr. Fremont. He's been hurt real bad."

"How? Where?"

"Uh," Stormy rolled his eyes and screwed up his
features, laboring to remember something he'd seen only
moments ago. "Oh, ah, he's stretched out in the barn. How
he got there, I don't know. But I think he's hurt real bad."

Cole gripped the man's elbow and dragged him alongside as
he hurried toward the double doors. "How bad is he, Stormy?"

"Pretty bad, Mr. Fremont." Turning away from his
employer, he looked down at the ground and muttered, "I
think he's daid."

"What?" Nathan's voice boomed from behind them.
"How can that be? You been drinking on the job again?"

Again Stormy's expressive brown eyes grew huge and
innocent. "Oh, no sir, no, I wouldn't do that. I don't never
do that no more."

Cole released his grip on the frightened hand and turned
to Nathan. "Come on, Dad. Let's go have a look."

They walked in silence, each mired in their own thoughts.
Once they stepped inside the barn, as they discovered Buck
sprawled in the stall, they spoke as one.

"Jesus Christ!"

Cole dropped into a crouch and automatically reached for
Buck's wrist even though he knew life no longer pulsed
through the man's veins. The open eyes stared at the
ceiling, but they could not see, and his features, twisted
more with surprise than pain, were frozen for all eternity.

Then he noticed the small, perfectly round hole in Buck's
shirt. Tearing it opened, both Nathan and Cole studied the
unusual wound, noting that it was too small to have been
caused by a bullet, too round for the blade of a knife to have

entered. In unison, the men's gazes moved upward to Buck's surprised features, then settled on the large bruise at his temple and its squared corners. The implications added up in a flash for Cole, then Nathan understood them as well.

"God almighty, son!" Nathan jumped to his feet and bellowed, "Bucky's been done in by one of those Goddamn half-breeds you brought home! One of them snuck into my office and stole that war club, but why in hell would they go and kill Buck?"

Cole had been wondering that same thing himself, but he said, "Don't go jumping to conclusions, Dad. Anyone could have taken the club from your office. Stay here with Buck. I'll find Sean and see if he knows anything about this."

Leaping to his feet, Cole hurried to the ladder and scrambled up the rungs. "Sean," he called as he stepped into the loft. "Answer me! We got trouble." *Please answer me, please be here,* he thought.

But the loft was empty.

Frantic and angry all at once, Cole tore the room apart. He tossed bales of alfalfa across the loft as if they were cotton, kicked piles of bedding straw into the air, and sputtered his frustration.

"Dammit all, Sean—where the hell are you? What am I supposed to tell Sunny? Or *Nellie*?"

But his own rapid breathing was the only sound to reach his ears. All Sean's belongings were gone, vanished as if he'd never been sheltered here. What had happened up here in the loft, and down in the stall?

"Why, Sean? *Why?*"

Cole covered his face with his hands and blew a hot breath against his palms. His father would be livid by now, out of his mind—out for blood. Shaking his head and muttering his frustration, Cole hurried back down to the barn floor.

He was too late. Nathan was gone. Cole glanced through the doors and saw his father standing in the yard waving his arms. He was gathering the ranch hands. Building a posse. Assembling a lynching party.

When Cole stepped into his view, Nathan called him over. "What'd you find up in the loft, son? Nuthin', right?"

A rider surrounded by his own cloud of dust born down on them as they spoke. Keeping one eye on the approaching man, Cole nodded and shrugged. "I can't understand it, but Sean is gone. So are his things."

The horse slid to a halt in front of Nathan. The elder Fremont turned his attention to the rider. "Well? What'd you find out?"

"The girl's pony is still in the pasture, but the mule is gone."

Nathan turned to Cole and leveled a caustic eye. "Ask me if I'm surprised, son."

Not only could Cole see that he was not, he thought he noticed an enthusiastic gleam in his tired blue eyes. Nathan's expression suggested he was enjoying Buck's murder and the hunt for his killer immensely. Not that any of the Fremonts, save Nellie, had a soft spot in their hearts for Wheeler. As a son-in-law, he had been more tolerated than loved. Still, Cole would have expected a little more emotion from his father, some sense of loss over Buck's death.

Watching as Nathan divided the ranch hands into two groups, Cole guessed there could be only one reason for his father's glee. He was hunting more than his favorite quarry—Indians. He was pursuing Sunny through her brother.

Cole glanced up at the bedroom windows and picked out the room in which she slept. The curtains were still drawn. No curious dark eyes peeked through the slit between them. She had a right to know what was going on out here. He turned and had taken only one step toward the house, when his father's voice halted his progress.

"You want to join us, son?"

Looking back, Cole saw the ranch hands scatter, split up in all directions as they ran to assemble their horses for the hunt. "Sure."

"Then you'd best get moving. You've got five minutes to be armed and saddled."

With that, Nathan was off to the barn.

Torn between his duty to Sunny and insuring Sean's safety, it occurred to Cole they might just be one in the same. If he took the time to wake her and tell her what had happened, the posse would ride off without him.

What would the ranch hands do when they caught up with Sean? Bind him over for trial, or visit their own brand of justice on him on the spot? With his father leading the pack, it was a question he didn't need to ask himself.

Just then, Nathan burst through the barn doors, shouting, "That son of a bitch is a horse thief, too! That murdering savage has stolen Dust Bucket!"

"Now hold on a minute, Dad. Jacob said he took his mule—why would he need a horse as well?"

"Ah, son," Nathan clucked, his bright blue eyes twinkling. "This wily savage is on the run. You have to assume he plans to run that ole mule to the ground and use Dust Bucket as his backup. Smart maybe, but not smart enough to get away from me!"

This statement erased any lingering doubts Cole had. He blew out a sigh and regarded his father. "What about Nellie? Who's going to tell her?"

"Your mother. I'll run and let her know what's happened, and then we'll ride."

Cole's sad green eyes followed his father's progress to the house. Then he picked out Sunny's gabled window. "Sleep well, little flower," he whispered, blowing a kiss into the air. "Enjoy your slumber while your mind is still at peace."

His heart heavy, Cole headed to the barn, knowing he'd done the right thing. Sunny would learn soon enough of her brother's grave mistake. No need to disturb her now.

As he reached the double doors, Stormy dashed through the opening on a thick-chested buckskin gelding. Looped over the horn of his saddle was a coil of rope—tied in a noose.

Cole raced into the barn.

FIFTEEN

A series of small thunderings vibrated against Sean's head. Particles of red earth screamed a warning into his ear. He finally woke enough to hear what they had to say. A stampede, or large group of riders, thundered across the desert. They were headed his way.

With a start, he bolted upright and tried to get his bearings. What had happened? How long had he slept?

Sean peered through the trees. His breath whooshed out at what he saw, and he sagged with the realization. The sun divided the horizon and the heavens. It was several hours past dawn.

"Mother of God!" Frantic, he turned to Eileen and shook her fragile shoulders. "Eileen, wake up."

Not hearing the urgency in his voice, she inched her eyes open and slowly rubbed them. Then she stifled a yawn and stretched her arms high overhead.

"Eileen," he barked. "Wake up!"

Fully conscious now, she pushed her elbows against the earth and sat up. "What's the matter with you? Why are you yelling at me like that?"

Maneuvering to his feet, Sean holstered his pistol and

reached for the rifle. "We slept too long. We should have left here hours ago."

"What's the harm? We'll just get a little later start, that's all." Eileen squinted newborn eyes into the sun and continued to rub the sleep from them.

"There could be much harm in our laziness. We are risking our lives as long as we stay in the area." His well-trained ears picked up the sounds he'd heard against the earth. Careful not to frighten her too much, he casually added, "I believe a group of riders are heading this way. I'll ride back a ways and have a look while you prepare for our journey. And hurry." He wheeled around and started for Whiskey.

"Sean, wait!" Eileen stumbled to her feet and lurched as she moved to his side. "What about Sunny? Is she here? Don't we have to wait for her?"

Sunny! He glanced around hopefully, but knew if she had joined them during the night, she'd have made her presence known by now. Masking his concern, he shrugged. "My sister was aware of our limited time, and understood she was to meet us before the first light of dawn. Perhaps she chose to remain. Don't worry about her. Sunflower can take care of herself." For now, he could only hope he was right.

Eileen sighed. "I wish I was more like her—stronger, somehow."

Sean smiled down at Eileen, at her fresh-scrubbed skin, the glow of sleep still coloring her freckled cheeks. Unable to resist the urge, he cupped her heart-shaped chin in his palm and softly said, "Maybe you are and you just haven't had the chance to find out before now. I think by the time our journey has ended, you will have discovered you have strength enough for ten women."

"Really? Do you really think so?"

Tickled by her enthusiasm, he laughed, then pinched her

cheek. "Yes, I think so. Now go, ready yourself for the trip.
I'll be right back."

Color rose in her cheeks, obscuring her freckles. Eileen
pursed her lips and fluttered her lashes as she turned, skirts
flouncing, and made her way through the fallen tree limbs
and rocks to her bedroll.

Still chuckling to himself, Sean marveled over how much
a little hope had brightened her sky-blue eyes. He heaved
the saddle onto Whiskey's back, more convinced than ever
he'd made the correct decision by helping Eileen, then
mounted and rode back towards the Triple F ranch.

He'd traveled less than a mile when he saw plumes of
dust rising in the distance and heard the unmistakable
sounds of horseshoes pounding against the hard dry earth.
Riders in a hurry. A posse of some kind.

To protect Eileen and himself, Sean had to believe those
riders were coming for him, and assume that Daniel must
have discovered he had taken his daughter with him. If that
were the case, he didn't have to wonder what to do next.
But he didn't have much time in which to get it done.

Giving Whiskey's reins a vicious jerk, he wheeled the
mule around and made a dash back to the tree grove.
"Eileen," he shouted as he slid from the animal's back.
"We're out of time, mount up!"

"Mount up? Just me?"

"Listen and do as I say. There is no time for questions."
Reaching for her bedroll, he hoisted it on Whiskey's back,
then directed her to place her foot in the stirrup. "Riders are
heading this way. They will most likely go right on by us,
but just in case they get nosy and stop in to have a look, it
is best you are not here with me."

"But why should I take the mule? I can go hide in—"

"Do as I say!"

The helpless orphaned calf expression that had originally
convinced him to take her with him overshadowed her
newfound enthusiasm. How could he explain the real

danger without frightening her half out of her mind, or reducing her to the trembling mouse she'd been a few hours ago?

Moving to Whiskey's side, he rested his hand on her knee. "You have to trust me, Eileen. If these men are after me, and I'm not saying they are, they'll find me. If that happens, I want you safely out of the way. If I am alone, maybe I can talk my way out of it and convince them you've left home of your own accord."

"Oh," she said brightly. "I see now. What do you want me to do?"

Pausing, he took a deep breath and explained as quickly yet gently as possible. "Ride down this wash at least three or four miles. Pick out a good hiding place for both you and Whiskey, then wait there."

An idea occurred to him as he spoke, and he circled around behind the mule and began to gather several of the thickest tree limbs lying around. "Once you feel safe, just settle in for the day. I'll do the same somewhere else."

Sean took two of the longest limbs and tied them, one on each side, to the back of his saddle. As he worked, he continued his instructions. "When it gets dark—and I do mean dark, not twilight—start back up the wash. I'll meet you right here. Do you have it?"

"Yes," she nodded, curious about his project at the rear of the mule. "But I don't see why I should take Whiskey. I don't mind the walk. It would seem less suspicious if you have him with—"

"Eileen," he cut in, wondering if there were an easy way to explain, "if they are after me, if I can't convince them I've done no wrong, they will . . . they'll want to take me in for questioning or something. I don't want to leave you out here alone without some form of transportation. If you should return here tonight and I am not to be found, Whiskey will take good care of you." As if to convince himself and the animal, he gave the mule an affectionate pat on the rump, then continued braiding the branches.

Eileen frowned and twisted the leather reins. It hadn't occurred to her that he might be captured, or that she might be left alone to fend for herself. If that happened, what would she do, where would she go? What would he expect of her?

Thinking of Sunflower's strength, of Sean's opinion of her, Eileen set her chin. "I—if they take you in, if I come back tonight and you're not here, I want you to know something. I won't be going back home. I'll go on ahead. By myself if I have to."

Sean glanced at her and nodded. He thought of warning her of the dangers she would face, of offering some advice, but then remembered his own words about finding her hidden strengths. She'd been resourceful enough to approach him for help. She would be all right if left to her own devices. She might not have any choice.

Sean smiled as he finished tying the smaller branches in a bundle. His grin spreading as he thought how much growing she'd already done in the last few hours, he attached the twigs crosswise to the longer limbs dragging the ground, and stood back to survey his work. "That ought to give you some privacy for awhile."

Eileen twisted around in the saddle and peered down to the ground. "What is that?"

"A broom of sorts. As Whiskey goes down the wash, this little contraption ought to wipe his hoofprints off the sand. It will be that much harder for anyone to find you."

"Oh, how clever! Will Whiskey mind dragging all that behind him?"

"Naw. He's pulled a lot bigger plows than this on our farm in Yuma." Sean no longer had to turn his head to hear the riders. They were approaching rapidly. "You must go now. I'll see you tonight, right on this spot."

But she couldn't leave. Not yet. Not like this. "Sean,"

she ventured in a tiny voice. "Please, before I go, could we, would you . . . kiss me goodbye?"

Should he risk it? Could he? If he were to touch her now, he might lose his reason, his control, and jump on Whiskey's back with her and make a run for it. But that would be foolish, and irresponsible—and it wouldn't stop the inevitable, either.

Sean looked up into her eager eyes and blurted out, "Quickly! Lean down."

When she bent over, he met her halfway, sliding his hands along her arms up to her sweet face. Her skin was soft and velvety as butterfly wings. The texture, the response it drew from deep inside, shook him and made him wonder if he'd ever have the chance to touch her again. Foolish thoughts. Dangerous thoughts.

Gruffly, with less tenderness than he'd intended, Sean crushed his mouth against hers for a brief moment, then pummeled Whiskey's rump with his hat.

"Go on! Get out of here!" he screamed after the fleeing mule.

Sean heard her gasp and watched for several seconds, making sure Eileen could keep her seat on the galloping animal. Then he hardened his heart and let his Quechan instincts for survival take over. He spun around in the sand and raced for cover.

Cole raised one arm in the air signaling the group of men behind him to hold up. He examined the well-traveled road, but was unable to pick out a clear set of tracks belonging to the mule or Dust Bucket.

Leaning back in his saddle, he took off his hat and fanned himself. Had he chosen the right direction in which to lead his men? Fresh tracks led away from the ranch in both northerly and south-westerly directions. Cole had decided to take the latter, leaving Nathan to head the group going north. Taking the trail leading towards Yuma seemed like the logical choice at the time. Now he wasn't so sure.

He nudged Sage and headed to the apex of the fork in the road. Tracks he was fairly certain belonged to the mule led toward the tree grove. But where were Dust Bucket's prints. Was this some kind of an elaborate trap?

"Hey, Cole!"

A voice behind him, low and dark, barely above a whisper, caught his attention. "What is it, Tom?"

"There's someone or something on the bluff above the wash over yonder."

Cole followed Tom's gaze and narrowed his eyes. "Where? I don't see anything."

"He's gone now, but I swear I seen a man's head just above that split rock on the left."

Then another voice. "Ain't but one way to find out fer sure." This was followed by a volley of rifle fire.

"Dammit, I didn't give any orders to shoot! Hold your fire!" Cole glared at Stormy, making sure he and the others knew he meant business, then he looked back at the bluff. A few small rocks tumbled down the side of the hill, but other than that the desert seemed unusually quiet.

Sliding his Colt from its leather holster, Cole whispered, "I'm going on up to have a look around. You men stay here."

"But—"

"If I need any help, I'll signal you by firing two quick shots. Got it?"

He glanced at the men, satisfied they would follow his directions, then dropped into a crouch and began to make his way across the wash. Using the narrow fissures from recent spring floods as toe holds, Cole began his ascent. He'd climbed halfway up the side of the hill when the order came.

"Don't come any closer."

The voice drifted above him, followed by the click of a rifle hammer. "Sean? Don't shoot—it's me, Cole."

"Stay where you are."

"I'm not budging. Show yourself and we'll talk. I know you must be running scared, but maybe we can work something out. Show yourself," he repeated, hoping to find a way to avoid a confrontation. "Let's talk about it."

Sean flattened himself against the boulder and inhaled. Wondering if he'd just tasted his last breath of freedom, of life, he squeezed his eyes shut. Beads of sweat formed on his brow. What chance did he have on foot? How far would he get before Cole or one of his men cut him down? And why was Fremont part of the search party?

Working to keep his voice steady, he asked, "What's your interest in this Cole? Does Sunny know you're tracking me down?"

"Let me come up there, Sean. Put the gun down and let—"

"No! Stay back and answer my questions!"

"All right, take it easy!" Cole scanned the hillside looking for a way to approach him undetected, but Sean had chosen his vantage point well. "I shouldn't have to explain family to you of all people, and no, I didn't tell Sunny I was going after you. I figured she'd have enough of a shock when she woke up and found both of us gone. Now, come on down—let's talk."

Sean inhaled again and wiped the sweat from his brow. Did he really have a choice? He could never outlast the group below if they chose to wait for evening and surround him. Cole might be offering him a way out—or at least a way to stay alive. If any of the rancher's feelings for Sunflower ran beyond lust, and apparently they did or she wouldn't have stayed on at the ranch, he might even be able to convince Cole to let him go.

Taking a gamble, Sean inched his way to the edge of the boulder and took a quick glance around the corner. Fremont sat in the open, apparently alone. "We'll talk, but first throw your gun on the ledge."

Sliding a reluctant finger across the steel barrel of his pistol, Cole squinted one eye towards the crest of the hill. Sunny had called her brother "crazy Callahan" the day he'd met him. How much of that description was true? Crazy in what sense?

In spite of his misgivings, Cole tossed his gun as directed, then finished the climb. He approached the boulder, hands high in the air, and Sean appeared, waving him into the clearing.

"Move over behind the boulder."

Cole sidestepped, then inclined his head towards the rifle. "You won't be needing that."

Indicating a spot, Sean said, "Sit. Then I will think about putting my gun to rest."

Sinking cross-legged into the sandy earth, Cole slowly inched his tobacco pouch from his shirt and rolled a cigarette. Looking up as he ran his tongue along the edge of the paper, he worked at ignoring the rifle barrel and said, "Why'd you do it, Sean?"

The half-breed shrugged. Then he released the hammer on the weapon and laid it across his legs as he considered his next move. How was he to find the correct answer for such a question, this from a man who rode off with his innocent sister, a man who made her his *puta*? Perhaps allowing the rancher access to his hiding place had been a mistake after all.

Unable to hide his scowl, or sense of injustice, Sean muttered, "I have done nothing you have not also done. The only real difference I see is in the color of our skin."

Cole's eyebrows drew together as he lit his cigarette. Maybe this Callahan really *was* crazy, he thought as he tried to make sense of his words. Maybe murder wasn't a crime to members of the Quechan nation. "I'm just trying to understand, that's all. I can't help you otherwise. Was it self-defense?"

Sean's brow shot up. "Self-defense?"

Feeling as if he was finally getting somewhere, Cole encouraged, "Yes. If it wasn't plain murder, if you were only defending yourself, it'll go a lot easier. Is that what happened?"

But Sean wasn't listening to Cole. Self-defense meant someone was dead. That could only mean Eileen had killed her father after all. How would she react when she found out? Shaking his head, he let out a small groan and said, "So he's dead."

"Hell yes, he's dead!" Cole boomed. "You put a hole two inches long through his heart! Did you really expect him to live through that?"

"A *hole*?" Sean wrinkled his nose and screwed his features into a grimace. How had Eileen managed to put a hole in her father with a frying pan? He rubbed his temples with his fingertips, then exhaled and shook his head. "I do not understand."

The Indian looked completely confused, as if he'd spent the evening swimming in a vat of firewater. Maybe he had. Keeping Sunny and her love for her brother in mind, Cole tried to help him remember. "Would you like a smoke?"

When Sean nodded, Cole tossed the pouch of Bull Durham to him and tried again. "Now think back," he urged. "Do you remember arguing with him or anything? How about bashing him alongside the head."

"Umph," Sean mumbled as he inhaled the first puff of smoke. "That's the first thing you've said that made any sense."

"Good. That's real good." Buoyed, Cole leaned forward. "Right after you hit him, you must have twirled the club around and stuck him in the chest. Do you remember now? Do you know why you did it?"

"What club? What in the name of sweet Jesus are you talking about now?"

"The war club, dammit."

Again he wrinkled his nose. "I only know about a frying pan."

Cole's patience snapped. He reached across the short distance and grabbed the collar of Sean's shirt. "I'm done playing games with you, so quit acting stupid! I know you stole the war club from my father's office and I know you went out to the barn and killed Buck Wheeler with it—what I don't know is *why*!"

Stunned, Sean's eyes grew round and dark. "Buck Wheeler? I thought you were talking about Daniel Hobbs."

"Dan Hobbs? Is he dead, too?"

"I—" Sean scratched his head, then turned his palms up. "Hell, I don't know."

The men stared at one another, owl-eyed and incredulous for several silent minutes. Gradually, Cole released his grip on Sean's shirt and eased back down in the sand. Retrieving his discarded cigarette, he took a long drag, then blew a series of smoke rings into the clear skies.

Lifting a honey-colored eyebrow, he quietly said, "Let's start over. Why are you up here hiding from my men?"

Sean looked at Cole, measuring his chances if he mentioned Eileen's name, and decided to remain evasive. "First tell me why your men chase me."

This time Cole remained in control of his instincts, and resisted the urge to take hold of the man's neck with his hands and squeeze until the truth popped out of him.

Instead, he said, "All right, we'll do it your way. Someone broke into Nathan's office, stole your grandfather's war club, and murdered Buck with it. We found Buck's body in the barn first thing this morning, then discovered you'd run off sometime during the night."

"And even white men who have never gone to school,"

Sean finished for him, "can add a half-breed to a dead man and come up with the correct answer. Is that it?"

"You've got to admit it looks bad, Sean. Are you saying you didn't do it?"

"That is exactly what I am saying. I didn't even see your foreman last night. Even if I had, what possible reason would I have to kill him?"

Cole shrugged. "Besides the fact he hates Indians, I don't know. I was hoping you could answer that for me."

"I'm sorry to disappoint you, but you have wasted your time chasing me. I have done nothing wrong."

Cole drummed his fingertips against the soft earth, wishing the end of their discussion could be that easy. "I believe you, but I'm afraid that's not good enough to call off the men. Why did you leave last night? What's all this about Dan Hobbs? Can he back you up if he's alive?"

Sean nearly laughed out loud. Instead, he choked on a puff of smoke before he said, "No, and please—forget I even mentioned his name."

"I can't do that, Sean. Tell me what happened between you and him last night."

"Nothing." At Cole's skeptical expression, he insisted, "Nothing at all. The man did not see me and I did not see him."

But Cole wasn't going to be put off, not with his brother-in-law lying dead and his murderer running free. He ground his cigarette into the base of a cactus plant and jabbed at the air with his finger. "You'll have to answer these questions sooner or later, so you might as well start with me, partner. What made you think Hobbs was dead? Does this have anything to do with Buck's murder?"

"I—no, I don't know."

"Come on, Sean." Cole's tone rose with his temper as he threatened, "If you don't start talking, I'm going to have to turn you over to those boys waiting down in the wash! Now give—why are you on the run?"

"I'm not exactly running!" Sean's Irish temper surfaced, leaving lucid thought behind in its wake. "I was only helping a friend last night."

"What friend? Tell me that and maybe we can get you out of this? Who were you with last night?"

"I can't tell you that. If I do, she'll be in as much trouble as I."

"She?" Cole exploded. "Good God, man. Have you been stupid enough to become involved with a white woman?"

"It's not like that!" Sean parried. "It's not like that at all. I—she—we are just good friends. I only tried to help her, that's all."

Calmer now, Cole leaned back on one elbow and took off his hat. He ran his hand through his thick, damp waves and blew out a heavy sigh. "Eileen Hobbs, right?" He glanced up long enough to take in Sean's reluctant nod. "And you and Dan got into it when you took her away?"

"No!" Sean shook his head vehemently. "I have been telling you the truth. I did not see the man. Eileen had a small argument with him, but it was not about me. Dan Hobbs does not know that I am with her."

There was no longer any question in Cole's mind that Sean spoke the truth. With a wave of his hand, he dropped his voice several tones and quietly said, "All right, I believe you. Let's try to work through this thing calmly from here on out."

"Yes," Sean agreed through a sigh. "That would be good."

"Where is Eileen now?"

Sean's chameleon-like eyes suddenly dulled, losing their hazel luster as he thought of her alone down in the wash. "She is safe."

"But where? We have to find her so she can clear you."

Sean studied Cole as he spoke, listening intently to his words, and found not a solution but a stab of envy. How simple life must be for a white man. How utterly impossible it must be for this one to understand how he was feeling.

"I cannot do that to her."

"I understand what you're driving at, Sean. I have a pretty good idea what folks will be saying about her when they learn she ran off with a half-breed, but—"

"Any hope she has for a happy life will be gone. Do you understand *that*?"

"Dammit, of course I do!" Frustrated, Cole picked up a large dirt clod and smashed it against the boulder. "Do *you* understand we're not talking about a happy life, but life *period*, if she doesn't clear you right now?"

Sean thought of Moonstar, of Patrick, and closed his eyes. His breath whistled out between his teeth. Then he murmured, "Yes. I understood the consequences when I agreed to help Eileen. I will not jeopardize her freedom now."

Caught between admiration and exasperation, Cole frowned. "I'm going to have to take you in, you know. Those boys are out for blood, and until I find out who really killed Buck, they're not going to settle for your word."

Sean nodded, his lips drawn and tight. Then he slowly unfolded his legs and rose. "I would ask, in my sister's name, that you give me some time—a head start on this posse you've collected."

Cole jumped to his feet and planted a boot on Sean's rifle as he bent to collect it. "Don't be a fool! Even if I could give you an hour, which I can't, these boys would hunt you down and shoot you on sight."

"I have no other choice."

"Yes, you do, and I just told you what it is."

Panic began to trickle into his mind, but Sean forced himself to listen to Cole's plan.

"Let me take you in. The sheriff's a decent, honest man. I'll explain as much as I have to about your innocence, then I swear I'll do everything I can to find out what happened back at the ranch. It's the only way out, Sean. You have to take it."

His features hard, more Quechan than Irish at that moment, Sean's intense gaze bore into Cole as he searched for deception in his words. Satisfied the man spoke the truth as he knew it, Sean stepped away from the rifle. "I would like a moment and another smoke, please."

"Sure." After Sean rolled his cigarette, Cole took the tobacco pouch and moved to the shade of a mesquite bush. Peering down into the wash, he could see the men were getting restless and knew they wouldn't wait for him much longer. Looking back to the big half-breed, he opened his mouth to call out a warning, but remained silent when he realized Sean was in some kind of trance.

His lips moved, but no sound issued forth. He raised an Indian profile to the heavens, but the sun lit the black strands of his hair with a copper halo of his Irish heritage. Which man would the good citizens of Phoenix put on trial? The Irishman or the Indian? The sinner or the saint?

Sean heard boots scraping against rock and knew the posse was coming for him with or without Cole's blessing. They were coming for the Indian. The trapped animal. For the first time, he understood how the jackrabbit must feel as a pack of coyotes ran it to ground. He knew helplessness, could almost hear the agonized screams as voracious teeth tore at the rabbit's limbs and disemboweled its body even before it hit the ground.

His own body shuddered then readied itself, poised to leap forward and force the men to come after him in the way of the coyote, but just then he saw his father's face and heard the mournful cry of a proud man robbed of both sons.

The tension in his muscles easing, Sean turned to Cole. Flipping the half-smoked cigarette to the ground, he said, "I suppose it would be best for you to tie me."

Heaving a sigh of relief, Cole crossed the distance between them in three long strides. "You've made a wise decision." He reached out and took Sean's hands in his. "I'll do everything I can to get you free, you know that."

"What I know," Sean said, allowing the hint of a smile, "is that my sister will find a way to make you very sorry if you don't."

With a short laugh, Cole instructed, "Stay close behind me. I'll alert the men we're coming down."

Inching his way to the crest of the hill, Cole fired one shot in the air and hollered, "I've got him! We're coming down. Hold your fire!"

He turned back to Sean. "Where's your mule?"

"Eileen has him."

"Dust Bucket, then. Where have you hidden her?"

"Your quarter mare?" Sean scooted away from the ledge and began to fumble with his bonds. "So I'm accused of horse theft, too, huh?"

Cole ducked and whirled around. "You took her, didn't you?"

"No," he spat, "but I can see I'm going to get the blame for everything that goes wrong from here on out. Maybe you'd better untie me and let me take my chances with prairie wolves and Apaches."

"Sean." Cole approached him, palms upward. "What else was I to think? You and my mare were missing. Buck was dead."

"And don't forget about the war club," Sean grumbled.

"A weapon," Cole said by way of apology, "anyone with access to the house could have taken." *But who would have taken it—why?* he suddenly wondered. The only ranch hands allowed in the house were Buck and the two cooks—Grubby, a man with a scorpion whip for a tongue but the body of a slug, and Tag, his young apprentice who was afraid of his own shadow. Neither was capable of standing up to, much less killing, Buck Wheeler. Other than his own family, the only person allowed to roam freely throughout the large house, was . . . Sunny.

Sunny! Sean's mind arrived at the same conclusion. He recalled her plan to take the war club for protection. Adding that to the missing horse, he tossed in the fact she hadn't met him at the fork as planned. Had she crossed paths with Buck as she tried to make her departure from the Triple F ranch? If so, what could he possibly have done or said to drive her to such a violent and bloody deed? And where was she now?

Cole watched the half-breed's expression, wondering if they shared the same thoughts. Ashamed and terrified by musings that included visualizing Sunny on the business end of the war club, Cole turned away as his men came over the edge of the hill. Rushing to greet them, he settled on a plan.

"Tom, Jacob! I want you boys to take Sean into town. Tell the sheriff to care for him as if he were a Fremont. Tell—"

"But boss!" Stormy objected. "I thought we was gonna hang him right here on—"

"That's enough of that kind of talk!" Cole drew his pistol and faced his men. "Anyone else thinking of having a hanging party?"

A few of the men grumbled, but none stepped forward. "Then hear me out," Cole continued. "I'm not so sure we've got the right man. I want the rest of you to go back to the ranch with me. We're going to tear that place apart looking for Buck's killer, and we're not going to stop until we're sure this time. Understood?"

Through muttered groans, the ranch hands shrugged, then turned and started back down the hill.

Regarding his two most trusted employees, Cole said, "As I was saying, I want this man treated like he's my long lost brother. He'd better arrive in Phoenix alive and well, and you'd best make sure the sheriff understands I want him to stay that way. Any questions?"

"No, sir," the men replied in unison.

With a nod, Cole turned his attention to Sean, and knew

as his gaze locked with the half-breed's that they had been entertaining the same horrifying thoughts about the girl they both loved.

"When you see my sister," Sean said, his gaze still locked and unblinking, "tell her to speak to no one but you."

Allowing Tom to lead him past Cole, he added under his breath, "And make sure she comes to talk to me before she does something else she may regret."

SIXTEEN

"Nell, please. You know I wouldn't bother you at a time like this if it wasn't important."

Nellie Fremont Wheeler sobbed into her pillow, both ashamed of her tears and disgusted with herself. She wept for purely selfish reasons, not for her dead husband. She thought only of her bleak future, not about the fact that Buck no longer had one. What kind of person was she, anyway? She didn't deserve her brother's attempts at consolation, or his love.

"Nell?" Cole whispered softly as he eased his weight onto the edge of the bed. "If there's anything I can do, something I can get for you, please tell me what it is. I'm sorry if I added to your grief."

If he could have, at that moment Cole would have kicked himself clear across the room. Why hadn't he taken a little more time soothing her, easing her sorrow before he started asking questions about Buck and throwing suspicion on his character? He should be comforting his sister, not casting doubt on her husband's memory.

His fingers tentative, Cole reached down and massaged Nell's trembling back. "Hush now," he encouraged, hoping to find a way to be of some use to her. "It's going to be all right."

"No, it's not!" she shrieked into her pillow. "It's never going to be all right again!"

"Take it easy, honey. Of course things will get better." Increasing the pressure, Cole moved his palm in a circular motion up and down Nellie's spine. "I know you'll never forget Buck and the love you had for him, but in time the memories won't hurt so much."

Instead of the calming affect he was looking for, Cole's words increased her sobs, raising the volume of her wailing until he could stand it no longer. He slid off the bed and straightened.

"I think it's best if I leave you to your grief. Maybe we can talk later."

He'd only taken one step when she pulled her head off the pillow and rolled to the edge of the bed. Stumbling, her arms outstretched, she cried, "No, don't go. Don't leave me alone. I need you. I need someone to talk to."

Then she was in his arms. Her pale hands fluttered against his chest as sobs racked her body. Uncomfortable, with no idea how to help her, Cole suggested, "You need to talk, but not to me. I'll go get Mother."

"No!" Nellie jerked out of his arms and wiped her eyes with the back of her hand. "You m-may not think you can h-help me, b-but I know y-you're the only one who can. Mother would *n-never* understand. I p-promise to calm down if you'll stay. P-Please stay."

"Yes, yes, of course." Kissing her forehead, he squeezed her shoulders then held her at arms length. "But I can't stay long. You realize why, don't you?"

Nodding, Nellie took in a great gulp of air. "I know. I'm worried about Sunny myself. I think she must have left sometime during the night, b-beca—" A sob robbed her of her breath and the rest of her sentence.

"Come on." Taking Nell's hand, Cole led her to the

gilded ivory dressing table and chair in the room from which Sunny had so recently fled. Urging her to take a seat, he leaned against the table. "Comfortable?"

"Yes. Thank you." Picking up a discarded yellow ribbon, the one Sunny had worn the day she arrived at the Triple F ranch, Nellie stroked the slick satin. "Anyway, Sunny wasn't here when Mother came to tell me about Buck. The room looked just like it does now, except the bed hadn't been disturbed. I don't think she even napped before she left. Why on earth would she—?"

Nellie cut off her own words when she remembered. "Oh, I almost forgot." Digging into her wrapper pocket, she pulled out a small sealed envelope. "This was on the pillow for you. Maybe it will answer some of your questions."

Snatching the envelope from his sister, Cole tore it open. He quickly read the contents, read them again, and groaned.

"Well?" Nellie raised an expectant eyebrow.

"She only says she's leaving, that she doesn't want to be the cause of any further discord among the fine Fremont family, thanks for everything, and that she'll . . ." Swallowing hard, Cole stuck the note in his pocket and whispered the final words, "And that she'll always love me."

"Oh, Cole." Reversing their roles, Nellie reached for her brother's hand and gave it a squeeze. "You have to go after her."

"I know, and I plan to, but I can't just leave Sean under arrest for a murder I know he didn't commit. Sunny won't be very happy to see me if I leave her brother behind to hang."

"Maybe Dad can—"

"No, forget him. He's just sure the Indian did it, and I don't have the time or patience to convince him otherwise. If it wouldn't upset you too much, I'd like to ask you a few questions about Buck. About, well—"

"Cole, it's no problem."

"But when I asked you earlier, when I first came in here, you—"

"I know. That's what I was talking about when I said I thought you'd understand. I wasn't crying over Bucky. I was crying over me." Shame burned her cheeks. Nellie wove the ribbon between her fingers, twisted the end around her thumb, then let it unravel and drop into her lap. "I know you all think Buck used me, that he married me just to get his hands on part of the ranch."

"Now stop that. We don't—"

"It's all right. I know that's why he married me, and it doesn't bother me at all. I used him, too. I'm just as guilty as he is."

Cole pushed away from the table and dropped into a crouch at his sister's knees. "Nellie? What are you trying to tell me?"

"That my grief is for myself," she cried. "Bucky wasn't much of a husband, but he *was* my husband. He gave me respectability, a reason for people to stop feeling sorry for me." Fighting off another sob, she clinched her fists. "Don't you see? I know I'll never find another man to share my life, and I'll die a lonely old woman!"

"That's just not so! You have a lot to offer a man, any man. I won't listen to you talk about yourself this way."

"But it's true! Oh, I don't know if I can explain it any better than that."

"Try. Help me to understand."

She hung her head and stared at the criss-cross pattern of her skirt and shrugged. "There aren't many men who want to marry a woman who can't bear his children."

"Is that what this is all about? You didn't tell Buck you were infertile before you married him?"

Nellie slowly shook her head. "No, I told him. That was all right with Buck. In fact, I think he was mighty happy to hear he wouldn't have to put up with a passel of brats."

Cole slid a finger under her chin and tilted her head until

she had to look at him. "I think you know there are other men in this world who don't mind not having a family— widowers in this town who'd snap you up in a minute. There's something else, isn't there?"

Nellie sniffed, but kept her tears in check. "How many men do you think there are who wouldn't mind having a wife whose insides are so messed up that she screams in pain every time he tries to touch her?"

"Oh, Nell," Cole sighed and reached for her hands. "I didn't know."

"*I* didn't know either. I didn't intentionally fool him into marrying what he thought was a whole woman, but deep inside I guessed things weren't right with me, that it might not be possible for me to . . . to consummate our marriage."

"And knowing Buck, I suppose that didn't set too well with him."

Again Nell sniffed, but this time it was with disdain. "Although he never said it in quite these words, he thought it was an awfully high price to pay for what he hoped would be half of this ranch." Dabbing at her nose, she added, "It didn't take him long to start satisfying his needs elsewhere. I know I shouldn't have blamed him for that, but it hurt just the same."

"Of course it did!" Cole rose and pulled Nellie from her chair. Cradling her in his arms, he whispered, "Believe me when I say there are good men out there who would be happy to marry you just the way you are, and remain true to you in the bargain."

Her tears were like a team of horses rearing to go. It took all Nellie's strength to rein them in and say to her brother, "That's hard to believe. What if it were you and Sunny? What if she h-had, w-what if she couldn't—"

"I love Sunny. Love always finds a way."

"Y-you mean you'd go to her anyway, you would s-stay by her side and never—"

"Never, little sister."

Nellie gasped, and a sob tore from her throat. Was it possible? Could she actually manage to have a complete relationship? Was there someone waiting for her somewhere—a man more gentle and caring than Buck had been?

Watching his sister's expression change from despair to hope, Cole grinned and took her face between his big hands. He stared into the depths of her golden eyes and said, "You see, there is always hope, and a very good chance that you will someday find the love you've been denied. You've got to believe that."

Nellie lost control. Tears sprang from her eyes, leaving her incapable of speech. She sobbed against her brother's leather vest until she could cry no more.

"S-sorry," she finally managed.

"Don't apologize. If you're able yet, the only thing I want from you is a little help."

"S-Sure." Pulling back from him, she reached for a lace-trimmed hanky and turned away as she blew her nose. Facing Cole again, she straightened her shoulders and thrust her chin out. "What do you need to know?"

Cole's grin widened and turned up the corners of his mustache. "You're gonna be just fine, little sis."

"I know I am," she grinned back. "Now, what can I do for you?"

"Tell me about Buck. Think back to when he returned from Maricopa. Was he acting any different or suspicious? Did he have any cuts or fresh wounds?"

Nellie screwed up her features and pressed a finger against her temple. "He did have a long cut just below his knee. He said he tripped over the spittoon at The Bucket and fell on his own knife. Said he bled like a stuck pig."

"How was he acting?"

Nellie shrugged and twisted her mouth to one side. "Same as usual, I guess. Loud and obnoxious."

"Did he make any comments about Sunny? Ask where she came from or why she was here?"

"He said several things about her, most of which I'm sure you wouldn't care to have me repeat. Let me think a minute." Intent on remembering anything, no matter how small a detail, concentration cut deep furrows between Nellie's eyes. "Hmmm. You know, he was acting a little loco, even for him, when I told him how you two met."

Picturing the scene, Nellie began to pace, her finger still pressed against her head. "I told him her mother had been murdered and that Sunny tracked the killer by following the unusual hoofprints. When I mentioned she followed those prints until she stumbled onto you, then nearly killed you, he laughed so hard I thought he was going to choke."

Nellie stopped her pacing as it all came together like the last piece in a puzzle. Whirling around, she took in her brother's appearance, trembling when she saw the rage building in his expression.

"Oh, my God! Cole? Did Bucky—could he have—?"

"I don't know, but I sure as hell intend to find out. And if it turns out Buck was involved in Moonstar's murder, he wasn't alone." Spinning on the heel of his boot, he left Nellie with an order before he crossed the threshold. "Keep this to yourself until I have all the answers. I don't want anyone spooked until I know what's what."

Then he barreled down the hallway and took the steps two at a time. After crashing through the front door of his home, he stomped across the yard and pushed his way inside the bunkhouse. Pausing only long enough to spot his quarry, Cole stalked across the room and grabbed a fistful of blue and grey checkered material.

"Get up off that bed!"

Aided by his employer's strong hands, Stormy lifted his tired body off the blanket and stood face-to-face with Cole Fremont. "W-What's you all excited about?"

"I've got a few very important questions for you, and I want some straight answers."

Never taking his intense gaze off the baffled man, Cole shouted out of the corner of his mouth, "The rest of you men—clear out! I need a little privacy."

Still staring down at Stormy with frigid green eyes, Cole heard rather than saw the room empty. Then he said, "Tell me all about your adventures with Buck after the three of us split up in Yuma." He wound more of Stormy's shirt into his palm, this time collecting both sides of the collar. "Tell me *everything*. Don't leave out so much as one disgusting detail."

Stormy's little boy features suddenly aged, growing hollow and ashen. "I-I don't know what yer gettin' at."

Cole twisted the material, bringing the helper's throat in contact with the back of his knuckles. "I'm short on patience and time. Out with it now, or so help me, I'll wring it out of you!"

The pressure increased against Stormy's throat until he could barely breathe. He squeaked out, "All right, I'll talk."

Cole relaxed his grip just enough to allow the man a minimal passage of air. "Spill it!"

"We, ah, we just had ourselves a little fun, Cole. That's all."

The pressure began to increase again, and he quickly added, "That's how it started out anyways! Buck, him and me, we just had some beers at the saloon, then we was gonna head on back to home."

"But you took a detour, isn't that right?"

Stormy's eyes bulged with as much fear as pressure. "You know Bucky, he likes them injun women. I just went along with him. I swear to God, it weren't my idear."

Cole ground his teeth together as he fought the urge to snap the man's neck and be done with it. Instead, he snarled, "And so you found an Indian woman, one you assumed was alone?"

Stormy nodded and his eyes grew rounder, brighter.

"Which one did you kill?" he spat. "The mother or the son?"

"I didn't kill nobody!" he shrieked. "Swear to God, swear to God!"

"Stop your damn babbling and tell me what happened!"

"I am, I am." He brought his hands up and pulled at Cole's wrists, but he couldn't loosen his grip. "Bucky done it. We went in the house and the squaw screamed. I swear, when the kid come runnin', Bucky shot him dead the second he walked in the door."

"That's not the way I heard it. I know that boy wasn't found in the house." He turned his wrist a half a notch.

"Stop!" Stormy cried. "Let me finish! The squaw got all hysterical and Buck, he said, go drag that kid outta here, so I done it. I took him out and hid him in the cornfield. When I come back, Bucky, he, well . . . he'd kilt her too."

"Aren't you forgetting something? Didn't you boys stop by to have a little fun? Don't try to tell me you and Buck didn't force your miserable selves on that helpless woman."

"I ain't forgettin! I admit it, we did get to the woman. I, it's just that, well it was . . . after."

"After?" This time, his hand twisted of its own volition. "After what, you lousy piece of buzzard bait?"

"After . . ." Stormy's voice was raspy, oxygen-starved. His ashen skin had begun to turn blue. "After she . . . were . . . dead."

Something Cole had no control over, some innate sense of propriety, kept him from tearing the man's head from his body. It didn't, however, stop him from heaving Stormy against the wall, crushing him against the thick wood slabs as if he were nothing more than a pesky fly.

The thud of flesh against solid pine and Stormy's agonized moans, coupled with the sight of his rumpled body lying on the floor like a pile of discarded laundry, gave Cole the strength to harness his rage. He had to organize his thoughts, and make his plans.

The seconds ticked by. Cole whipped into action when he decided what he must do first. Reaching down, he grabbed the back of Stormy's shirt and jerked him to his feet. "Get up! We're going for a ride."

Wincing, disoriented, the ranch hand protested. "I cain't. You done hurt me so bad, I cain't even walk."

Cole propelled the man backwards and propped him up against the wall. Then he drew his Colt .44. "You've got two choices. Pick one or I'll do it for you. You can ride into Phoenix with me, tell your story to the sheriff and take your medicine, or—" Pausing, Cole pulled back the hammer and pressed the gun barrel under Stormy's chin. "I'll be happy to put you on trial and carry out your sentence right here and now. Choose."

Looking exceptionally boyish, more ridiculous than ever, Stormy's eyes crossed as he stared down the length of the barrel. "I-I'm feeling lots better now. I-I believe I can make the ride to town."

Cole increased the pressure of the gun against his neck and added, "By the way, I've heard all I want to from that big stupid mouth of yours. One more word, here or on the trail, and—" Cole made a popping sound with his mouth. "I'll save myself a trip into town."

Stormy opened his mouth, but quickly shut it. Then Cole jerked him forward and pushed him towards the door.

Out in the yard, the other ranch hands milled around, pretending none had heard what went on inside the bunkhouse. Calling them over, Cole singled out one of the men. "Go saddle a fresh horse for me—get the strongest one you can find—and bring Stormy's horse around, too."

The man nodded and Cole turned to another hand. "Brownie, you go to the house. Tell Mrs. Fremont I'm taking Stormy to see the sheriff. When my father returns, make sure to tell him I'm on the trail of Buck's killer and I'm taking care of things. I'll wire him with my progress from Yuma. Understand?"

"*Yuma?* Well, not exactly. I thought that injun we caught was—"

"I'm not asking you to think, Brownie. We got the wrong man in jail. I can't explain any more than that right now. Do you know what to tell Nathan or not?"

"I guess I understand what to do."

"Good. And, there's one other thing. Tell Nellie not to worry, that I've got everything pretty well figured out. Tell her I'll be in touch as soon as possible."

"Yes, sir."

Cole thought of mentioning Buck's funeral, of excusing himself from the occasion, but found he couldn't even spit out his name. To think just minutes ago he'd felt sorry for Nell because she couldn't enjoy a physical relationship with the vile animal. It soured his stomach.

Cole's spirits lifted when he realized how fortunate Nellie actually was. Just know that his sister had never been forced to endure the touch of a filthy pig named Buck Wheeler nearly gave him cause to smile.

"Come on you piece of shit," Cole said almost cheerfully as he grabbed Stormy's arm. "I've got a long ride ahead of me."

Days later, camouflaged by thick bushes and reeds, Sunny and Dust Bucket drank their fill of cool water near the junction of the Gila and Colorado rivers in Yuma. Fanning herself with a yellowed copy of Godey's *Lady's Book* she'd found along the roadside, she sighed. Only a few weeks into spring, and already tongues of heat from the desert sun absorbed every precious drop of moisture the earth had to offer. The air was thick with the cloying aroma of fresh alfalfa crops baking in the mid-afternoon sun, and alive with bugs and mosquitoes.

Slap!

Sunny lifted the magazine from her arm and plucked a bloated, but very dead mosquito from her skin. The insects had arrived early with the heat. It was going to be a bad year for crops. An even worse year for bugs. And so far, it wasn't looking too good for Sunny, either.

What now?

She looked up river, longing to continue her journey to the farm, but forced herself to turn away. She and Pop would have their hands full trying to figure out how to save her hide. It would be best to wait until nightfall to bring a stolen horse onto her father's property and announce her crimes, her guilt. The decision made, Sunny slipped off her tattered trousers and eased into the cool river for a much-needed bath.

Several long hours later, exhausted, frightened, and dejected, Sunny trudged up a sandy path cut through the melon patches on the Callahan farm. Feeling her way in the darkness, she led Dust Bucket to a corner crop of feed corn and tethered the hungry animal on a nearby stake. Satisfied the tall stalks would hide as well as feed her ill-gotten mount, Sunny made her way to the only home she'd ever known.

Light from her father's kerosene lamp flickered in the window, beckoned her to come inside and seek comfort in Patrick's burly, understanding arms. Careful not to startle him, she crept silently across the wooden porch, then stood in the open doorway, waiting to be discovered.

Patrick sat at the family dining table. A large map was spread across the heavy pine like a tablecloth, and the greying Irishman studied it intently through spectacles held in place by his bulbous nose.

Sunny sighed as she noticed his bushy grey brows knot together as he spotted something of obvious importance. Patrick gave the paper a furious half-turn, then pushed the blunt edge of his index finger along some winding trail or river.

Another map leading to hidden gold, she surmised with a crooked grin. Knowing if that were the case, she could stand here all night and he would never notice her, Sunny kept her voice soft and low, and announced her arrival.

"Pop? I have come home."

Patrick whirled around in his chair. "Is that me girl I'm a hearin'? Me pretty yellow flower?"

Working the kinks out of his stubby legs, Patrick pushed away from the table and drew himself to his full height just in time to catch his daughter as she flew into his arms.

"Yes, Pop!" she cried against his stout shoulder. " 'Tis your Sunflower."

Patrick gave her a great hug, then pushed her at arms length. "Let me have a look at ye, lassie."

His robust grin and sparkling eyes dimmed as he took in her appearance. "Aye, and yer a sight for sore eyes, lass. Yer looking more like a refuge from a potato famine than me fine beautiful daughter. How could yer brother let ye skedaddle around the countryside looking like that?"

"Pop, he—ah—that is one of the things I must tell you about. Please." Sunny took his calloused hand and tried to lead him back to his chair. "Let us sit down."

But Patrick would have none of it. He jerked his hand free and limped to the door. "Where is my Sean boy? Ye out there, lad?"

"Pop," Sunny sighed. "Sean is not here. He remained in Phoenix and did not return with me."

Keeping his back to her, he quietly asked, "And do I want to know the reason why he'd let ye make such a journey without him, lass? Has Sean met with—? Is he—?"

"Oh, no, Pop!" Sunny hurried to his side. "I do not wish to fill your mind with more thoughts of grief. Sean was very happy and quite alive when I left him. He is healthy, my father."

Patrick turned and regarded his daughter. Cocking his head to one side, his ice blue eyes clouded, grew distant. "Ye know, lass, I never realized how much ye sound like your dear mum. With me eyes closed, listening to your sweet voice is almost like havin' her here with me again."

Sorrow choked her, but she held back her tears. The time for weeping would come soon enough. Swallowing hard, Sunny reached for her father's hand once again. "Come on, Pop. We have much to discuss."

As quickly as he'd retreated to the past, Patrick returned to the present. "Not so fast, lass. If yer brother has decided to remain in Phoenix, who has been so kind to see to yer safe return home?"

Avoiding the question, Sunny whirled around and made a great show of looking through the cupboards in the tiny kitchen. "Where do you hide the poteen these days?"

As if locked in place, Patrick's girth filled the doorway. A scowl peeking through a coarse grey beard, he said, "Ye'll not be tellin' me ye've returned the same way ye left—alone?"

"Ah, here it is!" Sunny looped her finger through the jug's crockery handle and took two glasses off the sideboard. Still feigning deafness, she marched to the table and began to pour the spirits.

Finally distracted, her father approached the table.

"*Two* glasses? What's this in me home?"

"I thought we could both use a drink."

"Then ye thought wrong, lass! 'Tis sin enough yer own father suffers from the curse of the Irish. I'll not be visitin' such a burden on me own young colleen!"

Sunny pushed one of the glasses across the table, then eased down into a chair and took the other in her hand. "I may have been no more than a little girl when I left Yuma, my father, but I have returned a woman. I have seen and learned much over the past weeks."

She lifted her glass. "This is to the souls of our beloved

Callahans who have gone on to their reward, and to the strength of those who remain behind."

Mimicking a feat she'd seen her father perform many times before, Sunny tossed the liquid down in one gulp.

At first she wasn't aware she'd swallowed anything other than warm water. Then a fireball exploded in her throat, shooting tendrils of liquid flame into her lungs and stomach. Sunny opened her mouth to draw in a breath, but even the oxygen seemed combustible, and ignited in a white hot flash in her throat.

Her eyes slammed shut as a tremendous shudder rippled throughout her. Then, her smile wan, as counterfeit as her earlier deafness had been, Sunny straightened her shoulders and said, "Mighty fine poteen you stock, Mr. Callahan. I believe I shall have another."

Patrick roared his laughter, then tossed his own drink down. Pulling out a chair, he straddled it and leveled one blue eye on his daughter.

"All right, lass. Ye've made yer point. But have ye growed up enough to know ye've no blitherin' fool for a father?"

Sunny poured another glass of poteen and nodded. "I never thought otherwise."

"Then it's time yer atellin' yer pop everything." Patrick held out his glass. "And fill 'er up while yer at it—me mouth's as dry as an owld miser's heart."

Sunny replenished the drink, then leaned back in her chair.

"I believe I am wanted for murder."

At her father's gasp, she quickly explained. "I have caused the death of two men. One was an outlaw who left me no other choice. The other—"

Sunny took a sip of poteen, and said, "The other exchanged his life for the murder of my mother."

Patrick's mouth dropped open. Then he removed his spectacles and finished his drink. With a long sigh, he softly said, "Go on, lass. Start at the beginning."

Slowly spinning her own glass of liquor around in her palm, she told her father about Cole, leaving out the most intimate details, then explained about the events leading to her confrontation with Buck Wheeler. When she finished, she slumped in her chair, bleary-eyed and exhausted.

Patrick rubbed stained and weathered fingertips across his brow, then glanced up at Sunny. Releasing the breath he'd been holding, he asked, "Are ye certain this Buck was killed then, girl? Could it be ye've only hurt the black heart a wee bit?"

Sunny laughed bitterly and took a sip. "I am afraid I hurt him a lot, Pop. He was deader than this jug of poteen last time I saw him."

Patrick jiggled the bottle, but no splash of liquid tickled his ears. "Then yer mum and I thank the Lord ye've managed to rid us of this blight of a man."

He rose and walked stiff-legged into the kitchen, observing as he looked through the cupboards, "The law may not think too kindly on yer generous deed, tho. There's somethin' about an Indian—man or woman—killing a white that just don't set well in these parts. We must prepare for what's to become of ye, lass."

Patrick dug through the pots and pans until he found the last jug of Moonstar's homemade poteen. Carrying it back to the table, he popped the cork and filled Sunny's glass before he poured his own.

Too late she protested, "No, thank you, Pop. The drink already lying in my belly has my head spinning and has given me a case of the walleyes. What I really need is some food."

"Ah, and I've just the thing." With an awkward pirouette, Patrick waltzed back into the kitchen. "I'll just be warmin' some soup for ye, girl. That'll put you in fine mettle."

"Do not take the time to warm it," she laughed feebly. "I am afraid I shall doze off before the flame reaches the pot."

"Aye, and I kin see that." Patrick filled a bowl with tepid soup and made a great show of serving it. "Made by me own hands with me own crop of the finest potatoes this side of the Atlantic Ocean."

Suddenly ravenous, Sunny forgot her manners and brought the bowl to her mouth. Sucking it down greedily, she only paused long enough to savor the few clumps of cabbage and onion tossed in among the chunks of potato, before setting the bowl on the table and pushing back in her chair.

"That did it, Pop," she groaned. "I must be off to bed now while I can still walk."

"Aye, and I'll be happy to give ye yer leave, but I must first inquire of me son's health. Why has Sean not returned with ye, girl?"

Sunny laughed and stretched her arms over her head. More tired than she could ever remember being, she yawned and said, "Do not concern yourself with Sean, Pop. He could not be better or happier. He is helping a damsel in distress. We will hear from him soon."

"First you, and now me son has lost his heart in Phoenix, as well? Humph. What d' ye suppose they put in the water in those parts?"

Sunny managed a short laugh, then shrugged. "I cannot be sure if he has lost his heart. The only thing I am sure of right now is that I will soon fall out of this chair. I have hardly slept these past four days."

"Four days, lass? How'd ye make the distance between here and Phoenix so fast?" Patrick shook his head and wagged a finger. "Ye must've run poor Paddy to the ground."

"No," she yawned, barely finding the strength to get to her feet. "Paddy's just fine. I left him at the Triple F ranch."

Sunny pushed in her chair and started for her bedroom.

"But Sunflower, girl. How'd ye make the trip home?"

"It was no problem, Pop," she said through another yawn. "I stole a fast horse. Goodnight."

Open-mouthed, Patrick watched his daughter disappear into the other room. Reaching for his glass, he muttered, "Bad cess. 'Tis awful bad cess I feel acomin' our way."

* * *

Late the following afternoon, Patrick returned to the farm, the buckboard filled with supplies. He fed and watered his mule, Flossie, then afforded Dust Bucket the same kindness. By the time he'd unloaded the last sack of flour and re-stocked his whiskey supply, the sun had dropped behind the mountains. Tip-toeing to the bedroom door, Patrick pushed it open a crack.

Still his Sunflower slept.

Pulling the door shut, Patrick went into the kitchen and began to prepare the leg of lamb he'd purchased to celebrate Sunny's return. He filled a kettle with water, onions, and the piece of meat and placed it on the wood-burning stove, but stopped short of lighting the fire.

Cocking his head he listened—was that the sound of a rider approaching?

Moving quickly for a man with arthritic knees, Patrick went to the front door and scanned the yard. In the vague light of dusk, all appeared calm.

No puffs of dust on the horizon announced a visitor. No startled crows shrieked and exploded from the corn fields where they fed.

Shrugging, the Irishman returned to the stove and struck a match on the heel of his boot.

"Evening."

Patrick wheeled on one leg, nearly falling, and gasped, "Wirra! And who'd be scarin' me half outta my wits?"

"Sorry, I didn't mean to alarm you, but I'm a stranger to these parts. I didn't want to walk into the barrel of a shotgun."

"Kindly state yer business, sir."

"I'm looking for the Callahan farm. Have I found it?"

Patrick stood rock still, the match burning in his left hand, and stared at the tall blond man in the black felt hat. Everything about him exuded confidence, an understated sense of wealth. Could this be the man his Sunflower spoke of? Was he here to help her—or arrest her?

The flame inched its way down the wooden match until it met Patrick's toughened flesh.

"Faith and begorra!" He flipped the match to the floor and stuck his fingers in his mouth, but managed to keep one eye on the stranger.

With a chuckle, Cole stepped into the room and removed his hat. "I'd say I found the Callahan farm. I'm Cole Fremont from Phoenix. A friend of Sunflower's."

Patrick narrowed a wary eye as he followed the progress of Cole's extended hand. He decided to accept the greeting. "Pleased to make yer acquaintance, sir. I am Patrick Callahan. What's yer business here?"

Cole glanced around the small house, then gestured towards the table. "May I?"

"Uh, I—I suppose there's no harm."

One side of his mustache lifting in a grin, Cole walked over to the table and tossed his hat down. Grabbing the back of a chair, he used it for support as he continued to look around. "I'd like to speak to Sunny."

"Uh, she's not here, I'm 'fraid."

"No?"

Making another visual sweep of the wood and sod home, Cole noticed the woman's touch, the flowered curtains and boldly colored Indian rugs hanging on the walls. The room was small by any standards, but every square inch of space had been utilized to the maximum. Two chairs circled the dining table, but three others hung upside down on the wall behind, their legs serving as temporary hat racks.

An extra-wide sofa, its wooden frame built right against the wall, looked as if it had doubled as a bed for one or both Callahan boys when it wasn't supporting visitors, and the curtained closets were carefully shelved to serve as pantries during the winter months. Neat, compact, efficient. With no visible sign of Sunflower.

Cole glanced at Patrick, then to the back wall and its two

doors. One was ajar, revealing the corner of a mussed bed. Patrick's? The other was shut tight.

Inclining his head in the direction of the latter, Cole said, "Is that Sunny's room?"

Patrick cleared his throat and walked over near her bedroom. "Now see here, lad. Yer makin' some mighty personal talkin' here and I do'na care to indulge ye any longer. Be on yer way."

But real or imagined, Sunny's scent was all around him. He hadn't come this far just to be turned away now. "Sorry, but I don't plan to leave here without seeing her. I've a lot to tell her. Where is she?"

"I'm tellin' ye, man! I do'na know."

Cole slammed the chair against the plank floor. "Sunny? Answer me, dammit!"

"Aw, now that's really quite enough of yer insolence, sir! I'll be askin' ye to take yer leave now." Patrick slapped his hands to his hips and spread his legs, blocking his daughter's doorway.

More certain than ever he'd found her, Cole searched for the words that would bring her out of hiding. But to appease her father, he took a backward step.

"All right, Mr. Callahan. I'll be leaving." He took his hat from the table and spun it in his hands. "Tell Sunny I'm not going to stop looking for her."

He took another step, then paused a few moments. "And please be sure to tell her that I love her."

When this drew no response from behind the closed door, Cole resumed his retreat. Just before he reached the threshold, he turned, his hat still in his hands, and tossed a final lure.

"Oh, by the way. There is one other thing she may be interested in hearing about."

Again he paused, then raised his voice a notch. "Sean has been arrested for the murder of Buck Wheeler."

SEVENTEEN

Sunny pushed her back against her bedroom wall near the door and drove her teeth into her knuckles. Had she heard Cole right? *He loved her?*

But then she thought of her crimes. Remembered the proof, Dust Bucket, stood tied in the corn field. Maybe Cole was trying to use her vulnerable heart as a way to trap her, to catch her off guard.

Torn with indecision, Sunny stood motionless and kept her silence.

Then Cole uttered his parting words.

Sunny gasped. Was it a trap? Or had her brother really been arrested for a murder she'd committed?

The heavy thud of Cole's boots grew dimmer. She listened to the unnaturally slow heel-to-toe gait resounding against the wood floor. Was he giving her plenty of time in which to make the most logical decision?

But time wouldn't help. Sunny knew what that decision had to be. She could take a chance with her own life, but not with her brother's. For Sean, if for no other reason, she would have to reveal herself.

Sunny tore open her bedroom door.

She expected to find her father standing in the frame, but instead, Patrick was already halfway across the room.

"If this be dooble talk!" Patrick threatened as he reached Cole. "If yer usin' me boy to get to me girl, I swear by all that's holy I'll have ye bound and roasted, I'll—"

"Pop!" Sunny cried. "Please, let him be. I have to talk to him. Cole? Is it true? Has Sean really been arrested?"

Looking past the red-faced Irishman, Cole's hungry gaze feasted on the woman he loved. Her skin was flushed with sleep and her long raven-black hair hung down to her waist in stark contrast to the fresh white cotton of her nightgown.

"Sunny," he whispered, too grateful to find her alive and unharmed to say anything else.

"Well?" she demanded.

"He's safe for the time being." Cole's green eyes warmed, growing moist as he softly said, "And how are you, little flower?"

Sunny's breath caught. Her throat swelled, and her heart felt as if it had grown to twice its size. Maybe he really did love her.

All pretenses of modesty forgotten, she hurried across the room, the hem of her long nightgown skipping along after her like a bridal train. She stopped just inches from him, her vision refusing to acknowledge her father's image at his side.

"Cole."

Impatient arms and eager fingers intertwined as they closed the gap and clung to one another. Cole rocked her, pressed her against his body as he filled her ear with his innermost thoughts.

"Oh, God, Sunny. You don't know how worried I've been, the dreadful thoughts I had when I didn't come across you on the trail. How could you just leave like that? Why didn't you come to me and tell me how you were feeling? Don't you know how much you mean to me?"

Pressing her mouth against his leather vest, she tried to

unravel the ball of string her mind had become. "Yes . . . no. I—I do not know."

Leaning back, Sunny looked into his eyes and tried to make him understand. "I can only be certain of how much you mean to me. The things I do, I do for you. When I heard you and your father arguing about me, I could not stay in your home any longer."

"What are you talking about?" Cole furrowed his brow, adding, "And what does my dad's opinion have to do with us, anyway?"

"A damn sight more than me own opinion, from the look of it!" Patrick cut in. "In the name o' decency, man, unhand me daughter and let us adjourn to the table."

Suddenly aware of her father, Sunny pushed away from Cole and lowered her gaze. "Pop, forgive me. I did not mean any disrespect."

"Later, lassie. Ye run make yerself decent fer now. I'll tend to this here young man. When yer dressed proper, we'll be gettin' our answers." Patrick shifted his gaze to Cole. "Isn't that right, lad?"

Sunny gave Cole a sideways glance, then rolled her eyes and scampered out of the room.

His gaze still spearing his visitor, Patrick pointed at the south wall. "Grab a chair and sit. I'll be tending to me chores before I join ye." Then he limped into the kitchen, his left knee stiffer than usual, and finished lighting the stove.

As he worked, he called to his unexpected guest, "Would ye be a drinking man?"

Cole measured his words—and Sunny's father—before he quietly said, "Occasionally."

A few moments later, Patrick appeared with a bottle and three glasses. "I kin see no harm in sharing a snort with ye even if y'ar the scalawag who introduced the evils of belly-wash to my innocent colleen."

Never taking one squinty blue eye off Cole, Patrick's

expression was a silent challenge as he banged the bottle on the table and dropped into a chair.

But Cole was ready for the man, if not his puzzling accusation. "Your daughter and I have never shared any spirits. Seems to me there might be a few misunderstandings here. What say you and me clear the air before Sunny joins us?"

Patrick pulled the cork out of the bottle with a resounding pop. "I do'na see the harm in the two of us sharin' a word s'long as me girl welcomes ye here. Just keep one thing in mind—ye can always tell an Irishman, but ye can't tell him much."

As soon as the words were out, Patrick began to laugh at his own joke. The response came from deep within, building strength and velocity as it spilled out. Cole automatically joined in, but his chuckles were strained with tension, and stuttered rather than roared with life.

Taking a deep breath, Cole promised, "I'll do my best to remember that, sir."

"Name's Patrick. Yer welcome to use it." The grey-haired man poured two glasses of amber liquid and shoved one across the table. "I'd like t' say I'm offering my best, but I cain't vouch for this whiskey. Just picked it up today since me girl and I drank up the last of Moonstar's poteen this past evenin'."

"Poteen?"

"That'd be homemade mescal to yer way of thinkin', I s'ppose."

"I once drank something the Apaches at Fort McDowell made by fermenting century plants. They called it mescal, and as I recall," Cole grimaced just thinking about it, "a shot of that rot gut could peel the hide off a Gila monster."

"Or grow hair on a sidewinder!"

Patrick slapped his knees as both men burst out in laughter. This time, they were in unison and equally boisterous.

Encouraged by Patrick's amicable nature, Cole lifted his glass. "How about a toast? To your beautiful daughter, Sunflower, and your fine son, Sean."

Patrick raised his glass, then he groaned and set it back down on the table.

"Sean," he murmured, his features suddenly pinched and wrinkled. "I have to know about him, and I'll be askin' ye to spare me the blarney, sir. What're me boy's chances with the hangman?"

Pushing out a heavy sigh, Cole shook his head then took a swallow of whiskey. After giving the spirits a moment to warm him, he looked up at Patrick. "I honestly can't answer that question until I talk with Sunny. The best I can do to ease your mind is to assure you that I've taken every precaution to make certain there won't be any hanging party or quick trial. Sheriff Brucker will take good care of him until I'm heard from."

"Humph!" Patrick downed his whiskey in one angry gulp. " 'Tis the best I kin hope for, I s'ppose. Still, it—"

The bedroom door swung open and Sunny swept into the room wearing a smoke-grey wrapper with small pink flowers embroidered throughout the fabric. Her hair was brushed and tied back with a length of charcoal velvet cut from the belt she'd tied around her waist.

Uncomfortable with the extra petticoats she'd donned, Sunny smoothed her skirt as she stepped up to the table. "Did I hear right? Have you two made your peace?"

The men exchanged glances. Then, with an almost imperceptible nod, Cole gave Patrick the floor.

"Our peace, or lack of it, 'tisn't the trouble, lass. I b'lieve yer knowin' that."

Her breath whooshed out in a faint "Oh!", but before she had a chance to speak further, Cole pushed out of his chair and moved to her side.

"She knows what the problems are, sir—Patrick. I'd appreciate it if you'd allow us a few minutes alone before we try to figure out what to do next." Glancing into Sunny's eyes, he offered a reassuring wink then turned back to Patrick. "Do you mind if we take a walk around the farm?"

Looking to his daughter, the Irishman raised his bushy brows. At her short nod, he scowled, but said, "Aye, but be quick about it. If ye stumbled on her so easily, so will others."

Clutching her skirts, Sunny started for the door, her expression grim. With Cole one step behind her, she waded through the chicken-strewn yard, but kept her stony silence until they reached the riverbank.

Scanning the area, she made sure no late-bathing Quechan braves floated in one of the calm recesses at water's edge, then turned on Cole. "How could you let them arrest Sean for murdering Buck Wheeler? Surely he told them he was not to blame! Why would they not believe him?"

"Sunny, we have a few other things to talk about first, matters that are—"

"Nothing is more important than my brother right now, and I will speak of nothing else until I know he is cleared!"

Cole narrowed his eyes, but held his temper in check. Trying to think rationally, calmly, he answered her questions the only way he could. With the truth.

"Sean was arrested for Buck's murder because he didn't have an alibi."

"But of course he did!" she protested. "Why he was with Ei—he . . ." Sunny bit her lip, knowing full well why her brother would never use Eileen as an excuse in such a manner. Suddenly wondering how much Cole knew, she tested him.

"You will just have to take my word for it. He was definitely somewhere else that night, with someone, but I cannot say who that person might be."

"Yes, you can. Sean was with Eileen."

"Then they were found together?" Sunny's heart raced as she thought of the consequences her brother would have to suffer for that kindness. "They will kill him for sure! We must go to him!"

"Relax, sweetheart. No one knows about Eileen but me. When I stopped by the sheriff's office, I had a long talk with Sean about you and his lady friend. He's stubborn." Cole reached over and pinched her cheek. "Just like you. I gave your brother my word I would keep my mouth shut, and assured him that Eileen's reputation will remain intact."

"And so she has gone back to her dreadful father?"

"No. Last time I saw her, she was going to apply for a job at Phoebe's Millinery so she could keep one eye on the jail. I don't think she plans to leave town until she can go with Sean."

Some of her fears were eased, but it wasn't nearly enough. Sunny stamped her foot. "I thought the Fremont name was very important in Phoenix. Could you not tell them Sean is innocent and make them believe it?"

"I could try, but it wouldn't do any good." Taking a step closer, he peered into her eyes. "There's a very good reason your brother is still in jail, darlin'. Sean hasn't told the sheriff he *didn't* kill Buck—and you know what? I don't think he plans to."

"W-Why, b-but, that is insane!" Sunny's hand fluttered to her breast and she gasped. "Sean did not kill that low-down, that . . . that son of a bitch! *I* did!"

Cole groaned and crushed her to his chest. Wishing he could absorb her pain, make her problems disappear, he whispered into her fragrant hair, "I know, sweetheart. I know."

Swallowing a sob, Sunny pushed away from him. "Then you tell the sheriff. I cannot bear to know Sean is being punished for my crime. You must insist he be set free!"

"Oh, honey, I wish it were that easy, but it's not." He held her shoulders between his hands and drew her close. "I can't hope to have him released without providing another suspect. You don't actually think for one minute I could turn you in, do you?"

Sunny lowered her lashes, but in the next instant, she filled her lungs and lifted her chin. "No. I would not ask such a thing of you. I shall do it myself."

"You will not!" Cole released her and turned his palms and attention to the skies. "Is this entire family loco?"

Then, shoving his hands in his pockets, he stomped along the river's edge, kicking at the ground, cursing the pebbles. "Damn, damn, double-down dammit! There has to be a way out of this for everyone. Something that will appease the law, yet keep you . . ."

Cole let his words die out as he turned back toward Sunny and shot her a scathing look. "I might have figured something out long before now if I hadn't spent the last few days looking for you, half out of my mind with worry. It's not that I don't care about your brother, you know. It's because I haven't had a chance to think about anything but *you*!"

"Cole, I—I do not know what to say."

"Don't say anything, especially to the law." He uttered a short laugh and added, "It wouldn't matter if you did. Sean will never let you be hauled in for Buck's murder any more than I will." He turned back to the river and scratched his head. "There has to be a way out of this."

Sunny stood on the bank looking down on Cole as he considered the options. He shrugged one shoulder to release the tension, rotated his head, then shrugged the other. He'd ridden as hard as she, driven himself to the same exhaustion on his journey from Phoenix. But he had done it all for her. She was asking, demanding, too much of him.

Lifting her skirts, Sunny worked her way down beside him. "Buck is the man who took my mother's life," she said, hoping to fill in the blanks.

But he surprised her, acknowledging, "I know. I beat it out of Stormy."

"Stormy?"

Nodding, Cole looked back out to the river. "He was on that trip to Yuma with me and Buck. He confessed to everything."

"He was the other? You mean he—he—?"

Cole slipped his arm around her shoulders. "He's in jail. Don't think about him now. We've much more important people to think about."

"But we have to think about him! If Stormy has told the sheriff what he and Buck did to my mother, I can turn myself in. They would not hang me for self-defense— would they?"

Cole ran a finger along her hairline. "I'd like to think not, but there's no way of telling what the fine citizens of Phoenix would do with you. They're not all so forgiving when it comes to people who are different than they are."

"I think I see." Sunny raised her chin and cocked her head. "The sheriff might just hang me anyway because I am a lowly Quechan?"

Unable to argue the point, Cole pressed his lips together.

"I believe that is answer enough." Disregarding her long skirts, Sunny grabbed Cole's hand and pulled. "Come. Let us return to my father's house. He has much experience with these pure-blooded idiots. He will know how to deal with them."

Because he was so tired, because he had no other answers for her, Cole allowed himself to be led.

After they returned to the house, Cole slipped back into his chair and quietly observed while Sunny and her father compared notes, worked at finding a reasonable solution, and argued over which Callahan would claim responsibility for the death in Phoenix.

As they bantered in their unique blend of Quechan/Irish expressions, Cole sipped his whiskey and mulled over several ideas. One in particular, one that had popped into his mind several times during his long journey tracking

Sunny, kept returning, blooming into something much more special than a solution to a problem. The idea, he suspected with an inward grin, had been churning in his mind for several days. Was now the time to present it?

Patrick made the decision for him. "I kin see the smoke billowin' outta yer ears from here, lad. Out with it! Have ye an idea for helpin' me girl outta this mess?"

"Maybe," Cole said with a short laugh.

Patrick refilled his glass. "Let's hear it, lad. Time's awastin'!"

"All right." Cole's expression became guarded, serious. "I've been sitting here doing a little thinking, and you know, I have to admit that Sunflower Callahan stands a pretty good chance of convincing the sheriff she killed Buck in self-defense."

"See, Pop!" Sunny cut in. "I thought that would be the best thing to do."

"Ah," Cole said, adding steam to his train of thought, "but there will be a price. I'm willing to bet the spring calving there'd be a sentence of some kind." Cole pinned Sunny with his gaze, then took a large gulp of whiskey. "You'd probably have to endure at *least* a short vacation in the Yuma Territorial Prison."

Sunny and Patrick shivered in unison.

Glancing from father to daughter, Cole leaned across the table and lifted one eyebrow. His grin crooked, boyish, he said, "But I'm also thinking I might know a way to get her off scot-free."

At their curious expressions, he explained.

"I'm willing to bet your farm, the sheriff would never dream of tossing Mrs. Cole Fremont into that hellhole."

EIGHTEEN

Sunny read the oak and brass name plate again: *Judge James R. Hoy*.

She glanced up and raised an eyebrow as she studied the man behind the title. She'd never had contact with any member of law enforcement, much less someone as distinguished as the aging gentleman sitting before her. She was awed, properly humble in his presence.

Even so, as she studied this bespectacled beacon of a socially correct society, Sunny had to work to keep from laughing.

Unaware of her amused gaze, Judge Hoy frowned as he scrutinized the papers in his hand. The expression caused the excess flesh in his brow to ripple into folds, and dropped his jowls, already sagging like the breasts of an old Apache squaw, even lower.

Sunny closed her eyes. Judge Hoy couldn't be real. None of this was real. It just couldn't be happening. She inched her eyelids open and carefully peeked around the room.

She was standing in the austere judge's chambers of the Yuma County Courthouse.

Cole Fremont was standing beside her, his fingers frantically counting the change in his pocket.

And she was draped in a satin dress of robin's egg blue trimmed with ostrich tips and lace. She looked more like a fancy model in the Montgomery Ward catalogue than Sunflower Callahan.

It was happening, all right.

But was it fitting? Was it fair to the handsome man standing beside her? Sunny stole a quick glance at Cole and nearly swooned. He was even more handsome today, resplendent, in fact, in his new store-bought suit of charcoal gabardine with matching vest and shiny black boots.

He deserves more, she thought, guilt skipping stones across her heart. He absolutely deserved more than a hastily arranged marriage to a half-breed girl dressed up as a white woman.

She bit her lip and turned to Cole. Whispering under her breath, she said, "You—we all—were very tired last night. I am thinking as we look on our decision in the morning light, it may no longer be such a good idea. I will understand if you wish to leave now."

Cole straightened his tie and whispered back, "This is one sentence you'll not escape, little stubborn flower."

"B-But, please look and see who you shall be tied to, see that the woman who will carry your name is not the fine lady you deserve."

Indulging her, Cole turned his head and smiled. "You're right. You're not the lady I deserve. You are much more than I could ever hope to be worthy of."

Struggling to keep her voice low, out of the judge's range, she said, "You do not understand, lizard-brain! I am not what I appear to be and shall never be again!"

His eyes wide, Cole slowly turned to her. "What the hell does that mean?"

"It means I am not pleased to be inside this dress, that you have wasted the entire morning and a lot of your money trying to turn me into a lady! I—I cannot stand to be

pinched by this dreadful corset, and I shall never wear these
awful bustles again!"

Eyebrows cocked, Cole examined her and said under his
breath, "Is that a promise?"

"That is a guarantee!"

"Good." He caught the end of his mustache between his
fingers and twirled before adding, "That'll make it a hell of
a lot easier to rip off your clothes when the mood strikes."

Judge Hoy raised his head. Pausing for a moment, he
narrowed his gaze, then returned to his work.

Blushing like a schoolgirl, Sunny brought her lace
handkerchief to her face and lowered her head. Her wedding bonnet, a fashionable pale blue shirred chiffon, tilted
forward sending the tip of an ostrich feather across her
brow.

Her composure returning, Sunny lifted her chin and blew
a puff of air toward the errant feather. Glaring at her
husband-to-be, she muttered under her breath, "Why do
you make jokes when all I wish to do is show you the future
with a half-breed wife? Have you thought how you will
explain me to your proper white neighbors? What will they
think of a wife who will not ride a horse in the manner of a
fine lady?"

"The women will be jealous, and the men—well, I
suppose I'll have to fight to keep them away from you."

Grumbling under her breath, she snapped, "That is
enough of your malarkey, Cole Fremont! Think of your
family, your father!"

"My father isn't marrying you. I am."

"But he will disown you. He will never forgive you for
such an insult to his name."

Cole shifted his position and pushed his toes against the
tight leather of his new boots. "My father will get used to
the idea, but I'm beginning to wonder if you will."

Sunny ignored his last remark and twisted the lace hanky

around her hand. "Your father will never get used to having an Indian in the family. He will—"

"Given a little time," Cole sliced in with a sigh, "when he realizes he'll lose his only son if he doesn't get used to you, you'll find he won't mind having your around one bit. Now that's enough of this conversation."

"I have not finished speaking." Suddenly indignant, Sunny was unaware her voice raised with each word. "This forgiving father of yours—will he not mind having a horse thief in the family?"

Again Judge Hoy looked up. This time, he openly stared at the young couple, his brows drawn tight, creating a small canyon between his eyes. Then he cleared his throat and resumed scratching his name on the papers.

Cole dropped his voice to a bare whisper, his green eyes twinkling with amusement, and said, "Consider Dust Bucket a wedding present from me to you. You only borrowed what was yours."

"Really?"

"Yes, really. Now be quiet."

"I am not finished yet."

"Yes, you are."

With a stamp of her foot, Sunny turned and slammed her hands onto her hips. "You are not thinking this through, Cole Fremont! How can you expect your father to welcome the woman who murdered his son-in-law as a member of the family?"

Judge Hoy's chin snapped up as if hit with a rabbit punch. He slowly moved his hand across the desk and jabbed his pen into the inkwell. Then, his syllables thick as sorghum and molasses, he drawled, "Excuse me, suh. Might I have a private word with y'all?"

Cole glanced at Sunny and ground his teeth before approaching the desk. "Yes, Your Honor?"

"Suh," the judge began, his gravelly voice as low as he could get it, "I wouldn't dream of tellen another man how

to run his business, but there are a few disturben things
reachen my ears here."

Judge Hoy leaned forward, the slightly rancid odor of the
sow belly he'd eaten for breakfast preceding his words.
"Are y'all absolutely certain you want to go through with
this weddin? I have completed the paperwork, but y'all
more than welcome to back out."

"Oh, no sir. Excuse our behavior, we're just a little
nervous."

"Uh huh." Judge Hoy inclined his head to the left,
looking past Cole. "Well," he muttered, his curious gaze
perusing the half-breed, "whatevah, suh. I just want to be
sure y'all know what you're getting into."

"That I do," Cole assured him. "That I do."

Several sharp raps on the chamber door ended the
speculation, the conversation. Judge Hoy glanced up at
Cole. "Would that be your witnesses, suh?"

"I sincerely hope so."

"Then go let them in and we'll get this thing over with."

"Ah, yes, Your Honor."

As he turned, the door banged open and Patrick Callahan
practically shoved a large pear of a woman through the
doorway.

"Top o' the mornin' to ye!" he exclaimed, guiding the
woman as if he pushed a wheelbarrow. "Looks like we've
come to the right place!"

The judge rolled his chair away from the desk and slowly
rose. Stepping down off the platform, he approached the
newcomers. "And who might y'all be?"

"Patrick Callahan, sir." The Irishman stuck out his hand
and pumped his greeting, then added, "Father of the bride
and proud of it!"

Raising a deliberate brow, Judge Hoy looked to the
plump woman. "And you, my dear?"

"Millicent," she giggled, covering her mouth with her
fingers. "Millicent Noland, ah, a . . . a friend of the

family." She wore a startling violet dress trimmed in magenta and bright pink, and sported a matching shepherdess hat adorned with several high-flying ostrich plumes.

Millicent leaned forward, her voluminous breasts spilling over the rim of her low-cut bodice, and tried to get Sunny's attention. "Yoo hoo, Cactus Flower," she called through a giggle. "Congratulations, sugar—he's a real dandy!"

Lifting his bifocals above the bridge of his nose, Judge Hoy peered at Millicent. Then he quickly dropped the spectacles back in place. Clearing his throat, he folded his hands across his girth and said, "Since we're all together now I suggest we get on with the proceedins."

"Amen," Cole said with a shake of his head.

"Mother of God," Sunny mumbled, stealing a glance at her maid of honor.

"Let the party begin!" Patrick exclaimed as he clutched his chest, grasping the outline of his whiskey flask.

Three pairs of eyes bobbed along with Millicent's backside as she waddled down the wooden sidewalk on her way back to The Bucket. When Sunny was certain the fancy woman was out of earshot, she turned to Patrick and exploded.

"Is that the best you could do, Pop? Could you not have found a woman who at least knows my name?"

"I think Cactus Flower is kinda cute," Cole said, hoping to smooth things. "The possibilities for nicknames are endless! You've got Cacci, Tussie, not to mention—"

"Please, I do not care to hear them. I was speaking to my father."

Patrick leaned over and kissed his daughter's cheek. "Now, lassie," he soothed, "do'na take it out on yer new husband. I told ye finding a proper lady to bear witness for ye wouldn't be so easy on short notice. I b'lieve we should praise the Lord that Millie were kind enough to offer her services."

"Humph." Sunny lifted her chin and blew the ostrich feather off her brow. "I would imagine there are many in this town who might well praise the Lord for Millicent and her services."

With a sigh and a shake of his head, Patrick turned to his new son-in-law. "Aye lad, and I can see ye'll be havin' some trouble taming this girl o' mine. May I be offerin' ye a wee bit of advice?"

Cole winked as he glanced at Sunny and said, "I expect I'll be needing all the advice I can get."

Patrick's grin spread as he took center stage. "We've a sayin' in the old country ye'll do well to keep in mind. There's more than a ring of truth in these blessed words, so listen careful, lad." Patrick slipped the flask out of his jacket before he offered his pearls of wisdom. "In yer upcoming life, my son, ye'll be findin' three without rule: a wife, a pig, and a mule!"

"Pop!"

"Tsk, tsk," Patrick chuckled as he unscrewed the top from the flask. "'Tis nothin' but the truth, lassie, and yer young man'll be knowin' it soon enough. Let us drink now to the happy times!" Patrick leaned back and took a swallow from the silver container, then passed it to Cole.

Raising the flask, he swiveled to Sunny and said in toast, "To the most beautiful bride a man could ask for." Then he tilted his head and took a drink.

Sunny didn't wait for her husband to pass the bottle. She reached over and snatched it from his hands. "To the sheriff and whatever he decides to do with me!" She took a swallow, then recklessly added, "And to the scorpions hiding in my room at the Yuma prison."

Her words were an arctic blast in the desert heat. Being reminded of the formidable hurdle they still must clear turned Cole's expression grim. "That isn't where you are going, Mrs. Fremont. Don't even think about it."

"I have no choice until my brother is freed and I am cleared."

"Then I guess we'd better get to it."

Cole raised his brows and shrugged, giving Patrick an out, but the older man strode back to the courthouse door. "Ye'll not be gettin' rid o' me till me children are free and we can celebrate as a family."

He stepped across the threshold, replacing the flask in the pocket nearest his heart, and gestured for them to follow. His grin beaming with confidence, Patrick turned to the right and pushed his way inside the office of the sheriff of Yuma County.

The Irishman rapped his knuckles on the desk, startling the sleeping deputy so badly that he nearly tipped over in his chair.

"Ah, w-what—yes?" the young man managed to spit out as his chair legs banged against the wooden floor. "Kin I help you?"

"I'm Patrick Callahan from up river a wee bit. I've brung Mr. and Mrs. Cole Fremont of Phoenix. We're lookin' fer a minute of Sheriff Moffit's time."

"I'll see if he's in." The deputy jumped to his feet and shuffled to the glass door at the back of the small room. He rapped on the frame with his knuckles, then opened it a crack. "Some folks from Phoenix out here to see ya, Allen. Should I let em in?"

With a short nod, the deputy turned back to the visitors. "You kin come on in."

"Thank ye kindly, sir." Patrick led the newlyweds through the doorway, then made the introductions. "Afternoon, Sheriff Moffit. Remember me?"

The sheriff cocked his head, then shook it. "Face is familiar, but I can't seem to recollect the name."

"Callahan," he snapped. "Patrick Callahan. This here's me daughter, Sunny, and her husband Cole Fremont from Phoenix."

Lifting his gaze to her, he squinted as he examined her features. "Oh, yes, now I remember. You had an Indian squ—wife who was killed a few weeks back. Right?"

"Good of ye t' keep it so fresh in yer mind," Patrick grumbled.

Allen Moffit pushed out of his chair and circled the desk, measuring the trio with careful eyes. "I'm Sheriff Moffit," he said, brushing past Patrick. "Nice to meet you both." Forcing a smile, he shook Cole's hand and tipped an imaginary hat to Sunny. His gaze still lingering on the woman, Allen arranged three chairs for his visitors, then walked to the back of his desk.

"Please sit down," he offered, easing into his own padded seat. He slid his palms against the sides of his head, making certain each slicked-back hair was still in place and said, "Haven't any new leads for you, Callahan. If you're here about your wife and son's untimely—"

"That's only one reason we stopped by," Cole cut in, already certain he wasn't going to enjoy doing business with the man. "You can call off your dogs. One of the killers confessed to the murder in Phoenix and the other's dead."

The sheriff whistled, then looked at Patrick. "I'm mighty glad to hear that. I expect knowing that has set your mind at ease somewhat."

"Somewhat," Patrick admitted, "but not nearly enough." He turned his ice blue eyes on Cole, clearly giving him the lead.

Accepting, the rancher explained. "Sean Callahan is sitting in jail in Phoenix for the death of the man who killed Moonstar. We need your help to set him free."

"And Sean would be . . . ?" The sheriff turned his palms up.

Patrick blurted out, "Me son. The one the dirty low-down pond scum didn't kill."

His expression indifferent, Allen leaned back in his chair and propped his boots on the corner of his desk. Folding his hand with the fingertips facing him, he studied his immaculate nails, looking for even the slightest bit of dirt.

With a heavy sigh, he finally made an observation. "I don't see the problem here—unless this boy, a half-breed I assume, shot the man in the back."

"It weren't like that, it . . . he, ah . . ."

Her patience thin, Sunny muttered, "It was me. I killed the son of a bitch, and I would do it again!"

The sheriff's boots slipped off the desk as he jerked forward and jackknifed to the floor with a resounding crash.

Patrick's mouth dropped open and he exclaimed, "Now where'd ye be pickin' up such cussin', me lassie?"

Sunny turned her face to the wall, ignoring them both.

Sheriff Moffit's interest peaked, he asked as he righted his chair, "Is that a true fact, ma'am?"

"That is only a small part of the facts," Cole jumped in. Telegraphing a warning to Sunny, he glanced at her then went on. "My wife is involved in this mess, but she is so distraught over the whole damn business, I feel I should relay the story for her."

Allen's high arching brows raised even farther as he considered Cole's proposal. With a shrug, he finally said, "Go ahead, but make it plain and simple."

"Thank you, Sheriff." Cole slid out of his chair and walked around behind Sunny. His hands resting lightly on her shoulders, he smiled pleasantly and said, "The dead man—Buck Wheeler—was the foreman of my ranch back in Phoenix. I brought him to Yuma along with another hand several weeks ago for a little cattle business."

Pausing, Cole gave the sheriff a few moments to absorb the information. "The three of us split up here. I took the Gila River trail on horseback. Buck and Stormy took the train to Maricopa. Only thing was—" Feeling Sunny's shoulders tense under his hands, Cole pressed his fingers into the muscles and lightly massaged them.

"Only thing was, those two decided to make a detour.

Moonstar and her son Mike were the casualties of their senseless slaughter."

Sheriff Moffit nodded. "I'm familiar with the story, Mr. Fremont. Just what is it you're driving at?"

With a reassuring squeeze to his wife's shoulders, Cole explained the events leading up to Buck Wheeler's death and Sean's subsequent arrest, omitting only Eileen's name. When he'd finished, he looked across the desk and said, "I think you'll have to agree there's been a serious miscarriage of justice here. Sean doesn't belong in jail any more than Sunny does."

Raising one whip-like eyebrow, the sheriff muttered, "Is that so?"

"Yes, sir. I believe Sean should be released immediately and my wife granted a full pardon. It's the only decent thing to do."

"We're talking justice here, not decency, Mr. Fremont." Frowning, he cocked his head. "Let me see if I have the facts straight. You say this Sean was with a woman—helping her in some way—yet, she didn't come forward to clear his name? Mighty strange—mighty suspicious to my way of thinking."

Vaguely uncomfortable, Cole tried to explain. "The woman, well, he was only trying to protect her reputation, you know." Hit by an inspiration, Cole winked. "He did spend the night in a field with her and all—you know how those things go."

"No, sir, I don't." Sheriff Moffit sat straight up in his chair. "Why would anyone give a good gall dang if two injuns decide to spend a night rutting in the bushes?" At Sunny's gasp, Allen inclined his head. "Begging your pardon, Mrs. Fremont, but that's a pure and simple fact."

Leaning back in his chair again, he narrowed one eye and stared at Cole. "Course, I could see a problem if that woman weren't an injun. That it?"

"Sheriff Moffit, I really don't think that has—"

"Let it be, lad. Sean'll be knowin' we were put on the fence." Rising from the chair, Patrick sucked in his belly and hiked up his trousers. "Me boy was with a white woman, as yer suspectin', but he weren't doin' her no dishonor, sir!"

His laugh short, ringed with disgust, Allen said, "You can say that all day long, but you got no proof of what he did or didn't do. I can see just by looking at your family, you folks don't care what or who you breed with."

Anticipating Patrick's reaction, Cole sidestepped and grabbed the back of his neck just as he tried to leap across the desk. "Take it easy," he whispered. "Let me handle this."

When the Irishman sank back into his chair, Cole picked up the lead. "Those remarks are uncalled for, and none of that really matters, does it? The point is, Sean has killed or harmed no one. Please send a wire to Phoenix and have him released—now, before some fool decides to carry out his own brand of justice."

"Hmm." Allen made a great show of pondering his words, and slid a well-scrubbed finger back and forth across his smooth chin.

Straightening in his chair, he leaned across his desk and picked up an old "wanted" poster. Slowly folding the paper into a series of pleats, he commented, "There's all kinds of laws to be broken in these parts. All kinds," he emphasized, spreading the poster into the shape of a fan. "I'm not so sure I have the authority to turn a fella like that loose without some sort of . . . justification."

"*Justification?* Yer awantin' justification, Sheriff? I'll be showing ye justification!" No longer able to contain his anger, Patrick balled up his fists and puffed up his chest as he struggled out of his chair, but before he could move, Cole gripped one of his bulky arms.

"Come on, Patrick. Have a seat. I think the sheriff and I can work something out." After he helped the irate Irishman back into his chair, Cole continued on around him and approached the desk. Laying his palms flat on the polished wood, he stared into the sheriff's eyes.

Allen rolled his chair back several inches and fanned the few drops of perspiration building on his brow. "Now look here," the sheriff boomed in his voice of authority. "If you people think you can come in here and threaten the law, you got another think coming."

His voice deceptively low and gentle, Cole smiled. "We wouldn't dream of such a thing, Sheriff." Certain he'd read the man's eyes and thoughts correctly, he went on. "I was just thinking how much plain folks like ourselves owe to you fine men behind the badge."

Visibly relieved, Allen's fan slowed and he arched his brows as Cole made his offer. "There must be some way for a common man like myself to show you how much we appreciate you and the high office you hold."

His gaze wary, calculating, Allen agreed. "It's always good to be appreciated, and most often seems to put me in a very . . . generous state of mind."

"It's a relief to know that about you." Glancing around the room, then back to the sheriff and his homemade fan, Cole hit on the perfect enticement. "Must get hotter than hell in here once summer rears its ugly head."

Just thinking about the heat yet to come increased the strokes of the sheriff's fan. Grumbling under his breath, he said, "It gets hotter than that while summer's still crawling uphill on her belly."

Cole forced a laugh, then made his offer. "You ever had a refreshing chunk of ice floating in your glass of lemonade or whiskey?"

More curious than wary by now, Allen shrugged. "I was at a wedding last summer where they put ice in the drinks. It was downright nice. Why'd you ask?"

"Oh, I was just thinking about all the hard work you and your office go through trying to settle a little problem like we got here. I think it'd be real fitting if the Fremont family were to donate one of those newfangled ice-making machines to the courthouse. Why, you could have iced drinks anytime you wanted."

The sheriff sat up rod-straight and fiddled with his string tie. "I have to admit," he finally said, his eyes round with enthusiasm, "that's a mighty temptin' offer and a hell of a good idea."

"Then consider it done."

"Now just a minute here!" Allen held his hands in the air as he rose. "I got to think on this a minute. You folks wait here—I'll be right back."

Three heads swiveled to watch his departure. After the sheriff disappeared around the corner, Sunny turned to Cole, her dark eyes wide and incredulous. "Did I hear right? Did you just offer that man a bribe, and did he accept it?"

"Hush," he cautioned, his index finger pressed against his lips. "Let's just say what you've witnessed here is a little territorial justice."

"B-but that's illegal!"

"And immoral as far as I'm concerned, but if it gains you and your brother your freedom, it's justice enough for me."

Patrick growled, a deep dangerous rumble in his throat. "I'd still like the chance to visit me own brand of justice on the blight! Just five minutes, that'd be all I need with the little cur!"

"I hope you get your chance one day, too, but for now," Cole glanced over his shoulder, "I think we'd better accept anything he'll give us and give whatever he'll take. Got it?"

With a grumble, Patrick nodded, then slipped his flask out of his pocket. Turning to Sunny, Cole looked for the same compromise, but he was met with her upturned chin and pursed lips. "*Got it*, Mrs. Fremont?"

"Oh," she complained, "I suppose I do if I must, but I do not have to like it!"

"No, you don't."

Patrick took a swig of whiskey then passed the flask. By the time Cole and Sunny had each taken a sip of the spirits and returned the container to her father, the sheriff returned. He escorted a grim-faced Judge James R. Hoy.

"Well now," the judge drawled as he strolled into the office. "And heah I thought I'd seen the last of y'all."

Sheriff Moffit stopped in his tracks. "You know these folks?"

"G'won, Allen. Have a seat and be still." Approaching the desk, the judge rested his hips against its edge as he faced the trio. "The sheriff has told me of your troubles. I think if we can clear up a few misunderstandings, we can settle these matters in a way to please everyone."

"That's all I've been hoping for, Judge Hoy. A little justice."

"Uh huh." Adjusting his bifocals, he cocked his head and peered at Sunny. "If you don' mind, li'l lady, please explain to me just how you come to end this Buck fella's life? I seem to recall you usin' the word murder in my chambers not one hour past. Was it self-defense, or did y'all go gunning for him?"

Sunny gulped, then took a deep breath. "I said the word murder because I believe causing the death of any person is nothing short of murder. But I did not go after Buck Wheeler. That is the truth, Your Honor." She looked down at the twisted hanky in her hand, shuddering as she remembered. "B-Buck came after me, tried to . . . to attack me. All I did was hit him, then, I don't know, it all happened so fast, everything is a blur. I do have to admit—"

Sunny glanced at Cole, then her father. Raising her chin a notch, she finished her testimony. "If Buck Wheeler were in this room now, I would kill him again."

Judge Hoy's features softened, and he came as close to smiling as he ever did. "I believe you would, too."

Patrick leaped out of his chair. "She do'na mean it, Yer Honor, she—"

"Please return to your seat, Mr. Callahan. Your daughter has cleared herself to my satisfaction." He leaned backward over the desk and said, "Run on over to the telegraph office, Allen. Send a wire to the sheriff in Phoenix tellin' him to drop the charges on the Callahan boy. Tell him we got the suspect here in Yuma and that I'll be sending the details by mail."

"Ah, yes, sir, but what about—"

"That'll be all, Jake. I can finish up with these folks."

The minute the sheriff left the room, Patrick was back on his feet again. "Thank ye kindly, me good man! I cannot thank ye enough—"

"Mr. Callahan, I've a few things to clear up with these two nice people here. Perhaps you'd join the deputy in the other room and give us a little privacy?"

"Faith, and I'll be happy ta be on me way." Chuckling, bowing, and waving, Patrick backed out of the office and closed the door.

Judge Hoy pushed away from the desk and stared down at Cole. "My sheriff here has leveled some serious charges again' you, suh. He says you tried to bribe him."

Jerking out of the chair, Cole faced the judge. "I'm afraid the man misunderstood. That offer had nothing to do with my wife's freedom. I merely wanted to give something to the land of her birth, leave a little something in her name when I take her away."

One thick caterpillar of an eyebrow responded, inched toward his hairline. "Do I understand you correctly, suh? Are y'all planning to take your leave of our fine town?"

"The minute my shipment of birds arrives in the next few days, Sunny and I will be heading east. We're making our home near the Verde River outside of Phoenix."

"Ummm, that's excellent news, suh. Just excellent." Stroking his chin, the judge began to walk toward the door.

"In that case, I'll just be drawing up some papers for you two to take to the authorities in Phoenix. They will include a full pardon for your wife."

"I thank you, Your Honor. We'll stop by after the birds have arrived to collect them. By then, I will have had the arrangements for the ice-making machine completed as well."

Turning as he opened the door, the judge nodded slowly. "That's excellent, suh. Just excellent." Then he was gone.

Stunned, Sunny climbed slowly out of her chair. "I—I cannot believe what has happened here, I cannot believe any of this."

Cole took two short strides and dragged her into his arms. "Believe it, my beautiful flower. You're free."

Squeezing her eyes shut, Sunny buried her face against his shoulder and returned his embrace as if it might be the last. Everything had happened so fast, so unexpectedly. She was Sunflower Fremont now, married to the only man she would ever love. Did she love him enough to release him from the reckless bargain he'd made just to insure her freedom, her life? That Cole Fremont loved her, Sunny no longer had any doubt. Was it deep enough to remain tied to her for the rest of his life? Condemned, as his father might say, to be the father of a passel of half-breeds?

She had to be sure. Forcing a smile, Sunny pulled back and said, "I am free, but you are not. Is there some way for us to end this marriage and return you to the fine ladies of your world?"

Holding her at arms length, Cole grumbled, "You just don't get it do you?"

"I—I only want what is best for you."

"This," Cole jerked her hand up between them and pointed at the shiny gold ring on her finger, "and this," he patted the marriage certificate sticking out of his jacket pocket, "are what I think is best for me. What do you want, Sunflower?"

"I want you, Cole. You are all I have ever wanted, but it is not fair, it is—"

"I love you. What else can I say? What else can I do to prove my love to you?"

Sunny gasped and brought her hand to her mouth. He *did* love her enough to endure the trials ahead. He did. Tears glistened in the corners of her eyes. She couldn't speak.

Glancing through the sheriff's dusty window, Cole spotted the Yuma Hotel across the street. Looking back at Sunny, his grin spread his mustache almost to his earlobes. "Come on, Mrs. Fremont. Once we get this marriage consummated, you'll play hell getting out of it."

She found her voice. "Consummated? What does this mean?"

Taking her by the hand, he winked as they strolled out of the room. "Well, it means . . . Why don't you let me show you what it means."

Laughing as they stepped out into the sunshine, he glanced at her with a wicked gleam in his eye. "What was it you were saying awhile back about that damnable corset and bustle?"

NINETEEN

Cole captured a dusky rose nipple in his mouth and teased the crown with a languid tongue. Submersed in pleasure, awash with contentment, he murmured, "I love you, Sunny. I'll always love you."

"I know," she whispered against the top of his blond head. "And I shall always love you, my husband."

"I will always *be* your husband."

"And I shall always be your wife."

"I'm glad we finally got that little problem solved," he laughed. "But now we've another."

Reading the mirth in his expression, Sunny's dark eyes widened and sparkled as she playfully said, "If the problem has anything to do with more consummating, I do not believe I can help you for awhile." Dramatically flinging her arms on the pillow above her head, Sunny sighed. "I am *very* tired, my vigorous husband."

With a lusty chuckle, Cole planted a kiss between her damp breasts, then rolled onto his back and closed his eyes. "Thank God for small favors. You haven't been out of this bed for damn near twenty-four hours. How can you expect to get anything out of this marriage *but* consummation, if every time I leave and come back to this room you're lying there with your hair spread all over that pillow just asking for trouble?"

Through a giggle, she asked, "And this bothers you so?"

"No," he admitted as he leaned up on one elbow and gazed down at her. "I feel like you've been robbed of what should have been a very special day. I want to make it up to you, so I'm offering to marry you all over again. Here or in Phoenix—or both if you wish."

"But we are married already, are we not?"

Cole shrugged. "Legally, yes, but don't you want more? Don't you want a real wedding dress, and lots of guests at a big party after, and most of all—" he laughed at the memory, "your own choice of attendants?"

The suggestion and memories gave her a good laugh before she replied. "It means a lot to know that you would do that for me, but I believe the most important thing to me is knowing we had a truly memorable wedding. And believe me, my husband, I shall never, *ever* forget the day we wed!"

"It's a day I'm not likely to forget either, but are you sure it's enough? Won't you always feel a little robbed?"

"I am sure. And I only feel robbed when you are not with me." Reaching behind Cole's neck, she drew him to her and fit his mouth to the contours of hers. The kiss was meant as a bond, a gentle token of their love and dedication to one another, but it quickly flared to passion, left Sunny breathless with its intensity.

With the last of her strength, she pushed him away and gasped, "I thought you wanted me out of this bed."

"I thought I did, too, my wicked little flower."

Breaking into a grin, Sunny purred, "Do we not have to go to the railroad station?"

"We do, but not for another hour."

"An hour, my love? Whatever shall we do to help the time pass?"

His mustache crooked, twitching in anticipation, Cole slid his hand beneath the bedsheet. Finding the sleek expanse of satiny skin he sought, he murmured, "I'll think of something."

To make sure that he did, Sunny tossed the sheets aside, and said, "See? No bustles, no corset!"

Sunny slipped her gloved hand in the crook of Cole's arm as the pair rounded the corner and headed up the dusty street toward the railroad depot. In spite of the fact that she wore *two* bustles lashed to her behind, she held her head high, secure in the knowledge her appearance was as fashionable as any woman she'd passed in town. As comfortable as it was practical, her grey serge travelling suit was of the newest style, decorated with rows of black silk braiding across the bodice, and set off at the throat with a bit of primrose lace to soften the look.

The bustles, entirely Sunny's idea and decision, finished the ensemble with a silhouette of feminine elegance. But at the end of the train ride to Maricopa, she thought with a delicious smile, these hideous "fanny pillows" would be prized only by buzzards and roadrunners as nesting materials. This time Sunny meant it—she had donned them for the last time.

Pleased as she imagined herself tossing the bustles over a cliff, Sunny increased the tempo as she walked, and wore a smile bright enough to challenge the Arizona sun.

"Top o' the mornin' to ye there!" Patrick called as he shuffled across the dusty street. "Hold up a bit. I've received word from Sean!"

He limped up beside them, dragging a leg left dangling on a bar stool for too long the night before, and paused to catch his breath. He waved a yellow paper in his hand and explained, "Me boy's been released! He is well!"

"Oh, thank God for that," Sunny breathed, pressing her hand to her breast. "When will he return home?"

"Aye, of that I'm not too sure."

Cole slapped his father-in-law on the back. "Walk along with us to the depot and fill us in on the way."

Falling in alongside, Patrick shrugged as he trudged down Madison Avenue with them. " 'Tis precious little I've t' report. Me boy has taken up his cause agin'." He elbowed Cole in the ribs and winked. "Takes after his sister, I b'lieve he do!"

Waiting until the train's shrill whistle completed its declaration, Sunny exclaimed, "You mean he's with Eileen again?"

The squeal of engine brakes filled the air as the train slowed for its approach, and Patrick had to shout. "He's bound to help the lass he says, but would not put in writin' the direction they'll be aheadin'. He'll wire again when they stop at another town."

They'd reached the depot and Cole helped Sunny onto the platform, then turned and offered her father his arm.

"Thank ye, lad," Patrick muttered, accepting the aid. "I fear a Gila monster may have crawled in me mouth as I took me rest last night. Poisoned me something powerful, it did."

Sunny rested a fist on her hip. "The only way that bit of malarkey could be true is if that Gila monster crawled into your pocket while you were taking your rest at The Bucket."

"Ye see what I mean, lad! Ye kin never get ahead of 'em, nor gather enough advice to live in peace!" Patrick's bushy brows arched and he became animated, but the rest of his complaints were lost as the Southern Pacific roared up beside them.

Coughing and belching out thick dark columns of smoke, the engine slowly screeched to a halt. Occasionally interrupted by the rhythmic billows of steam hissing from the train's boilers, Sunny turned to Cole.

"I am so excited! When can I see these birds?"

"Birrds?" Patrick bellowed. "What birrds?"

Cole gestured for them to follow as he made his way down the wooden planks toward the box cars. "I'm going to start raising ostriches!" he shouted over a whoosh of steam.

"Ostriches, lad? Glory be."

They walked past several passenger and livestock cars before Cole finally spotted his unusual cargo. "There they are!"

The trio rushed up alongside the wooden car and peered through the slats. The enormous birds were a sight none were prepared for.

Sunny's mouth dropped open, but no sound issued forth.

Patrick squeezed his eyes shut and rubbed them, but when he lifted his lids, the scene was unchanged. "Faith and begorra!"

"God almighty!" Cole exclaimed as he took a backward step. "They must be seven feet tall!"

"Eight, mister," a voice from above supplied.

Stunned, Cole looked toward the back of the car and observed a man sliding down off the ladder. His right leg was bracketed between two slats of wood bound together with strips of cloth.

Leaning heavily on a cane fashioned from a mesquite branch, the man limped to the front of the boxcar and inquired, "You Fremont?"

"Yes." Cole reached out to greet him, but the man merely nodded and wiped the back of his free hand under his nose.

"Brought you twenty-nine of the thirty-two birds you ordered. Lost three once we hit the Californey desert. Now if you'll excuse me, I gotta go find out if this town has a sawbones."

"Wait!" Cole stepped in front of the man, apologizing. "I see you've got some trouble there with your leg, but couldn't you give me just a little advice on what to do with these birds before you go?"

"Yeah!" The man turned his head to the side and spit a thick stream of tobacco juice onto the railroad tie. "Stay the hell away from 'em! I didn't get this busted leg playing poker in the caboose."

"An ostrich did that?"

"Oh, yes, and that's an almighty fact. You have bought yourself twenty-nine of the dumbest critters ever dropped on God's green earth. And if dumb ain't enough, they kick like a cow and got three times the strength. Good luck, mister—you're going to need it."

Frantic for more information, Cole glanced at the birds and noticed their odd headgear. "Those hoods—what are they for?"

The man laughed and spit another stream of tobacco. "Cute ain't they? But I strongly suggest you keep your new little friends wearing their bonnets. If you don't, and they get a look around and see they ain't at home, well, they're just likely to take off on you; and stopping a runaway ostrich isn't no easy trick. 'Sides," he laughed, "even if they stick around, without them bonnets, their little heads will get sunburned and they'll keel over, deader than a rock but still twice as dumb!" He pushed off with his cane and began to hobble away. "Good luck, and make sure you hire a doc for your ranch. I got a feeling he's going to be a hell of a lot more important than a cook."

Knowing the man wouldn't be delayed any further, Cole waved and called, "Thanks. Sorry for your trouble."

Sunny moved up along side him, her eyes filled with wonder. "I cannot believe this. These birds are so big! I thought . . ." She bent over and gestured a few feet off the ground.

Behind her, Patrick muttered, "Faith and begorra."

Then a stranger approached. "Excuse me, these your birds?"

Cole tore his gaze from his new enterprise and said, "Ah, yes, they are."

"We'll be pulling out of Yuma in about two hours. Don't you want to feed and water these critters before we head out to Maricopa?"

"Oh, of course."

The official from the railroad craned his neck and shook his head as he studied the bonneted birds. "I'll send some men over to give you a hand."

When the official had left, Cole turned to his wife. "Sunny, I'm not sure what the hell I've gotten us into."

After a long moment and another glance at the herd, Sunny said, "I am not sure either, my husband."

Stunned, the trio stood in front of the boxcar, peering inside, until a railroad worker stepped up to them. "You want to unload these birds in a stockyard, mister? I can—" The kid's mouth dropped open as he followed their gaze. "Jumping Jehoshaphat!" He wheeled around calling, "Hey, Jimmy, get on over here and lookie at this, would you?"

Soon after, Cole had more help than he could have used herding a hundred head of cattle the length of Arizona. By the time the last ostrich lurched down the gangplank and padded into the fenced stockyard, a crowd of curious onlookers had gathered.

"Please stay back!" Cole beseeched the excited crowd as they crushed against the railing. "You're making them nervous."

But no one budged, and their delighted voices grew louder.

Nearby, pens of cattle bawled their terror, strained against their confines as the scent of something new and frightening reached their nostrils.

Sheep bleated and converged in the center of their corral.

Pigs squealed and frantically dug at the soft earth as they sought escape from the unknown.

Things were getting out of control. Thinking if he could just manage to get the crowd to disperse, all the livestock would relax, Cole climbed to the top rail of the fence to make an announcement.

But it was too late.

An eager bystander reached across the barrier and removed the bonnet from one of the birds.

An enormous pair of dark eyes darted around. The tiny bald head jerked a couple of times. And then, as if it faced nothing more than a small puddle, the ostrich leaped over the six-foot fence.

Great puffs of sand followed the creature as it loped past the boxcars and down the streets of Yuma, scattering women, children, and livestock in all directions. It lurched like a drunk on payday as it lumbered onto Main Street, then stumbled around the corner and disappeared in a cloud of dust.

"What the *hell*?" Cole moaned, watching part of his sixteen-thousand-dollar investment gain its freedom.

"Mother of God," Sunny breathed as the ostrich reappeared, only to crash through the swinging doors of The Bucket.

Patrick jerked a silver whiskey flask from his back pocket and raised it on high.

"Let the party begin!"

369